"Thus the gods point my way," Caramon murmured. Creeping up to the side of the bed, he paused, the dagger in his hand, listening to the quiet breathing of his victim, trying to detect any change in the deep, even rhythm that would tell him he had been discovered.

In and out . . . in and out . . . the breathing was strong, deep, peaceful. The breathing of a healthy young man. Caramon shuddered, recalling how old this wizard was supposed to be, recalling the dark tales he had heard about how Fistandantilus renewed his youth. The man's breathing was steady, even. There was no break, no quickening. The moonlight poured in, cold, unwavering, a sign. . . .

Caramon raised the dagger. One thrust—swift and neat—deep in the chest . . . and it would be over.

by Margaret Weis and Tracy Hickman

DRAGONLANCE CHRONICLES

Dragons of Autumn Twilight

Dragons of Winter Night

Dragons of Spring Dawning

DRAGONLANCE LEGENDS

Time of the Twins

War of the Twins

Test of the Twins

The Second Generation

Dragons of Summer Flame

THE WAR OF SOULS

Dragons of a Fallen Sun

Dragons of a Lost Star

Dragons of a Vanished Moon

LEGENDS

VOLUME ONE

TIME OF THE TWINS

Margaret Weis & Tracy Hickman

Poetry By Michael Williams
Cover Art By Matt Stawicki
Interior Art By Valerie Valusek

DRAGONLANCE® LEGENDS
Volume One
TIME OF THE TWINS
©1986 TSR, Inc.
©2004 Wizards of the Coast, Inc.

All characters in this book are fictitious. Any resemblance to actual persons, living or dead, is purely coincidental.

This book is protected under the copyright laws of the United States of America. Any reproduction or unauthorized use of the material or artwork contained herein is prohibited without the express written permission of Wizards of the Coast, Inc.

Distributed in the United States by Holtzbrinck Publishing. Distributed in Canada by Fenn Ltd.

Distributed to the hobby, toy, and comic trade in the United States and Canada by regional distributors.

Distributed worldwide by Wizards of the Coast, Inc. and regional distributors.

DRAGONLANCE, WIZARDS OF THE COAST, and their respective logos are trademarks of Wizards of the Coast, Inc., in the U.S.A. and other countries.

All Wizards of the Coast characters, character names, and the distinctive likenesses thereof are trademarks of Wizards of the Coast, Inc.

Printed in the U.S.A.

The sale of this book without its cover has not been authorized by the publisher. If you purchased this book without a cover, you should be aware that neither the author nor the publisher has received payment for this "stripped book."

Cover art by Matt Stawicki
First Printing: February 1986
Library of Congress Catalog Card Number: 00-190764

9 8 7 6 5 4

US ISBN: 0-7869-1804-7
UK ISBN: 0-7869-2027-0
620-21804-001-EN

U.S., CANADA,	EUROPEAN HEADQUARTERS
ASIA, PACIFIC, & LATIN AMERICA	Wizards of the Coast, Belgium
Wizards of the Coast, Inc.	T Hofveld 6d
P.O. Box 707	1702 Groot-Bijgaarden
Renton, WA 98057-0707	Belgium
+1-800-324-6496	+322 467 3360

Visit our web site at **www.wizards.com**

To Samuel G. and Alta Hickman

My grandpa who tossed me into bed in his own special way
and my grandma nanny who is always so very wise.
Thank you all for the bedtime stories, life, love, and history.
You will live forever.
—Tracy Raye Hickman

This book about the physical and spiritual bonds binding
brothers together could be dedicated to only one
person—my sister. To Terry Lynn Weis Wilhelm, with love.
—Margaret Weis

ACKNOWLEDGMENTS

We wish to gratefully acknowledge the work of the following:

Michael Wllliams—for splendid poetry and warm friendship.

Steve Sullivan—for his wonderful maps. (Now you know where you are, Steve!)

Patrick Price—for his helpful advice and thoughtful criticism.

Jean Black—our editor, who had faith in us from the beginning.

Ruth Hoyer—for cover and interior design.

Roger Moore—for DRAGON® magazine articles and the story of Tasslehoff and the wolly mammoth.

The DRAGONLANCE® team: Harold Johnson, Laura Hickman, Douglas Niles, Jeff Grubb, Michael Dobson, Michael Breault, Bruce Heard.

The 1987 DRAGONLANCE Calendar artists: Clyde Caldwell, Larry Elmore, Keith Parkinson, and Jeff Easley.

The Meeting

A lone figure trod softly toward the distant light. Walking unheard, his footfalls were sucked into the vast darkness all around him. Bertrem indulged in a rare flight of fancy as he glanced at the seemingly endless rows of books and scrolls that were part of the *Chronicles of Astinus* and detailed the history of this world, the history of Krynn.

"It's like being sucked into time," he thought, sighing as he glanced at the still, silent rows. He wished, briefly, that he were being sucked away somewhere, so that he did not have to face the difficult task ahead of him.

"All the knowledge of the world is in these books," he said to himself wistfully. "And I've never found one thing to help make the intrusion upon their author any easier."

Bertrem came to a halt outside the door to summon his courage. His flowing Aesthetic's robes settled themselves about him, falling into correct and orderly folds. His stomach, however, refused to follow the robes' example and lurched about wildly. Bertrem ran his hand across his scalp, a nervous gesture left over from a younger age, before his chosen profession had cost him his hair.

What was bothering him? he wondered bleakly—other than going in to see the Master, of course, something he had not done since . . . since . . . He shuddered. Yes, since the young mage had nearly died upon their doorstep during the last war.

War . . . change, that was what it was. Like his robes, the world had finally seemed to settle around him, but he felt change coming once again, just as he had felt it two years ago. He wished he could stop it. . . .

Bertrem sighed. "I'm certainly not going to stop anything by standing out here in the darkness," he muttered. He felt uncomfortable anyway, as though surrounded by ghosts. A bright light shone from under the door, beaming out into the hallway. Giving a quick glance backward at the shadows of the books, peaceful corpses resting in their tombs, the Aesthetic quietly opened the door and entered the study of Astinus of Palanthas.

Though the man was within, he did not speak, nor even look up.

Walking with gentle, measured tread across the rich rug of lamb's wool that lay upon the marble floor, Bertrem paused before the great, polished wooden desk. For long moments he said nothing, absorbed in watching the hand of the historian guide the quill across the parchment in firm, even strokes.

"Well, Bertrem?" Astinus did not cease his writing.

Bertrem, facing Astinus, read the letters that—even upside down—were crisp and clear and easily decipherable.

This day, as above Darkwatch rising 29, Bertrem entered my study.

"Crysania of the House of Tarinius is here to see you, Master. She says she is expected. . . ." Bertrem's voice trailed off in a whisper, it having taken a great deal of the Aesthetic's courage to get that far.

Astinus continued writing.

"Master," Bertrem began faintly, shivering with his daring. "I—we are at a loss. She is, after all, a Revered Daughter of Paladine and I—we found it impossible to refuse her admittance. What sh—"

"Take her to my private chambers," Astinus said without ceasing to write or looking up.

Bertrem's tongue clove to the roof of his mouth, rendering him momentarily speechless. The letters flowed from the quill pen to the white parchment.

This day, as above Afterwatch rising 28, Crysania of Tarinius arrived for her appointment with Raistlin Majere.

"Raistlin Majere!" Bertrem gasped, shock and horror prying his tongue loose. "Are we to admit hi—"

Astinus looked up now, annoyance and irritation creasing his brow. As his pen ceased its eternal scratching on the parchment, a deep unnatural silence settled upon the room. Bertrem paled. The historian's face might have been reckoned handsome in a timeless, ageless fashion. But none who saw his face ever remembered it. They simply remembered the eyes—dark, intent, aware, constantly moving, seeing everything. Those eyes could also communicate vast worlds of impatience, reminding Bertrem that time was passing. Even as the two spoke, whole minutes of history were ticking by, unrecorded.

"Forgive me, Master!" Bertrem bowed in profound reverence, then backed precipitately out of the study, closing the door quietly on his way. Once outside, he mopped his shaved head that was glistening with perspiration, then hurried down the silent, marble corridors of the Great Library of Palanthas.

Astinus paused in the doorway to his private residence, his gaze on the woman who sat within.

Located in the western wing of the Great Library, the residence of the historian was small and, like all other rooms in the library, was filled with books of every type and binding, lining the shelves on the walls and giving the central living area a faint musty odor, like a mausoleum that had been sealed for centuries. The furniture was sparse, pristine. The chairs, wooden and handsomely carved, were hard and uncomfortable to sit upon. A low table, standing by a window, was absolutely free of any ornament or object, reflecting the light from the setting sun upon its smooth black surface. Everything in the room was in the most perfect order. Even the wood for the evening fire—the late spring nights were cool, even this far north—was stacked in such orderly rows it resembled a funeral pyre.

And yet, cool and pristine and pure as was this private chamber of the historian, the room itself seemed only to mirror the cold, pristine, pure beauty of the woman who sat, her hands folded in her lap, waiting.

Crysania of Tarinius waited patiently. She did not fidget or sigh or glance often at the water-run timing device in the corner. She did not read—though Astinus was certain Bertrem would have her offered a book. She did not pace the room or examine the few rare ornaments that stood in shadowed nooks within the bookcases. She sat in the straight, uncomfortable, wooden chair, her clear, bright eyes fixed upon the red-stained fringes of the clouds above the mountains as if she were watching the sun set for possibly the first—or last—time upon Krynn.

So intent was she upon the sight beyond the window that Astinus entered without attracting her attention. He regarded her with intense interest. This was not unusual for the historian, who scrutinized all beings living upon Krynn with the same fathomless, penetrating gaze. What was unusual was that, for a moment, a look of pity and of profound sorrow passed across the historian's face.

Astinus recorded history. He had recorded it since the beginning of time, watching it pass before his eyes and setting it down in his books. He could not foretell the future, that was the province of the gods. But he could sense all the signs of change, those same signs that had so disturbed Bertrem. Standing there, he could hear the drops of water falling in the timing device. By placing his hand beneath them, he could cease the flow of the drops, but time would go on.

Sighing, Astinus turned his attention to the woman, whom he had heard of but never met.

Her hair was black, blue-black, black as the water of a calm sea at night. She wore it combed straight back from a central part, fastened at the back of her head with a plain, unadorned, wooden comb. The severe style was not becoming to her pale, delicate features, emphasizing their pallor. There was no color at all in her face. Her eyes were gray and seemingly much too large. Even her lips were bloodless.

Some years ago, when she had been young, servants had braided and coiled that thick, black hair into the latest, fashionable styles, tucking in pins of silver and of gold, decorating the somber hues with sparkling jewels. They had tinted her cheeks with the juice of crushed berries and dressed her in sumptuous gowns of palest pinks and powdery blues. Once she had been beautiful. Once her suitors had waited in lines.

The gown she wore now was white, as befitted a cleric of Paladine, and plain though made of fine material. It was unadorned save for the belt of gold that encircled her slim waist. Her only ornament was Paladine's—the medallion of the Platinum Dragon. Her hair was covered by a loose white hood that enhanced the marble smoothness and coldness of her complexion.

She might have been made of marble, Astinus thought, with one difference—marble could be warmed by the sun.

"Greetings, Revered Daughter of Paladine," Astinus said, entering and shutting the door behind him.

"Greetings, Astinus," Crysania of Tarinius said, rising to her feet.

As she walked across the small room toward him, Astinus was somewhat startled to note the swiftness and almost masculine length of her stride. It seemed oddly incongruous with her delicate features. Her handshake, too, was firm and strong, not typical of Palanthian women, who rarely shook hands and then did so only by extending their fingertips.

"I must thank you for giving up your valuable time to act as a neutral party in this meeting," Crysania said coolly. "I know how you dislike taking time from your studies."

"As long as it is not wasted time, I do not mind," Astinus replied, holding her hand and regarding her intently. "I must admit, however, that I resent this."

"Why?" Crysania searched the man's ageless face in true perplexity. Then—in sudden understanding—she smiled, a cold smile that brought no more life to her face than the moonlight upon snow. "You don't believe he will come, do you?"

Astinus snorted, dropping the woman's hand as though he had completely lost interest in her very existence. Turning away, he walked to the window and looked out over the city of Palanthas, whose gleaming white buildings glowed in the sun's radiance with a breathtaking beauty, with one exception. One building remained untouched by the sun, even in brightest noontime.

And it was upon this building that Astinus's gaze fixed. Thrusting itself up in the center of the brilliant, beautiful city, its black stone towers twisted and writhed, its minarets—newly repaired and constructed by the powers of magic—glistened blood-red in the sunset, giving the appearance of rotting, skeletal fingers clawing their way up from some unhallowed burial ground.

"Two years ago, he entered the Tower of High Sorcery," Astinus said in his calm, passionless voice as Crysania joined him at the window. "He entered in the dead of night in darkness, the only moon in the sky was the moon that sheds no light. He walked through the Shoikan Grove—a stand of accursed oak trees that no mortal—not even those of the kender race—dare approach. He made his way to the gates upon which hung still the body of the evil mage who, with his dying breath, cast the curse upon the Tower and leapt from the upper windows, impaling himself upon its gates—a fearsome watchman. But when *he* came there, the watchman bowed before him, the gates opened at his touch, then they shut behind him. And they have not opened again these past two years. He has not left and, if any have been admitted, none have seen them. And you expect *him* . . . *here*?"

"The master of past and of present," Crysania shrugged. "He came, as was foretold."

Astinus regarded her with some astonishment.

"You know his story?"

"Of course," the cleric replied calmly, glancing up at him for an instant, then turning her clear eyes back to look at the Tower, already shrouding itself with the coming night's shadows. "A good general always studies the enemy before engaging in battle. I know Raistlin Majere very well, very well indeed. And I know—he will come this night."

Crysania continued gazing at the dreadful Tower, her chin lifted, her bloodless lips set in a straight, even line, her hands clasped behind her back.

Astinus's face suddenly became grave and thoughtful, his eyes troubled, though his voice was cool as ever. "You seem very sure of yourself, Revered Daughter. How do you know this?"

"Paladine has spoken to me," Crysania replied, never taking her eyes from the Tower. "In a dream, the Platinum Dragon appeared before me and told me that evil—once banished from the world—had returned in the person of this black-robed wizard, Raistlin Majere. We face dire peril, and it has been given to me to prevent it." As Crysania spoke, her marble face grew smooth, her gray eyes were clear and bright. "It will be the test of my faith I have prayed for!" She glanced at Astinus. "You see, I have known since childhood that my destiny was to perform some great deed, some great service to the world and its people. This is my chance."

Astinus's face grew graver as he listened, and even more stern.

"Paladine told you this?" he demanded abruptly.

Crysania, sensing, perhaps, this man's disbelief, pursed her lips. A tiny line appearing between her brows was, however, the only sign of her anger, that and an even more studied calmness in her reply.

"I regret having spoken of it, Astinus, forgive me. It was between my god and myself, and such sacred things should not be discussed. I brought it up simply to prove to you that this evil man will come. He cannot help himself. Paladine will bring him."

Astinus's eyebrows rose so that they very nearly disappeared into his graying hair.

"This 'evil man' as you call him, Revered Daughter, serves a goddess as powerful as Paladine—Takhisis, Queen of Darkness! Or perhaps I should not say *serves*," Astinus remarked with a wry smile. "Not of him...."

Crysania's brow cleared, her cool smile returned. "Good redeems its own," she answered gently. "Evil turns in upon itself. Good will triumph again, as it did in the War of the Lance against Takhisis and her evil dragons. With Paladine's help, *I* shall triumph over this evil as the hero, Tanis Half-Elven, triumphed over the Queen of Darkness herself."

"Tanis Half-Elven triumphed with the help of Raistlin Majere," Astinus said imperturbably. "Or is that a part of the legend you choose to ignore?"

Not a ripple of emotion marred the still, placid surface of Crysania's expression. Her smile remained fixed. Her gaze was on the street.

"Look, Astinus," she said softly. "He comes."

The sun sank behind the distant mountains, the sky, lit by the afterglow, was a gemlike purple. Servants entered quietly, lighting the fire in the small chamber of Astinus. Even it burned quietly, as if the flames themselves had been taught by the historian to maintain the peaceful repose of the Great Library. Crysania sat once more in the uncomfortable chair, her hands folded once more in her lap. Her outward mein was calm and cool as always. Inwardly, her heart beat with excitement that was visible only by a brightening of her gray eyes.

Born to the noble and wealthy Tarinius family of Palanthas, a family almost as ancient as the city itself, Crysania had received every comfort and benefit money and rank could bestow. Intelligent, strong-willed, she might easily have grown into a stubborn and willful woman. Her wise and loving parents, however, had carefully nurtured and pruned their daughter's strong spirit so that it had blossomed into a deep and steadfast belief in herself. Crysania had done only one thing in her entire life to grieve her doting parents, but that one thing had cut them deeply. She had turned from an ideal marriage with a fine and noble young man to a life devoted to serving long-forgotten gods.

She first heard the cleric, Elistan, when he came to Palanthas at the end of the War of the Lance. His new religion—or perhaps it should have been called the *old* religion—was spreading like wildfire through Krynn, because new-born legend credited this belief in old gods with having helped defeat the evil dragons and their masters, the Dragon Highlords.

On first going to hear Elistan talk, Crysania had been skeptical. The young woman—she was in her mid-twenties—had been raised on stories of how the gods had inflicted the Cataclysm upon Krynn, hurling down the fiery mountain that rent the lands asunder and plunged the holy city of Istar into the Blood Sea. After this, so people related, the gods turned from men, refusing to have any more to do with them. Crysania was prepared to listen politely to Elistan, but had arguments at hand to refute his claims.

She was favorably impressed on meeting him. Elistan, at that time, was in the fullness of his power. Handsome, strong, even in his middle years, he seemed like one of the clerics of old, who had ridden to battle—so some legends said—with the mighty knight, Huma. Crysania began the evening finding cause to admire him. She ended on her knees at his feet, weeping in humility and joy, her soul at last having found the anchor it had been missing.

The gods had not turned from men, was the message. It was men who had turned from the gods, demanding in their pride what Huma had sought in humility. The next day, Crysania left her home, her wealth, her servants, her parents, and her betrothed to move into the small, chill house that was the forerunner of the new Temple Elistan planned to build in Palanthas.

Now, two years later, Crysania was a Revered Daughter of Paladine, one of a select few who had been found worthy to lead the church through its youthful growing pangs. It was well the church had this strong, young blood. Elistan had given unstintingly of his life and his energy. Now, it seemed, the god he served so faithfully would soon be summoning his cleric to his side. And when that sorrowful event occurred, many believed Crysania would carry on his work.

Certainly Crysania knew that she was prepared to accept the leadership of the church, but was it enough? As she had told Astinus, the young cleric had long felt her destiny was to perform some great service for the world. Guiding the church through its daily routines, now that the war was over, seemed dull and mundane. Daily she had prayed to Paladine to assign her some hard task. She would sacrifice anything, she vowed, even life itself, in the service of her beloved god.

And then had come her answer.

Now, she waited, in an eagerness she could barely restrain. She was not frightened, not even of meeting this man, said to be the most powerful force for evil now living on the face of Krynn. Had her breeding permitted it, her lip would have curled in a disdainful sneer. What evil could withstand the mighty sword of her faith? What evil could penetrate her shining armor?

Like a knight riding to a joust, wreathed with the garlands of his love, knowing that he cannot possibly lose with such tokens fluttering in the wind, Crysania kept her eyes fixed on the door, eagerly awaiting the tourney's first blows. When the door opened, her hands—until now calmly folded—clasped together in excitement.

Bertrem entered. His eyes went to Astinus, who sat immovable as a pillar of stone in a hard, uncomfortable chair near the fire.

"The mage, Raistlin Majere," Bertrem said. His voice cracked on the last syllable. Perhaps he was thinking about the last time he had announced this visitor—the time Raistlin had been dying, vomiting blood on the steps of the Great Library. Astinus frowned at Bertrem's lack of self-control, and the Aesthetic disappeared back through the door as rapidly as his fluttering robes permitted.

Unconsciously, Crysania held her breath. At first she saw nothing, only a shadow of darkness in the doorway, as if night itself had taken form and shape within the entrance. The darkness paused there.

"Come in, old friend," Astinus said in his deep, passionless voice.

The shadow was lit by a shimmer of warmth—the firelight gleamed on velvety soft, black robes—and then by tiny sparkles, as the light glinted off silver threads, embroidered runes around a velvet cowl. The shadow became a figure, black robes completely draping the body. For a brief moment, the figure's only human appendage that could be seen was a thin, almost skeletal hand clutching a wooden staff. The staff itself was topped by a crystal ball, held fast in the grip of a carved golden dragon's claw.

As the figure entered the room, Crysania felt the cold chill of disappointment. She had asked Paladine for some difficult task! What great evil was there to fight in this? Now that she could see him clearly, she saw a frail, thin man, shoulders slightly stooped, who leaned upon his staff as he walked, as if too weak to move without its aid. She knew his age, he would be about twenty-eight now. Yet he moved like a human of ninety—his steps slow and deliberate, even faltering.

What test of my faith lies in conquering this wretched creature? Crysania demanded of Paladine bitterly. I have no need to fight him. He is being devoured from within by his own evil!

Facing Astinus, keeping his back to Crysania, Raistlin folded back his black hood.

"Greetings again, Deathless One," he said to Astinus in a soft voice.

"Greetings, Raistlin Majere," Astinus said without rising. His voice had a faint sardonic note, as if sharing some private joke with the mage. Astinus gestured. "May I present Crysania of the House of Tarinius."

Raistlin turned.

Crysania gasped, a terrible ache in her chest caused her throat to close, and for a moment she could not draw a breath. Sharp, tingling pins jabbed her fingertips, a chill convulsed her body. Unconsciously, she shrank back in her chair, her hands clenching, her nails digging into her numb flesh.

All she could see before her were two golden eyes shining from the depths of darkness. The eyes were like a gilt mirror, flat, reflective, revealing nothing of the soul within. The pupils—Crysania stared at the dark pupils in rapt horror. The pupils within the golden eyes were the shape of hourglasses! And the face—Drawn with suffering, marked with the pain of the tortured existence the young man had led for seven years, ever since the cruel Tests in the Tower of High Sorcery left his body shattered and his skin tinged gold, the mage's face was a metallic mask, impenetrable, unfeeling as the golden dragon's claw upon his staff.

"Revered Daughter of Paladine," he said in a soft voice, a voice filled with respect and—even reverence.

Crysania started, staring at him in astonishment. Certainly that was not what she had expected.

Still, she could not move. His gaze held her, and she wondered in panic if he had cast a spell upon her. Seeming to sense her fear, he walked across the room to stand before her in an attitude that was both patronizing and reassuring. Looking up, she could see the firelight flickering in his golden eyes.

"Revered Daughter of Paladine," Raistlin said again, his soft voice enfolding Crysania like the velvety blackness of his robes. "I hope I find you well?" But now she heard bitter, cynical sarcasm in that voice. This she had expected, this she was prepared for. His earlier tone of respect had taken her by surprise, she admitted to herself angrily, but her first weakness was past. Rising to her feet, bringing her eyes level with his, she unconsciously clasped the medallion of Paladine with her hand. The touch of the cool metal gave her courage.

"I do not believe we need to exchange meaningless social amenities," Crysania stated crisply, her face once more smooth and cold. "We are keeping Astinus from his studies. He will appreciate our completing our business with alacrity."

"I could not agree more," the black-robed mage said with a slight twist of his thin lip that might have been a smile. "I have come in response to your request. What is it you want of me?"

Crysania sensed he was laughing at her. Accustomed only to the highest respect, this increased her anger. She regarded him with cold gray eyes. "I have come to warn you, Raistlin Majere, that your evil designs are known to Paladine. Beware, or he will destroy you—"

"How?" Raistlin asked suddenly, and his strange eyes flared with a strange, intense light. "How will he destroy me?" he repeated. "Lightning bolts? Flood and fire? Perhaps another fiery mountain?"

He took another step toward her. Crysania moved coolly away from him, only to back into her chair. Gripping the hard wooden back firmly, she walked around it, then turned to face him.

"It is your own doom you mock," she replied quietly.

Raistlin's lip twisted further still, but he continued talking, as if he had not heard her words. "Elistan?" Raistlin's voice sank to a hissing whisper. "He will send Elistan to destroy me?" The mage shrugged. "But no, surely not. By all reports, the great and holy cleric of Paladine is tired, feeble, dying. . . ."

"No!" Crysania cried, then bit her lip, angry that this man had goaded her into showing her feelings. She paused, drawing a deep breath. "Paladine's ways are not to be questioned or mocked," she said with icelike calm, but she could not help her voice from softening almost imperceptibly. "And Elistan's health is no concern of yours."

"Perhaps I take a greater interest in his health than you realize," Raistlin replied with what was, to Crysania, a sneering smile.

Crysania felt blood pound in her temples. Even as he had spoken, the mage moved around the chair, coming nearer the young woman. He was so close to her now that Crysania could feel a strange, unnatural heat radiate from his body through his black robes. She could smell a faintly cloying but pleasant scent about him. A spiciness—His spell components, she realized suddenly. The thought sickened and disgusted her. Holding the medallion of Paladine in her hand, feeling its smoothly chiseled edges bite into her flesh, she moved away from him again.

"Paladine came to me in a dream—" she said haughtily.

Raistlin laughed.

Few there were who had ever heard the mage laugh, and those who had heard it remembered it always, resounding through their darkest dreams. It was thin, high-pitched, and sharp as a blade. It denied all goodness, mocked everything right and true, and it pierced Crysania's soul.

"Very well," Crysania said, staring at him with a disdain that hardened her bright, gray eyes to steel blue, "I have done my best to divert you from this course. I have given you fair warning. Your destruction is now in the hands of the gods."

Suddenly, perhaps realizing the fearlessness with which she confronted him, Raistlin's laughter ceased. Regarding her intently, his golden eyes narrowed. Then he smiled, a secret inner smile of such strange joy that Astinus, watching the exchange between the two, rose to his feet. The historian's body blocked the light of the fire. His shadow fell across them both. Raistlin started, almost in alarm. Half-turning, he regarded Astinus with a burning, menacing stare.

"Beware, old friend," the mage warned, "or would you meddle with history?"

"I do not meddle," Astinus replied, "as you well know. I am an observer, a recorder. In all things, I am neutral. I know your schemes, your plans as I know the schemes and plans of all who draw breath this day. Therefore, hear me, Raistlin Majere, and heed this warning. This one is beloved of the gods—as her name implies."

"Beloved of the gods? So are we all, are we not, Revered Daughter?" Raistlin asked, turning to face Crysania once more. His voice was soft as the velvet of his robes. "Is that not written in the Disks of Mishakal? Is that not what the godly Elistan teaches?"

"Yes," Crysania said slowly, regarding him with suspicion, expecting more mockery. But his metallic face was serious, he had the appearance, suddenly, of a scholar—intelligent, wise. "So it is written." She smiled coldly. "I am pleased to find you have read the sacred Disks, though you obviously have not learned from them. Do you not recall what is said in the—"

She was interrupted by Astinus, snorting.

"I have been kept from my studies long enough." The historian crossed the marble floor to the door of the antechamber. "Ring for Bertrem when you are ready to depart. Farewell, Revered Daughter. Farewell . . . old friend."

Astinus opened the door. The peaceful silence of the library flowed into the room, bathing Crysania in refreshing coolness. She felt herself in control and she relaxed. Her hand let loose of the medallion. Formally and gracefully, she bowed her farewell to Astinus, as did Raistlin. And then the door shut behind the historian. The two were alone.

For long moments, neither spoke. Then Crysania, feeling Paladine's power flowing through her, turned to face Raistlin. "I had forgotten that it was you and those with you who recovered the sacred Disks. Of course, you would have read them. I would like to discuss them with you further but, henceforth, in any future dealings we might have, Raistlin Majere," she said in her cool voice, "I will ask you to speak of Elistan more respectfully. He—"

She stopped amazed, watching in alarm as the mage's slender body seemed to crumble before her eyes.

Wracked by spasms of coughing, clutching his chest, Raistlin gasped for breath. He staggered. If it had not been for the staff he leaned upon. he would have fallen to the floor. Forgetting her aversion and her disgust, reacting instinctively, Crysania reached out and, putting her hands upon his shoulders, murmured a healing prayer. Beneath her hands, the black robes were soft and warm. She could feel Raistlin's muscles twisting in spasms, sense his pain and suffering. Pity filled her heart.

Raistlin jerked away from her touch, shoving her to one side. His coughing gradually eased. Able to breathe freely once more, he regarded her with scorn.

"Do not waste your prayers on me, Revered Daughter," he said bitterly. Pulling a soft cloth from his robes, he dabbed his lips and Crysania saw that it came away stained with blood. "There is no cure for my malady. This is the sacrifice, the price I paid for my magic."

"I don't understand," she murmured. Her hands twitched, as she remembered vividly the velvety soft smoothness of the black robes, and she unconsciously clasped her fingers behind her back.

"Don't you?" Raistlin asked, staring deep into her soul with his strange, golden eyes. "What was the sacrifice you made for *your* power?"

A faint flush, barely visible in the dying firelight, stained Crysania cheeks with blood, much as the mage's lips were stained. Alarmed at this invasion of her being, she averted her face, her eyes looking once more out the window. Night had fallen over Palanthas. The silver moon, Solinari, was a sliver of light in the dark sky. The red moon that was its twin had not yet risen. The black moon—She caught herself wondering, where is it? Can *he* truly see it?

"I must go," Raistlin said, his breath rasping in his throat. "These spasms weaken me. I need rest."

"Certainly," Crysania felt herself calm once more. All the ends of her emotions tucked back neatly into place, she turned to face him again. "I thank you for coming—"

"But our business is not concluded," Raistlin said softly. "I would like a chance to prove to you that these fears of your god are unfounded. I have a suggestion. Come visit me in the Tower of High Sorcery. There you will see me among my books and understand my studies. When you do, your mind will be at ease. As it teaches in the Disks, we fear only that which is unknown." He took a step nearer her.

Astounded at his proposal, Crysania's eyes opened wide. She tried to move away from him, but she had inadvertently let herself become trapped by the window. "I cannot go . . . to the Tower," she faltered as his nearness smothered her, stole her breath. She tried to walk around him, but he moved his staff slightly, blocking her path. Coldly, she continued, "The spells laid upon it keep out all—"

"Except those I choose to admit," Raistlin whispered. Folding the blood-stained cloth, he tucked it back into a secret pocket of his robes. Then, reaching out, he took hold of Crysania's hand.

"How brave you are, Revered Daughter," he commented. "You do not tremble at my evil touch."

"Paladine is with me," Crysania replied disdainfully.

Raistlin smiled, a warm smile, dark and secret—a smile for just the two of them. It fascinated Crysania. He drew her near to him. Then, he dropped her hand. Resting the staff against the chair, he reached out and took hold of her head with his slender hands, placing his fingers over the white hood she wore. Now, Crysania trembled at his touch, but she could not move, she could not speak or do anything more than stare at him in a wild fear she could neither suppress nor understand.

Holding her firmly, Raistlin leaned down and brushed his blood-flecked lips across her forehead. As he did so, he muttered strange words. Then he released her.

Crysania stumbled, nearly falling. She felt weak and dizzy. Her hand went to her forehead where the touch of his lips burned into her skin with a searing pain. "What have you done?" she cried brokenly. "You cannot cast a spell upon me! My faith protects—"

"Of course," Raistlin sighed wearily, and there was an expression of sorrow in his face and voice, the sorrow of one who is constantly suspected, misunderstood. "I have simply given you a charm that will allow you to pass through Shoikan Grove. The way will not be easy"— his sarcasm returned—"but, undoubtedly your *faith* will sustain you!"

Pulling his hood low over his eyes, the mage bowed silently to Crysania, who could only stare at him, then he walked toward the door with slow, faltering steps. Reaching out a skeletal hand, he pulled the bell rope. The door opened and Bertrem entered so swiftly and suddenly that Crysania knew he must have been posted outside. Her lips tightened. She flashed the Aesthetic such a furious, imperious glance that the man paled visibly, though totally unaware of what crime he had committed, and mopped his shining forehead with the sleeve of his robe.

Raistlin started to leave, but Crysania stopped him. "I-I apologize for not trusting you, Raistlin Majere," she said softly. "And, again, I thank you for coming."

Raistlin turned. "And I apologize for my sharp tongue," he said. "Farewell, Revered Daughter. If you truly do not fear knowledge, then come to the Tower two nights from this night, when Lunitari makes its first appearance in the sky."

"I will be there," Crysania answered firmly, noting with pleasure Bertrem's look of shocked horror. Nodding in good-bye, she rested her hand lightly on the back of the ornately carved wooden chair.

The mage left the room, Bertrem followed, shutting the door behind him.

Left alone in the warm, silent room, Crysania fell to her knees before the chair. "Oh, thank you, Paladine!" she breathed. "I accept your challenge. I will not fail you! I will not fail!"

BOOK 1

Chapter I

Behind her, she could hear the sound of clawed feet, scrapping through the leaves of the forest. Tika tensed, but tried to act as if she didn't hear, luring the creature on. Firmly, she gripped her sword in her hand. Her heart pounded. Closer and closer came the footsteps, she could hear the harsh breathing. The touch of a clawed hand fell upon her shoulder. Whirling about, Tika swung her sword and . . . knocked a tray full of mugs to the floor with a crash.

Dezra shrieked and sprang backward in alarm. Patrons sitting at the bar burst into raucous laughter. Tika knew her face must be as red as her hair. Her heart was pounding, her hands shook.

"Dezra," she said coldly, "you have all the grace and brains of a gully dwarf. Perhaps you and Raf should switch places. *You* carry out the garbage and I'll let *him* wait tables!"

Dezra looked up from where she knelt, picking broken pieces of crockery up off the floor, where they floated in a sea of beer. "Perhaps I should!" the waitress cried, tossing the pieces back onto the floor. "Wait tables yourself . . . or is that beneath you now, Tika Majere, Heroine of the Lance?"

Flashing Tika a hurt, reproachful glance, Dezra stood up, kicked the broken crockery out of her way, and flounced out of the Inn.

As the front door banged open, it hit sharply against its frame, making Tika grimace as she envisioned scratches on the woodwork. Sharp words rose to her lips, but she bit her tongue and stopped their utterance, knowing she would regret them later.

The door remained standing open, letting the bright light of fading afternoon flood the Inn. The ruddy glow of the setting sun gleamed in the bar's freshly polished wood surface and sparkled off the glasses. It even danced on the surface of the puddle on the floor. It touched Tika's flaming red curls teasingly, like the hand of a lover, causing many of the sniggering patrons to choke on their laughter and gaze at the comely woman with longing.

Not that Tika noticed. Now ashamed of her anger, she peered out the window, where she could see Dezra, dabbing at her eyes with an apron. A customer entered the open door, dragging it shut behind him. The light vanished, leaving the Inn once more in cool, half-darkness.

Tika brushed her hand across her own eyes. *What kind of monster am I turning into?* she asked herself remorsefully. *After all, it wasn't Dezra's fault. It's this horrible feeling inside of me! I almost wish there were draconians to fight again. At least then I knew what I feared, at least then I could fight it with my own hands! How can I fight something I can't even name?*

Voices broke in on her thoughts, clamoring for ale, for food. Laughter rose, echoing through the Inn of the Last Home.

This is what I came back to find. Tika sniffed and wiped her nose with the bar rag. *This is my home. These people are as right and beautiful and warm as the setting sun. I'm surrounded by the sounds of love—laughter, good fellowship, a lapping dog. . . .*

Lapping dog! Tika groaned and hurried out from behind the bar.

"Raf!" she exclaimed, staring at the gully dwarf in despair.

"Beer spill. Me mop up," he said, looking at her and cheerfully wiping his hand across his mouth.

Several of the old-time customers laughed, but there were a few, new to the Inn, who were staring at the gully dwarf in disgust.

"Use this rag to clean it up!" Tika hissed out of the corner of her mouth as she grinned weakly at the customers in apology. She tossed Raf the bar rag and the gully dwarf caught it. But he only held it in his hand, staring at it with a mystified expression.

"What me do with this?"

"Clean up the spill!" Tika scolded, trying unsuccessfully to shield him from the customer's view with her long, flowing skirt.

"Oh! Me not need that," Raf said solemnly. "Me not get nice rag dirty." Handing the cloth back to Tika, the gully dwarf got down on all fours again and began to lick up the spilled beer, now mingled with tracked-in mud.

Her cheeks burning, Tika reached down and jerked Raf up by his collar, shaking him. "Use the rag!" she whispered furiously. "The customers are losing their appetites! And when you're finished with that, I want you to clear off that big table near the fire pit. I'm expecting friends—" Tika stopped.

Raf was staring at her, wide-eyed, trying to absorb the complicated instructions. He was exceptional, as gully dwarves go. He'd only been there three weeks and Tika had already taught him to count to three (few gully dwarves ever get past two) and had finally gotten rid of his stench. This new-found intellectual prowess combined with cleanliness would have made him a king in a gully dwarf realm, but Raf had no such ambitions. He knew no king lived like he did—"mopping up" spilled beer (if he were quick) and "taking out" the garbage. But there were limits to Raf's talents, and Tika had just reached them.

"I'm expecting friends and—" she started again, then gave up. "Oh, never mind. Just mop this up—*with the rag*," she added severely, "then come to me to find out what to do next."

"Me no drink?" Raf began, then caught Tika's furious glare. "Me do."

Sighing in disappointment, the gully dwarf took the rag back and slopped it around, muttering about "waste good beer." Then he picked up pieces of the broken mugs and, after staring at them a moment, grinned and stuck them in the pockets of his shirt.

Tika wondered briefly what he planned to do with them, but knew it was wiser not to ask. Returning to the bar, she grabbed some more mugs and filled them, trying not to notice that Raf had cut himself on some of the sharper pieces and was now leaning back on his heels, watching, with intense interest, the blood drip from his hand.

"Have you ... uh ... seen Caramon?" Tika asked the gully dwarf casually.

"Nope." Raf wiped his bloody hand in his hair. "But me know where to look." He leaped up eagerly. "Me go find?"

"No!" snapped Tika, frowning. "Caramon's at home."

"Me no think so," Raf said, shaking his head. "Not after sun go down—"

"He's home!" Tika snapped so angrily that the gully dwarf shrank away from her.

"You want to make bet?" Raf muttered, but well under his breath. Tika's temper these days was as fiery as her flaming hair.

Fortunately for Raf, Tika didn't hear him. She finished filling the beer mugs, then carried the tray over to a large party of elves, seated near the door.

I'm expecting friends, she repeated to herself dully. Dear friends. Once she would have been so excited, so eager to see Tanis and Riverwind. Now ... She sighed, handing out the beer mugs without conscious awareness of what she was doing. Name of the true gods, she prayed, let them come and go quickly! Yes, above all, go quickly! If they stayed ... If they found out....

Tika's heart sank at the thought. Her lower lip trembled. If they stayed, that would be the end. Plain and simple. Her life would be over. The pain was suddenly more than she could bear. Hurriedly setting the last beer mug down, Tika left the elves, blinking her eyes rapidly. She did not notice the bemused gazes the elves exchanged among themselves as they stared at the beer mugs, and she never did remember that they had all ordered wine.

Half blinded by her tears, Tika's only thought was to escape to the kitchen where she could weep unseen. The elves looked about for another waitress, and Raf, sighing in contentment, got back down on his hands and knees, happily lapping up the rest of the beer.

Tanis Half-Elven stood at the bottom of a small rise, staring up the long, straight, muddy road that stretched ahead of him. The woman he escorted and their mounts waited some distance behind him. The woman had been in need of rest, as had their horses. Though her pride had kept her from saying a word, Tanis saw her face was gray and drawn with fatigue. Once today, in fact, she had nodded off to sleep in the saddle, and would have fallen but for Tanis's strong arm. Therefore, though eager to reach her destination, she had not protested when Tanis stated that he wanted to scout the road ahead alone. He helped her from her horse and saw her settled in a hidden thicket.

He had misgivings about leaving her unattended, but he sensed that the dark creatures pursuing them had fallen far behind. His insistence on speed had paid off, though both he and the woman were aching and exhausted. Tanis hoped to stay ahead of the things until he could turn his companion over to the one person on Krynn who might be able to help her.

They had been riding since dawn, fleeing a horror that had followed them since leaving Palanthas. What it was exactly, Tanis—with all his experience during the wars—could not name. And that made it all the more frightening. Never there when confronted, it was only seen from the corner of the eye that was looking for something else. His companion had sensed it, too, he could tell, though, characteristically, she was too proud to admit to fear.

Walking away from the thicket, Tanis felt guilty. He shouldn't be leaving her alone, he knew. He shouldn't be wasting precious time. All his warrior senses protested. But there was one thing he had to do, and he had to do it alone. To do otherwise would have seemed sacrilege.

And so Tanis stood at the bottom of the hill, summoning his courage to move forward. Anyone looking at him might have supposed he was advancing to fight an ogre. But that was not the case. Tanis Half-Elven was returning home. And he both longed for and dreaded his first sight.

The afternoon sun was beginning its downward journey toward night. It would be dark before he reached the Inn, and he dreaded traveling the roads by night. But, once there, this nightmarish journey would be over. He would leave the woman in capable hands and continue on to Qualinesti. But, first, there was this he had to face. With a deep sigh, Tanis Half-Elven drew his green hood up over his head and began the climb.

Topping the rise, his gaze fell upon a large, moss-covered boulder. For a moment, his memories overwhelmed him. He closed his eyes, feeling the sting of swift tears beneath the lids. "Stupid quest," he heard the dwarf's voice echo in his memory. "Silliest thing I ever did!"

Flint! My old friend!

I can't go on, Tanis thought. This is too painful. Why did I ever agree to come back? It holds nothing for me now . . . nothing except the pain of old wounds. My life is good, at last. Finally I am at peace, happy. Why . . . why did I tell them I would come?

Drawing a shuddering sigh, he opened his eyes and looked at the boulder. Two years ago—it would be three this autumn—he had topped this rise and met his long-time friend, the dwarf, Flint Fireforge, sitting on that boulder, carving wood, and complaining—as usual. That meeting had set in motion events that had shaken the world, culminating in the War of the Lance, the battle that cast the Queen of Darkness back into the Abyss, and broke the might of the Dragon Highlords.

Now I am a hero, Tanis thought, glancing down ruefully at the gaudy panoply he wore: breastplate of a Knight of Solamnia; green silken sash, mark of the Wildrunners of Silvanesti, the elves' most honored legions; the medallion of Kharas, the dwarves' highest honor; plus countless others. No one—human, elf, or half-elf—had been so honored. It was ironic. He who hated armor, who hated ceremony, now forced to wear it as befitting his station. How the old dwarf would have laughed.

"You—a hero!" He could almost hear the dwarf snort. But Flint was dead. He had died two years ago this spring in Tanis's arms.

"Why the beard?" He could swear once again that he heard Flint's voice, the first words he had said upon seeing the half-elf in the road. "You were ugly enough. . . ."

Tanis smiled and scratched the beard that no elf on Krynn could grow, the beard that was the outward, visible sign of his half-human heritage. Flint knew well enough why the beard, Tanis thought, gazing fondly at the sun-warmed boulder. He knew me better than I knew myself. He knew of the chaos that raged inside my soul. He knew I had a lesson to learn.

"And I learned it," Tanis whispered to the friend who was with him in spirit only. "I learned it, Flint. But . . . oh, it was bitter!"

The smell of wood smoke came to Tanis. That and the slanting rays of the sun and the chill in the spring air reminded him he still had some distance to travel. Turning, Tanis Half-Elven looked down into the valley where he had spent the bittersweet years of his young manhood. Turning, Tanis Half-Elven looked down upon Solace.

It had been autumn when he last saw the small town. The vallenwood trees in the valley had been ablaze with the season's colors, the brilliant reds and golds fading into the purple of the peaks of the Kharolis mountains beyond, the deep azure of the sky mirrored in the still waters of Crystalmir Lake. There had been a haze of smoke over the valley, the smoke of home fires burning in the peaceful town that had once roosted in the vallenwood trees like contented birds. He and Flint had watched the lights flicker on, one by one, in the houses that sheltered among the leaves of the huge trees. Solace—tree city—one of the beauties and wonders of Krynn.

For a moment, Tanis saw the vision in his mind's eye as clearly as he had seen it two years before. Then the vision faded. Then it had been autumn. Now it was spring. The smoke was there still, the smoke of the home fires. But now it came mostly from houses built on the ground. There was the green of living, growing things, but it only seemed—in Tanis's mind—to emphasize the black scars upon the land; scars that could never be totally erased, though here and there he saw the marks of the plow across them.

Tanis shook his head. Everyone thought that, with the destruction of the Queen's foul temple at Neraka, the war was over. Everyone was anxious to plow over the black and burned land, scorched by dragonfire, and forget their pain.

His eyes went to a huge circle of black that stood in the center of town. Here, nothing would grow. No plow could turn the soil ravaged by dragonfire and soaked by the blood of innocents, murdered by the troops of the Dragon Highlords.

Tanis smiled grimly. He could imagine how an eyesore like that must irritate those who were working to forget. He was glad it was there. He hoped it would remain, forever.

Softly, he repeated words he had heard Elistan speak, as the cleric dedicated in solemn ceremony the High Clerist's Tower to the memory of those knights who had died there.

"We must remember or we will fall into complacency—as we did before—and the evil will come again."

If it is not already upon us, Tanis thought grimly. And, with that in mind, he turned and walked rapidly back down the hill.

The Inn of the Last Home was crowded that evening.

While the war had brought devastation and destruction to the residents of Solace, the end of the war had brought such prosperity that there were already some who were saying it hadn't been "such a bad thing." Solace had long been a crossroads for travelers through the lands of Abanasinia. But, in the days before the war, the numbers of travelers had been relatively few. The dwarves—except for a few renegades like Flint Fireforge—had shut themselves up in their mountain kingdom of Thorbardin or barricaded themselves in the hills, refusing to have anything to do with the rest of the world. The elves had done the same, dwelling in the beautiful lands of Qualinesti to the southwest and Silvanesti on the eastern edge of the continent of Ansalon.

The war had changed all that. Elves and dwarves and humans traveled extensively now, their lands and their kingdoms open to all. But it had taken almost total annihilation to bring about this fragile state of brotherhood.

The Inn of the Last Home—always popular with travelers because of its fine drink and Otik's famous spiced potatoes—became more popular still. The drink was still fine and the potatoes as good as ever—though Otik had retired—but the real reason for the Inn's increase in popularity was that it had become a place of some renown. The Heroes of the Lance—as they were now called—had been known to frequent this Inn in days gone by.

Otik had, in fact, before his retirement, seriously considered putting up a plaque over the table near the firepit—perhaps something like "Tanis Half-Elven and Companions Drank Here." But Tika had opposed the scheme so vehemently (the mere thought of what Tanis would say if he caught sight of that made Tika's cheeks burn) that Otik had let it drop. But the rotund barkeep never tired of telling his patrons the story of the night the barbarian woman had sung her strange song and healed Hederick the Theocrat with her blue crystal staff, giving the first proof of the existence of the ancient, true gods.

Tika, who took over management of the Inn upon Otik's retirement and was hoping to save enough money to buy the business, fervently hoped Otik would refrain from telling that story again tonight. But she might have spent her hope on better things.

There were several parties of elves who had traveled all the way from Silvanesti to attend the funeral of Solostaran—Speaker of the Suns and ruler of the elven lands of Qualinesti. They were not only urging Otik to tell his story, but were telling some of their own, about the Heroes' visit to their land and how they freed it from the evil dragon, Cyan Bloodbane.

TIME OF THE TWINS

Tika saw Otik glance her direction wistfully at this—Tika had, after all, been one of the members of the group in Silvanesti. But she silenced him with a furious shake of her red curls. *That* was one part of their journey she refused ever to relate or even discuss. In fact, she prayed nightly that she would forget the hideous nightmares of that tortured land.

Tika closed her eyes a moment, wishing the elves would drop the conversation. She had her own nightmares now. She needed no past ones to haunt her. "Just let them come and go quickly," she said softly to herself and to whatever god might be listening.

It was just past sunset. More and more customers entered, demanding food and drink. Tika had apologized to Dezra, the two friends had shed a few tears together, and now were kept busy running from kitchen to bar to table. Tika started every time the door opened, and she scowled irritably when she heard Otik's voice rise above the clatter of mugs and tongues.

". . . beautiful autumn night, as I recall, and I was, of course, busier than a draconian drill sergeant." That always got a laugh. Tika gritted her teeth. Otik had an appreciative audience and was in full swing. There would be no stopping him now. "The Inn was up in the vallenwood trees then, like the rest of our lovely city before the dragons destroyed it. Ah, how beautiful it was in the old days." He sighed—he always sighed at this point—and wiped away a tear. There was a sympathetic murmur from the crowd. "Where was I?" He blew his nose, another part of the act. "Ah, yes. There I was, behind the bar, when the door opened. . . ."

The door opened. It might have been done on cue, so perfect was the timing. Tika brushed back a strand of red hair from her perspiring forehead and glanced over nervously. Sudden silence filled the room. Tika stiffened, her nails digging into her hands.

A tall man, so tall he had to duck to enter the door, stood in the doorway. His hair was dark, his face grim and stern.

Although cloaked in furs, it was obvious from his walk and stance that his body was strong and muscular. He cast a swift glance around the crowded Inn, sizing up those who were present, wary and watchful of danger.

But it was an instinctive action only, for when his penetrating, somber gaze rested on Tika, his stern face relaxed into a smile and he held his arms open wide.

Tika hesitated, but the sight of her friend suddenly filled her with joy and a strange wave of homesickness. Shoving her way through the crowd, she was caught in his embrace.

"Riverwind, my friend!" she murmured brokenly.

Grasping the young woman in his arms, Riverwind lifted her effortlessly, as though she were a child. The crowd began to cheer, banging their mugs on the table. Most couldn't believe their luck. Here was a Hero of the Lance himself, as if carried on the wings of Otik's story. And he even looked the part! They were enchanted.

For, upon releasing Tika, the tall man had thrown his fur cloak back from his shoulders, and now all could see the Mantle of the Chieftain that the Plainsman wore, its V-shaped sections of alternating furs and tooled leathers each representing one of the Plains tribes over which he ruled. His handsome face, though older and more careworn than when Tika had seen him last, was burned bronze by the sun and weather, and there was an inner joy within the man's eyes which showed that he had found in his life the peace he had been searching for years before.

Tika felt a choking sensation in her throat and turned quickly away, but not quickly enough.

"Tika," he said, his accent thick from living once more among his people, "it is good to see you well and beautiful still. Where's Caramon? I cannot wait to see—Why, Tika, what's wrong?"

"Nothing, nothing," Tika said briskly, shaking her red curls and blinking her eyes. "Come, I have a place saved for you by the fire. You must be exhausted and hungry."

She led him through the crowd, talking nonstop, never giving him a chance to say a word. The crowd inadvertently helped her, keeping Riverwind occupied as they gathered around to touch and marvel over his fur cloak, or tried to shake his hand (a custom Plainsmen consider barbaric) or thrust drinks into his face.

Riverwind accepted it all stoically, as he followed Tika through the excited throng, clasping the beautiful sword of elven make close to his side. His stern face grew a shade darker, and he glanced often out the windows as though already longing to escape the confines of this noisy, hot room and return to the outdoors he loved. But Tika skillfully shoved the more exuberant patrons aside and soon had her old friend seated by the fire at an isolated table near the kitchen door.

"I'll be back," she said, flashing him a smile and vanishing into the kitchen before he could open his mouth.

The sound of Otik's voice rose once again, accompanied by a loud banging. His story having been interrupted, Otik was using his cane—one of the most feared weapons in Solace—to restore order. The barkeep was crippled in one leg now and he enjoyed telling that story, too—about how he had been injured during the fall of Solace, when, by his own account, he single-handedly fought off the invading armies of draconians.

Grabbing a panful of spiced potatoes and hurrying back to Riverwind, Tika glared at Otik irritably. She knew the true story, how he had hurt his leg being dragged out of his hiding place beneath the floor. But she never told it. Deep within, she loved the old man like a father. He had taken her in and raised her, when her own father disappeared, giving her honest work when she might have turned to thievery. Besides, just reminding him that *she* knew the truth was useful in keeping Otik's tall tales from stretching to new heights.

The crowd was fairly quiet when Tika returned, giving her a chance to talk to her old friend.

"How is Goldmoon and your son?" she asked brightly, seeing Riverwind looking at her, studying her intently.

"She is fine and sends her love," Riverwind answered in his deep, low baritone. "My son"—his eyes glowed with pride—"is but two, yet already stands this tall and sits a horse better than most warriors."

"I was hoping Goldmoon would come with you," Tika said with a sigh she didn't mean Riverwind to hear. The tall Plainsman ate his food for a moment in silence before he answered.

"The gods have blessed us with two more children," he said, staring at Tika with a strange expression in his dark eyes.

"Two?" Tika looked puzzled, then, "oh, twins!" she cried joyfully. "Like Caramon and Rais—" She stopped abruptly, biting her lip.

Riverwind frowned and made the sign that wards off evil. Tika flushed and looked away. There was a roaring in her ears. The heat and the noise made her dizzy. Swallowing the bitter taste in her mouth, she forced herself to ask more about Goldmoon and, after awhile, could even listen to Riverwind's answer.

". . . still too few clerics in our land. There are many converts, but the powers of the gods come slowly. She works hard, too hard to my mind, but she grows more beautiful every day. And the babies, our daughters, both have silver-golden hair—"

Babies. . . . Tika smiled sadly. Seeing her face, Riverwind fell silent, finished eating, and pushed his plate away. "I can think of nothing I would rather do than continue this visit," he said slowly, "but I cannot be gone long from my people. You know the urgency of my mission. Where is Cara—"

"I must go check on your room," Tika said, standing up so quickly she jostled the table, spilling Riverwind's drink. "That gully dwarf is supposed to be making the bed. I'll probably find him sound asleep—"

She hurried away. But she did not go upstairs to the rooms. Standing outside by the kitchen door, feeling the night wind cool her fevered cheeks, she stared out into the darkness. "Let him go away!" she whispered. "Please. . . ."

Chapter 2

Perhaps most of all, Tanis feared his first sight of the Inn of the Last Home. Here it had all started, three years ago this autumn. Here he and Flint and the irrepressible kender, Tasslehoff Burrfoot, had come that night to meet old friends. Here his world had turned upside down, never to exactly right itself again.

But, riding toward the Inn, Tanis found his fears eased. It had changed so much it was like coming to some place strange, a place that held no memories. It stood on the ground, instead of in the branches of a great vallenwood. There were new additions, more rooms had been built to accommodate the influx of travelers, it had a new roof, much more modern in design. All the scars of war had been purged, along with the memories.

Then, just as Tanis was beginning to relax, the front door of the Inn opened. Light streamed out, forming a golden path of welcome, the smell of spiced potatoes and the sound of laughter came to him on the evening breeze. The memories returned in a rush, and Tanis bowed his head, overcome.

But, perhaps fortunately, he did not have time to dwell upon the past. As he and his companion approached the Inn, a stableboy ran out to grab the horses' reins.

"Food and water," said Tanis, sliding wearily from the saddle and tossing the boy a coin. He stretched to ease the cramps in his muscles. "I sent word ahead that I was to have a fresh horse waiting for me here. My name is Tanis Half-Elven."

The boy's eyes opened wide; he had already been staring at the bright armor and rich cloak Tanis wore. Now his curiosity was replaced by awe and admiration.

"Y-yes, sir," he stammered, abashed at being addressed by such a great hero. "T-the horse is ready, sh-shall I bring him around n-now, sir?"

"No" Tanis smiled. "I will eat first. Bring him in two hours."

"T-two hours. Yes, sir. Thank you, sir." Bobbing his head, the boy took the reins Tanis pressed into his unfeeling hand, then stood there, gaping, completely forgetting his task until the impatient horse nudged him, nearly knocking him over.

As the boy hurried off, leading Tanis's horse away, the half-elf turned to assist his companion down from her saddle.

"You must be made of iron," she said, looking at Tanis as he helped her to the ground. "Do you really intend to ride further tonight?"

"To tell the truth, every bone in my body aches," Tanis began, then paused, feeling uncomfortable. He was simply unable to feel at ease around this woman.

Tanis could see her face reflected in the light beaming from the Inn. He saw fatigue and pain. Her eyes were sunken into pale, hollow cheeks. She staggered as she stepped upon the ground, and Tanis was quick to give her his arm to lean upon. This she did, but only for a moment. Then, drawing herself up she gently but firmly pushed him away and stood alone, glancing at her surroundings without interest.

Every move hurt Tanis, and he could imagine how this woman must feel, unaccustomed as she was to physical exertion or hardship, and he was forced to regard her with grudging admiration. She had not complained once on their long and frightening journey. She had kept up with him, never lagging behind and obeying his instructions without question.

Why, then, he wondered, couldn't he feel anything for her? What was there about her that irritated him and annoyed him? Looking at her face, Tanis had his answer. The only warmth there was the warmth reflected from the Inn's light. Her face itself—even exhausted—was cold, passionless, devoid of—what? Humanity? Thus she had been all this long, dangerous journey. Oh, she had been coolly polite, coolly grateful, coolly distant and remote. She probably would have coolly buried me, Tanis thought grimly. Then, as if to reprimand him for his irreverent thoughts, his gaze was drawn to the medallion she wore around her neck, the Platinum Dragon of Paladine. He remembered Elistan's parting words, spoken in private just before their journey's beginning.

"It is fitting that you escort her, Tanis," said the now-frail cleric. "In many ways, she begins a journey much like your own years ago—seeking self-knowledge. No, you are right, she doesn't know this herself yet." This in answer to Tanis's dubious look. "She walks forward with her gaze fixed upon the heavens," Elistan smiled sadly. "She has not yet learned that, in so doing, one will surely stumble. Unless she learns, her fall may be hard." Shaking his head, he murmured a soft prayer. "But we must put our trust in Paladine."

Tanis had frowned then and he frowned now, thinking about it. Though he had come to a strong belief in the true gods—more through Laurana's love and faith in them than anything else—he felt uncomfortable trusting his life to them, and he grew impatient with those like Elistan who, it seemed, placed too great a burden upon the gods. Let man be responsible for himself for a change, Tanis thought irritably.

"What is it, Tanis?" Crysania asked coldly.

Realizing he had been staring at her all this while, Tanis coughed in embarrassment, cleared his throat, and looked away. Fortunately, the boy returned for Crysania's horse at this moment, sparing Tanis the need to answer. He gestured at the Inn, and the two walked toward it.

"Actually," Tanis said when the silence grew awkward, "I would like nothing better than to stay here and visit with my friends. But I have to be in Qualinesti the day after tomorrow, and only by hard riding will I arrive in time. My relations with my brother-in-law are not such that I can afford to offend him by missing Solostaran's funeral." He added with a grim smile, "Both politically and personally, if you take my meaning."

Crysania smiled in turn, but—Tanis saw—it was not a smile of understanding. It was a smile of tolerance, as if this talk of politics and family were beneath her.

They had reached the door to the Inn. "Besides," Tanis added softly, "I miss Laurana. Funny, isn't it. When she is near and we're busy about our own tasks, we'll sometimes go for days with just a quick smile or a touch and then we disappear into our worlds. But when I'm far away from her, it's like I suddenly awaken to find my right arm cut off. I may not go to bed thinking of my right arm, but when it is gone. . . ."

Tanis stopped abruptly, feeling foolish, afraid he sounded like a lovesick adolescent. But Crysania, he realized, was apparently not paying the least bit of attention to him. Her smooth, marble face had grown, if anything, more cold until the moon's silver light seemed warm by comparison. Shaking his head, Tanis pushed open the door.

I don't envy Caramon and Riverwind, he thought grimly.

The warm, familiar sounds and smells of the Inn washed over Tanis and, for long moments, everything was a blur. Here was Otik, older and fatter, if possible, leaning upon a cane and pounding him on the back. Here were people he had not seen in years, who had never had much to do with him before, now shaking his hand and claiming his friendship. Here was the old bar, still brightly polished, and somehow he managed to step on a gully dwarf. . . .

And then there was a tall man cloaked in furs, and Tanis was clasped inside his friend's warm embrace.

"Riverwind," he whispered huskily, holding onto the Plainsman tightly.

"My brother," Riverwind said in Que-shu, the language of his people. The crowd in the Inn was cheering wildly, but Tanis didn't hear them, because a woman with flaming red hair and a smattering of freckles had her hand upon his arm.

Reaching out still holding fast to Riverwind, Tanis gathered Tika into their embrace and for long moments the three friends clung to each other—bound together by sorrow and pain and glory.

Riverwind brought them to their senses. Unaccustomed to such public displays of emotion, the tall Plainsman regained his composure with a gruff cough and stood back, blinking his eyes rapidly and frowning at the ceiling until he was master of himself again. Tanis, his reddish beard wet with his own tears, gave Tika another swift hug, then looked around.

"Where's that big lummox of a husband of yours?" he asked cheerfully. "Where's Caramon?"

It was a simple question, and Tanis was totally unprepared for the response. The crowd fell completely silent; it seemed as if someone had shut them all up in a barrel. Tika's face flushed an ugly red, she muttered something unintelligible, and, bending down, dragged a gully dwarf up off the floor and shook him so his teeth rattled in his head.

Startled, Tanis looked at Riverwind, but the Plainsman only shrugged and raised his dark eyebrows. The half-elf turned to ask Tika what was going on, but just then felt a cool touch upon his arm. Crysania! He had completely forgotten her!

His own face flushing, he made his belated introductions.

"May I present Crysania of Tarinius, Revered Daughter of Paladine," Tanis said formally. "Lady Crysania, Riverwind, Chieftain of the Plainsmen, and Tika Waylan Majere."

Crysania untied her traveling cloak and drew back her hood. As she did so, the platinum medallion she wore around her neck flashed in the bright candlelight of the Inn. The woman's pure white lamb's wool robes peeped through the folds of her cloak. A murmur—both reverent and respectful—went through the crowd.

"A holy cleric!"

"Did you catch her name? Crysania! Next in line . . ."

"Elistan's successor . . ."

Crysania inclined her head. Riverwind bowed from the waist, his face solemn, and Tika, her own face still so flushed she appeared feverish, shoved Raf hurriedly behind the bar, then made a deep curtsey.

At the sound of Tika's married name, Majere, Crysania glanced at Tanis questioningly and received his nod in return.

"I am honored," Crysania said in her rich, cool voice, "to meet two whose deeds of courage shine as an example to us all."

Tika flushed in pleased embarrassment. Riverwind's stern face did not change expression, but Tanis saw how much the cleric's praise meant to the deeply religious Plainsman. As for the crowd, they cheered boisterously at this honor to their own and kept on cheering. Otik, with all due ceremony, led his guests to a waiting table, beaming on the heroes as if he had arranged the entire war especially for their benefit.

Sitting down, Tanis at first felt disturbed by the confusion and noise but soon decided it was beneficial. At least he could talk to Riverwind without fear of being overheard. But first, he had to find out—where was Caramon?

Once again, he started to ask, but Tika—after seeing them seated and fussing over Crysania like a mother hen—saw him open his mouth and, turning abruptly, disappeared into the kitchen.

Tanis shook his head, puzzled, but before he could think about it further, Riverwind was asking him questions. The two were soon deeply involved in talk.

"Everyone thinks the war is over," Tanis said, sighing. "And that places us in worse danger than before. Alliances between elves and humans that were strong when times were dark are beginning to melt in the sun. Laurana's in Qualinesti now, attending the funeral of her father and also trying to arrange an agreement with that stiff-necked brother of hers, Porthios, and the Knights of Solamnia. The only ray of hope we have is in Porthios's wife, Alhana Starbreeze," Tanis smiled. "I never thought I would live to see that elf woman not only tolerant of humans and other races, but even warmly supporting them to her intolerant husband."

"A strange marriage," Riverwind commented, and Tanis nodded in agreement. Both men's thoughts were with their friend, the knight, Sturm Brightblade, now lying dead—hero of the High Clerist's Tower. Both knew Alhana's heart had been buried there in the darkness with Sturm.

"Certainly not a marriage of love," Tanis shrugged. "But it may be a marriage that will help restore order to the world. Now, what of you, my friend? Your face is dark and drawn with new worries, as well as beaming with new joy. Goldmoon sent Laurana word of the twins."

Riverwind smiled briefly. "You are right. I begrudge every minute I am away," the Plainsman said in his deep voice, "though seeing you again, my brother, lightens my heart's burden. But I left two tribes on the verge of war. So far, I have managed to keep them talking, and there has been no blood shed yet. But malcontents work against me, behind my back. Every minute I am away gives them a chance to stir up old blood feuds."

Tanis clasped his arm. "I am sorry, my friend, and I am grateful you came." Then he sighed again and glanced at Crysania, realizing he had new problems. "I had hoped you would be able to offer this lady your guidance and protection." His voice sank to a murmur. "She travels to the Tower of High Sorcery in Wayreth Forest."

Riverwind's eyes widened in alarm and disapproval. The Plainsman distrusted mages and anything connected with them.

Tanis nodded. "I see you remember Caramon's stories about the time he and Raistlin traveled there. And *they* had been invited. This lady goes without invitation, to seek the mages' advice about—"

Crysania gave him a sharp, imperious glance. Frowning, she shook her head. Tanis, biting his lip, added lamely, "I was hoping you could escort her—"

"I feared as much," said Riverwind, "when I received your message, and that was why I felt I had to come—to offer you some explanation for my refusal. If it were any other time, you know I would gladly help and, in particular, I would be honored to offer my services to a person so revered." He bowed slightly to Crysania, who accepted his homage with a smile that vanished instantly when she returned her gaze to Tanis. A small, deep line of anger appeared between her brows.

Riverwind continued, "But there is too much at stake. The peace I have established between the tribes, many who have been at war for years, is a fragile one. Our survival as a nation and a people depend upon us uniting and working together to rebuild our land and our lives."

"I understand," Tanis said, touched by Riverwind's obvious unhappiness in having to refuse his request for help. The half-elf caught Lady Crysania's displeased stare, however, and he turned to her with grim politeness. "All will be well, Revered Daughter," he said, speaking with elaborate patience. "Caramon will guide you, and he is worth three of us ordinary mortals, right, Riverwind?"

The Plainsman smiled, old memories returning. "He can eat as much as three ordinary mortals, certainly. And he is as strong as three or more. Do you remember, Tanis, when he used to lift stout Pig-faced William off his feet, when we put on that show in . . . where was it . . . Flotsam?"

"And the time he killed those two draconians by bashing their heads together," Tanis laughed, feeling the darkness of the world suddenly lift in sharing those times with his friend. "And do you remember when we were in the dwarven kingdom and Caramon sneaked up behind Flint and—" Leaning forward, Tanis whispered in Riverwind's ear. The Plainsman's face flushed with laughter. He recounted another tale, and the two men continued, recalling stories of Caramon's strength, his skill with a sword, his courage and honor.

"And his gentleness," Tanis added, after a moment's quiet reflection. "I can see him now, tending to Raistlin so patiently, holding his brother in his arms when those coughing fits nearly tore the mage apart—"

He was interrupted by a smothered cry, a crash, and a thud. Turning in astonishment, Tanis saw Tika staring at him, her face white, her green eyes glimmering with tears.

"Leave now!" she pleaded through pale lips. "Please, Tanis! Don't ask any questions! Just go!" She grabbed his arm, her nails digging painfully into his flesh.

"Look, what in the name of the Abyss is going on, Tika?" Tanis asked in exasperation, standing up and facing her.

A splintering crash came in answer. The door to the Inn burst open, hit from outside by some tremendous force. Tika jumped back, her face convulsed in such fear and horror as she looked at the door that Tanis turned swiftly, his hand on his sword, and Riverwind rose to his feet.

A large shadow filled the doorway, seeming to spread a pall over the room. The crowd's cheerful noise and laughter ceased abruptly, changing to low, angry mutterings.

Remembering the dark and evil things that had been chasing them, Tanis drew his sword, placing himself between the darkness and Lady Crysania. He sensed, though he did not see, Riverwind's stalwart presence behind him, backing him up.

So, it's caught up with us, Tanis thought, almost welcoming the chance to fight this vague, unknown terror. Grimly he stared at the door, watching as a bloated, grotesque figure entered into the light.

It was a man, Tanis saw, a huge man, but, as he looked more closely, he saw it was a man whose giant girth had run to flab. A bulging belly hung over cinched up leather leggings. A filthy shirt gaped open at the navel, there being too little shirt to cover too much flesh. The man's face—partially obscured by a three-day growth of beard—was unnaturally flushed and splotchy, his hair greasy and unkempt. His clothes, while fine and well-made, were dirty and smelled strongly of vomit and the raw liquor known as dwarf spirits.

Tanis lowered his sword, feeling like a fool. It was just some poor drunken wretch, probably the town bully, using his great size to intimidate the citizenry. He looked at the man with pity and disgust, thinking, even as he did so, that there was something oddly familiar about him. Probably someone he had known when he lived in Solace long ago, some poor slob who had fallen on hard times.

The half-elf started to turn away, then noticed—to his amazement—that everyone in the Inn was looking at him expectantly.

What do they want me to do, Tanis thought in sudden, swift anger. Attack him? Some hero I'd look—beating up the town drunk!

Then he heard a sob at his elbow. "I told you to leave," Tika moaned, sinking down into a chair. Burying her face in her hands, she began to cry as if her heart would break.

Growing more and more mystified, Tanis glanced at Riverwind, but the Plainsman was obviously as much in the dark as his friend. The drunk, meanwhile, staggered into the room and gazed about in anger.

"Wash ish thish? A party?" he growled. "And nobody in-in-invited their old . . . invited me?"

No one answered. They were fixedly ignoring the slovenly man, their eyes still on Tanis, and now even the drunk's attention turned to the half-elf. Attempting to bring him into focus, the drunk stared at Tanis in a kind of puzzled anger, as though blaming him for being the cause of all his troubles. Then, suddenly, the drunk's eyes widened, his face split into a foolish grin, and he lurched forward, hands outstretched.

"Tanish . . . my fri—"

"Name of the gods," Tanis breathed, recognizing him at last.

The man staggered forward and stumbled over a chair. For a moment he stood swaying unsteadily, like a tree that has been cut and is ready to fall. His eyes rolled back in his head, people scrambled to get out of his way. Then—with a thud that shook the Inn—Caramon Majere, Hero of the Lance, passed out cold at Tanis's feet.

CHAPTER 3

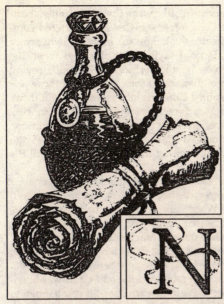

"Name of the gods," Tanis repeated in sorrow as he stooped down beside the comatose warrior. "Caramon . . ."

"Tanis—" Riverwind's voice caused the half-elf to glance up quickly. The Plainsman held Tika in his arms, both he and Dezra trying to comfort the distraught young woman. But people were pressing close, trying to question Riverwind or asking Crysania for a blessing. Others were demanding more ale or just standing around, gawking.

Tanis rose swiftly to his feet. "The Inn is closed for the night," he shouted.

There were jeers from the crowd, except for some scattered applause near the back where several customers thought he was buying a round of drinks.

"No, I mean it," Tanis said firmly, his voice carrying over the noise. The crowd quieted. "Thank you all for this welcome. I cannot tell you what it means to me to come back to my homeland. But, my friends and I would like to be alone now. Please, it is late. . . ."

There were murmurs of sympathy and some good-natured clapping. Only a few scowled and muttered comments about the greater the knight the more his own armor glares in his eyes (an old saying from the days when the Solamnic Knights were held in derision). Riverwind, leaving Dezra to take care of Tika, came forward to prod those few stragglers who assumed Tanis meant everyone except them. The half-elf stood guard over Caramon, who was snoring blissfully on the floor, keeping people from stepping on the big man. He exchanged glances with Riverwind as the Plainsman passed, but neither had time to speak until the Inn was emptied.

Otik Sandeth stood by the door, thanking everyone for coming and assuring each that the Inn would be open again tomorrow night. When everyone else had gone, Tanis stepped up to the retired proprietor, feeling awkward and embarrassed. But Otik stopped him before he could speak.

Gripping Tanis's hand in his, the elderly man whispered, "I'm glad you've come back. Lock up when you're finished." He glanced at Tika, then motioned the half-elf forward conspiratorially. "Tanis," he said in a whisper, "if you happen to see Tika take a little out of the money box, pay it no mind. She'll pay it back someday. I just pretend not to notice." His gaze went to Caramon, and he shook his head sadly. "I know you'll be able to help," he murmured, then he nodded and stumped off into the night, leaning on his cane.

Help! Tanis thought wildly. We came seeking *his* help. Caramon snored particularly loudly, half-woke himself up, belched up great fumes of dwarf spirits, then settled back down to sleep. Tanis looked bleakly at Riverwind, then shook his head in despair.

Crysania stared down at Caramon in pity mingled with disgust. "Poor man," she said softly. The medallion of Paladine shone in the candlelight. "Perhaps I—"

"There's nothing you can do for him," Tika cried bitterly. "He doesn't need healing. He's drunk, can't you see that? Dead drunk!"

Crysania's gaze turned to Tika in astonishment, but before the cleric could say anything, Tanis hurried back to Caramon.

"Help me, Riverwind," he said, bending down. "Let's get him hom—"

"Oh, leave him!" Tika snapped, wiping her eyes with the corner of her apron. "He's spent enough nights on the barroom floor. Another won't matter." She turned to Tanis. "I wanted to tell you. I really did. But I thought . . . I kept hoping . . . He was excited when your letter arrived. He was . . . well, more like himself than I've seen him in a long time. I thought maybe this might do it. He might change. So I let you come." She hung her head. "I'm sorry. . . ."

Tanis stood beside the big warrior, irresolute. "I don't understand. How long—"

"It's why we couldn't come to your wedding, Tanis," Tika said, twisting her apron into knots. "I wanted to, so much! But—" She began to cry again. Dezra put her arms around her.

"Sit down, Tika," Dezra murmured, helping her to a seat in a high-backed, wooden booth.

Tika sank down, her legs suddenly giving out beneath her, then she hid her head in her arms.

"Let's all sit down," Tanis said firmly, "and get our wits about us. You there"—the half-elf beckoned to the gully dwarf, who was peering out at them from beneath the wooden bar. "Bring us a pitcher of ale and some mugs, wine for Lady Crysania, some spiced potatoes—"

Tanis paused. The confused gully dwarf was staring at him, round-eyed, his mouth hanging open in confusion.

"Better let me get it for you, Tanis," Dezra offered, smiling. "You'd probably end up with a pitcher of potatoes if Raf went after it."

"Me help!" Raf protested indignantly.

"You take out the garbage!" Dezra snapped.

"Me big help. . . ." Raf mumbled disconsolately as he shuffled out, kicking at the table legs to relieve his hurt feelings.

"Your rooms are in the new part of the Inn," Tika mumbled. "I'll show you. . . ."

"We'll find them later," Riverwind said sternly, but as he looked at Tika, his eyes were filled with gentle sympathy. "Sit and talk to Tanis. He has to leave soon."

"Damn! My horse!" Tanis said, starting up suddenly. "I asked the boy to bring it around—"

"I will go have them wait," Riverwind offered.

"No, I'll go. It'll just take a moment—"

"My friend," Riverwind said softly as he went past him, "I need to be outdoors! I'll come back to help with—" He nodded his head toward the snoring Caramon.

Tanis sat back down, relieved. The Plainsman left. Crysania sat down beside Tanis on the opposite side of the table, staring at Caramon in perplexity. Tanis kept talking to Tika about small, inconsequential matters until she was able to sit up and even smile a little. By the time Dezra returned with drinks, Tika seemed more relaxed, though her face was still drawn and strained. Crysania, Tanis noticed, barely touched her wine. She simply sat, glancing occasionally at Caramon, the dark line appearing once again between her brows. Tanis knew he should explain to her what was going on, but he wanted someone to explain it to him first.

"When did this—" he began, hesitantly.

"Start?" Tika sighed. "About six months after we got back here." Her gaze went to Caramon. "He was so happy—at first. The town was a mess, Tanis. The winter had been terrible for the survivors. Most of them were starving, the draconians and goblin soldiers took everything. Those whose houses had been destroyed were living in whatever shelter they could find—caves, lean-to hovels. The draconians had abandoned the town by the time we got back, and people were beginning to rebuild. They welcomed Caramon as a hero—the bards had been here already, singing their songs about the defeat of the Queen."

Tika's eyes shimmered with tears and remembered pride.

"He was so happy, Tanis, for a while. People needed him. He worked day and night—cutting trees, hauling timber from the hills, putting up houses. He even took up smithy work, since Theros was gone. Oh, he wasn't very good at it." Tika smiled sadly. "But he was happy, and no one really minded. He made nails and horseshoes and wagon wheels. That first year was good for us—truly good. We were married, and Caramon seemed to forget about . . . about . . ."

Tika swallowed. Tanis patted her hand and, after eating a little and drinking some wine in silence, Tika was able to continue.

"A year ago last spring, though, everything started to change. Something happened to Caramon. I'm not sure what. It had something to do with—" She broke off, shook her head. "The town was prosperous. A blacksmith who had been held captive at Pax Tharkas moved here and took over the smithy trade. Oh, people still needed homes built, but there was no hurry. I took over running the Inn," Tika shrugged. "I guess Caramon just had too much time on his hands."

"No one needed him," Tanis said grimly.

"Not even me. . . ." Tika said, gulping and wiping her eyes. "Maybe it's my fault—"

"No," said Tanis, his thoughts—and his memories—far away. "Not your fault, Tika. I think we know whose fault this is."

"Anyway"—Tika drew a deep breath—"I tried to help, but I was so busy here. I suggested all sorts of things he could do and he tried—he really did. He helped the local constable, tracking down renegade draconians. He was a bodyguard, for a while, hiring out to people traveling to Haven. But no one ever hired him twice." Her voice dropped. "Then one day, last winter, the party he'd been supposed to protect returned, dragging him on a sled. He was dead drunk. *They'd* ended up protecting *him*! Since then, he's spent all his time either sleeping, eating, or hanging out with some ex-mercenaries at the Trough, that filthy place at the other end of town."

Wishing Laurana were here to discuss such matters, Tanis suggested softly, "Maybe a—um—baby?"

"I was pregnant, last summer," Tika said dully, leaning her head on her hand. "But not for long. I miscarried. Caramon never even knew. Since then"—she stared down at the wooden table—"well, we haven't been sleeping in the same room."

Flushing in embarrassment, Tanis could do nothing more than pat her hand and hurriedly change the subject. "You said a moment before 'it had something to do with—' . . . with what?"

Tika shivered, then took another drink of wine. "Rumors started, then, Tanis," she said in a low, hushed voice. "Dark rumors. You can guess who they were about!"

Tanis nodded.

"Caramon wrote to him, Tanis. I saw the letter. It was—it tore my heart. Not a word of blame or reproach. It was filled with love. He begged his brother to come back and live with us. He pleaded with him to turn his back on the darkness."

"And what happened?" Tanis asked, though he already guessed the answer.

"It came back," Tika whispered. "Unopened. The seal wasn't even broken. And on the outside was written, 'I have no brother. I know no one named Caramon.' And it was signed, *Raistlin!*"

"Raistlin!" Crysania looked at Tika, as if seeing her for the first time. Her gray eyes were wide and startled as they went from the red-haired young woman to Tanis, then to the huge warrior on the floor, who belched comfortably in his drunken sleep. "Caramon . . . This is *Caramon Majere*? This is *his* brother? The twin you were telling me about? The man who could guide me—"

"I'm sorry, Revered Daughter," Tanis said, flushing. "I had no idea he—"

"But Raistlin is so . . . intelligent, powerful. I thought his twin must be the same. Raistlin is sensitive, he exerts such strong control over himself and those who serve him. He is a perfectionist, while this"— Crysania gestured—"this pathetic wretch, while he deserves our pity and our prayers, is—"

"Your 'sensitive and intelligent perfectionist' had a hand in making this man the 'pathetic wretch' you see, Revered Daughter," Tanis said acidly, keeping his anger carefully under control.

"Perhaps it was the other way around," Crysania said, regarding Tanis coldly. "Perhaps it was for lack of love that Raistlin turned from the light to walk in darkness."

Tika looked up at Crysania, an odd expression in her eyes. "Lack of love?" she repeated gently.

Caramon moaned in his sleep and began thrashing about on the floor. Tika rose quickly to her feet.

"We better get him home." She glanced up to see Riverwind's tall figure appear in the doorway, then turned to Tanis. "I'll see you in the morning, won't I? Couldn't you stay . . . just overnight?"

Tanis looked at her pleading eyes and felt like biting off his tongue before he answered. But there was no help for it. "I'm sorry, Tika," he said, taking her hands. "I wish I could, but I must go. It is a long ride to Qualinost from here, and I dare not be late. The fate of two kingdoms, perhaps, depends on my being there."

"I understand," Tika said softly. "This isn't your problem anyway. I'll cope."

Tanis could have torn out his beard with frustration. He longed to stay and help, if he even could help. At least he might talk with Caramon, try to get some sense into that thick skull. But Porthios would take it as a personal affront if Tanis did not come to the funeral, which would affect not only his personal relationships with Laurana's brother, but would affect the treaty of alliance being negotiated between Qualinesti and Solamnia.

And then, his eyes going to Crysania, Tanis realized he had another problem. He groaned inwardly. He couldn't take her to Qualinost. Porthios had no use for human clerics.

"Look," Tanis said, suddenly getting an idea, "I'll come back, after the funeral." Tika's eyes brightened. He turned to Lady Crysania. "I'll leave you here, Revered Daughter. You'll be safe in this town, in the Inn. Then I can escort you back to Palanthas since your journey has failed—"

"My journey has not failed," Crysania said resolutely. "I will continue as I began. I intend to go to the Tower of High Sorcery at Wayreth, there to council with Par-Salian of the White Robes."

Tanis shook his head. "I cannot take you there," he said. "And Caramon obviously is incapable. Therefore I suggest—"

"Yes," Crysania interrupted complacently. "Caramon is clearly incapacitated. Therefore I will wait for the kender friend of yours to meet me here with the person he was sent to find, then I will continue on my own."

"Absolutely not!" Tanis shouted. Riverwind raised his eyebrows, reminding Tanis who he was addressing. With an effort, the half-elf regained control. "My lady, you have no idea of the danger! Besides those dark things that pursued us—and I think we all know who sent them—I've heard Caramon's stories about the Forest of Wayreth. It's darker still! We'll go back to Palanthas, I'll find some Knights—"

For the first time, Tanis saw a pale stain of color touch Crysania's marble cheeks. Her dark brows contracted as she seemed to be thinking. Then her face cleared. Looking up at Tanis, she smiled.

"There is no danger," she said. "I am in Paladine's hands. The dark creatures may have been sent by Raistlin, but they have no power to harm *me*! They have merely strengthened my resolve." Seeing Tanis's face grow even grimmer, she sighed. "I promise this much. I will think about it. Perhaps you are right. Perhaps the journey is too dangerous—"

"And a waste of time!" Tanis muttered, sorrow and exhaustion making him speak bluntly what he had felt all along about this woman's crazy scheme. "If Par-Salian could have destroyed Raistlin, he would have done it long before—"

"Destroy!" Crysania regarded Tanis in shock, her gray eyes cold. "I do not seek his destruction."

Tanis stared at her in amazement.

"I seek to reclaim him," Crysania continued. "I will go to my rooms now, if someone will be so kind as to guide me to them."

Dezra hurried forward. Crysania calmly bade them all goodnight, then followed Dezra from the room. Tanis gazed after her, totally at a loss for words. He heard Riverwind mutter something in Que-shu. Then Caramon groaned again. Riverwind nudged Tanis. Together they bent over the slumbering Caramon and—with an effort—hauled the big man to his feet.

"Name of the Abyss, he's heavy!" Tanis gasped, staggering under the man's dead weight as Caramon's flacid arms flopped over his shoulders. The putrid smell of the dwarf spirits made him gag.

"How can he drink that stuff?" Tanis said to Riverwind as the two dragged the drunken man to the door, Tika following along anxiously behind.

"I saw a warrior fall victim to that curse once," Riverwind grunted. "He perished leaping over a cliff, being chased by creatures that were there only in his mind."

"I should stay—" Tanis murmured.

"You cannot fight another's battle, my friend," Riverwind said firmly. "Especially when it is between a man and his own soul."

It was past midnight when Tanis and Riverwind had Caramon safely at home and dumped—unceremoniously—into his bed. Tanis had never been so tired in his life. His shoulders ached from carrying the dead weight of the giant warrior. He was worn out and felt drained, his memories of the past—once pleasant—were now like old wounds, open and bleeding. And he still had hours to ride before morning.

"I wish I could stay," he repeated again to Tika as they stood together with Riverwind outside her door, gazing out over the sleeping, peaceful town of Solace. "I feel responsible—"

"No, Tanis," Tika said quietly. "Riverwind's right. You can't fight *this* war. You have your own life to live, now. Besides, there's nothing you can do. You might only make things worse."

"I suppose," Tanis frowned. "At any rate, I'll be back in about a week. I'll talk to Caramon then."

"That would be nice," Tika sighed, then, after a pause, changed the subject. "By the way, what did Lady Crysania mean about a kender coming here? Tasslehoff?"

"Yes," Tanis said, scratching his beard. "It has something to do with Raistlin, though I'm not sure what. We ran into Tas in Palanthas. He started in on some of his stories—I warned her that only about half of what he says is true and even that half's nonsense, but he probably convinced her to send him after some person she thinks can help her *reclaim* Raistlin!"

"The woman may be a holy cleric of Paladine," Riverwind said sternly, "and may the gods forgive me if I speak ill of one of their chosen. But I think she's mad." Having made this pronouncement, he slung his bow over his shoulder and prepared to depart.

Tanis shook his head. Putting his arm around Tika, he kissed her. "I'm afraid Riverwind's right," he said to her softly. "Keep an eye on Lady Crysania while she's here. I'll have a talk with Elistan about her when we return. I wonder how much he knew about this wild scheme of hers. Oh, and if Tasslehoff does show up, hang onto him, will you? I don't want him turning up in Qualinost! I'm going to have enough trouble with Porthios and the elves as it is!"

"Sure, Tanis," Tika said softly. For a moment she nestled close to him, letting herself be comforted by his strength and the compassion she could sense in both his touch and his voice.

Tanis hesitated, holding her, reluctant to let her go. Glancing inside the small house, he could hear Caramon crying out in his sleep.

"Tika—" he began.

But she pushed herself away. "Go along, Tanis," she said firmly. "You've got a long ride ahead of you."

"Tika. I wish—" But there was nothing he could say that would help, and they both knew it.

Turning slowly, he trudged off after Riverwind.

Watching them go, Tika smiled.

"You are very wise, Tanis Half-Elven. But this time you are wrong," she said to herself as she stood alone on her porch. "Lady Crysania *isn't* mad. She's in love."

Chapter 4

An army of dwarves was marching around the bedroom, their steelshod boots going THUD, THUD, THUD. Each dwarf had a hammer in his hand and, as he marched past the bed, he banged it against Caramon's head. Caramon groaned and flapped his hands feebly.

"Get away!" he muttered. "Get away!"

But the dwarves only responded by lifting his bed up onto their strong shoulders and whirling it around at a rapid pace, as they continued to march, their boots striking the wooden floor THUD, THUD, THUD.

Caramon felt his stomach heave. After several desperate tries, he managed to leap out of the revolving bed and make a clumsy dash for the chamber pot in the corner. Having vomited, he felt better. His head cleared. The dwarves disappeared—although he suspected they were hiding beneath the bed, waiting for him to lie down again.

Instead, he opened a drawer in the tiny bedside table where he kept his small flask of dwarf spirits. Gone! Caramon scowled. So Tika was playing *this* game again, was she? Grinning smugly, Caramon stumbled over to the large clothes chest on the other side of the room. He lifted the lid and rummaged through tunics and pants and shirts that would no longer fit over his flabby body. There it was—tucked into an old boot.

Caramon withdrew the flask lovingly, took a swig of the fiery liquor, belched, and heaved a sigh. There, the hammering in his head was gone. He glanced around the room. Let the dwarves stay under the bed. He didn't care.

There was the clink of crockery in the other room. Tika! Hurriedly, Caramon took another sip, then closed the flask and tucked it back into the boot again. Shutting the lid very, very quietly, he straightened up, ran a hand through his tangled hair, and started to go out into the main living area. Then he caught a glimpse of himself in a mirror as he passed.

"Change my shirt," he muttered thickly.

After much pulling and tugging, he dragged off the filthy shirt he was wearing and tossed it in a corner. Perhaps he should wash? Bah! What was he—a sissy? So he smelled—it was a manly smell. Plenty of women liked it, found it attractive—found *him* attractive! Never complained or nagged, not like Tika. Why couldn't she take him as he was? Struggling into a clean shirt he found at the foot of the bed, Caramon felt very sorry for himself. No one understood him . . . life was hard . . . he was going through a bad time just now . . . but that would change . . . just wait . . . someday—tomorrow maybe. . . .

Lurching out of the bedroom, trying to appear nonchalant, Caramon walked unsteadily across the neat, clean living room and collapsed into a chair at the eating table. The chair creaked beneath his great weight. Tika turned around.

Catching her glance, Caramon sighed. Tika was mad—again. He tried grinning at her, but it was a sickly grin and didn't help. Her red curls bouncing in anger, she whirled around and disappeared through a door into the kitchen. Caramon winced as he heard heavy iron pots bang. The sound brought the dwarves and their hammers back. Within a few moments, Tika returned, carrying a huge dish of sizzling bacon, fried maize cakes, and eggs. She slammed the plate down in front of him with such force the cakes leaped three inches into the air.

Caramon winced again. He wondered briefly about eating—considering the queasy state of his stomach—then grouchily reminded his stomach who was boss. He was starved, he couldn't remember when he'd eaten last. Tika flounced down in a chair next to him. Glancing up, he saw her green eyes blazing. Her freckles stood out clearly against her skin—a certain sign of fury.

"All right," Caramon growled, shoveling food into his mouth. "What'd I do now?"

"You don't remember." It was a statement.

Caramon cast about hastily in the foggy regions of his mind. Something stirred vaguely. He was supposed to have been somewhere last night. He'd stayed home all day, getting ready. He'd promised Tika . . . but he'd grown thirsty. His flask was empty. He'd just go down to the Trough for a quick nip, then to . . . where . . . why . . .

"I had business to attend to," Caramon said, avoiding Tika's gaze.

"Yes, *we* saw your business," Tika snapped bitterly. "The business that made you pass out right at Tanis's feet!"

"*Tanis!*" Caramon dropped his fork. "Tanis . . . last night . . ." With a heartsick moan, the big man let his aching head sink into his hands.

"You made quite a spectacle of yourself," Tika continued, her voice choked. "In front of the entire town, plus half the elves in Krynn. Not to mention our old friends." She was weeping quietly now. "Our best friends. . . ."

Caramon moaned again. Now he was crying, too. "Why? Why?" he blubbered. "Tanis, of all of them . . ." His self-recriminations were interrupted by a banging on the front door.

"Now what?" Tika muttered, rising and wiping her tears away with the sleeve of her blouse. "Maybe it's Tanis, after all." Caramon lifted his head. "Try at least to *look* like the man you once were." Tika said under her breath as she hurried to the door.

Throwing the bolt, she unlatched it. "Otik?" she said in astonishment. "What are—Whose food?"

The rotund, elderly innkeeper stood in the doorway, a plate of steaming food in his hand. He peered past Tika.

"Isn't she here?" he asked, startled.

"Isn't who here?" Tika replied, confused. "There's no one here."

"Oh, dear," Otik's face grew solemn. Absently, he began to eat the food from the plate. "Then I guess the stableboy was right. She's gone. And after I fixed this nice breakfast."

"Who's gone?" Tika demanded in exasperation, wondering if he meant Dezra.

"Lady Crysania. She's not in her room. Her things aren't there, either. And the stableboy said she came this morning, told him to saddle her horse, and left. I thought—"

"Lady Crysania!" Tika gasped. "She's gone off, by herself. Of course, she would. . . ."

"What?" asked Otik, still munching.

"Nothing," Tika said, her face pale. "Nothing Otik. Uh, you better get back to the Inn. I'll—I may be a little late today."

"Sure, Tika," Otik said kindly, having seen Caramon hunched over the table. "Get there when you can." Then he left, eating as he walked. Tika shut the door behind him.

Seeing Tika return, and knowing he was in for a lecture, Caramon rose clumsily to his feet. "I'm not feeling too good," he said. Lurching across the floor, he staggered into the bedroom, slamming the door shut behind him. Tika could hear the sound of wracking sobs from inside.

She sat down at the table, thinking. Lady Crysania had gone, she was going to find Wayreth Forest by herself. Or rather, she had gone in search of it. No one ever found it, according to legend. *It* found *you*! Tika shivered, remembering Caramon's stories. The dread Forest was on maps, but—comparing them— no two maps ever agreed on its location. And there was always a symbol of warning beside it. At its center stood the Tower of High Sorcery of Wayreth, where all the power of the mages of Ansalon was now concentrated. Well, almost all—

In sudden resolution, Tika got up and thrust open the bedroom door. Going inside, she found Caramon flat upon the bed, sobbing and blubbering like a child. Hardening her heart against this pitiful sight, Tika walked with firm steps over to the large chest of clothes. As she threw open the lid and began sorting through the clothes, she found the flask, but simply tossed it into a corner of the room. Then—at the very bottom—she came upon what she had been searching for.

Caramon's armor.

Lifting out a cuisse by its leather strap, Tika stood up and turning around, hurled the polished metal straight at Caramon.

It struck him in the shoulder, bouncing off to fall to the floor with a clatter.

"Ouch!" the big man cried, sitting up. "Name of the Abyss, Tika! Leave me alone for—"

"You're going after her," Tika said firmly, lifting out another piece of armor. "You're going after her, if I have to haul you out of here in a wheelbarrow!"

"Uh, pardon me," said a kender to a man loitering near the edge of the road on the outskirts of Solace. The man instantly clapped his hand over his purse. "I'm looking for the home of a friend of mine. Well, actually two friends of mine. One's a woman, pretty, with red curls. Her name is Tika Waylan—"

Glaring at the kender, the man jerked a thumb. "Over there yonder."

Tas looked. "There?" he said pointing, impressed. "That truly magnificent house in the new vallenwood?"

"What?" The man gave a brief, sharp laugh. "What'd you call it? Truly magnificent? That's a good one." Still chuckling, he walked off, laughing and hastily counting the coins in his purse at the same time.

How rude! Tas thought, absently slipping the man's pocket knife into one of his pouches. Then, promptly forgetting the incident, the kender headed for Tika's home. His gaze lingered fondly on each detail of the fine house nestled securely in the limbs of the still-growing vallenwood tree.

"I'm so glad for Tika." Tas remarked to what appeared to be a mound of clothes with feet walking beside him. "And for

Caramon, too," he added. "But Tika's never really had a true home of her own. How proud she must be!"

As he approached the house, Tas saw it was one of the better homes in the township. It was built in the ages-old tradition of Solace. The delicate turns of the vaulting gables were shaped to appear to be part of the tree itself. Each room extended off from the main body of the house, the wood of the walls carved and polished to resemble the tree trunk. The structure conformed to the shape of the tree, a peaceful harmony existed between man's work and nature's to create a pleasing whole. Tas felt a warm glow in his heart as he thought of his two friends working on and living in such a wonderful dwelling. Then—

"That's funny," said Tas to himself, "I wonder why there's no roof."

As he drew closer, looking at the house more intently, he noticed it was missing quite a few things—a roof among them.

The great vaulting gables actually did nothing more than form a framework for a roof that wasn't there. The walls of the rooms extended only part way around the building. The floor was only a barren platform.

Coming to stand right beneath it, Tas peered upwards, wondering what was going on. He could see hammers and axes and saws lying out in the open, rusting away. From their looks, they hadn't been used in months. The structure itself was showing the effects of long exposure to weather. Tas tugged his topknot thoughtfully. The building had all the makings of the most magnificent structure in all of Solace—if it was ever finished!

Then Tas brightened. One section of the house *was* finished. All of the glass had been carefully placed into the window frames, the walls were intact, a roof protected the room from the elements. At least Tika has one room of her own, the kender thought. But, as he studied the room more closely, his smile faded. Above the door, he could see clearly, despite some weathering, the carefully crafted mark denoting a wizard's residence.

"I might have known," Tas said, shaking his head. He glanced around. "Well, Tika and Caramon certainly can't be living there. But that man said—Oh."

As he walked around the huge vallenwood tree, he came upon a small house, almost lost amidst overgrown weeds, hidden by the shadow of the vallenwood tree. Obviously built only as a temporary measure, it had the look of becoming all too permanent. If ever a building could look unhappy, Tas mused, this one did. Its gables sagged into a frown. Its paint was cracked and peeling. Still, there were flowers in the windowboxes and frilly curtains in the windows. The kender sighed. So this was Tika's house, built in the shadow of a dream.

Approaching the little house, he stood outside the door, listening attentively. There was the most awful commotion going on inside. He could hear thuds and glass breaking and shouts and thumping.

"I think you better wait out here." Tas said to the bundle of clothes.

The bundle grunted and plopped itself comfortably down into the muddy road outside the house. Tas glanced at it uncertainly, then shrugged and walked up to the door. Putting his hand on the doorknob, he turned it and took a step forward, confidently expecting to walk right in. Instead he smashed his nose on the wood. The door was locked.

"That's odd," Tas said, stepping back and looking around. "What is Tika thinking about? Locking doors! How barbaric. And a bolt lock at that. I'm sure I was expected...." He stared at the lock gloomily. The shouts and yells continued inside. He thought he could hear Caramon's deep voice.

"It sure sounds interesting in there." Tas glanced around, and felt cheered immediately. "The window! Of course!"

But, on hurrying over to the window, Tas found it locked, too! "I never would have expected that of Tika, of all people," the kender commented sadly to himself. Studying the lock, he noticed it was a simple one and would open quite easily. From the set of tools in his pouch, Tas removed the lock-picking device that is a kender's birthright. Inserting it, he gave it an expert twist and had the satisfaction of hearing the lock click. Smiling happily, he pushed the paned glass open and crawled inside. He hit the floor without a sound. Peering back out the window, he saw the shapeless bundle napping in the gutter.

Relieved on that point, Tasslehoff paused to look around the house, his sharp eyes taking in everything, his hands touching everything.

"My, isn't this interesting," went Tas's running commentary as he headed for the closed door from beyond which came the crashing sounds. "Tika won't mind if I study it for a moment. I'll put it right back." The object tumbled, of its accord, into his pouch. "And look at this! Uh-oh, there's a crack in it. She'll thank me for telling her about it." That object slipped into another pouch. "And what's the butter dish doing clear over here? I'm sure Tika kept it in the pantry. I better return it to its proper place." The butter dish settled into a third pouch.

By this time, Tas had reached the closed door. Turning the handle— (he was thankful to see Tika hadn't locked it as well!)—he walked inside.

"Hullo," he said merrily. "Remember me? Say, this looks like fun! Can I play? Give me something to throw at him, too, Tika. Gee, Caramon"—Tas entered the bedroom and walked over to where Tika stood, a breastplate in her hand, staring at him in profound astonishment—"what *is* the matter with you—you look *awful*, just *awful*! Say, why are we throwing armor at Caramon, Tika?" Tas asked, picking up a chain mail vest and turning to face the big warrior, who had barricaded himself behind the bed. "Is this something you two do regularly? I've heard married couples do some strange things, but this seems kind of weird—"

"Tasslehoff Burrfoot!" Tika recovered her power of speech. "What in the name of the gods are you doing here?"

"Why, I'm sure Tanis must have told you I was coming," Tas said, hurling the chain mail at Caramon. "Hey—this *is* fun! I found the front door locked." Tas gave her a reproachful glance. "In fact, I had to come in a window, Tika," he said severely. "I think you might have more consideration. Anyway, I'm supposed to meet Lady Crysania here and—"

To Tas's amazement, Tika dropped the breastplate, burst into tears, and collapsed onto the floor. The kender looked over at Caramon, who was rising up from behind the backboard like a spectre rising from the grave. Caramon stood looking at Tika with a lost and wistful expression. Then he picked his way through pieces of armor that lay scattered about on the floor and knelt down beside her.

"Tika," he whispered pathetically, patting her shoulder. "I'm sorry. I didn't mean all those things I said, you know that. I love you! I've always loved you. It's just . . . I don't know what to do!"

"You know what to do!" Tika shouted. Pulling away from him, she sprang to her feet. "I just told you! Lady Crysania's in danger. You've got to go to her!"

"Who is this Lady Crysania?" Caramon yelled back. "Why should I give a damn whether she's in danger or not?"

"Listen to me for once in your life," Tika hissed through clenched teeth, her anger drying her tears. "Lady Crysania is a powerful cleric of Paladine, one of the most powerful in the world, next to Elistan. She was warned in a dream that Raistlin's evil could destroy the world. She is going to the Tower of High Sorcery in Wayreth to talk to Par-Salian to—"

"To get help destroying him, isn't that it?" Caramon snarled.

"And what if they did?" Tika flared. "Does he deserve to live? He'd kill you without a second thought!"

Caramon's eyes flashed dangerously, his face flushed. Tas gulped, seeing the big man's fist clench, but Tika walked right up to stand in front of him. Though her head barely came to his chin, Tas thought the big man cowered at her anger. His hand opened weakly.

"But, no, Caramon," Tika said grimly, "she doesn't want to destroy him. She's just as big a fool as you are. She loves your brother, may the gods help her. She wants to save him, to turn him from evil."

Caramon stared at Tika in wonder. His expression softened.

"Truly?" he said.

"Yes, Caramon," Tika said wearily. "That's why she came here, to see you. She thought you might be able to help. Then, when she saw you last night—"

Caramon's head drooped. His eyes filled with tears. "A woman, a stranger, wants to help Raist. And risks her life to do it." He began to blubber again.

Tika stared at him in exasperation. "Oh, for the love of— Go after her, Caramon!" she cried, stamping her foot on the floor. "She'll never reach the Tower alone. You know that! You've been through the Forest of Wayreth."

"Yes," Caramon said, sniffing. "I went with Raist. I took him there, so he could find the Tower and take the Test. That evil Test! I guarded him. He needed me . . . then."

"And Crysania needs you now!" Tika said grimly. Caramon was still standing, irresolute, and Tas saw Tika's face settle in firm, hard lines. "You don't have much time to lose, if you're going to catch up with her. Do you remember the way?"

"I do!" shouted Tas in excitement. "That is, I have a map," Tika and Caramon turned around to stare at the kender in astonishment, both having forgotten his existence.

"I dunno," Caramon said, regarding Tas darkly. "I remember your maps. One of them took us to a seaport that didn't have any sea!"

"That wasn't my fault!" Tas cried indignantly. "Even Tanis said so. My map was drawn before the Cataclysm struck and took the sea away. But you *have* to take me with you, Caramon! I'm supposed to meet Lady Crysania. She sent me on a quest, a real quest. And I completed it. I found"—sudden movement caught Tas's attention—"oh, here she is."

He waved his hand, and Tika and Caramon turned to see the shapeless bundle of clothes standing in the door to their bedroom. Only now the bundle had grown two black, suspicious eyes.

"Me hungry," said the bundle to Tas accusingly. "When we eat?"

"I went on a quest for Bupu," Tasslehoff Burrfoot said proudly.

"But what in the name of the Abyss does Lady Crysania want with a gully dwarf?" Tika said in absolute mystification. She had taken Bupu to the kitchen, given her some stale bread and half a cheese, then sent her back outside—the gully dwarf's smell doing nothing to enhance the comfort of the small house. Bupu returned happily to the gutter, where she supplemented her meal by drinking water out of a puddle in the street.

"Oh, I promised I wouldn't tell," Tas said importantly. The kender was helping Caramon to strap on his armor—a rather involved task, since the big man was considerably bigger since the last time he'd worn it. Both Tika and Tas worked until they were sweating, tugging on straps, pushing and prodding rolls of fat beneath the metal.

Caramon groaned and moaned, sounding very much like a man being stretched on the rack. The big man's tongue licked his lips and his longing gaze went more than once to the bedroom and the small flask Tika had so casually tossed into the corner.

"Oh, come now, Tas," Tika wheedled, knowing the kender couldn't keep a secret to save his life. "I'm sure Lady Crysania wouldn't mind—"

Tas's face twisted in agony. "She-she made me promise and swear to Paladine, Tika!" The kender's face grew solemn. "And you know that Fizban—I mean Paladine—and I are *personal* friends." The kender paused. "Suck in your gut, Caramon," he ordered irritably. "How did you ever get yourself into this condition, anyway?"

Putting his foot against the big man's thigh, Tas tugged. Caramon yelped in pain.

"I'm in fine shape," the big man mumbled angrily. "It's the armor. It's shrunk or something."

"I didn't know this kind of metal shrinks," Tas said with interest. "I'll bet it has to be heated! How did you do that? Or did it just get real, real hot around here?"

"Oh, shut up!" Caramon snarled.

"I was only being helpful," Tas said, wounded. "Anyway, oh, about Lady Crysania." His face took on a lofty look. "I gave my sacred oath. All I can say is she wanted me to tell her everything I could remember about Raistlin. And I did. And this has to do with that. Lady Crysania's truly a wonderful person, Tika," Tas continued solemnly. "You might not have noticed, but I'm not very religious. Kender aren't as a rule. But you don't have to be religious to know that there is something *truly good* about Lady Crysania. She's smart, too. Maybe even smarter than Tanis."

Tas's eyes were bright with mystery and importance. "I think I can tell you this much," he said in a whisper. "She has a plan! A plan to help save Raistlin! Bupu's part of the plan. She's taking her to Par-Salian!"

Even Caramon looked dubious at this, and Tika was privately beginning to think maybe Riverwind and Tanis were right. Maybe Lady Crysania was mad. Still, anything that might help Caramon, might give him some hope—

But Caramon had apparently been working things out in his own mind. "You know. It's all the fault of this Fis-Fistandoodle or whatever his name was," he said, tugging uncomfortably at the leather straps where they bit into his flabby flesh. "You know, that mage Fizban—er—Paladine told us about. And Par-Salian knows something about that, too!" His face brightened. "We'll fix everything. I'll bring Raistlin back here, like we planned, Tika! He can move into the room we've got fixed up for him. We'll take care of him, you and I. In our new house. It's going to be fine, fine!" Caramon's eyes shone.

Tika couldn't look at him. He sounded so much like the old Caramon, the Caramon she had loved. . . .

Keeping her expression stern, she turned abruptly and headed for the bedroom. "I'll go get the rest of your things—"

"Wait!" Caramon stopped her. "No, uh—thanks, Tika. I can manage. How about you—uh—pack us something to eat."

"I'll help," Tas offered, heading eagerly for the kitchen.

"Very well,' Tika said. Reaching out, she caught hold of the kender by the topknot of hair that tumbled down his back. "Just one minute, Tasslehoff Burrfoot. You're not going anywhere until you sit down and empty out every one of your pouches!"

Tas wailed in protest. Under cover of the confusion, Caramon hurried into the bedroom and shut the door. Without pausing, he went straight for the corner and retrieved the flask. Shaking it, he found it over half-full. Smiling to himself in satisfaction, he thrust it deep into his pack, then hastily crammed some additional clothes in on top of it.

"Now, I'm all set!" he called out cheerfully to Tika.

"I'm all set," Caramon repeated, standing disconsolately on the porch.

He was a ludicrous sight. The stolen dragon armor he had worn during the last months of the campaign had been completely refurbished by the big warrior when he arrived back in Solace. He had beaten the dents out, cleaned and polished and redesigned it so completely that it no longer resembled the original. He had taken a great deal of care with it, then packed it away lovingly. It was still in excellent condition. Only now, unfortunately, there was a large gap between the shining black chain mail that covered his chest and the big belt that girdled his rotund waist. Neither he nor Tas had been able to strap the metal plates that guarded his legs around his flabby thighs. He had stowed these away in his pack. He groaned when he lifted his shield and looked at it suspiciously, as if certain someone had filled it with lead weights during the last two years. His sword belt would not fit around his sagging gut. Blushing furiously, he strapped the sword in its worn scabbard onto his back.

At this point, Tas was forced to look somewhere else. The kender thought he was going to laugh but was startled to find himself on the verge of tears.

"I look a fool," Caramon muttered, seeing Tas turn away hurriedly. Bupu was staring at him with eyes as wide as teacups, her mouth hanging open.

"Him look just like my Highbulp, Phudge I," Bupu sighed.

A vivid memory of the fat, slovenly king of the gully dwarf clan in Xak Tsaroth came to Tas's mind. Grabbing the gully dwarf, he stuffed a hunk of bread in her mouth to shut her up. But the damage had been done. Apparently Caramon, too, remembered.

"That does it," he snarled, flushing darkly and hurling his shield to the wooden porch where it banged and clattered loudly. "I'm not going! This was a stupid idea anyway!" He stared accusingly at Tika, then, turning around, he started for the door. But Tika moved to stand in front of him.

"No," she said quietly. "You're not coming back into my house, Caramon, until you come back one whole person."

"Him more like *two* whole person," mumbled Bupu in a muffled voice. Tas stuffed more bread in her mouth.

"You're not making any sense!" Caramon snapped viciously, putting his hand on her shoulder. "Get out of my way, Tika!"

"Listen to me, Caramon," Tika said. Her voice was soft, but penetrating; her eyes caught and held the big man's attention. Putting her hand on his chest, she looked up at him earnestly. "You offered to follow Raistlin into darkness, once. Do you remember?"

Caramon swallowed, then nodded silently, his face pale.

"He refused." Tika continued gently, "saying it would mean your death. But, don't you see, Caramon—you *have* followed him into darkness! And you're dying by inches! Raistlin himself told you to walk your own path and let him walk his. But you haven't done that! You're trying to walk both paths, Caramon. Half of you is living in darkness and the other half is trying to drink away the pain and the horror you see there."

"It's my fault!" Caramon began to blubber, his voice breaking. "It's my fault he turned to the Black Robes. I drove him to it! That's what Par-Salian tried to make me see—"

Tika bit her lip. Tas could see her face grow grim and stern with anger, but she kept it inside. "Perhaps," was all she said. Then she drew a deep breath. "But you are not coming back to me as husband or even friend until you come back at peace with yourself."

Caramon stared at her, looking as though he was seeing her for the first time. Tika's face was resolute and firm, her green eyes were clear and cold. Tas suddenly remembered her fighting draconians in the Temple at Neraka that last horrible night of the War. She had looked just the same.

"Maybe that'll be never," Caramon said surlily. "Ever think of that, huh, my fine lady?"

"Yes," Tika said steadily. "I've thought of it. Good-bye, Caramon."

Turning away from her husband, Tika walked back through the door of her house and shut it. Tas heard the bolt slide home with a click. Caramon heard it, too, and flinched at the sound. He clenched his huge fists, and for a minute Tas feared he might break down the door. Then his hands went limp. Angrily, trying to salvage some of his shattered dignity, Caramon stomped off the porch.

"I'll show her," he muttered, striding off, his armor clanking and clattering. "Come back, three or four days, with that Lady Cryslewhatever. Then we'll talk about this. She can't do this to me! No, by all the gods! Three, four days, she'll be begging me to come back. But maybe I will and maybe I won't...."

Tas stood, irresolute. Behind him, inside the house, his sharp kender ears could hear grief-stricken sobbing. He knew that Caramon, between his own self-pitying ramblings and his clanking armor, could hear nothing. But what could he do?

"I'll take care of him, Tika!" Tas shouted, then, grabbing Bupu, they hurried along after the big man. Tas sighed. Of all the adventures he had been on, this one was certainly starting out all wrong.

Chapter 5

alanthas—fabled city of beauty.

A city that has turned its back upon the world and sits gazing, with admiring eyes, into its mirror.

Who had described it thus? Kitiara, seated upon the back of her blue dragon, Skie, pondered idly as she flew within sight of the city walls. The late, unlamented Dragon Highlord Ariakas, perhaps. It sounded pretentious enough, like something he would say. But he had been right about the Palanthians, Kit was forced to admit. So terrified were they of seeing their beloved city laid waste, they had negotiated a separate peace with the Highlords. It wasn't until right before the end of the war—when it was obvious they had nothing to lose—that they had reluctantly joined with others to fight the might of the Dark Queen.

Because of the heroic sacrifice of the Knights of Solamnia, the city of Palanthas was spared the destruction that had laid other cities—such as Solace and Tarsis—to waste. Kit, flying within arrow shot of the walls, sneered. Now, once more, Palanthas had turned her eyes to her mirror, using the new influx of prosperity to enhance her already legendary charm.

Thinking this, Kitiara laughed out loud as she saw the stir upon the Old City walls. It had been two years since a blue dragon had flown above the walls. She could picture the chaos, the panic. Faintly, on the still night air, she could hear the beating of drums and the clear calls of trumpets.

Skie, too, could hear. His blood stirred at the sounds of war, and he turned a blazing red eye round to Kitiara, begging her to reconsider.

"No, my pet," Kitiara called, reaching down to pat his neck soothingly. "Now is not the time! But soon—if we prove successful! Soon, I promise you!"

Skie was forced to content himself with that. He achieved some satisfaction, however, by breathing a bolt of lightning from his gaping jaws, blackening the stone wall as he soared past, keeping just out of arrow range. The troops scattered like ants at his coming, the dragonfear sweeping over them in waves.

Kitiara flew slowly, leisurely. None dared touch her—a state of peace existed between her armies in Sanction and the Palanthians, though there were some among the Knights who were trying to persuade the free peoples of Ansalon to unite and attack Sanction where Kitiara had retreated following the war. But the Palanthians couldn't be bothered. The war was over, the threat gone.

"And daily I grow in strength and in might," Kit said to them as she flew above the city, taking it all in, storing it in her mind for future reference.

Palanthas is built like a wheel. All of the important buildings—the palace of the reigning lord, government offices, and the ancient homes of the nobles—stand in the center. The city revolves around this hub. In the next circle are built the homes of the wealthy guildsmen—the "new" rich—and the summer homes of those who live outside the city walls. Here, too, are the educational centers, including the Great Library of Astinus. Finally, near the walls of Old City, is the marketplace and shops of every type and description.

Eight wide avenues lead out from the center of Old City, like spokes on the wheel. Trees line these avenues, lovely trees, whose leaves are like golden lace all year long. The avenues lead to the seaport to the north and to the seven gates of Old City Wall.

Surrounding the wall, Kit saw New City, built just like Old City, in the same circular pattern. There are no walls around New City, since walls "detract from the overall design," as one of the lords put it.

Kitiara smiled. She did not see the beauty of the city. The trees were nothing to her. She could look upon the dazzling marvels of the seven gates without a catch in her throat— well, perhaps, a small one. How easy it would be, she thought with a sigh, to capture!

Two other buildings attracted her interest. One was a new one being built in the center of the city—a Temple, dedicated to Paladine. The other building was her destination. And, on this one, her gaze rested thoughtfully.

It stood out in such vivid contrast to the beauty of the city around it that even Kitiara's cold, unfeeling gaze noted it. Thrusting up from the shadows that surrounded it like a bleached fingerbone, it was a thing of darkness and twisted ugliness, all the more horrible because once it must have been the most wonderful building in Palanthas—the ancient Tower of High Sorcery.

Shadow surrounded it by day and by night, for it was guarded by a grove of huge oak trees, the largest trees growing on Krynn, some of the more well-traveled whispered in awe. No one knew for certain because there were none, even of the kender race which fears little on this world, who could walk in the trees' dread darkness.

"The Shoikan Grove," Kitiara murmured to an unseen companion. "No living being of any race dared enter it. Not until *he* came—*the master of past and of present.*" If she said this with a sneer in her voice, it was a sneer that quivered as Skie began to circle nearer and nearer that patch of blackness.

The blue dragon settled down upon the empty, abandoned streets near the Shoikan Grove. Kit had urged Skie with everything from bribes to dire threats to fly her over the

Grove to the Tower itself. But Skie, although he would have shed the last drop of his blood for his master, refused her this. It was beyond his power. No mortal being, not even a dragon, could enter that accursed ring of guardian oaks.

Skie stood glaring into the grove with hatred, his red eyes burning, while his claws nervously tore up the paving stones. He would have prevented his master from entering, but he knew Kitiara well. Once her mind was set upon something, nothing could deter her. So Skie folded his great, leathery wings around his body and gazed at this fat, beautiful city while thoughts of flames and smoke and death filled him with longing.

Kitiara dismounted from her dragonsaddle slowly. The silver moon, Solinari, was a pale, severed head in the sky. Its twin, the red moon Lunitari, had just barely risen and now flickered on the horizon like the wick of a dying candle. The faint light of both moons shimmered in Kitiara's dragonscale armor, turning it a ghastly blood-hued color.

Kit studied the grove intently, took a step toward it, then stopped nervously. Behind her, she could hear a rustle—Skie's wings giving unspoken advice—*Let us flee this place of doom, lady! Flee while we still have our lives!*

Kitiara swallowed. Her tongue felt dry and swollen. Her stomach muscles knotted painfully. Vivid memories of her first battle returned to her, the first time she had faced an enemy and known that she must kill this man—or she herself would be dead. Then, she had conquered with the skillful thrust of her sword blade. But this?

"I have walked many dark places upon this world," Kit said to her unseen companion in a deep, low voice, "and I have not known fear. But I cannot enter here."

"Simply hold the jewel he gave you high in your hand," said her companion, materializing out of the night. "The Guardians of the Grove will be powerless to harm you."

Kitiara looked into the dense ring of tall trees. Their vast, spreading branches blotted out the light of moons and stars by night, of the sun by day. Around their roots flowed perpetual night. No soft breeze touched their hoary arms, no storm wind moved the great limbs. It was said that even during the awful days before the Cataclysm, when storms the like of which had not been known before on Krynn swept the land, the trees of Shoikan Grove alone had not bent to the anger of the gods.

But, more horrible even than their everlasting darkness, was the echo of everlasting life that pulsed from deep within. Everlasting life, everlasting misery and torment . . .

"What you say my head believes," Kitiara answered, shivering, "but my heart does not, Lord Soth."

"Turn back, then," the death knight answered, shrugging. "Show *him* that the most powerful Dragon Highlord in the world is a coward."

Kitiara stared at Soth from the eye slits of her dragonhelm.

Her brown eyes glinted, her hand closed spasmodically over the hilt of her sword. Soth returned her gaze, the orange flame flickering within his eye sockets burned bright in hideous mockery. And if *his* eyes laughed at her, what would those golden eyes of the mage reveal? Not laughter—triumph!

Compressing her lips tightly, Kitiara reached for the chain around her neck where hung the charm Raistlin had sent her. Grasping hold of the chain, she gave it a quick jerk, snapping it easily. Then she held the jewel in her gloved hand.

Black as dragon's blood, the jewel felt cold to the touch, radiating a chill even through her heavy, leather gloves. Unshining, unlovely, it lay heavy in her palm.

"How can these Guardians see it?" Kitiara demanded, holding it to the moons' light. "Look, it does not gleam or sparkle. It seems I hold nothing more than a lump of coal in my hand."

"The moon that shines upon the night jewel you cannot see, nor can any see save those who worship it," Lord Soth replied. "Those—and the dead who, like me, have been damned to eternal life. *We* can see it! For us, it shines more clearly than any light in the sky. Hold it high, Kitiara, hold it high and walk forward. The Guardians will not stop you. Take off your helm, that they may look upon your face and see the light of the jewel reflected in your eyes."

Kitiara hesitated a moment longer. Then—with thoughts of Raistlin's mocking laughter ringing in her ears—the Dragon Highlord removed the horned dragonhelm from her head. Still she stood, glancing around. No wind ruffled her dark curls. She felt cold sweat trickle down her temple. With an angry flick of her glove, she wiped it away. Behind her, she could hear the dragon whimper—a strange sound, one she had never heard Skie make before. Her resolution faltered. The hand holding the jewel shook.

"They feed off fear, Kitiara," said Lord Soth softly. "Hold the jewel high, let them see it reflected in your eyes!"

Show him you are a coward! Those words echoed in her mind. Clutching the nightjewel, lifting it high above her head, Kitiara entered Shoikan Grove.

Darkness descended, dropping over her so suddenly Kitiara thought for one horrible, paralyzing moment she had been struck blind. Only the sight of Lord Soth's flaming eyes flickering within his pale, skeletal visage reassured her. She forced herself to stand there calmly, letting that debilitating moment of fear fade. And then she noticed, for the first time, a light gleam from the jewel. It was like no other light she had ever seen. It did not illuminate the darkness so much as allow Kitiara to distinguish all that lived within the darkness from the darkness itself.

By the jewel's power, Kitiara could begin to make out the trunks of the living trees. And now she could see a path forming at her feet. Like a river of night, it flowed onward, into the trees, and she had the eerie sensation that she was flowing along with it.

Fascinated, she watched her feet move, carrying her forward without her volition. The Grove had tried to keep her out, she realized in horror. Now, it was drawing her in!

Desperately she fought to regain control of her own body. Finally, she won—or so she presumed. At least, she quit moving. But now she could do nothing but stand in that flowing darkness and shiver, her body racked by spasms of fear. Branches creaked overhead, cackling at the joke. Leaves brushed her face. Frantically, Kit tried to bat them away, then she stopped. Their touch was chill, but not unpleasant. It was almost a caress, a gesture of respect. She had been recognized, known for one of their own. Immediately, Kit was in command of herself once more. Lifting her head, she made herself look at the path.

It was not moving. That had been an illusion borne of her own terror. Kit smiled grimly. The trees themselves were moving! Standing aside to let her pass. Kitiara's confidence rose. She walked the path with firm steps and even turned to glance triumphantly at Lord Soth, who walked a few paces behind her. The death knight did not appear to notice her, however.

"Probably communing with his fellow spirits," Kit said to herself with a laugh that was twisted, suddenly, into a shriek of sheer terror.

Something had caught hold of her ankle! A bone-freezing chill was seeping slowly through her body, turning her blood and her nerves to ice. The pain was intense. She screamed in agony. Clutching at her leg, Kitiara saw what had grabbed her— a white hand! Reaching up from the ground, its bony fingers were wrapped tightly around her ankle. It was sucking the life out of her, Kit realized, feeling the warmth leave. And then, horrified, she saw her foot begin to disappear into the oozing soil.

Panic swept her mind. Frantically she kicked at the hand, trying to break its freezing grip. But it held her fast, and yet another hand reached up from the black path and grabbed hold of her other ankle. Screaming in terror, Kitiara lost her balance and plunged to the ground.

"Don't drop the jewel!" came Lord Soth's lifeless voice. "They will drag you under!"

Kitiara kept hold of the jewel, clutching it in her hand even as she fought and twisted, trying to escape the deathly grasp that was slowly drawing her down to share its grave. "Help me!" she cried, her terror-stricken gaze seeking Soth.

"I cannot," the death knight answered grimly. "My magic will not work here. The strength of your own will is all that can save you now, Kitiara. Remember the jewel. . . ."

For a moment, Kitiara lay quite still, shivering at the chilling touch. And then anger coursed through her body. *How dare he do this to me!* she thought, seeing, once more, mocking golden eyes enjoying her torture. Her anger thawed the chill of fear and burned away the panic. She was calm now. She knew what she must do. Slowly, she pushed herself up out of the dirt. Then, coldly and deliberately, she held the jewel down next to the skeletal hand and, shuddering, touched the jewel to the pallid flesh.

A muffled curse rumbled from the depths of the ground. The hand quivered, then released its grip, sliding back into the rotting leaves beside the trail.

Swiftly, Kitiara touched the jewel to the other hand that grasped her. It, too, vanished. The Dragon Highlord scrambled to her feet and stared around. Then she held the jewel aloft.

"See this, you accursed creatures of living death?" she screamed shrilly. "You will not stop me! I will pass! Do you hear me? I *will* pass!"

There was no answer. The branches creaked no longer, the leaves hung limply. After standing a moment longer in silence, the jewel in her hand, Kitiara started walking down the trail once more, cursing Raistlin beneath her breath. She was aware of Lord Soth near her.

"Not much farther," he said. "Once again, Kitiara, you have earned my admiration."

Kitiara did not answer. Her anger was gone, leaving a hollow place in the pit of her stomach that was rapidly filling up again with fear. She did not trust herself to speak. But she kept walking, her eyes now focused grimly on the path ahead of her. All around her now, she could see the fingers digging through the soil, seeking the living flesh they both craved and hated. Pale, hollow visages glared at her from the trees, black and shapeless things flitted about her, filling the cold, clammy air with a foul scent of death and decay.

But, though the gloved hand that held the jewel shook, it never wavered. The fleshless fingers did not stop her. The faces with their gaping mouths howled in vain for her warm blood. Slowly, the oak trees continued to part before Kitiara, the branches bending back out of the way.

There, standing at the trail's end, was Raistlin.

"I should kill you, you damned bastard!" Kitiara said through numb lips, her hand on the hilt of her sword.

"I am overjoyed to see you, too, my sister," Raistlin replied in his soft voice.

It was the first time brother and sister had met in over two years. Now that she was out from among the darkness of the trees, Kitiara could see her brother, standing in Solinari's pale light. He was dressed in robes of the finest black velvet. Hanging from his slightly stooped, thin shoulders, they fell in soft folds around his slender body. Silver runes were stitched about the hood that covered his head, leaving all but his golden eyes in shadow. The largest rune was in the center—an hourglass. Other silver runes sparkled in the moons' light upon the cuffs of his wide, full sleeves. He leaned upon the Staff of Magius, its crystal, which flamed into light only upon Raistlin's command—dark and cold, clutched in a golden dragon's claw.

"I should kill you!" Kitiara repeated, and, before she was quite aware of what she did, she cast a glance at the death knight, who seemed to form out of the darkness of the grove. It was a glance, not of command, but of invitation—an unspoken challenge.

Raistlin smiled, the rare smile that few ever saw. It was, however, lost in the shadows of his hood.

"Lord Soth," he said, turning to greet the death knight.

Kitiara bit her lip as Raistlin's hourglass eyes studied the undead knight's armor. Here were still the graven symbols of a Knight of Solamnia—the Rose and the Kingfisher and the Sword—but all were blackened as if the armor burned in a fire.

"Knight of the Black Rose," continued Raistlin, "who died in flames in the Cataclysm before the curse of the elfmaid you wronged dragged you back to bitter life."

"Such is my tale," the death knight said without moving. "And you are Raistlin, master of past and present, the one foretold."

The two stood, staring at each other, both forgetting Kitiara, who—feeling the silent, deadly contest being waged between the two—forgot her own anger, holding her breath to witness the outcome.

"Your magic is strong," Raistlin commented. A soft wind

stirred the branches of the oak trees, caressed the black folds of the mage's robes.

"Yes," said Lord Soth quietly. "I can kill with a single word. I can hurl a ball of fire into the midst of my enemies. I rule a squadron of skeletal warriors, who can destroy by touch alone. I can raise a wall of ice to protect those I serve. The invisible is discernible to my eyes. Ordinary magic spells crumble in my presence."

Raistlin nodded, the folds of his hood moving gently.

Lord Soth stared at the mage without speaking. Walking close to Raistlin, he stopped only inches from the mage's frail body. Kitiara's breath came fast.

Then, with a courtly gesture, the cursed Knight of Solamnia placed his hand over that portion of his anatomy that had once contained his heart.

"But I bow in the presence of a master," Lord Soth said.

Kitiara chewed her lip, checking an exclamation.

Raistlin glanced over at her quickly, amusement flashing in his golden, hourglass eyes.

"Disappointed, my dear sister?"

But Kitiara was well accustomed to the shifting winds of fate. She had scouted out the enemy, discovered what she needed to know. Now she could proceed with the battle. "Of course not, little brother," she answered with the crooked smile that so many had found so charming. "After all, it was you I came to see. It's been too long since we visited. You look well."

"Oh, I am, dear sister," Raistlin said. Coming forward, he put his thin hand upon her arm. She started at his touch, his flesh felt hot, as though he burned with fever. But—seeing his eyes intent upon her, noting every reaction—she did not flinch. He smiled.

"It has been so long since we saw each other last. What, two years? Two years ago this spring, in fact," he continued, conversationally, holding Kitiara's arm within his hand. His voice was filled with mockery. "It was in the Temple of the Queen of Darkness at Neraka, that fateful night when my queen met her downfall and was banished from the world—"

"Thanks to your treachery," Kitiara snapped, trying, unsuccessfully, to break free of his grip. Raistlin kept his hand upon Kitiara's arm. Though taller and stronger than the frail mage, and seemingly capable of breaking him in two with her bare hands, Kitiara—nevertheless—found herself longing to pull away from that burning touch, yet not daring to move.

Raistlin laughed and, drawing her with him, led her to the outer gates of the Tower of High Sorcery.

"Shall we talk of treachery, dear sister? Didn't you rejoice when I used my magic to destroy Lord Ariakas's shield of protection, allowing Tanis Half-Elven the chance to plunge his sword into the body of *your* lord and master? Did not I— by that action—make you the most powerful Dragon Highlord in Krynn?"

"A lot of good it has done me!" Kitiara returned bitterly. "Kept almost a prisoner in Sanction by the foul Knights of Solamnia, who rule the lands all about! Guarded day and night by golden dragons, my every move watched. My armies scattered, roaming the land...."

"Yet you came here," Raistlin said simply. "Did the gold dragons stop you? Did the Knights know of your leaving?"

Kitiara stopped on the path leading to the tower, staring at her brother in amazement. "Your doing?"

"Of course!" Raistlin shrugged. "But, we will talk of these matters later, dear sister," he said as they walked. "You are cold and hungry. The Shoikan Grove shakes the nerves of the most stalwart. Only one other person has successfully passed through its borders, with my help, of course. I expected you to do well, but I must admit I was a bit surprised at the courage of Lady Crysania—"

"Lady Crysania!" Kitiara repeated, stunned. "A Revered Daughter of Paladine! You allowed her—here?"

"I not only allowed her, I invited her," Raistlin answered imperturbably. "Without that invitation and a charm of warding, of course, she could never have passed."

"And she came?"

"Oh, quite eagerly, I assure you." Now it was Raistlin who paused. They stood outside the entrance to the Tower of High

Sorcery. Torchlight from the windows shone upon his face. Kitiara could see it clearly. The lips were twisted in a smile, his flat golden eyes shone cold and brittle as winter sunlight. "Quite eagerly," he repeated softly.

Kitiara began to laugh.

Late that night, after the two moons had set, in the still dark hours before the dawn, Kitiara sat in Raistlin's study, a glass of dark-red wine in her hands, her brows creased in a frown.

The study was comfortable, or so it seemed to look upon. Large, plush chairs of the best fabric and finest construction stood upon hand-woven carpets only the wealthiest people in Krynn could afford to own. Decorated with woven pictures of fanciful beasts and colorful flowers, they drew the eye, tempting the viewer to lose himself for long hours in their beauty. Carved wooden tables stood here and there, objects rare and beautiful—or rare and ghastly—ornamented the room.

But its predominant feature were the books. It was lined with deep wooden shelves, holding hundreds and hundreds of books. Many were similar in appearance, all bound with a nightblue binding, decorated with runes of silver. It was a comfortable room, but, despite a roaring fire blazing in a huge, gaping fireplace at one end of the study, there was a bone-chilling cold in the air. Kitiara was not certain, but she had the feeling it came from the books.

Lord Soth stood far from the fire's light, hidden in the shadows. Kit could not see him, but she was aware of his presence—as was Raistlin. The mage sat opposite his half-sister in a large chair behind a gigantic desk of black wood, carved so cunningly that the creatures decorating it seemed to watch Kitiara with their wooden eyes.

Squirming uncomfortably, she drank her wine, too fast. Although well accustomed to strong drink, she was beginning to feel giddy, and she hated that feeling. It meant she was losing control. Angrily, she thrust the glass away from her, determined to drink no more.

"This plan of yours is crazy!" she told Raistlin irritably. Not liking the gaze of those golden eyes upon her, Kitiara stood up and began to pace the room. "It's senseless! A waste of time.

With your help, we could rule Ansalon, you and I. In fact"—Kitiara turned suddenly, her face alight with eagerness—"with your power we could rule the world! We don't need Lady Crysania or our hulking brother—"

"Rule the world," Raistlin repeated softly, his eyes burning. "Rule the *world*? You still don't understand, do you, my dear sister? Let me make this as plain as I know how." Now it was his turn to stand up. Pressing his thin hands upon the desk, he leaned toward her, like a snake.

"I don't give a damn about the world!" he said softly. "I could rule it tomorrow if I wanted it! I don't."

"You don't want the world," Kit shrugged, her voice bitter with sarcasm. "Then that leaves only—"

Kitiara almost bit her tongue. She stared at Raistlin in wonder. In the shadows of the room, Lord Soth's flaming eyes blazed more brightly than the fire.

"*Now* you understand," Raistlin smiled in satisfaction and resumed his seat once more. "Now you see the importance of this Revered Daughter of Paladine! It was fate brought her to me, just when I was nearing the time for my journey."

Kitiara could only stare at him, aghast. Finally, she found her voice. "How—how do you know she will follow you? Surely you didn't tell her!"

"Only enough to plant the seed in her breast," Raistlin smiled, looking back to that meeting. Leaning back, he put his thin fingers to his lips. "My performance was, frankly, one of my best. Reluctantly I spoke, my words drawn from me by her goodness and purity. They came out, stained with blood, and she was mine . . . lost through her own pity." He came back to the present with a start. "She will come," he said coldly, sitting forward once more. "She and that buffoon of a brother. He will serve me unwittingly, of course. But then, that's how he does everything."

Kitiara put her hand to her head, feeling her blood pulse. It was not the wine, she was cold sober now. It was fury and frustration. He could help me! she thought angrily. He is truly as powerful as they said. More so! But he's insane. He's lost his mind. . . . Then, unbidden, a voice spoke to her from somewhere deep inside.

What if he isn't insane? What if he really means to go through with this?

Coldly, Kitiara considered his plan, looking at it carefully from all angles. What she saw horrified her. No. He could not win! And, worse, he would probably drag her down with him!

These thoughts passed through Kit's mind swiftly, and none of them showed on her face. In fact, her smile grew only more charming. Many were the men who had died, that smile their last vision.

Raistlin might have been considering that as he looked at her intently. "You can be on a winning side for a change, my sister."

Kitiara's conviction wavered. If he *could* pull it off, it would be glorious! Glorious! Krynn would be hers.

Kit looked at the mage. Twenty-eight years ago, he had been a newborn baby, sick and weakly, a frail counterpart to his strong, robust twin brother.

"Let 'im die. 'Twill be best in the long run," the midwife had said. Kitiara had been a teenager then. Appalled, she heard her mother weepingly agree.

But Kitiara had refused. Something within her rose to the challenge. The baby would live! She would *make* him live, whether he wanted to or not. "My first fight," she used to tell people proudly, "was with the gods. And I won!"

And now! Kitiara studied him. She saw the man. She saw—in her mind's eye—that whining, puking baby. Abruptly, she turned away.

"I must get back," she said, pulling on her gloves. "You will contact me upon your return?"

"If I am successful, there will be no need to contact you," Raistlin said softly. "You will *know*."

Kitiara almost sneered but caught herself quickly. Glancing at Lord Soth, she prepared to leave the room. "Farewell then, my brother." Controlled as she was, she could not keep an edge of anger from her voice. "I am sorry you do not share my desire for the good things of *this* life! We could have done much together, you and I!"

"Farewell, Kitiara," Raistlin said, his thin hand summoning the shadowy forms of those who served him to show his guests to the door. "Oh, by the way," he added as Kit stood in the doorway, "I owe you my life, dear sister. At least, so I have been told. I just wanted to let you know that—with the death of Lord Ariakas, who would, undoubtedly, have killed you—I consider my debt paid. I owe you nothing!"

Kitiara stared into the mage's golden eyes, seeking threat, promise, what? But there was nothing there. Absolutely nothing. And then, in an instant, Raistlin spoke a word of magic and vanished from her sight.

The way out of Shoikan Grove was not difficult. The guardians had no care for those who left the Tower. Kitiara and Lord Soth walked together, the death knight moving soundlessly through the Grove, his feet leaving no impression on the leaves that lay dead and decaying on the ground. Spring did not come to Shoikan Grove.

Kitiara did not speak until they had passed the outer perimeter of trees and once more stood upon the solid paving stones of the city of Palanthas. The sun was rising, the sky brightening from its deep night blue to a pale gray. Here and there, those Palanthians whose business called for them to rise early were waking. Far down the street, past the abandoned buildings that surrounded the Tower, Kitiara could hear marching feet, the changing of the watch upon the wall. She was among the living once again.

She drew a deep breath, then, "He must be stopped," she said to Lord Soth.

The death knight made no comment, one way or the other.

"It will not be easy, I know," Kitiara said, drawing the dragonhelm over her head and walking rapidly toward Skie, who had reared his head in triumph at her approach. Patting her dragon lovingly upon his neck, Kitiara turned to face the death knight.

"But we do not have to confront Raistlin directly. His scheme hinges upon Lady Crysania. Remove her, and we stop him. He need never know I had anything to do with it, in fact. Many have died, trying to enter the Forest of Wayreth. Isn't that so?"

Lord Soth nodded, his flaming eyes flaring slightly.

"You handle it. Make it appear to be . . . fate," Kitiara said. "My little brother believes in that, apparently." She mounted her dragon. "When he was small, I taught him that to refuse to do my bidding meant a whipping. It seems he must learn that lesson again!"

At her command, Skie's powerful hind legs dug into the pavement, cracking and breaking the stones. He leaped into the air, spread his wings, and soared into the morning sky. The people of Palanthas felt a shadow lift from their hearts, but that was all they knew. Few saw the dragon or its rider leave.

Lord Soth remained standing upon the fringes of Shoikan Grove.

"I, too, believe in fate, Kitiara," the death knight murmured. "The fate a man makes himself."

Glancing up at the windows of the Tower of High Sorcery, Soth saw the light extinguished from the room where they had been. For a brief instant, the Tower was shrouded in the perpetual darkness that seemed to linger around it, a darkness the sun's light could not penetrate. Then one light gleamed forth, from a room at the top of the tower.

The mage's laboratory, the dark and secret room where Raistlin worked his magic.

"Who will learn this lesson, I wonder?" Soth murmured. Shrugging, he disappeared, melting into the waning shadows as daylight approached.

Chapter 6

"Let's stop at this place," Caramon said, heading for a ramshackle building that stood huddled back away from the trail, lurking in the forest like a sulking beast. "Maybe she's been in here."

"I really doubt it," said Tas, dubiously eyeing the sign that hung by one chain over the door. "The 'Cracked Mug' doesn't seem quite the place—"

"Nonsense," growled Caramon, as he had growled more times on this journey already than Tas could count, "she has to eat. Even great, muckety-muck clerics have to eat. Or maybe someone in here will have seen some sign of her on the trail. *We're* not having any luck."

"No," muttered Tasslehoff beneath his breath, "but we might have more luck if we searched the road, not taverns."

They had been on the road three days, and Tas's worst misgivings about this adventure had proved true.

Ordinarily, kender are enthusiastic travelers. All kender are stricken with wanderlust somewhere near their twentieth year. At this time, they gleefully strike out for parts unknown, intent on finding nothing except adventure and whatever beautiful, horrible, or curious items might by chance fall into their bulging pouches. Completely immune to the self-preserving emotion of fear, afflicted by unquenchable curiosity, the kender population on Krynn was not a large one, for which most of Krynn was devoutly grateful.

Tasslehoff Burrfoot, now nearing his thirtieth year (at least as far as he could remember), was, in most regards, a typical kender. He had journeyed the length and breadth of the continent of Ansalon, first with his parents before they had settled down in Kenderhome. After coming of age, he wandered by himself until he met Flint Fireforge, the dwarven metalsmith and his friend, Tanis Half-Elven. After Sturm Brightblade, Knight of Solamnia, and the twins, Caramon and Raistlin, joined them, Tas became involved in the most wonderful adventure of his life—the War of the Lance.

But, in some respects, Tasslehoff was *not* a typical kender, although he would have denied this if it were mentioned. The loss of two people he loved dearly—Sturm Brightblade and Flint—touched the kender deeply. He had come to know the emotion of fear, not fear for himself, but fear and concern for those he cared about. His concern for Caramon, right now, was deep.

And it grew daily.

At first, the trip had been fun. Once Caramon got over his fit of sulks about Tika's hard-heartedness and the inability of the world in general to understand him, he had taken a few swigs from his flask and felt better. After several more swigs, he began to relate stories about his days helping to track down draconians. Tas found this amusing and entertaining and, though he continually had to watch Bupu to make certain she didn't get run over by a wagon or wander into a mudhole, he enjoyed his morning.

By afternoon, the flask was empty, and Caramon was even in such a good humor as to be ready to listen to some of Tas's stories, which the kender never tired of relating. Unfortunately, right at the best part, when he was escaping with the woolly mammoth and the wizards were shooting lightning bolts at him, Caramon came to a tavern.

"Just fill up the flask," he mumbled and went inside.

Tas started to follow, then saw Bupu staring in open-mouthed wonder at the red-hot blacksmith's forge across the road. Realizing she would either set herself or the town or both on fire, and knowing that he couldn't take her into the tavern (most refused to serve gully dwarves), Tas decided to stay out and keep an eye on her. After all, Caramon would probably be only a few minutes....

Two hours later, the big man stumbled out.

"Where in the Abyss have you been?" Tas demanded, pouncing on Caramon like a cat.

"Jusht having a . . . having a little . . ." Caramon swayed unsteadily, "one for the . . . road."

"I'm on a quest!" Tas yelled in exasperation. "My first quest, given to me by an Important Person, who may be in danger. And I've been stuck out here two hours with a gully dwarf!" Tas pointed at Bupu, who was asleep in a ditch. "I've never been so bored in my life, and *you're* in there soaking up dwarf spirits!"

Caramon glared at him, his lips pursed into a pout. "You know something," the big man muttered as he staggered off down the road, "you're st-starting to shound a lot like Tika..."

Things went rapidly downhill from there.

That night they came to the crossroads.

"Let's go this way," Tas said, pointing. "Lady Crysania's certain to know people are going to try to stop her. She'll take a route that's not very well traveled to try and throw off pursuit. I think we should follow the same trail we took two years ago, when we left Solace—"

"Nonsense!" Caramon snorted. "She's a woman and a cleric to boot. She'll take the easiest road. We'll go by way of Haven."

Tas had been dubious about this decision, and his doubts proved well-founded. They hadn't traveled more than a few miles when they came to another tavern.

Caramon went in to find out if anyone had seen a person matching Lady Crysania's description, leaving Tas—once again—with Bupu. An hour later the big man emerged, his face flushed and cheerful.

"Well, has anyone seen her?" Tas asked irritably.

"Seen who? Oh—her. No...."

And now, two days later, they were only about halfway to

Haven. But the kender could have written a book describing the taverns along the way.

"In the old days," Tas fumed, "we could have walked to Tarsis and back in this time!"

"I was younger then, and immature. My body's mature now, and I have to build up my strength," Caramon said loftily, "little by little."

"He's building up something little by little," Tas said to himself grimly, "but strength isn't it!"

Caramon could not walk much more than an hour before he was forced to sit down and rest. Often he collapsed completely, moaning in pain, sweat rolling off his body. It would take Tas, Bupu, and the flask of dwarf spirits to get him back on his feet again. He complained bitterly and continually. His armor chafed, he was hungry, the sun was too hot, he was thirsty. At night, he insisted that they stop in some wretched inn. Then Tas had the thrill of watching the big man drink himself senseless. Tas and the bartender would haul him to his room where he would sleep until half the morning was gone.

After the third day of this (and their twentieth tavern) and still no sign of Lady Crysania, Tasslehoff was beginning to think seriously about returning to Kenderhome, buying a nice little house, and retiring from adventuring.

It was about midday when they arrived at the Cracked Mug. Caramon immediately disappeared inside. Heaving a sigh that came from the toes of his new, bright green shoes, Tas stood with Bupu, looking at the outside of the slovenly place in grim silence.

"Me no like this anymore," Bupu announced. She glared at Tas accusingly. "You say we go find pretty man in red robes. All we find is one fat drunk. I go back home, back to Highbulp, Phudge I."

"No, don't leave! Not yet!" Tas cried desperately. "We'll find the—uh—pretty man. Or at least a pretty lady who wants to help the pretty man. Maybe . . . maybe we'll learn something here.

It was obvious Bupu didn't believe him. Tas didn't believe himself.

"Look," he said, "just wait for me here. It won't be much farther. I know—I'll bring you something to eat. Promise you won't leave?"

Bupu smacked her lips, eyeing Tas dubiously. "Me wait," she said, plopping down into the muddy road. "At least till after lunch."

Tas, his pointed chin jutting out firmly, followed Caramon into the tavern. He and Caramon were going to have a little talk—

As it turned out, however, that wasn't necessary.

"Your health, gentlemen," Caramon said, raising a glass to the slovenly crowd gathered in the bar. There weren't many—a couple of traveling dwarves, who sat near the door, and a party of humans, dressed like rangers, who lifted their mugs in return to Caramon's salute.

Tas sat down next to Caramon, so depressed that he actually returned a purse his hands had (without his knowing it) removed from the belt of one of the dwarves as he passed.

"I think you dropped this," Tas mumbled, handing it back to the dwarf, who stared at him in amazement.

"We're looking for a young woman," Caramon said, settling down for the afternoon. He recited her description as he had recited it in every tavern from Solace on. "Black hair, small, delicate, pale face, white robes. She's a cleric—"

"Yeah, we've seen her," said one of the rangers.

Beer spurted from Caramon's mouth. "You have?" he managed to gasp, choking.

Tas perked up. "Where?" he asked eagerly.

"Wandering about the woods east of here," said the ranger, jerking his thumb.

"Yeah?" Caramon said suspiciously. "What're you doing out in the woods yourselves?"

"Chasing goblins. There's a bounty for them in Haven."

"Three gold pieces for goblin ears," said his friend, with a toothless grin, "if you care to try your luck."

"What about the woman?" Tas pursued.

"She's a crazy one, I guess." The ranger shook his head. "We told her the land out around here was crawling with goblins and she shouldn't be out alone. She just said she was in the hands of Paladine, or some such name, and he would take care of her."

Caramon heaved a sigh and lifted his drink to his lips. "That sounds like her all right—"

Leaping up, Tas snatched the glass from the big man's hand.

"What the—" Caramon glared at him angrily.

"Come on!" Tas said, tugging at him. "We've got to go! Thanks for the help," he panted, dragging Caramon to the door. "Where did you say you saw her?"

"About ten miles east of here. You'll find a trail out back, behind the tavern. Branches off the main road. Follow it and it'll take you through the forest. Used to be a short cut to Gateway, before it got too dangerous to travel."

"Thanks again!" Tas pushed Caramon, still protesting, out the door.

"Confound it, what's the hurry?" Caramon snarled angrily, jerking away from Tas's prodding hands. "We coulda at least had dinner. . . ."

"Caramon!" said Tas urgently, dancing up and down. "Think! Remember! Don't you realize where she is? Ten miles east of here! Look—" Yanking open one of his pouches, Tas pulled out a whole sheaf of maps. Hurriedly, he sorted through them, tossing them onto the ground in his haste. "Look," he repeated finally, unrolling one and thrusting it into Caramon's flushed face.

The big man peered at it, trying to bring it into focus. "Huh?"

"Oh, for—Look, here's where we are, near as I can figure. And here's Haven, still south of us. Across here is Gateway. Here's the path they were talking about and here—" Tas's finger pointed.

Caramon squinted. "Dark-dar-dar Darken Wood," he mumbled. "Darken Wood. That seems familiar. . . ."

"Of course it seems familiar! We nearly died there!" Tas yelled, waving his arms. "It took Raistlin to save us—"

Seeing Caramon scowl, Tas hurried on. "What if she should wander in there alone?" he asked pleadingly.

Caramon looked out into the forest, his bleary eyes peering at the narrow, overgrown trail. His scowl deepened. "I suppose you expect me to stop her," he grumbled.

"Well, naturally we'll have to stop her!" Tas began, then came to a sudden halt. "You never meant to," the kender said softly, staring at Caramon. "All along, you never meant to go after her. You were just going to stumble around here for a few days, have a few drinks, a few laughs, then go back to

Tika, tell her you're a miserable failure, figuring she'd take you back, same as usual—"

"So what did you expect me to do?" Caramon growled, turning away from Tas's reproachful gaze. "How can I help this woman find the Tower of High Sorcery, Tas?" He began to whimper. "I don't *want* to find it! I swore I'd never go near that foul place again! They destroyed him there, Tas. When he came out, his skin was that strange gold color. They gave him those cursed eyes so that all he sees is death. They shattered his body. He couldn't take a breath without coughing. And they made him . . . they made him kill me!" Caramon choked and buried his face in his hands, sobbing in pain, trembling in terror.

"He-he didn't kill you, Caramon," Tas said, feeling completely helpless. "Tanis told me. It was just an image of you. And he was sick and scared and hurting real bad inside. He didn't know what he was doing—"

But Caramon only shook his head. And the tender-hearted kender couldn't blame him. No wonder he doesn't want to go back there, Tas thought remorsefully. Perhaps I should take him home. He certainly isn't much good to anyone in this state. But then Tas remembered Lady Crysania, out there all alone, blundering into Darken Wood. . . .

"I talked to a spirit there once," Tas murmured, "but I'm not certain they'd remember me. And there're goblins out there. And, while I'm not afraid of them, I don't suppose I'd be much good fighting off more than three or four."

Tasslehoff was at a loss. If only Tanis were here! The half-elf always knew what to say, what to do. He'd make Caramon listen to reason. But Tanis isn't here, said a stern voice inside of the kender that sounded at times suspiciously like Flint. It's up to you, you doorknob!

I don't want it to be up to me! Tas wailed, then waited for a moment to see if the voice answered. It didn't. He was alone.

"Caramon," Tas said, making his voice as deep as possible and trying very hard to sound like Tanis, "look, just come with us as far as the edges of the Forest of Wayreth. Then you can go home. We'll probably be safe after that—"

But Caramon wasn't listening. Awash in liquor and self-pity he collapsed onto the ground. Leaning back against a tree, he babbled incoherently about nameless horrors, begging Tika to take him back.

Bupu stood up and came to stand in front of the big warrior. "Me go," she said in disgust. "Me want fat, slobbering drunk me find plenty back home." Nodding her head, she started off down the path. Tas ran after her, caught her, and dragged her back.

"No, Bupu! You can't! We're almost there!"

Suddenly Tasslehoff's patience ran out. Tanis wasn't here. No one was here to help. It was just like the time when he'd broken the dragon orb. Maybe what he was doing wasn't the right thing, but it was the only thing he could think of to do.

Tas walked up and kicked Caramon in the shins.

"Ouch!" Caramon gulped. Startled, he stared at Tas, a hurt and puzzled look on his face. "What'dya do that for?"

In answer, Tas kicked him again, hard. Groaning, Caramon grabbed his leg.

"Hey, now we have some fun," Bupu said. Running forward gleefully, she kicked Caramon in the other leg. "Me stay now."

The big man roared. Blundering to his feet, he glared at Tas. "Blast it, Burrfoot, if this is one of your games—"

"It's no game, you big ox!" the kender shouted. "I've decided to kick some sense into you, that's all! I've had enough of your whining! All you've done, all these years, is whine! The noble Caramon, sacrificing everything for his ungrateful brother. Loving Caramon, always putting Raistlin first! Well—maybe you did and maybe you didn't. I'm starting to think you always put Caramon first! And maybe Raistlin knew, deep inside, what I'm just beginning to figure out! You only did it because it made *you* feel good! Raistlin didn't need you—you needed him! You lived his life because you're too scared to live a life of your own!"

Caramon's eyes glowed feverishly, his face paled with anger. Slowly, he stood up, his big fists clenched. "You've gone too far this time, you little bastard—"

"Have I?" Tas was screaming now, jumping up and down. "Well, listen to this, Caramon! You're always blubbering about how no one needs you. Did you ever stop to think that Raistlin needs you now more than he's ever needed you before? And Lady Crysania—she needs you!

And there you stand, a big blob of quivering jelly with your brain all soaked and turned to mush!"

Tasslehoff thought for a moment he *had* gone too far. Caramon took an unsteady step forward, his face blotched and mottled and ugly. Bupu gave a yelp and ducked behind Tas. The kender stood his ground—just as he had when the furious elf lords had been about to slice him in two for breaking the dragon orb. Caramon loomed over him, the big man's liquor-soaked breath nearly making Tas gag. Involuntarily, he closed his eyes. Not from fear, but from the look of terrible anguish and rage on Caramon's face.

He stood, braced, waiting for the blow that would likely smash his nose back through to the other side of his head.

But the blow never fell. There was the sound of tree limbs ripping apart, huge feet stomping through dense brush.

Cautiously, Tas opened his eyes. Caramon was gone, crashing down the trail into the forest. Sighing, Tas stared after him. Bupu crept out from behind his back.

"That fun," she announced. "I stay after all. Maybe we play game again?"

"I don't think so, Bupu," Tas said miserably. "Come on. I guess we better go after him."

"Oh, well," the gully dwarf reflected philosophically. "Some other game come along, just as fun."

"Yeah," Tas agreed absently. Turning around, afraid that perhaps someone in the wretched inn had overheard and might start trouble, the kender's eyes opened wide.

The Cracked Mug tavern was gone. The dilapidated building, the sign swinging on one chain, the dwarves, the rangers, the bartender, even the glass Caramon had lifted to his lips. All had disappeared into the midafternoon air like an evil dream upon awakening.

Chapter 7

Sing as the spirits move you,
Sing to your doubling eye,
Plain Jane becomes Lovable Lindas
When six moons shine in the sky.

Sing to a sailor's courage,
Sing while the elbows bend,
A ruby port your harbor,
Hoist three sheets to the wind.

Sing while the heart is cordial,
Sing to the absinthe of cares,
Sing to the one for the weaving road,
And the dog, and each of his hairs.

All of the waitresses love you,
Every dog is your friend,
Whatever you say is just what you mean,
So hoist three sheets to the wind.

By evening, Caramon was roaring drunk.

Tasslehoff and Bupu caught up with the big man as he was standing in the middle of the trail, draining the last of the dwarf spirits from the flask. He leaned his head back, tilting it to get every drop. When he finally lowered the flask, it was to peer inside it in disappointment. Wobbling unsteadily on his feet, he shook it.

"All gone," Tas heard him mumble unhappily.

The kender's heart sank.

"Now I've done it," Tas said to himself in misery. "I can't tell him about the disappearing inn. Not when he's in this condition! I've only made things worse!"

But he hadn't realized quite how much worse until he came up to Caramon and tapped him on the shoulder. The big man whirled around in drunken alarm.

"What ish it? Who'sh there?" He peered around the rapidly darkening forest.

"Me, down here," said Tas in a small voice. "I—I just wanted to say I was sorry, Caramon, and—"

"Uh? Oh . . ." Staggering backwards, Caramon stared at him, then grinned foolishly. "Oh, hullo there, little fellow. A kender"—his gaze wandered to Bupu—"and a gu-gul-gull-gullydorf," he finished with a rush. He bowed. "Whash-yournames?"

"What?" Tas asked.

"Whashyournames?" Caramon repeated with dignity.

"You know me, Caramon," Tas said, puzzled. "I'm Tasslehoff."

"Me Bupu," answered the gully dwarf, her face lighting up, obviously hoping this was another game. "Who you?"

"You know who he is," Tas began irritably, then nearly swallowed his tongue as Caramon interrupted.

"I'm Raistlin," said the big man solemnly with another, unsteady bow. "A—a great and pow—pow—powerfulmagicuser."

"Oh, come off it, Caramon!" Tas said in disgust. "I said I was sorry, so don't—"

"Caramon?" The big man's eyes opened wide, then narrowed shrewdly. "Caramon's dead. I killed him. Long ago in the Tow—the Twowr—the TwerHighSorshry."

"By Reorx's beard!" Tas breathed.

"Him not Raistlin!" snorted Bupu. Then she paused, eyeing him dubiously. "Is him?"

"N-no! Of course not," Tasslehoff snapped.

"This not fun game!" Bupu said with firm decision. "Me no like! Him not pretty man so nice to me. Him fat drunk. Me go home." She looked around. "Which way home?"

"Not now, Bupu!" What was going on? Tas wondered bleakly. Clutching at his topknot, he gave his hair a hard yank. His eyes watered with the pain, and the kender sighed in relief. For a moment, he thought he'd fallen asleep without knowing it and was walking around in some weird dream.

But apparently it was all real—too real. Or at least for him. For Caramon, it was quite a different story.

"Watch," Caramon was saying solemnly, weaving back and forth. "I'll casht a magicshpell." Raising his hands, he blurted out a string of gibberish. "Ashanddust and ratsnests! Burrung!" He pointed at a tree. "Poof," he whispered, stumbling backward. "Up in flames! Up! Up! Burning, burning, burning . . . jusht like poor Caramon." He staggered forward, wobbling down the trail.

"All of the waitresshes love you," he sang. "Every dog ish your friend. Whatever you shay is jusht what you m-mean—"

Wringing his hands, Tas hurried after him. Bupu trotted along behind.

"Tree *not* burn," she said to Tas sternly.

"I know!" Tas groaned. "It's just . . . he thinks—"

"Him one bad magician. My turn." Rummaging around in the huge bag that kept tripping her periodically, Bupu gave a triumphant yell and pulled out a very stiff, very dead rat.

"Not now, Bupu—" Tas began, feeling what was left of his own sanity start to slip. Caramon, ahead of them, had quit singing and was shouting something about covering the forest in cobwebs.

"I going to say secret magic word," Bupu stated. "You no listen. Spoil secret."

"I won't listen," Tas said impatiently, trying to catch up with Caramon, who, for all his wobbling, was moving along at a fair rate of speed.

"You listening?" Bupu asked, panting along after him.

"No," Tas said, sighing.

"Why not?"

"You told me not to!" Tas shouted in exasperation.

"But how you know when to no listen if you no listen?" Bupu demanded angrily. "You try to steal secret magic word! Me go home."

The gully dwarf came to a dead stop, turned around, and trotted back down the path. Tas skidded to a halt. He could see Caramon now, clinging to a tree, conjuring up a host of dragons, by the sounds of it. The big man looked like he would stay put for a while at least. Cursing under his breath, the kender turned and ran after the gully dwarf.

"Stop, Bupu!" he cried frantically, catching hold of a handful of filthy rags that he mistook for her shoulder. "I swear, I'd never steal your secret magic word!"

"You stole it!" she shrieked, waving the dead rat at him. "You said it!"

"Said what?" Tasslehoff asked, completely baffled.

"Secret magic word! You say!" Bupu screamed in outrage. "Here! Look!" Holding out the dead rat, she pointed ahead of them, down the trail, and yelled, "I say secret magic word now—*secret magic word*! There. *Now* we see some hot magic."

Tas put his hand to his head. He felt giddy.

"Look! Look!" Bupu shouted in triumph, pointing a grubby finger. "See? I start fire. Secret magic word never fail. Umphf. Some bad magic-user—him."

Glancing down the path, Tas blinked. There *were* flames visible ahead of them on the trail.

"I'm definitely going back to Kenderhome," Tas mused quietly to himself. "I'll get a little house . . . or maybe move in with the folks for a few months until I feel better."

"Who's out there?" called a clear, crystalline voice.

Relief flooded over Tasslehoff. "It's a campfire!" he babbled, nearly hysterical with joy. And the voice! He hurried forward, running through the darkness toward the light. "It's me—Tasslehoff Burrfoot. I've—oof!"

The "oof" was occasioned by Caramon plucking the kender off of his feet, lifting him in his strong arms, and clapping his hand over Tas's mouth.

"Shhhh," whispered Caramon close to Tas's ear. The fumes from his breath made the kender's head swim. "There's shomeone out there!"

"Mpf blsxtchscat!" Tas wriggled frantically, trying to loosen Caramon's hold. The kender was slowly being smothered to death.

"That's who I thought it was," Caramon whispered, nodding to himself solemnly as his hand clamped even more firmly over the kender's mouth.

Tas began to see bright blue stars. He fought desperately, tearing at Caramon's hands with all his strength, but it would have been the end of the kender's brief but exciting life had not Bupu suddenly appeared at Caramon's feet.

"Secret magic word!" she shrieked, thrusting the dead rat into Caramon's face. The distant firelight was reflected in the corpse's black eyes and glittered off the sharp teeth fixed in a perpetual grin.

"Ayiii!" Caramon screamed and dropped the kender. Tas fell heavily to the ground, gasping for breath.

"What is going on out there?" said a cold voice.

"We've come . . . to rescue you. . . ." said Tasslehoff, standing up dizzily.

A white-robed figure cloaked in furs appeared on the path in front of them. Bupu looked up at it in deep suspicion.

"Secret magic word," said the gully dwarf, waving the dead rat at the Revered Daughter of Paladine.

"You'll forgive me if I'm not wildly grateful," said Lady Crysania to Tasslehoff as they sat around the fire later that evening.

"I know. I'm sorry," Tasslehoff said, sitting hunched in misery on the ground. "I made a mess of things. I generally do," he continued woefully. "Ask anyone. I've often been told I drive people crazy—but this is the first time I ever did it for real!"

Snuffling, the kender cast an anxious gaze at Caramon. The big man sat near the fire, huddled in his cape. Still under the influence of the potent dwarf spirits, he was now sometimes Caramon and sometimes Raistlin. As Caramon, he ate voraciously, cramming food into his mouth with gusto. He then regaled them with several bawdy ballads—to the delight of Bupu, who clapped along out of time and came in strong on the choruses. Tas was torn by a strong desire to giggle wildly or crawl beneath a rock and die in shame.

But, the kender decided with a shudder, he would take Caramon—bawdy songs and all—over Caramon/Raistlin. The transformation occurred suddenly, right in the middle of a song, in fact. The big man's frame collapsed, he began to cough, then—looking at them with narrow eyes—he coldly ordered himself to shut up.

"You didn't do this to him," Lady Crysania said to Tas, regarding Caramon with a cool gaze. "It is the drink. He is gross, thick-headed, and obviously lacking in self-control. He has let his appetites rule him. Odd, isn't it, that he and Raistlin are twins? His brother is so much in control, so disciplined, intelligent, and refined."

She shrugged. "Oh, there is no doubt this poor man is to be greatly pitied." Standing up, she walked over to where her horse was tethered and began to unstrap her bedroll from its place behind her saddle. "I shall remember him in my prayers to Paladine."

"I'm sure prayers won't hurt," Tas said dubiously, "but I think some strong tarbean tea might be better just now."

Lady Crysania turned and regarded the kender with a reproving stare. "I am certain you did not mean to blaspheme. Therefore I will take your statement in the sense it was uttered. Do endeavor to look at things with a more serious attitude, however."

"I *was* serious," Tas protested. "All Caramon needs is a few mugs of good, thick tarbean tea—"

Lady Crysania's dark eyebrows rose so sharply that Tas fell silent, though he hadn't the vaguest idea what he had said to upset her. He began to unpack his own blankets, his spirits just about as low as he could ever remember them being. He felt just as he had when he had ridden dragonback with Flint during the Battle of Estwilde Plains. The dragon had soared into the clouds, then it dove out, spinning round and round. For a few moments, up had been down, sky had been below, ground above, and then—whoosh! into a cloud, and everything was lost in the haze.

His mind felt just like it did then. Lady Crysania admired Raistlin and pitied Caramon. Tas wasn't certain, but that seemed all backward. Then there was Caramon who was Caramon and then wasn't Caramon. Inns that were there one minute and gone the next. A secret magic word he was supposed to listen for so he'd know when not to listen. Then he'd made a perfectly logical, commonsense suggestion about tarbean tea and been reprimanded for blasphemy!

"After all," he mumbled to himself, jerking at his blankets, "Paladine and I are *close* personal friends. *He'd* know what I meant."

Sighing, the kender pillowed his head upon a rolled-up cloak. Bupu—now quite convinced that Caramon was Raistlin—was sound asleep, curled up with her head resting adoringly on the big man's foot. Caramon himself was sitting quietly now, his eyes closed, humming a song to himself. Occasionally he would cough, and once he demanded in a loud voice that Tas bring him his spellbook so that he could study his magic. But he seemed peaceful enough. Tas hoped he would soon doze and sleep off the effects of the dwarf spirits.

The fire burned low. Lady Crysania spread out her blankets on a bed of pine needles she had gathered to keep out the damp. Tas yawned. She was certainly getting on better than he'd expected. She had chosen a good, sensible location to make camp—near the trail, a stream of clear running water close by. Just as well not to have to wander too far in these dark and spooky woods—

Spooky wood ... what did that remind him of? Tas caught himself as he was slipping over the edge of sleep. Something important. Spooky wood. Spooks ... talk to spooks ...

"Darken Wood!" he said in alarm, sitting bolt upright.

"What?" asked Lady Crysania, wrapping her cloak around her and preparing to lie down.

"Darken Wood!" Tas repeated in alarm. He was now thoroughly awake. "We're close to Darken Wood. We came to warn you! It's a horrible place. You might have blundered into it. Maybe we're in it already—"

"Darken Wood?" Caramon's eyes flared open. He stared around him vaguely.

"Nonsense," Lady Crysania said comfortably, adjusting beneath her head a small traveling pillow she had brought with her. "We are not in Darken Wood, not yet. It is about five miles distant. Tomorrow we will come to a path that will take us there."

"You—you *want* to go there!" Tas gasped.

"Of course," Lady Crysania said coldly. "I go there to seek the Forestmaster's help. It would take me many long months to travel from here to the Forest of Wayreth, even on horseback. Silver dragons dwell in Darken Wood with the Forestmaster. They will fly me to my destination."

"But the spectres, the ancient dead king and his followers—"

"—were released from their terrible bondage when they answered the call to fight the Dragon Highlords," Lady Crysania said, somewhat sharply. "You really should study the history of the war, Tasslehoff. Especially since you were involved in it. When the human and elven forces combined to recapture Qualinesti, the spectres of Darken Wood fought with them and thus broke the dark enchantment that held them bound to dreadful life. They left this world and have been seen no more."

"Oh," said Tas stupidly. After glancing about for a moment, he sat back down on his bedroll. "I talked to them," he continued wistfully. "They were very polite—sort of abrupt in their comings and goings, but very polite. It's kind of sad to think—"

"I am quite tired," interrupted Lady Crysania. "And I have a long journey ahead of me tomorrow. I will take the gully dwarf and continue on to Darken Wood. You can take your besotted friend back home where he will—hopefully—find the help he needs. Now go to sleep."

"Shouldn't one of us . . . stay on watch?" Tas asked hesitantly. "Those rangers said—" He stopped suddenly. Those "rangers" had been in the inn that wasn't.

"Nonsense. Paladine will guard our rest," said Lady Crysania sharply. Closing her eyes, she began to recite soft words of prayer.

Tas gulped. "I wonder if we know the same Paladine?" he asked, thinking of Fizban and feeling very lonesome. But he said it under his breath, not wanting to be accused of blasphemy again. Lying down, he squirmed in his blankets but could not get comfortable. Finally, still wide awake, he sat back up and leaned against a tree trunk. The spring night was cool but not unpleasantly chill. The sky was clear, and there was no wind. The trees rustled with their own conversations, feeling new life running through their limbs, waking after their long winter's sleep. Running his hand over the ground, Tas fingered the new grass poking up beneath the decaying leaves.

The kender sighed. It was a nice night. Why did he feel uneasy? Was that a sound? A twig breaking? Tas started and looked around, holding his breath to hear better. Nothing. Silence. Glancing up into the heavens, he saw the constellation of Paladine, the Platinum Dragon, revolving around the constellation of Gilean, the Scales of Balance. Across from Paladine—each keeping careful watch upon the other—was the constellation of the Queen of Darkness—Takhisis, the Five-Headed Dragon.

"You're awfully far away up there," Tas said to the Platinum Dragon. "And you've got a whole world to watch, not just us. I'm sure you won't mind if *I* guard our rest tonight, too. No disrespect intended, of course. It's just that I have the feeling Someone Else up there is watching us tonight, too, if you take my meaning." The kender shivered. "I don't know why I feel so queer all of a sudden. Maybe it's just being so close to Darken Wood and—well, I'm responsible for everyone apparently!"

It was an uncomfortable thought for a kender. Tas was accustomed to being responsible for himself, but when he'd traveled with Tanis and the others, there had always been someone else responsible for the group. There had been strong, skilled warriors—

What was that? He'd definitely heard something *that* time! Jumping up, Tas stood quietly, staring into the darkness. There was silence, then a rustle, then—

A squirrel. Tas heaved a sigh that came from his toes.

"While I'm up, I'll just go put another log on the fire," he said to himself. Hurrying over, he glanced at Caramon and felt a pang. It would have been much easier standing watch in the darkness if he knew he could count on Caramon's strong arm. Instead, the warrior had fallen over on his back, his eyes closed, his mouth open, snoring in drunken contentment. Curled about Caramon's boot, her head on his foot, Bupu's snores mingled with his. Across from them, as far away as possible, Lady Crysania slept peacefully, her smooth cheek resting on her folded hands.

With a trembling sigh, Tas cast the logs on the fire. Watching it blaze up, he settled himself down to watch, staring intently into the night-shrouded trees whose whispering words now had an ominous tone. Then, there it was again.

"Squirrel!" Tas whispered resolutely.

Was that something moving in the shadows? There was a distinct crack—like a twig snapping in two. No squirrel did that! Tas fumbled about in his pouch until his hand closed over a small knife.

The forest was moving! The trees were closing in!

Tas tried to scream a warning, but a thin-limbed branch grabbed hold of his arm. . . .

"Aiiii," Tas shouted, twisting free and stabbing at the branch with his knife.

There was a curse and yelp of pain. The branch let loose its hold, and Tas breathed a sigh. No tree he had ever met yelped in pain. Whatever they were facing was living, breathing. . . .

"Attack!" the kender yelled, stumbling backward. "Caramon! Help! Caramon—"

Two years before, the big warrior would have been on his feet instantly, his hand closing over the hilt of his sword, alert and ready for battle. But Tas, scrambling to get his back to the fire, his small knife the only thing keeping whatever it was at bay, saw Caramon's head loll to one side in drunken contentment.

"Lady Crysania!" Tas screamed wildly, seeing more dark shapes creep from the woods. "Wake up! Please, wake up!"

He could feel the heat of the fire now. Keeping an eye on the menacing shadows, Tas reached down and grabbed a smoldering log by one end—he hoped it was the cool end. Lifting it up, he thrust the firebrand out before him.

There was movement as one of the creatures made a dive for him. Tas swiped out with his knife, driving it back. But in that instant, as it came into the light of his brand, he'd caught a glimpse of it.

"Caramon!" he shrieked. "Draconians!"

Lady Crysania was awake now; Tas saw her sit up, staring around in sleepy confusion.

"The fire!" Tas shouted to her desperately. "Get near the fire!" Stumbling over Bupu, the kender kicked Caramon. "Draconians!" he yelled again.

One of Caramon's eyes opened, then the other, glaring around muzzily.

"Caramon! Thank the gods!" Tas gasped in relief.

Caramon sat up. Peering around the camp, completely disoriented and confused, he was still warrior enough to be hazily aware of danger. Rising unsteadily to his feet, he gripped the hilt of his sword and belched.

"Washit?" he mumbled, trying to focus his eyes.

"Draconians!" Tasslehoff screeched, hopping around like a small demon, waving his firebrand and his knife with such vigor that he actually succeeded in keeping his enemies at bay.

"Draconians?" Caramon muttered, staring around in disbelief. Then he caught a glimpse of a twisted reptilian face in the light of the dying fire. His eyes opened wide. "Draconians!" he snarled. "Tanis! Sturm! Come to me! Raistlin—your magic! We'll take them."

Yanking his sword from its scabbard, Caramon plunged ahead with a rumbling battle cry—and fell flat on his face.

Bupu clung to his foot.

"Oh, no!" Tas groaned.

Caramon lay on the ground, blinking and shaking his head in wonder, trying to figure out what hit him. Bupu, rudely awakened, began to howl in terror and pain, then bit Caramon on the ankle.

Tas started forward to help the fallen warrior—at least drag Bupu off him—when he heard a cry. Lady Crysania! Damn! He'd forgotten about her! Whirling around, he saw the cleric struggling with one of the dragon men.

Tas hurtled forward and stabbed viciously at the draconian. With a shriek, it let loose of Crysania and fell backward, its body turning to stone at Tas's feet. Just in time, the kender remembered to retrieve his knife or the stony corpse would have kept it fast.

Tas dragged Crysania back with him toward the fallen Caramon, who was trying to shake the gully dwarf off his leg.

The draconians closed in. Glancing about feverishly, Tas saw they were surrounded by the creatures. But why weren't they attacking full force? What were they waiting for?

"Are you all right?" he managed to ask Crysania.

"Yes," she said. Though very pale, she appeared calm and—if frightened—was keeping her fear under control. Tas saw her lips move—presumably in silent prayer. The kender's own lips tightened.

"Here, lady," he said, shoving the firebrand in her hand. "I guess you're going to have to fight and pray at the same time."

"Elistan did. So can I," Crysania said, her voice shaking only slightly.

Shouted commands rang out from the shadows. The voice wasn't draconian. Tas couldn't make it out. He only knew that just hearing it gave him cold chills. But there wasn't time to wonder about it. The draconians, their tongues flicking out of their mouths, jumped for them.

Crysania lashed out with the smoldering brand clumsily, but it was enough to make the draconians hesitate. Tas was still trying to pry Bupu off Caramon. But it was a draconian who, inadvertently, came to their aid. Shoving Tas backward, the dragon man laid a clawed hand on Bupu.

Gully dwarves are noted throughout Krynn for their extreme cowardice and total unreliability in battle. But—when driven into a corner—they can fight like rabid rats.

"Glupsludge!" Bupu screamed in anger and, turning from gnawing on Caramon's ankle, she sank her teeth into the scaly hide of the draconian's leg.

Bupu didn't have many teeth, but what she did have were sharp and she bit into the draconian's green flesh with a relish occasioned by the fact that she hadn't eaten much dinner.

The draconian gave a hideous yell. Raising its sword, it was about to end Bupu's days upon Krynn when Caramon—bumbling around trying to see what was going on—accidentally sliced off the creature's arm. Bupu sat back, licking her lips, and looked about eagerly for another victim.

"Hurrah! Caramon!" Tas cheered wildly, his small knife stabbing here and there as swiftly as a striking snake. Lady Crysania smashed one draconian with her firebrand, crying out the name of Paladine. The creature pitched over.

There were only two or three draconians still standing that Tas could see, and the kender began to feel elated. The creatures lurked just outside the firelight, eyeing the big warrior, Caramon, warily as he staggered to his feet. Seen only in the shadows, he still cut the menacing figure he had in the old days. His sword blade gleamed wickedly in the red flames.

"Get 'em, Caramon!" Tas yelled shrilly. "Clunk their heads—"

The kender's voice died as Caramon turned slowly to face him, a strange look on his face.

"I'm not Caramon," he said softly. "I'm his twin, Raistlin. Caramon's dead. I killed him." Glancing down at the sword in his hand, the big warrior dropped it as if it stung him. "What am I doing with cold steel in my hands?" he asked harshly. "I can't cast spells with a sword and shield!"

Tasslehoff choked, casting an alarmed glance at the draconians. He could see them exchanging shrewd looks. They began to move forward slowly, though they all kept their gazes fixed upon the big warrior, probably suspecting a trap of some sort.

"You're not Raistlin! You're Caramon!" Tas cried in desperation, but it was no use. The man's brain was still pickled in dwarf spirits. His mind completely unhinged, Caramon closed his eyes, lifted his hands, and began to chant.

"Antsnests silverash bookarah," he murmured, weaving back and forth.

The grinning face of a draconian loomed up before Tas. There was a flash of steel, and the kender's head seemed to explode in pain. . . .

Tas was on the ground. Warm liquid was running down his face, blinding him in one eye, trickling into his mouth. He tasted blood. He was tired . . . very tired. . . .

But the pain was awful. It wouldn't let him sleep. He was afraid to move his head, afraid if he did it might separate into two pieces. And so he lay perfectly still, watching the world from one eye.

He heard the gully dwarf screaming on and on, like a tortured animal, and then the screams suddenly ended. He heard a deep cry of pain, a smothered groan, and a large body crashed to the ground beside him. It was Caramon, blood flowing from his mouth, his eyes wide open and staring.

Tas couldn't feel sad. He couldn't feel anything except the terrible pain in his head. A huge draconian stood over him, sword in hand. He knew that the creature was going to finish him off. Tas didn't care. End the pain, he pleaded. End it quickly.

Then there was a flurry of white robes and a clear voice calling upon Paladine. The draconian disappeared abruptly with the sound of clawed feet scrambling through the brush. The white robes knelt beside him, Tas felt the touch of a gentle hand upon his head, and heard the name of Paladine again. The pain vanished. Looking up, he saw the cleric's hand touch Caramon, saw the big man's eyelids flutter and close in peaceful sleep.

It's all right! Tas thought in elation. They've gone! We're going to be all right. Then he felt the hand tremble. Regaining some of his senses as the cleric's healing powers flooded through his body, the kender raised his head, peering ahead with his good eye.

Something was coming. Something had called off the draconians. Something was walking into the light of the fire.

Tas tried to cry out a warning, but his throat closed. His mind tumbled over and over. For a moment, too frightened and dizzy to think clearly, he thought someone had mixed up adventures on him.

He saw Lady Crysania rise to her feet, her white robes sweeping the dirt near his head. Slowly, she began backing away from the thing that stalked her. Tas heard her call to Paladine, but the words fell from lips stiff with terror.

Tas himself wanted desperately to close his eyes. Fear and curiosity warred in his small body. Curiosity won out. Peering out of his one good eye, Tas watched the horrible figure draw nearer and nearer to the cleric. The figure was dressed in the armor of a Solamnic Knight, but that armor was burned and blackened. As it drew near Crysania, the figure stretched forth an arm that did not end in a hand. It spoke words that did not come from a mouth. Its eyes flared orange, its transparent legs strode right through the smoldering ashes of the fire. The chill of the regions where it was forced to eternally dwell flowed from its body, freezing the very marrow in Tas's bones.

Fearfully, Tas raised his head. He saw Lady Crysania backing away. He saw the death knight walk toward her with slow, steady steps.

The knight raised its right hand and pointed at Crysania with a pale, shimmering finger.

Tas felt a sudden, uncontrollable terror seize him. "No!" he moaned, shivering, though he had no idea what awful thing was about to happen.

The knight spoke one word.

"Die."

At that moment, Tas saw Lady Crysania raise her hand and grasp the medallion she wore around her neck. He saw a bright flash of pure white light well from her fingers and then she fell to the ground as though stabbed by the fleshless finger.

"No!" Tasslehoff heard himself cry. He saw the orange flaring eyes turn their attention to him, and a chill, dank darkness, like the darkness of a tomb, sealed shut his eyes and closed his mouth. . . .

Chapter 8

Dalamar approached the door to the mage's laboratory with trepidation, tracing a nervous finger over the runes of protection stitched onto the fabric of his black robes as he hastily rehearsed several spells of warding in his mind. A certain amount of caution would not have been thought unseemly in any young apprentice approaching the inner, secret chambers of a dark and powerful master. But Dalamar's precautions were extraordinary. And with good reason. Dalamar had secrets of his own to hide, and he dreaded and feared nothing more in this world than the gaze of those golden, hourglass eyes.

And yet, deeper than his fear, an undercurrent of excitement pulsed in Dalamar's blood as it always did when he stood before this door. He had seen wonderful things inside this chamber, wonderful . . . fearful. . . .

Raising his right hand, he made a quick sign in the air before the door and muttered a few words in the language of magic. There was no reaction. The door had no spell cast upon it. Dalamar breathed a bit easier, or perhaps it was a sigh of disappointment. His master was not engaged in any potent, powerful magic, otherwise Raistlin would have cast a spell of holding upon the door. Glancing down at the floor, the dark elf saw no flickering, flaring lights beaming from beneath the heavy wooden door. He smelled nothing except the usual smells of spice and decay. Dalamar placed the five fingertips of his left hand upon the door and waited in silence.

Within the space of time it took the dark elf to draw a breath came the softly spoken command, "Enter, Dalamar."

Bracing himself, Dalamar stepped into the chamber as the door swung silently open before him. Raistlin sat at a huge and ancient stone table, so large that one of the tall, broad-shouldered race of minotaurs living upon Mithas might have lain down upon it, stretched out his full height, and still had room to spare. The stone table, in fact the entire laboratory, were part of the original furnishings Raistlin had discovered when he claimed the Tower of High Sorcery in Palanthas as his own.

The great, shadowy chamber seemed much larger than it could possibly have been, yet the dark elf could never determine whether it was the chamber itself that seemed larger or he himself who seemed smaller whenever he entered it. Books lined the walls, here as in the mage's study. Runes and spidery writing glowed through the dust gathered on their spines. Glass bottles and jars of twisted design stood on tables around the sides of the chamber, their bright-colored contents bubbling and boiling with hidden power.

Here, in this laboratory long ago, great and powerful magic had been wrought. Here, the wizards of all three Robes—the White of Good, the Red of Neutrality, and the Black of Evil—joined in alliance to create the Dragon Orbs—one of which was now in Raistlin's possession. Here, the three Robes had come together in a final, desperate battle to save their Towers, the bastions of their strength, from the Kingpriest of Istar and the mobs. Here they had failed, believing it was better to live in defeat than fight, knowing that their magic could destroy the world.

The mages had been forced to abandon this Tower, carrying their spellbooks and other paraphernalia to the Tower of High Sorcery, hidden deep within the magical Forest of Wayreth. It was when they abandoned this Tower that the curse had been cast upon it. The Shoikan Grove had grown to guard it from all comers until—as foretold— "the master of past and present shall return with power."

And the master had returned. Now he sat in the ancient laboratory, crouched over the stone table that had been dragged, long ago, from the bottom of the sea. Carved with runes that ward off all enchantments, it was kept free of any outside influences that might affect the mage's work. The table's surface was ground smooth and polished to an almost mirrorlike finish. Dalamar could see the nightblue bindings of the spellbooks that sat upon it reflected in the candlelight.

Scattered about on its surface were other objects, too—objects hideous and curious, horrible and lovely: the mage's spell components. It was on these Raistlin was working now, scanning a spellbook, murmuring soft words as he crushed something between his delicate fingers, letting it trickle into a phial he held.

"*Shalafi,*" Dalamar said quietly, using the elven word for "master."

Raistlin looked up.

Dalamar felt the stare of those golden eyes pierce his heart with an indefinable pain. A shiver of fear swept over the dark elf, the words, *He knows!* seethed in his brain. But none of this emotion was outwardly visible. The dark elf's handsome features remained fixed, unchanged, cool. His eyes returned Raistlin's gaze steadily. His hands remained folded within his robes as was proper.

So dangerous was this job that—when *They* had deemed it necessary to plant a spy inside the mage's household—They had asked for volunteers, none of them willing to take responsibility for cold-bloodedly commanding anyone to accept this deadly assignment. Dalamar had stepped forward immediately.

Magic was Dalamar's only home. Originally from Silvanesti, he now neither claimed nor was claimed by that noble race of elves. Born to a low caste, he had been taught only the most rudimentary of the magical arts, higher learning being for those of royal blood. But Dalamar had tasted the power, and it became his obsession. Secretly he worked, studying the forbidden, learning wonders reserved for only the high-ranking elven mages. The dark arts impressed him most, and thus, when he was discovered wearing the Black Robes that no true elf could even bear to look upon, Dalamar was cast out of his home and his nation. And he became known as a "dark elf," one who is outside of the light. This suited Dalamar well for, early on, he had learned that there is power in darkness.

And so Dalamar had accepted the assignment. When asked to give his reasons why he would willingly risk his life performing this task, he had answered coldly, "I would risk my soul for the chance to study with the greatest and most powerful of our order who has *ever* lived!"

"You may well be doing just that," a sad voice had answered him.

The memory of that voice returned to Dalamar at odd moments, generally in the darkness of the night—which was so *very* dark inside the Tower. It returned to him now. Dalamar forced it out of his mind.

"What is it?" Raistlin asked gently.

The mage always spoke gently and softly, sometimes not even raising his voice above a whisper. Dalamar had seen fearful storms rage in this chamber. The blazing lightning and crashing thunder had left him partially deaf for days. He had been present when the mage summoned creatures from the planes above and below to do his bidding; their screams and wails and curses still sounded in his dreams at night. Yet, through it all, he had never heard Raistlin raise his voice. Always that soft, sibilant whisper penetrated the chaos and brought it under control.

"Events are transpiring in the outside world, *Shalafi*, that demand your attention."

"Indeed?" Raistlin looked down again, absorbed in his work.

"Lady Crysania—"

Raistlin's hooded head lifted quickly. Dalamar, reminded forcibly of a striking snake, involuntarily fell back a step before that intense gaze.

"What? Speak!" Raistlin hissed the word.

"You—you should come, *Shalafi*," Dalamar faltered. "The Live Ones report...."

The dark elf spoke to empty air. Raistlin had vanished.

Heaving a trembling sigh, the dark elf pronounced the words that would take him instantly to his master's side.

Far below the Tower of High Sorcery, deep beneath the ground, was a small round room magically carved from the rock that supported the Tower. This room had *not* been in the Tower originally. Known as the Chamber of Seeing, it was Raistlin's creation.

Within the center of the small room of cold stone was a perfectly round pool of still, dark water. From the center of the strange, unnatural pond spurted a jet of blue flame. Rising to the ceiling of the chamber, it burned eternally, day and night. And around it, eternally, sat the Live Ones.

Though the most powerful mage living upon Krynn, Raistlin's power was far from complete, and no one realized that more than the mage himself. He was always forcibly reminded of his weaknesses when he came into this room—one reason he avoided it, if possible. For here were the visible, outward symbols of his failures—the Live Ones.

Wretched creatures mistakenly created by magic gone awry, they were held in thrall in this chamber, serving their creator. Here they lived out their tortured lives, writhing in a larva-like, bleeding mass about the flaming pool. Their shining wet bodies made a horrible carpet for the floor, whose stones, made slick with their oozings, could be seen only when they parted to make room for their creator.

Yet, despite their lives of constant, twisted pain, the Live Ones spoke no word of complaint. Far better their lot than those who roamed the Tower, those known as the Dead Ones. . . .

Raistlin materialized within the Chamber of Seeing, a dark shadow emerging out of darkness. The blue flame sparkled off the silver threads that decorated his robes, shimmered within the black cloth. Dalamar appeared beside him, and the two walked over to stand beside the surface of the still, black water.

"Where?" Raistlin asked.

"Here, M-master," blurbled one of the Live Ones, pointing a misshapen appendage.

Raistlin hurried to stand beside it, Dalamar walking by his side, their black robes making a soft, whispering sound upon the slimy stone floor. Staring into the water, Raistlin motioned Dalamar to do the same. The dark elf looked into the still surface, seeing for an instant only the reflection of the jet of blue flame. Then the flame and the water merged, then parted, and he was in a forest. A big human male, clad in ill-fitting armor, stood staring down at the body of a young human female, dressed in white robes. A kender knelt beside the body of the woman, holding her hand in his. Dalamar heard the big man speak as clearly as if he had been standing by his side.

"She's dead...."

"I—I'm not sure, Caramon. I think—"

"I've seen death often enough, believe me. She's dead. And it's all my fault ... my fault...."

"Caramon, you imbecile!" Raistlin snarled with a curse. "What happened? What went wrong?"

As the mage spoke, Dalamar saw the kender look up quickly.

"Did you say something?" the kender asked the big human, who was working in the soil.

"No. It was just the wind."

"What are you doing?"

"Digging a grave. We've got to bury her."

"Bury her?" Raistlin gave a brief, bitter laugh. "Oh, of course, you bumbling idiot! That's all you can think of to do!" The mage fumed. "Bury her! I must know what happened!" He turned to the Live One. "What did you see?"

"T-they c-camp in t-trees, M-master." Froth dribbled from the creature's mouth, its speech was practically unrecognizable. "Ddraco k-kill—"

"Draconians?" Raistlin repeated in astonishment. "Near Solace? Where did they come from?"

"D-dunno! Dunno!" The Live One cowered in terror. "I-I—"

"Shhh," Dalamar warned, drawing his master's attention back to the pond where the kender was arguing.

"Caramon, you can't bury her! She's—"

"We don't have any choice. I know it's not proper, but Paladine will see that her soul journeys in peace. We don't dare build a funeral pyre, not with those dragonmen around—"

"But, Caramon, I really think you should come look at her! There's not a mark on her body!"

"I don't want to look at her! She's dead! It's my fault! We'll bury her here, then I'll go back to Solace, go back to digging my own grave—"

"Caramon!"

"Go find some flowers and leave me be!"

Dalamar saw the big man tear up the moist dirt with his bare hands, hurling it aside while tears streamed down his face. The kender remained beside the woman's body, irresolute, his face covered with dried blood, his expression a mixture of grief and doubt.

"No mark, no wound, draconians coming out of nowhere..." Raistlin frowned thoughtfully. Then, suddenly, he knelt beside the Live One, who shrank away from him. "Speak. Tell me everything. I must know. Why wasn't I summoned earlier?"

"Th-the d-draco k-kill, M-master," the Live One's voice bubbled in agony. "B-but the b-big m-man k-kill, too. T-then b-big ddark c-come! E-eyes of f-fire. I-I s-scared. I-I f-fraid f-fall in wa-water...."

"I found the Live One lying at the edge of the pool," Dalamar reported coolly, "when one of the others told me something strange was going on. I looked into the water. Knowing of your interest in this human female, I thought you—"

"Quite right," Raistlin murmured, cutting off Dalamar's explanation impatiently. The mage's golden eyes narrowed, his thin lips compressed. Feeling his anger, the poor Live One dragged its body as far from the mage as possible. Dalamar held his breath. But Raistlin's anger was not directed at them.

" 'Big dark, eyes of fire'—Lord Soth! So, my sister, you betray me," Raistlin whispered. "I smell your fear, Kitiara! You coward! I could have made you queen of this world. I could have given you wealth immeasurable, power unlimited. But no. You are, after all, a weak and petty-minded worm!"

Raistlin stood quietly, pondering, staring into the still pond. When he spoke next, his voice was soft, lethal. "I will not forget this, my dear sister. You are fortunate that I have more urgent, pressing matters at hand, or you would be residing with the phantom lord who serves you!" Raistlin's thin fist clenched, then—with an obvious effort—he forced himself to relax. "But, now, what to do about this? I must do something before my brother plants the cleric in a flower bed!"

"*Shalafi*, what has happened?" Dalamar ventured, greatly daring. "This—woman. What is she to you? I do not understand."

Raistlin glanced at Dalamar irritably and seemed about to rebuke him for his impertinence. Then the mage hesitated. His golden eyes flared once with a flash of inner light that made Dalamar cringe, before returning to their flat, impassive stare.

"Of course, apprentice. You shall know everything. But first—"

Raistlin stopped. Another figure had entered the scene in the forest they watched so intently. It was a gully dwarf, bundled in layers and layers of bright, gaudy clothing, a huge bag dragging behind her as she walked.

"Bupu!" Raistlin whispered, the rare smile touching his lips. "Excellent. Once more you shall serve me, little one."

Reaching out his hand, Raistlin touched the still water. The Live Ones around the pool cried out in horror, for they had seen many of their own kind stumble into that dark water, only to shrivel and wither and become nothing more than a wisp of smoke, rising with a shriek into the air. But Raistlin simply murmured soft words, then withdrew his hand. The fingers were white as marble, a spasm of pain crossed his face. Hurriedly, he slid his hand into a pocket of his robe.

"Watch," he whispered exultantly.

Dalamar stared into the water, watching the gully dwarf approach the still, lifeless form of the woman.

"*Me help.*"

"*No, Bupu!*"

"*You no like my magic! Me go home. But first me help pretty lady.*"

"What in the name of the Abyss—" Dalamar muttered.

"Watch!" Raistlin commanded.

Dalamar watched as the gully dwarf's small, grubby hand dove into the bag at her side. After fumbling about for several moments, it emerged with a loathsome object—a dead, stiff lizard with a leather thong wrapped around its neck. Bupu approached the woman and—when the kender tried to stop her—thrust her small fist into his face warningly. With a sigh and a sideways glance at Caramon, who was digging furiously, his face a mask of grief and blood, the kender stepped back. Bupu plopped down beside the woman's lifeless form and carefully placed the dead lizard on the unmoving chest.

Dalamar gasped.

The woman's chest moved, the white robes shivered. She began breathing, deeply and peacefully.

The kender let out a shriek.

"Caramon! Bupu's cured her! She's alive! Look!"

"What the—" The big man stopped digging and stumbled over, staring at the gully dwarf in amazement and fear.

"Lizard cure," Bupu said in triumph. *"Work every time."*

"Yes, my little one," Raistlin said, still smiling. "It works well for coughs, too, as I remember." He waved his hand over the still water. The mage's voice became a lulling chant. "And now, sleep, my brother, before you do anything else stupid. Sleep, kender, sleep, little Bupu. And sleep as well, Lady Crysania, in the realm where Paladine protects you."

Still chanting, Raistlin made a beckoning motion with his hand. "And now come, Forest of Wayreth. Creep up on them as they sleep. Sing them your magical song. Lure them onto your secret paths."

The spell was ended. Rising to his feet, Raistlin turned to Dalamar. "And you come, too, apprentice"—there was the faintest sarcasm in the voice that made the dark elf shudder—"come to my study. It is time for us to talk."

Chapter 9

Dalamar sat in the mage's study in the same chair Kitiara had occupied on her visit. The dark elf was far less comfortable, far less secure than Kitiara had been. Yet his fears were well-contained. Outwardly he appeared relaxed, composed. A heightened flush upon his pale elven features could be attributed, perhaps, to his excitement at being taken into his master's confidence.

Dalamar had been in the study often, though not in the presence of his master. Raistlin spent his evenings here alone, reading, studying the tomes that lined his walls. No one dared disturb him then. Dalamar entered the study only during the daylight hours, and then only when Raistlin was busy elsewhere. At that time the dark elf apprentice was allowed—no, required—to study the spellbooks himself, some of them, that is. He had been forbidden to open or even touch those with the nightblue binding.

Dalamar had done so once, of course. The binding felt intensely cold, so cold it burned his skin. Ignoring the pain, he managed to open the cover, but after one look, he quickly shut it. The words inside were gibberish, he could make nothing of them. And he had been able to detect the spell of protection cast over them. Anyone looking at them too long without the proper key to translate them would go mad.

Seeing Dalamar's injured hand, Raistlin asked him how it happened. The dark elf replied coolly that he had spilled some acid from a spell component he was mixing. The archmage smiled and said nothing. There was no need. Both understood.

But now he was in the study by Raistlin's invitation, sitting here on a more or less equal basis with his master. Once again, Dalamar felt the old fear laced by intoxicating excitement.

Raistlin sat before him at the carved wooden table, one hand resting upon a thick nightblue-bound spellbook. The archmage's fingers absently caressed the book, running over the silver runes upon the cover. Raistlin's eyes stared fixedly at Dalamar. The dark elf did not stir or shift beneath that intense, penetrating gaze.

"You were very young, to have taken the Test," Raistlin said abruptly in his soft voice.

Dalamar blinked. This was not what he had expected.

"Not so young as you, *Shalafi*," the dark elf replied. "I am in my nineties, which figures to about twenty-five of your human years. You, I believe, were only twenty-one when you took the Test."

"Yes," Raistlin murmured, and a shadow passed across the mage's golden-tinted skin. "I was . . . twenty-one."

Dalamar saw the hand that rested upon the spellbook clench in swift, sudden pain; he saw the golden eyes flare. The young apprentice was not surprised at this show of emotion. The Test is required of any mage seeking to practice the arts of magic at an advanced level. Administered in the Tower of High Sorcery at Wayreth, it is conducted by the leaders of all three Robes. For, long ago, the magic-users of Krynn realized what had escaped the clerics—if the balance of the world is to be maintained, the pendulum must swing freely back and forth among all three—Good, Evil, Neutrality. Let one grow too powerful—any one—and the world would begin to tilt toward its destruction.

The Test is brutal. The higher levels of magic, where true power is obtained, are no place for inept bunglers. The Test was designed to get rid of those—permanently; death being the penalty for failure. Dalamar still had nightmares about his own testing, so he could well understand Raistlin's reaction.

"I passed," Raistlin whispered, his eyes staring back to that time. "But when I came out of that terrible place I was as you see me now. My skin had this golden tint, my hair was white, and my eyes..." He came back to the present, to look fixedly at Dalamar. "Do you know what I see with these hourglass eyes?"

"No, *Shalafi*."

"I see time as it affects all things," Raistlin replied. "Human flesh withers before these eyes, flowers wilt and die, the rocks themselves crumble as I watch. It is always winter in my sight. Even you, Dalamar"—Raistlin's eyes caught and held the young apprentice in their horrible gaze—"even elven flesh that ages so slowly the passing of the years are as rain showers in the spring—even upon your young face, Dalamar—I see the mark of death!"

Dalamar shivered, and this time could not hide his emotion. Involuntarily, he shrank back into the cushions of the chair. A shield spell came quickly to his mind, as did— unbidden—a spell designed to injure, not defend. Fool! he sneered at himself, quickly regaining control, what puny spell of mine could kill *him*?

"True, true," Raistlin murmured, answering Dalamar's thoughts, as he often did. "There live none upon Krynn who has the power to harm me. Certainly not you, apprentice. But you are brave. You have courage. Often you have stood beside me in the laboratory, facing those I have dragged from the planes of their existence. You knew that if I but drew a breath at the wrong time, they would rip the living hearts from our bodies and devour them while we writhed before them in torment."

"It was my privilege," Dalamar murmured.

"Yes," Raistlin replied absently, his thoughts abstracted. Then he raised an eyebrow. "And you knew, didn't you, that if such an event occurred, I would save myself but not you?"

"Of course, *Shalafi*," Dalamar answered steadily. "I understand and I take the risk"—the dark elf's eyes glowed. His fears forgotten, he sat forward eagerly in his chair—"no, *Shalafi*, I *invite* the risks! I would sacrifice anything for the sake of—"

"The magic," Raistlin finished.

"Yes! The sake of the magic!" Dalamar cried.

"And the power it confers," Raistlin nodded. "You are ambitious. But—how ambitious, I wonder? Do you, perhaps, seek rulership of your kinsmen? Or possibly a kingdom somewhere, holding a monarch in thrall while you enjoy the wealth of his lands? Or perhaps an alliance with some dark lord, as was done in the days of the dragons not far back. My sister, Kitiara, for example, found you quite attractive. She would enjoy having you about. Particularly if you have any magic arts you practice in the bedroom—"

"*Shalafi*, I would not desecrate—"

Raistlin waved a hand. "I joke, apprentice. But you take my meaning. Does one of those reflect your dreams?"

"Well, certainly, *Shalafi*." Dalamar hesitated, confused. Where was all this leading? To some information he could use and pass on, he hoped, but how much of himself to reveal? "I—"

Raistlin cut him off. "Yes, I see I have come close to the mark. I have discovered the heights of your ambition. Have you never guessed at mine?"

Dalamar felt a thrill of joy surge through his body. *This* is what he had been sent to discover. The young mage answered slowly, "I have often wondered, *Shalafi*. You are so powerful"—Dalamar motioned at the window where the lights of Palanthas could be seen, shining in the night— "this city, this land of Solamnia, this continent of Ansalon could be yours."

"This *world* could be mine!" Raistlin smiled, his thin lips parting slightly. "We have seen the lands beyond the seas, haven't we, apprentice. When we look into the flaming water, we can see them and those who dwell there. To control them would be simplicity itself—"

Raistlin rose to his feet. Walking to the window, he stared out over the sparkling city spread out before him.

Feeling his master's excitement, Dalamar left his chair and followed him.

"I could give you that kingdom, Dalamar," Raistlin said softly. His hand drew back the curtain, his eyes lingered upon the lights that gleamed more warmly than the stars above. "I could give you not only rulership of your miserable kinsmen, but control of the elves everywhere in Krynn." Raistlin shrugged. "I could give you my sister."

Turning from the window, Raistlin faced Dalamar, who watched him eagerly.

"But I care nothing for that"—Raistlin gestured, letting the curtain fall— "nothing. My ambition goes further."

"But, *Shalafi*, there is not much left if you turn down the world." Dalamar faltered, not understanding. "Unless you have seen worlds beyond this one that are hidden from my eyes. . . ."

"Worlds beyond?" Raistlin pondered. "Interesting thought. Perhaps someday I should consider that possibility. But, no, that is not what I meant." The mage paused and, with a motion of his hand, beckoned Dalamar closer. "You have seen the great door in the very back of the laboratory? The door of steel, with runes of silver and of gold set within? The door without a lock?"

"Yes, *Shalafi*," Dalamar replied, feeling a chill creep over him that not even the strange heat of Raistlin's body so near him could dispel.

"Do you know where that door leads?"

"Yes . . . *Shalafi*." A whisper.

"And you know why it is not opened?"

"You cannot open it, *Shalafi*. Only one of great and powerful magic and one of true holy powers may together open—" Dalamar stopped, his throat closing in fear, choking him.

"Yes," Raistlin murmured, "you understand. 'One of true holy powers.' Now you know why I ne ! Now you understand the heights—and the depths—of my ambition."

"This is madness!" Dalamar gasped, then lowered his eyes in shame. "Forgive me, *Shalafi*, I meant no disrespect."

"No, and you are right. It *is* madness, with my limited powers." A trace of bitterness tinged the mage's voice. "That is why I am about to undertake a journey."

"Journey?" Dalamar looked up. "Where?"

"Not where—when," Raistlin corrected. "You have heard me speak of Fistandantilus?"

"Many times, *Shalafi*," Dalamar said, his voice almost reverent. "The greatest of our Order. Those are his spellbooks, the ones with the nightblue binding."

"Inadequate," Raistlin muttered, dismissing the entire library with a gesture. "I have read them all, many times in these past years, ever since I obtained the Key to their secrets from the Queen of Darkness herself. But they only frustrate me!" Raistlin clenched his thin hand. "I read these spellbooks and I find great gaps—entire volumes missing! Perhaps they were destroyed in the Cataclysm or, later, in the Dwarfgate Wars that proved Fistandantilus's undoing. These missing volumes, this knowledge of his that has been lost, will give me the power I need!"

"And so your journey will take you—" Dalamar stopped in disbelief.

"Back in time," Raistlin finished calmly. "Back to the days just prior to the Cataclysm, when Fistandantilus was at the height of his power."

Dalamar felt dizzy, his thoughts swirled in confusion. What would *They* say? Amidst all Their speculation, They had certainly not foreseen this!

"Steady, my apprentice." Raistlin's soft voice seemed to come to Dalamar from far away. "This has unnerved you. Some wine?"

The mage walked over to a table. Lifting a carafe, he poured a small glass of blood-red liquid and handed it to the dark elf. Dalamar took it gratefully, startled to see his hand shaking. Raistlin poured a small glass for himself.

"I do not drink this strong wine often, but tonight it seems we should have a small celebration. A toast to—how did you put it?—one of true holy powers. This, then, to Lady Crysania!"

Raistlin drank his wine in small sips. Dalamar gulped his down. The fiery liquid bit into his throat. He coughed.

"*Shalafi*, if the Live One reported correctly, Lord Soth cast a death spell upon Lady Crysania, yet she still lives. Did you restore her life?"

Raistlin shook his head. "No, I simply gave her visible signs of life so that my dear brother would not bury her. I cannot be certain what happened, but it is not difficult to guess. Seeing the death knight before her and knowing her fate, the Revered Daughter fought the spell with the only weapon she had, and a powerful one it was—the holy medallion of Paladine. The god protected her, transporting her soul to the realms where the gods dwell, leaving her body a shell upon the ground. There are none—not even I—who can bring her soul and body back together again. Only a high cleric of Paladine has that power."

"Elistan?"

"Bah, the man is sick, dying. . . ."

"Then she is lost to you!"

"No," said Raistlin gently. "You fail to understand, apprentice. Through inattention, I lost control. But I have regained it quickly. Not only that, I will make this work to my advantage. Even now, they approach the Tower of High Sorcery. Crysania was going there, seeking the help of the mages. When she arrives, she will find that help, and so will my brother."

"You *want* them to help her?" Dalamar asked in confusion. "She plots to destroy you!"

Raistlin quietly sipped his wine, watching the young apprentice intently. "Think about it, Dalamar," he said softly, "think about it, and you will come to understand. But"—the mage set down his empty glass—"I have kept you long enough."

Dalamar glanced out the window. The red moon, Lunitari, was starting to sink out of sight behind the black jagged edges of the mountains. The night was nearing its midpoint.

"You must make *your* journey and be back before I leave in the morning," Raistlin continued. "There will undoubtedly be some last-minute instructions, besides many things I must leave in your care. You will be in charge here, of course, while I am gone."

Dalamar nodded, then frowned. "You spoke of *my* journey, *Shalafi*? I am not going anywhere—" The dark elf stopped, choking as he remembered that he did, indeed, have somewhere to go, a report to make.

Raistlin stood regarding the young elf in silence, the look of horrified realization dawning on Dalamar's face reflected in the mage's mirrorlike eyes. Then, slowly, Raistlin advanced upon the young apprentice, his black robes rustling gently about his ankles. Stricken with terror, Dalamar could not move. Spells of protection slipped from his grasp. His mind could think of nothing, see nothing, except two flat, emotionless, golden eyes.

Slowly, Raistlin lifted his hand and laid it gently upon Dalamar's chest, touching the young man's black robes with the tips of five fingers.

The pain was excruciating. Dalamar's face turned white, his eyes widened, he gasped in agony. But the dark elf could not withdraw from that terrible touch. Held fast by Raistlin's gaze, Dalamar could not even scream.

"Relate to them accurately both what I have told you," Raistlin whispered, "and what you may have guessed. And give the great Par-Salian my regards ... apprentice!"

The mage withdrew his hand.

Dalamar collapsed upon the floor, clutching his chest, moaning. Raistlin walked around him without even a glance. The dark elf could hear him leave the room, the soft swish of the black robes, the door opening and closing.

In a frenzy of pain, Dalamar ripped open his robes. Five red, glistening trails of blood streamed down his breast, soaking into the black cloth, welling from five holes that had been burned into his flesh.

CHAPTER 10

"Caramon! Get up! Wake up!"

No. I'm in my grave. It's warm here beneath the ground, warm and safe. You can't wake me, you can't reach me. I'm hidden in the clay, you can't find me.

"Caramon, you've got to see this! Wake up!"

A hand shoved aside the darkness, tugged at him.

No, Tika, go away! You brought me back to life once, back to pain and suffering. You should have left me in the sweet realm of darkness below the Blood Sea of Istar. But I've found peace now at last. I dug my grave and I buried myself.

"Hey, Caramon, you better wake up and take a look at this!"

Those words! They were familiar. Of course, I said them! I said them to Raistlin long ago, when he and I first came to this forest. So how can I be hearing them? Unless I *am* Raistlin. . . . Ah, that's—

There was a hand on his eyelid! Two fingers were prying it open! At the touch, fear ran prickling through Caramon's bloodstream, starting his heart beating with a jolt.

"Arghhhh!" Caramon roared in alarm, trying to crawl into the dirt as that one, forcibly opened eye saw a gigantic face hovering over him—the face of a gully dwarf!

"Him awake," Bupu reported. "Here," she said to Tasslehoff, "you hold this eye. I open other one."

"No!" Tas cried hastily. Dragging Bupu off the warrior, Tas shoved her behind him. "Uh . . . you go get some water."

"Good idea," Bupu remarked and scuttled off.

"It—it's all right, Caramon," Tas said, kneeling beside the big man and patting him reassuringly. "It was only Bupu. I'm sorry, but I was—uh—looking at the . . . well, you'll see . . . and I forgot to watch her."

Groaning, Caramon covered his face with his hand. With Tas's help, he struggled to sit up. "I dreamed I was dead," he said heavily. "Then I saw that face—I knew it was all over. I was in the Abyss."

"You may wish you were," Tas said somberly.

Caramon looked up at the sound of the kender's unusually serious tone. "Why? What do you mean?" he asked harshly.

Instead of answering, Tas asked, "How do you feel?"

Caramon scowled. "I'm sober, if that's what you want to know," the big man muttered. "And I wish to the gods I wasn't. So there."

Tasslehoff regarded him thoughtfully for a moment, then, slowly, he reached into a pouch and drew forth a small leather-bound bottle. "Here, Caramon," he said quietly, "if you really think you need it."

The big man's eyes flashed. Eagerly, he stretched out a trembling hand and snatched the bottle. Uncorking the top, he sniffed at it, smiled, and raised it to his lips.

"Quit staring at me!" he ordered Tas sullenly.

"I'm s-sorry," Tas flushed. He rose to his feet. "I-I'll just go look after Lady Crysania—"

"Crysania . . ." Caramon lowered the flask, untasted. He rubbed his gummed eyes. "Yeah, I forgot about her. Good idea, you looking after her. Take her and get out of here, in fact. You and that vermin-ridden gully dwarf of yours! Get out and leave me alone!" Raising the bottle to his lips again, Caramon took a long pull. He coughed once, lowered the bottle, and wiped his mouth with the back of his hand. "Go on," he repeated, staring at Tas dully, "get out of here! All of you! Leave me alone!"

"I'm sorry, Caramon," Tas said quietly. "I really wish we could. But we can't."

"Why?" snarled Caramon.

Tas drew a deep breath. "Because, if I remember the stories Raistlin told me, I think the Forest of Wayreth has found us."

For a moment, Caramon stared at Tas, his blood-shot eyes wide.

"That's impossible," he said after a moment, his words little more than a whisper. "We're miles from there! I—it took me and Raist . . . it took us months to find the Forest! And the Tower is far south of here! It's clear past Qualinesti, according to your map," Caramon regarded Tas balefully. "That isn't the same map that showed Tarsis by the sea, is it?"

"It could be," Tas hedged, hastily rolling up the map and hiding it behind his back. "I have so many. . . ." He hurriedly changed the subject. "But Raistlin said it was a magic forest, so I suppose it could have found us, if it was so inclined."

"It *is* a magic forest," Caramon murmured, his voice deep and trembling. "It's a place of horror." He closed his eyes and shook his head, then—suddenly—he looked up, his face full of cunning. "This is a trick, isn't it? A trick to keep me from drinking! Well, it won't work—"

"It's no trick, Caramon," Tas sighed. Then he pointed. "Look over there. It's just like Raistlin described to me once."

Turning his head, Caramon saw, and he shuddered, both at the sight and at the bitter memories of his brother it brought back.

The glade they were camped in was a small, grassy clearing some distance from the main trail. It was surrounded by maple trees, pines, walnut trees, and even a few aspens. The trees were just beginning to bud out. Caramon had looked at them while digging Crysania's grave. The branches shimmered in the early morning sunlight with the faint yellow-green glow of spring. Wild flowers bloomed at their roots, the early flowers of spring—crocuses and violets.

As Caramon looked around now, he saw that these same trees surrounded them still—on three sides. But now—on the fourth, the southern side—the trees had changed.

These trees, mostly dead, stood side-by-side, lined up evenly, row after row. Here and there, as one looked deeper into the Forest, a living tree might be seen, watching like an officer over the silent ranks of his troops. No sun shone in this Forest. A thick, noxious mist flowed out of the trees, obscuring the light. The trees themselves were hideous to look upon, twisted and deformed, their limbs like great claws dragging the ground. Their branches did not move, no wind stirred their dead leaves. But—most horrible—things within the Forest moved. As Caramon and Tas watched, they could see shadows flitting among the trunks, skulking among the thorny underbrush.

"Now, look at this," Tas said. Ignoring Caramon's alarmed shout, the kender ran straight for the Forest. As he did so, the trees parted! A path opened wide, leading right into the Forest's dark heart. "Can you beat that?" Tas cried in wonder, coming to a halt right before he set foot upon the path. "And when I back away—"

The kender walked backward, away from the trees, and the trunks slid back together again, closing ranks, presenting a solid barrier.

"You're right," Caramon said hoarsely. "It is the Forest of Wayreth. So it appeared, one morning, to us." He lowered his head. "I didn't want to go in. I tried to stop Raist. But he wasn't afraid! The trees parted for him, and he entered. 'Stay by me, my brother,' he told me, 'and I will keep you from harm.' How often had I said those words to *him*? He wasn't afraid! I was!"

Suddenly, Caramon stood up. "Let's get out of here!" Feverishly grabbing his bedroll with shaking hands, he slopped the contents of the bottle all over the blanket.

"No good," Tas said laconically. "I tried. Watch."

Turning his back on the trees, the kender walked north. The trees did not move. But—inexplicably—Tasslehoff was walking *toward* the Forest once more. Try as he might, turn as he might, he always ended up walking straight into the tree's fog-bound, nightmarish ranks.

Sighing, Tas came over to stand beside Caramon. The kender looked solemnly up into the big man's tear-stained, red-rimmed eyes and reached out a small hand, resting it on the warrior's once-strong arm.

"Caramon, you're the only one who's been through here! You're the only one who knows the way. And, there's something else," Tas pointed. Caramon turned his head. "You asked about Lady Crysania. There she is. She's alive, but she's dead at the same time. Her skin is like ice. Her eyes are fixed in a terrible stare. She's breathing, her heart's beating, but it might just as well be pumping through her body that spicy stuff the elves use to preserve their dead!" The kender drew a deep, quivering breath.

"We've got to get help for her, Caramon. Maybe in there"—Tas pointed to the Forest—"the mages can help her! I can't carry her." He raised his hands helplessly. "I need you, Caramon. She needs you! I guess you could say you owe it to her."

"Since it's my fault she's hurt?" Caramon muttered savagely.

"No, I didn't mean that," Tas said, hanging his head and brushing his hand across his eyes. "It's no one's fault, I guess."

"No, it *is* my fault," Caramon said. Tas glanced up at him, hearing a note in Caramon's voice he hadn't heard in a long, long time. The big man stood, staring at the bottle in his hands. "It's time I faced up to it. I've blamed everyone else—Raistlin, Tika. . . . But all the time I knew—deep inside—it was me. It came to me, in that dream. I was lying at the bottom of a grave, and I realized—this *is* the bottom! I can't go any lower. I either stay here and let them throw dirt on top of me—just like I was going to bury Crysania—or I climb out," Caramon sighed, a long, shuddering sigh. Then, in sudden resolution, he put the cork on the bottle and handed it back to Tas. "Here," he said softly. "It's going to be long climb, and I'm going to need help, I expect. But not that kind of help."

"Oh, Caramon!" Tas threw his arms around the big man's waist as far as he could reach, hugging him tightly. "I wasn't afraid of that spooky wood, not really. But I *was* wondering how I was going to get through by myself. Not to mention Lady Crysania and—Oh, Caramon! I'm so glad you're back! I—"

"There, there," Caramon muttered, flushing in embarrassment and shoving Tasslehoff gently away from him. "It's all right. I'm not sure how much help I'll be—I was scared to death the first time I went into that place. But, you're right. Maybe they can help Crysania." Caramon's face hardened. "Maybe they can answer a few questions I have about Raist, too. Now, where's that gully dwarf gotten to? And"—he glanced down at his belt—"where's my dagger?"

"What dagger?" Tas asked, skipping around, his gaze on the Forest.

Reaching out, his face grim, Caramon caught hold of the kender. His gaze went to Tas's belt. Tas's followed. His eyes opened wide in astonishment.

"You mean *that* dagger? My goodness, I wonder how it got there? You know," he said thoughtfully, "I'll bet you dropped it, during the fight."

"Yeah," Caramon muttered. Growling, he retrieved his dagger and was just putting it back into its sheath when he heard a noise behind him. Whirling around in alarm, he got a bucketful of icy water, right in the face.

"Him awake now," Bupu announced complacently, dropping the bucket.

While drying his clothes, Caramon sat and studied the trees, his face drawn with the pain of his memories. Finally, heaving a sigh, he dressed, checked his weapons, then stood up. Instantly, Tasslehoff was right next to him.

"Let's go!" he said eagerly.

Caramon stopped. "Into the Forest?" he asked in a hopeless voice.

"Well, of course!" Tas said, startled. "Where else?"

Caramon scowled, then sighed, then shook his head. "No, Tas," he said gruffly. "You stay here with Lady Crysania. Now, look," he said in answer to the kender's indignant squawk of protest, "I'm just going into the Forest for a little ways—to, er, check it out."

"You think there's something in there, don't you?" Tas accused the big man. "That's why you're making me stay out!

You'll go in there and there'll be a big fight. You'll probably kill it, and I'll miss the whole thing!"

"I doubt that," Caramon muttered. Glancing into the fog-ridden Forest apprehensively, he tightened his sword belt.

"At least you might tell me what you think it is," Tas said. "And, say, Caramon, what am I supposed to do if *it* kills *you*? Can I go in then? How long should I wait? Could it kill you in—say—five minutes? Ten? Not that I think it will," he added hastily, seeing Caramon's eyes widen. "But I really should know, I mean, since you're leaving me in charge."

Bupu studied the slovenly warrior speculatively. "Me say—two minutes. It kill him in two minutes. You make bet?" She looked at Tas.

Caramon glared grimly at both of them, then heaved another sigh. Tas was only being logical, after all.

"I'm not sure what to expect," Caramon muttered. "I-I remember last time, we . . . we met this thing . . . a wraith. It—Raist . . ." Caramon fell silent. "I don't know what you should do," he said after a moment. Shoulders slumping, he turned away and began to walk slowly toward the Forest. "The best you can, I guess."

"I got nice snake here, me say he last two minutes," Bupu said to Tas, rummaging around in her bag. "What stakes you put up?"

"Shhhh," Tas said softly, watching Caramon walk away. Then, shaking his head, he scooted over to sit beside Crysania, who lay on the ground, her sightless eyes staring up at the sky. Gently, Tas drew the cleric's white hood over her head, shading her from the sun's rays. He had tried unsuccessfully to shut those staring eyes, but it was as if her flesh had turned to marble.

Raistlin seemed to walk beside Caramon every step of the way into the Forest. The warrior could almost hear the soft whisper of his brother's red robes—they had been red then! He could hear his brother's voice—always gentle, always soft, but with that faint hiss of sarcasm that grated so on their friends. But it had never bothered Caramon. He had understood—or anyway thought he had.

The trees in the Forest suddenly shifted at Caramon's approach, just as they had shifted at the kender's approach.

Just as they shifted when we approached . . . how many years ago, Caramon thought. Seven? Has it only been seven years? No, he realized sadly. It's been a lifetime, a lifetime for both of us.

As Caramon came to the edge of the wood, the mist flowed out along the ground, chilling his ankles with a cold that seared through flesh and bit into bone. The trees stared at him, their branches writhing in agony. He remembered the tortured woods of Silvanesti, and that brought more memories of his brother. Caramon stood still a moment, looking into the Forest. He could see the dark and shadowy shapes waiting for him. And there was no Raistlin to keep them at bay. Not this time.

"I was never afraid of anything until I entered the Forest of Wayreth," Caramon said to himself softly. "I only went in last time because you were with me, my brother. Your courage alone kept me going. How can I go in there now without you? It's magic. I don't understand magic! I can't fight it! What hope is there?" Caramon put his hands over his eyes to blot out the hideous sight. "I can't go in there," he said wretchedly. "It's too much to ask of me!"

Pulling his sword from its sheath, he held it out. His hand shook so he nearly dropped the weapon. "Hah!" he said bitterly. "See? I couldn't fight a child. This is too much to ask. No hope. There is no hope. . . ."

"It is easy to have hope in the spring, warrior, when the weather is warm and the vallenwoods are green. It is easy to have hope in the summer when the vallenwoods glitter with gold. It is easy to have hope in the fall when the vallenwoods are as red as living blood. But in the winter, when the air is sharp and bitter and the skies are gray, does the vallenwood die, warrior?"

"Who spoke?" Caramon cried, staring around wildly, clutching his sword in his trembling hand.

"What does the vallenwood do in the winter, warrior, when all is dark and even the ground is frozen? It digs deep, warrior. It sends its root down, down, into the soil, down to warm heart of the world. There, deep within, the vallenwood finds nourishment to

help it survive the darkness and the cold, so that it may bloom again in the spring."

"So?" Caramon asked suspiciously, backing up a step and looking around.

"So you stand in the darkest winter of your life, warrior. And so you must dig deep to find the warmth and the strength that will help you survive the bitter cold and the terrible darkness. No longer do you have the bloom of spring or the vigor of summer. You must find the strength you need in your heart, in your soul. Then, like the vallenwoods, you will grow once more."

"Your words are pretty—" Caramon began, scowling, distrusting this talk of spring and trees. But he could not finish, his breath caught in his throat.

The Forest was changing before his eyes.

The twisting, writhing trees straightened as he watched, lifting their limbs to the skies, growing, growing, growing. He bent his head back so far he nearly lost his balance, but still he couldn't see their tops. They were vallenwood trees! Just like those in Solace before the coming of the dragons. As he watched in awe, he saw dead limbs burst into life—green buds sprouted, burst open, blossomed into green glistening leaves that turned summer gold—seasons changing as he drew a shivering breath.

The noxious fog vanished, replaced by a sweet fragrance drifting from beautiful flowers that twined among the roots of the vallenwoods. The darkness in the forest vanished, the sun shed its bright light upon the swaying trees. And as the sunlight touched the trees' leaves, the calls of birds filled the perfumed air.

Easeful the forest, easeful its mansions perfected
Where we grow and decay no longer, our trees ever green,
Ripe fruit never falling, streams still and transparent
As glass, as the heart in repose this lasting day.

Beneath these branches the willing surrender of movement,
The business of birdsong, of love, left on the borders
With all of the fevers, the failures of memory.
Easeful the forest, easeful its mansions perfected.

And light upon light, light as dismissal of darkness,
Beneath these branches no shade, for shade is forgotten
In the warmth of the light and the cool smell of the leaves
Where we grow and decay; no longer, our trees ever green.

Here there is quiet, where music turns in upon silence,
Here at the world's imagined edge, where clarity
Completes the senses, at long last where we behold
Ripe fruit never falling, streams still and transparent.

Where the tears are dried from our faces. or settle,
Still as a stream in accomplished countries of peace,
And the traveler opens, permitting the voyage of light
As air, as the heart in repose this lasting day.

Easeful the forest, easeful its mansions perfected
Where we grow and decay no longer, our trees ever green,
Ripe fruit never falling, streams still and transparent
As air, as the heart in repose this lasting day.

Caramon's eyes filled with tears. The beauty of the song pierced his heart. There was hope! Inside the Forest, he would find all the answers! He'd find the help he sought.

"Caramon!" Tasslehoff was jumping up and down with excitement. "Caramon, that's wonderful! How did you do it? Hear the birds? Let's go! Quickly."

"Crysania—" Caramon said, starting to turn back. "We'll have to make a litter. You'll have to help—" But before he could finish, he stopped, staring in astonishment at two white-robed figures, who glided out of the golden woods. Their white hoods were pulled low over their heads, he could not see their faces. Both bowed before him solemnly, then walked across the glade to where Crysania lay in her deathlike sleep. Lifting her still body with ease, they bore her gently back to where Caramon stood. Coming to the edge of the Forest, they stopped, turning their hooded heads, looking at him expectantly.

"I think they're waiting for you to go in first, Caramon," Tas said cheerfully. "You go on ahead, I'll get Bupu."

The gully dwarf remained standing in the center of the glade, regarding the Forest with deep suspicion, which Caramon looking at the white-robed figures, suddenly shared.

"Who are you?" he asked.

They did not answer. They simply stood, waiting.

"Who cares who they are!" Tas said, impatiently grabbing hold of Bupu and dragging her along, her sack bumping against her heels.

Caramon scowled. "You go first." He gestured at the white-robed figures. They said nothing, nor did they move.

"Why are you waiting for me to enter that Forest?" Caramon stepped back a pace. "Go ahead"—he gestured—"take her to the Tower. You can help her. You don't need me—"

The figures did not speak, but one raised his hand, pointing.

"C'mon, Caramon," Tas urged. "Look, it's like he was inviting us!"

They will not bother us, brother. . . . We have been invited! Raistlin's words, spoken seven years ago.

"Mages invited us. I don't trust 'em." Caramon softly repeated the answer he had made then.

Suddenly, the air was filled with laughter—strange, eerie, whispering laughter. Bupu threw her arms around Caramon's leg, clinging to him in terror. Even Tasslehoff seemed a bit disconcerted. And then came a voice, as Caramon had heard it seven years before.

Does that include me, dear brother?

Chapter II

The hideous apparition came closer and closer to her. Crysania was possessed by a fear such as she had never known, a fear she could never have believed existed. As she shrank back before it, Crysania, for the first time in her life, contemplated death—her own death. It was not the peaceful transition to a blessed realm she had always believed existed. It was savage pain and howling darkness, eternal days and nights spent envying the living.

She tried to cry out for help, but her voice failed. There was no help anyway. The drunken warrior lay in a pool of his own blood. Her healing arts had saved him, but he would sleep long hours. The kender could not help her. Nothing could help her against this. . . .

On and on the dark figure walked, nearer and nearer he came. Run! her mind screamed. Her limbs would not obey. It was all she could do to creep backward, and then her body seemed to move of its own volition, not through any direction of hers. She could not even look away from him. The orange flickering lights that were his eyes held her fast.

He raised a hand, a spectral hand. She could see through it, see through him, in fact, to the night-shadowed trees behind.

The silver moon was in the sky, but it was not its bright light that gleamed off the antique armor of a long-dead Solamnic Knight. The creature shone with an unwholesome light of his own, glowing with the energy of his foul decay. His hand lifted higher and higher, and Crysania knew that when his hand reached a level even with her heart, she would die.

Through lips numb with fear, Crysania called out a name, "Paladine," she prayed. The fear did not leave her, she still could not wrench her soul away from the terrible gaze of those fiery eyes. But her hand went to her throat. Grasping hold of the medallion, she ripped it from her neck. Feeling her strength draining, her consciousness ebbing, Crysania raised her hand. The platinum medallion caught Solinari's light and flared bluewhite. The hideous apparition spoke— "Die!"

Crysania felt herself falling. Her body hit the ground, but the ground did not catch her. She was falling through it, or away from it. Falling . . . falling . . . closing her eyes . . . sleeping. . . . dreaming. . . .

She was in a grove of oak trees. White hands clutched at her feet, gaping mouths sought to drink her blood. The darkness was endless, the trees mocked her, their creaking branches laughing horribly.

"Crysania," said a soft, whispering voice.

What was that, speaking her name from the shadows of the oaks? She could see it, standing in a clearing, robed in black.

"Crysania," the voice repeated.

"Raistlin!" She sobbed in thankfulness. Stumbling out of the terrifying grove of oak trees, fleeing the bone-white hands that sought to drag her down to join their endless torment, Crysania felt thin arms hold her. She felt the strange burning touch of slender fingers.

"Rest easy, Revered Daughter," the voice said softly. Trembling in his arms, Crysania closed her eyes. "Your trials are over. You have come through the Grove safely. There was nothing to fear, lady. You had my charm."

"Yes," Crysania murmured. Her hand touched her forehead where his lips had pressed against her skin. Then, realizing what she had been through, and realizing, too, that she had allowed him to see her give way to weakness, Crysania pushed the mage's arms away. Standing back from him, she regarded him coldly.

"Why do you surround yourself with such foul things?" she demanded. "Why do you feel the need for such . . . such guardians!" Her voice quavered in spite of herself.

Raistlin looked at her mildly, his golden eyes shining in the light of his staff. "What kind of guardians do you surround yourself with, Revered Daughter?" he asked. "What torment would I endure if I set foot upon the Temple's sacred grounds?"

Crysania opened her mouth for a scathing reply, but the words died on her lips. Indeed, the Temple *was* consecrated ground. Sacred to Paladine, if any who worshipped the Queen of Darkness entered its precincts, they would feel Paladine's wrath. Crysania saw Raistlin smile, his thin lips twitch. She felt her skin flush. How was he capable of doing this to her? Never had any man been able to humiliate her so! Never had any man cast her mind in such turmoil!

Ever since the evening she had met Raistlin at the home of Astinus, Crysania had not been able to banish him from her thoughts. She had looked forward to visiting the Tower this night, looked forward to it and dreaded it at the same time. She had told Elistan all about her talk with Raistlin, all—that is—except the "charm" he had given her. Somehow, she could not bring herself to tell Elistan that Raistlin had touched her, had—No, she wouldn't mention it.

Elistan had been upset enough as it was. He knew Raistlin, he had known the young man of old—the mage having been among the companions who rescued the cleric from Verminaard's prison at Pax Tharkas. Elistan had never liked or trusted Raistlin, but then no one had, not really. The cleric had not been surprised to hear that the young mage had donned the Black Robes. He was not surprised to hear about Crysania's warning from Paladine. He *was* surprised at Crysania's reaction to meeting Raistlin, however. He was surprised—and alarmed—at hearing Crysania had been invited to visit

Raistlin in the Tower—a place where now beat the heart of evil in Krynn. Elistan would have forbidden Crysania to go, but freedom of will was a teaching of the gods.

He told Crysania his thoughts and she listened respectfully. But she had gone to the Tower, drawn by a lure she could not begin to understand—although she told Elistan it was to "save the world."

"The world is getting on quite well," Elistan replied gravely.

But Crysania did not listen.

"Come inside," Raistlin said. "Some wine will help banish the evil memories of what you have endured." He regarded her intently. "You are very brave, Revered Daughter," he said and she heard no sarcasm in his voice. "Few there are with the strength to survive the terror of the Grove."

He turned away from her then, and Crysania was glad he did. She felt herself blushing at his praise.

"Keep near me," he warned as he walked ahead of her, his black robes rustling softly around his ankles. "Keep within the light of my staff."

Crysania did as she was bidden, noticing as she walked near him how the staff's light made her white robes shine as coldly as the light of the silver moon, a striking contrast to the strange warmth it shed over Raistlin's soft velvety black robes.

He led her through the dread Gates. She stared at them in curiosity, remembering the gruesome story of the evil mage who had cast himself down upon them, cursing them with his dying breath. *Things* whispered and jabbered around her. More than once, she turned at the sound, feeling cold fingers upon her neck or the touch of a chill hand upon hers. More than once, she saw movement out of the corner of her eye, but when she looked, there was never anything there. A foul mist rose up from the ground, rank with the smell of decay, making her bones ache. She began to shake uncontrollably and when, suddenly, she glanced behind her and saw two disembodied, staring eyes—she took a hurried step forward and slipped her hand around Raistlin's thin arm.

He regarded her with curiosity and a gentle amusement that made her blush again.

"There is no need to be afraid," he said simply. "I am master here. I will not let you come to harm."

"I-I'm not afraid," she said, though she knew he could feel her body quivering. "I . . . was just . . . unsure of my steps, that was all."

"I beg your pardon, Revered Daughter," Raistlin said, and now she could not be certain if she heard sarcasm in his voice or not. He came to a halt. "It was impolite of me to allow you to walk this unfamiliar ground without offering you my assistance. Do you find the walking easier now?"

"Yes, much," she said, flushing deeply beneath that strange gaze.

He said nothing, merely smiled. She lowered her eyes, unable to face him, and they resumed walking. Crysania berated herself for her fear all the way to the Tower, but she did not remove her hand from the mage's arm. Neither of them spoke again until they reached the door to the Tower itself. It was a plain wooden door with runes carved on the outside of its surface. Raistlin said no word, made no motion that Crysania could see, but—at their approach—the door slowly opened. Light streamed out from inside, and Crysania felt so cheered by its bright and welcoming warmth, that—for an instant—she did not see another figure standing silhouetted within it.

When she did, she stopped and drew back in alarm.

Raistlin touched her hand with his thin, burning fingers.

"That is only my apprentice, Revered Daughter," he said. "Dalamar is flesh and blood, he walks among the living—at least for the moment."

Crysania did not understand that last remark, nor did she pay it much attention, hearing the underlying laughter in Raistlin's voice. She was too startled by the fact that live people *lived* here. How silly, she scolded herself. What kind of monster have I pictured this man? He *is* a man, nothing more. He is human, he is flesh and blood. The thought relieved her, made her relax. Stepping through the doorway, she felt almost herself. She extended her hand to the young apprentice as she would have given it to a new acolyte.

"My apprentice, Dalamar," Raistlin said, gesturing toward him. "Lady Crysania, Revered Daughter of Paladine."

"Lady Crysania," said the apprentice with becoming gravity, accepting her hand and bringing it to his lips, bowing slightly. Then he lifted his head, and the black hood that shadowed his face fell back.

"An elf!" Crysania gasped. Her hand remained in his. "But, that's not possible, she began in confusion. "Not serving evil—"

"I am a dark elf, Revered Daughter," the apprentice said, and she heard a bitterness in his voice. "At least, that is what my people call me."

Crysania murmured in embarrassment. "I'm sorry. I didn't mean—"

She faltered and fell silent, not knowing where to look. She could almost feel Raistlin laughing at her. Once again, he had caught her off-balance. Angrily, she snatched her hand away from the apprentice's cool grip and withdrew her other hand from Raistlin's arm.

"The Revered Daughter has had a fatiguing journey, Dalamar," Raistlin said. "Please show her to my study and pour her a glass of wine. With your permission, Lady Crysania"— the mage bowed— "there are a few matters that demand my attention. Dalamar, anything the lady requires, you will provide at once."

"Certainly, *Shalafi*," Dalamar answered respectfully.

Crysania said nothing as Raistlin left, suddenly overwhelmed with a sense of relief and a numbing exhaustion. Thus must the warrior feel, battling for his life against a skilled opponent, she observed silently as she followed the apprentice up a narrow, winding staircase.

Raistlin's study was nothing like she had expected.

What *had* I expected, she asked herself. Certainly not this pleasant room filled with strange and fascinating books. The furniture was attractive and comfortable, a fire burned on the hearth, filling the room with warmth that was welcome after the chill of the walk to the Tower. The wine that Dalamar poured was delicious. The warmth of the fire seemed to seep into her blood as she drank a small sip.

Dalamar brought forward a small, ornately carved table and set it at her right hand. Upon this, he placed a bowl of fruit and a loaf of fragrant, still-warm bread.

"What is this fruit?" Crysania asked, picking up a piece and examining it in wonder. "I've never seen anything like this before."

"Indeed not, Revered Daughter," Dalamar answered, smiling. Unlike Raistlin, Crysania noticed, the young apprentice's smile was reflected in his eyes. "*Shalafi* has it brought to him from the Isle of Mithas."

"Mithas?" Crysania repeated in astonishment. "But that's on the other side of the world! The minotaurs live there. They allow none to enter their kingdom! Who brings it?"

She had a sudden, terrifying vision of the servant who might have been summoned to bring such delicacies to such a master. Hastily, she returned the fruit to the bowl.

"Try it, Lady Crysania," Dalamar said without a trace of amusement in his voice. "You will find it quite delicious. The *Slalafi's* health is delicate. There are so few things he can tolerate. He lives on little else but this fruit, bread, and wine."

Crysania's fear ebbed. "Yes," she murmured, her eyes going to the door involuntarily. "He is dreadfully frail, isn't he. And that terrible cough . . ." Her voice was soft with pity.

"Cough? Oh, yes," Dalamar said smoothly, "his . . . cough." He did not continue and, if Crysania thought this odd, she soon forgot it in her contemplation of the room.

The apprentice stood a moment, waiting to see if she required anything else. When Crysania did not speak, he bowed. "If you need nothing more, lady, I will retire. I have my own studies to pursue."

"Of course. I will be fine here," Crysania said, coming out of her thoughts with a start. "He is your teacher, then," she said in sudden realization. Now it was her turn to look at Dalamar intently. "Is he a good one? Do you learn from him?"

"He is the most gifted of any in our Order, Lady Crysania," Dalamar said softly. "He is brilliant, skilled, controlled. Only one has lived who was as powerful—the great Fistandantilus. And my *Shalafi* is young, only twenty-eight. If he lives, he may well—"

"If he lives?" Crysania repeated, then felt irritated that she had unintentionally let a note of concern creep into her voice.

It is right to feel concern, she told herself. After all, he is one of the gods' creatures. All life is sacred.

"The Art is fraught with danger, my lady," Dalamar was saying. "And now, if you will excuse me...."

"Certainly," Crysania murmured.

Bowing again, Dalamar padded quietly from the room, shutting the door behind him. Toying with her wine glass, Crysania stared into the dancing flames, lost in thought. She did not hear the door open—if indeed it did. She felt fingers touching her hair. Shivering, she looked around, only to see Raistlin sitting in a high-backed wooden chair behind his desk.

"Can I send for anything else? Is everything to your liking?" he asked politely.

"Y-yes," Crysania stammered, setting her wine glass down so that he would not see her hand shake. "Everything is fine. More than fine, actually. Your apprentice—Dalamar? He is quite charming."

"Isn't he," said Raistlin dryly. He placed the tips of the five fingers of each hand together and rested them upon the table.

"What marvelous hands you have," Crysania said, without thinking. "How slender and supple the fingers are, and so delicate." Suddenly realizing what she had been saying, she flushed and stammered. "B-but I-I suppose that is requisite to your Art—"

"Yes," Raistlin said, smiling, and this time Crysania thought she saw actual pleasure in his smile. He held his hands to the light cast by the flames. "When I was just a child, I could amaze and delight my brother with the tricks these hands could—even then—perform." Taking a golden coin from one of the secret pockets of his robes, Raistlin placed the coin upon the knuckles of his hand. Effortlessly, he made it dance and spin and whirl across his hand. It glistened in and out of his fingers. Flipping into the air, it vanished, only to reappear in his other hand. Crysania gasped in delight. Raistlin glanced up at her, and she saw the smile of pleasure twist into one of bitter pain.

"Yes," he said, "it was my one skill, my one talent. It kept the other children amused. Sometimes it kept them from hurting me."

"Hurting you?" Crysania asked hesitantly, stung by the pain in his voice.

He did not answer at once, his eyes on the golden coin he still held in his hand. Then he drew a deep breath. "I can picture your childhood," he murmured. "You come from a wealthy family, so they tell me. You must have been beloved, sheltered, protected, given anything you wanted. You were admired, sought after, liked."

Crysania could not reply. She felt suddenly overwhelmed with guilt.

"How different was my childhood." Again, that smile of bitter pain. "My nickname was the Sly One. I was sickly and weak. And too smart. They were such fools! Their ambitions so petty—like my brother, who never thought deeper than his food dish! Or my sister, who saw the only way to attain her goals was with her sword. Yes, I was weak. Yes, they protected me. But some day, I vowed I wouldn't need their protection! I would rise to greatness on my own, using my gift—*my magic.*"

His hand clenched, his golden-tinted skin turned pale. Suddenly he began to cough, the wrenching, wracking cough that twisted his frail body. Crysania rose to her feet, her heart aching with pain. But he motioned her to sit down. Drawing a cloth from a pocket, he wiped the blood from his lips.

"And this was the price I paid for my magic," he said when he could speak again. His voice was little more than a whisper. "They shattered my body and gave me this accursed vision, so that all I look upon I see dying before my eyes. But it was worth it, worth it all! For I have what I sought—power. I don't need them—any of them—anymore."

"But this power is evil!" Crysania said, leaning forward in her chair and regarding Raistlin earnestly.

"Is it?" asked Raistlin suddenly. His voice was mild. "Is ambition evil? Is the quest for power, for control over others evil? If so, then I fear, Lady Crysania, that you may as well exchange those white robes for black."

"How dare you?" Crysania cried, shocked. "I don't—"

"Ah, but you do," Raistlin said with a shrug. "You would not have worked so hard to rise to the position you have in the church without having your share of ambition, of the desire for power." Now it was his turn to lean forward. "Haven't you always said to yourself—there is something *great* I am destined to do? *My* life will be different from the lives of others. *I* am not content to sit and watch the world pass by. I want to shape it, control it, mold it!"

Held fast by Raistlin's burning gaze, Crysania could not move or utter a word. How could he know? she asked herself, terrified. Can he read the secrets of my heart?

"Is that evil, Lady Crysania?" Raistlin repeated gently, insistently.

Slowly, Crysania shook her head. Slowly, she raised her hand to her throbbing temples. No, it wasn't evil. Not the way he spoke of it, but something wasn't quite right. She couldn't think. She was too confused. All that kept running through her mind was: *How alike we are, he and I!*

He was silent, waiting for her to speak. She had to say something. Hurriedly, she took a gulp of wine to give herself time to collect her scattered thoughts.

"Perhaps I do have those desires," she said, struggling to find the words, "but, if so, my ambition is not for myself. I use my skills and talents for others, to help others. I use it for the church—"

"The church!" Raistlin sneered.

Crysania's confusion vanished, replaced by cold anger. "Yes," she replied, feeling herself on safe and secure ground, surrounded by the bastion of her faith. "It was the power of good, the power of Paladine, that drove away the evil in the world. It is that power I seek. That power that—"

"Drove away the evil?" Raistlin interrupted.

Crysania blinked. Her thoughts had carried her forward.

She hadn't even been totally aware of what she was saying. "Why, yes—"

"But evil and suffering still remain in the world," Raistlin persisted.

"Because of such as you!" Crysania cried passionately.

"Ah, no, Revered Daughter," Raistlin said. "Not through any act of mine. Look—" He motioned her near with one hand, while with the other he reached once again into the secret pockets of his robe.

Suddenly wary and suspicious, Crysania did not move, staring at the object he drew forth. It was a small, round piece of crystal, swirling with color, very like a child's marble. Lifting a silver stand from where it stood on a corner of his desk, Raistlin placed the marble on top of it. The thing appeared ludicrous, much too small for the ornate stand. Then Crysania gasped. The marble was growing! Or perhaps *she* was shrinking! She couldn't be certain. But the glass globe was now the right size and rested comfortably upon the silver stand.

"Look into it," Raistlin said softly.

"No," Crysania drew back, staring fearfully at the globe. "What is that?"

"A dragon orb," Raistlin replied, his gaze holding her fast. "It is the only one left on Krynn. It obeys my commands. I will not allow you to come to harm. Look inside the orb, Lady Crysania—unless you fear the truth."

"How do I know it will show me the truth?" Crysania demanded, her voice shaking. "How do I know it won't show me just what you tell it to show me?"

"If you know the way the dragons orbs were made long ago," Raistlin replied, "you know they were created by all three of the Robes—the White, the Black, and the Red. They are not tools of evil, they are not tools of good. They are everything and nothing. You wear the medallion of Paladine"—the sarcasm had returned— "and you are strong in your faith. Could I force you to see what you did not want to see?"

"What will I see?" Crysania whispered, curiosity and a strange fascination drawing her near the desk.

"Only what your eyes have seen, but refused to look at."

Raistlin placed his thin fingers upon the glass, chanting words of command. Hesitantly, Crysania leaned over the desk and looked into the dragon orb. At first she saw nothing inside the glass globe but a faint swirling green color. Then she drew back. There were hands inside the orb! Hands that were reaching out....

"Do not fear," murmured Raistlin. "The hands come for me."

And, indeed, even as he spoke, Crysania saw the hands inside the orb reach out and touch Raistlin's hands. The image vanished. Wild, vibrant colors whirled madly inside the orb for an instant, making Crysania dizzy with their light and their brilliance. Then they, too, were gone. She saw . . .

"Palanthas," she said, startled. Floating on the mists of morning, she could see the entire city, gleaming like a pearl, spread out before her eyes. And then the city began to rush up at her, or perhaps she was falling down into it. Now she was hovering over New City, now she was over the Wall, now she was inside Old City. The Temple of Paladine rose before her, the beautiful, sacred grounds peaceful and serene in the morning sunlight. And then she was *behind* the Temple, looking over a high wall.

She caught her breath. "What is this?" she asked.

"Have you never seen it?" Raistlin replied. "This alley so near the sacred grounds?"

Crysania shook her head, "N-no," she answered, her voice breaking. "And, yet, I must have. I have lived in Palanthas all my life. I know all of—"

"No, lady," Raistlin said, his fingertips lightly caressing the dragon orb's crystalline surface. "No, you know very little."

Crysania could not answer. He spoke the truth, apparently, for she did not know this part of the city. Littered with refuse, the alley was dark and dismal. Morning's sunlight did not find its way past the buildings that leaned over the street as if they had no more energy to stand upright. Crysania recognized the buildings now. She had seen them from the front. They were used to store everything from grain to casks of wine and ale. But how much different they looked from the front! And who were these people, these wretched people?

"They live there," Raistlin answered her unspoken question.

"Where?" Crysania asked in horror. "There? Why?"

"They live where they can. Burrowing into the heart of the city like maggots, they feed off its decay. As for why?" Raistlin shrugged. "They have nowhere else to go."

"But this is terrible! I'll tell Elistan. We'll help them, give them money—"

"Elistan knows," Raistlin said softly.

"No, he can't! That's impossible!"

"You knew. If not about this, then you knew of other places in your fair city that are not so fair."

"I didn't—" Crysania began angrily, then stopped. Memories washed over her in waves—her mother averting her face as they rode in their carriage through certain parts of town, her father quickly drawing shut the curtains in the carriage windows or leaning out to tell the driver to take a different road.

The scene shimmered, the colors swirled, it faded and was replaced by another, and then another. Crysania watched in agony as the mage ripped the pearl-white facade from the city, showing her blackness and corruption beneath. Bars, brothels, gambling dens, the wharves, the docks . . . all spewed forth their refuse of misery and suffering before Crysania's shocked vision. No longer could she avert her face, there were no curtains to pull shut. Raistlin dragged her inside, brought her close to the hopeless, the starving, the forlorn, the forgotten.

"No," she pleaded, shaking her head and trying to back away from the desk. "Please show me no more."

But Raistlin was pitiless. Once again the colors swirled, and they left Palanthas. The dragon orb carried them around the world, and everywhere Crysania looked, she saw more horrors. Gully dwarves, a race cast off from their dwarven kin, living in squalor in whatever part of Krynn they could find that no one else wanted. Humans eking out a wretched existence in lands where rain had ceased to fall. The Wilder elves, enslaved by their own people. Clerics, using their power to cheat and amass great wealth at the expense of those who trusted them.

It was too much. With a wild cry, Crysania covered her face with her hands. The room swayed beneath her feet. Staggering, she nearly fell. And then Raistlin's arms were around her. She felt that strange, burning warmth from his body and the soft touch of the black velvet. There was a smell of spices, rose petals, and other, more mysterious odors. She could hear his shallow breathing rattle in his lungs.

Gently, Raistlin led Crysania back to her chair. She sat down, quickly drawing away from his touch. His nearness was both repelling and attracting at the same time, adding to her feelings of loss and confusion. She wished desperately that Elistan were here. He would know, he would understand. For there had to be an explanation! Such terrible suffering, such evil should not be allowed. Feeling empty and hollow, she stared into the fire.

"We are not so very different." Raistlin's voice seemed to come from the flames. "I live in my Tower, devoting myself to my studies. You live in your Tower, devoting yourself to your faith. And the world turns around us."

"And that is true evil," Crysania said to the flames. "To sit and do nothing."

"Now you understand," Raistlin said. "No longer am I content to sit and watch. I have studied long years for one reason, with one aim. And now that is within my grasp. *I* will make a difference, Crysania. *I* will change the world. *That* is my plan."

Crysania looked up swiftly. Her faith had been shaken, but its core was strong. "Your plan! It is the plan Paladine warned me of in my dream. This plan to change the world will cause the world's destruction!" Her hand clenched in her lap. "You must not go through with it! Paladine—"

Raistlin made an impatient gesture with his hand. His golden eyes flashed and, for a moment, Crysania shrank back, catching a glimpse of the smoldering fires within the man.

"Paladine will not stop me," Raistlin said, "for I seek to depose his greatest enemy."

Crysania stared at the mage, not understanding. What enemy could that be? What enemy could Paladine have upon this world. Then Raistlin's meaning became clear. Crysania felt the blood drain from her face, cold fear made her shudder convulsively. Unable to speak, she shook her head. The enormity of his ambition and his desires was too fearful, too impossible to even contemplate.

"Listen," he said, softly. "I will make it clear. . . ."

And he told her his plans. She sat for what seemed like hours before the fire, held by the gaze of his strange, golden eyes, mesmerized by the sound of his soft, whispering voice, hearing him tell her of the wonders of his magic and of the magic now long lost, the wonders discovered by Fistandantilus.

Raistlin's voice fell silent. Crysania sat for long moments, lost and wandering in a realm far from any she had ever known. The fire burned low in the gray hour before dawn. The room became lighter. Crysania shivered in the suddenly chill chamber.

Raistlin coughed, and Crysania looked up at him, startled. He was pale with exhaustion, his eyes seemed feverish, his hands shook. Crysania rose to her feet.

"I am sorry," she said, her voice low. "I have kept you awake all night, and you are not well. I must go."

Raistlin rose with her. "Do not worry about my health, Revered Daughter," he said with a twisted smile. "The fire that burns within me is fuel enough to warm this shattered body. Dalamar will accompany you back through Shoikan Grove, if you like."

"Yes, thank you," Crysania murmured. She had forgotten that she must go back through that evil place. Taking a deep breath, she held her hand out to Raistlin. "Thank you for meeting with me," she began formally. "I hope—"

Raistlin took her hand in his, the touch of his smooth flesh burned. Crysania looked into his eyes. She saw herself reflected there, a colorless woman dressed in white, her face framed by her dark, black hair.

"You cannot do this," Crysania whispered. "It is wrong, you must be stopped." She held onto his hand very tightly.

"Prove to me that it is wrong," Raistlin answered, drawing her near. "Show me that this is evil. Convince me that the ways of good are the means of saving the world."

"Will you listen?" Crysania asked wistfully. "You are surrounded by darkness. How can I reach you?"

"The darkness parted, didn't it," Raistlin said. "The darkness parted, and you came in."

"Yes..." Crysania was suddenly aware of the touch of his hand, the warmth of his body. Flushing uncomfortably, she stepped back. Removing her hand from his grasp, she absently rubbed it, as if it hurt.

"Farewell, Raistlin Majere," she said, without meeting his eyes.

"Farewell, Revered Daughter of Paladine," he said.

The door opened and Dalamar stood within it, though Crysania had not heard Raistlin summon the young apprentice. Drawing her white hood up over her hair, Crysania turned from Raistlin and walked through the door. Moving down the gray, stone hallway, she could feel his golden eyes burning through her robes. When she arrived at the narrow winding staircase leading down, his voice reached her.

"Perhaps Paladine did not send you to stop me, Lady Crysania. Perhaps he sent you to help."

Crysania paused and looked back. Raistlin was gone, the gray hall was bleak and empty. Dalamar stood beside her in silence, waiting.

Slowly, gathering the folds of her white robes in her hand so that she did not trip, Crysania descended the stairs.

And kept on descending . . . down . . . down . . . into unending sleep.

Chapter 12

The Tower of High Sorcery in Wayreth had been, for centuries, the last outpost of magic upon the continent of Ansalon. Here the mages had been driven, when the Kingpriest ordered them from the other Towers. Here they had come, leaving the Tower in Istar, now under the waters of the Blood Sea, leaving the accursed and blackened Tower in Palanthas.

The Tower in Wayreth was an imposing structure, an unnerving sight. The outer walls formed an equilateral triangle. A small tower stood at each angle of the perfect geometric shape. In the center stood the two main towers, slanted slightly, twisting just a little, enough to make the viewer blink and say to himself—aren't those crooked?

The walls were built of black stone. Polished to a high gloss, it shone brilliantly in the sunlight and, in the night, reflected the light of two moons and mirrored the darkness of the third. Runes were carved upon the surface of the stone, runes of power and strength, shielding and warding; runes that bound the stones to each other; runes that bound the stones to the ground. The tops of the walls were smooth. There were no battlements for soldiers to man. There was no need.

Far from any centers of civilization, the Tower at Wayreth was surrounded by its magic wood. None could enter who did not belong, none came to it without invitation. And so the mages protected their last bastion of strength, guarding it well from the outside world.

Yet, the Tower was not lifeless. Ambitious apprentice magic-users came from all over the world to take the rigorous—and sometimes fatal—Test. Wizards of high standing arrived daily, continuing their studies, meeting, discussing, conducting dangerous and delicate experiments. To these, the Tower was open day and night. They could come and go as they chose—Black Robes, Red Robes, White Robes.

Though far apart in philosophies—in their ways of viewing and of living with the world—all the Robes met in peace in the Tower. Arguments were tolerated only as they served to advance the Art. Fighting of any sort was prohibited—the penalty was swift, terrible death.

The Art. It was the one thing that united them all. It was their first loyalty—no matter who they were, whom they served, what color robes they wore. The young magic-users who faced death calmly when they agreed to take the Test understood this. The ancient wizards who came here to breathe their last and be entombed within the familiar walls understood this. The Art—Magic. It was parent, lover, spouse, child. It was soil, fire, air, water. It was life. It was death. It was beyond death.

Par-Salian thought of all this as he stood within his chambers in the northernmost of the two tall towers, watching Caramon and his small retinue advance toward the gates.

As Caramon remembered the past, so, too, did Par-Salian. Some wondered if it was with regret.

No, he said silently, watching Caramon come up the path, his battlesword clanking against his flabby thighs. I do not regret the past. I was given a terrible choice and I made it.

Who questions the gods? They demanded a sword. I found one. And—like all swords—it was two-edged.

Caramon and his group had arrived at the outer gate. There were no guards. A tiny silver bell rang in Par-Salian's quarters.

The old mage raised his hand. The gates swung open.

It was twilight when they entered the outer gates of the Tower of High Sorcery. Tas glanced around, startled. It had been morning only moments ago. Or at least it seemed like it had been morning! Looking up, he could see red rays streaking across the sky, gleaming eerily off the polished stone walls of the Tower.

Tas shook his head. "How does anyone tell time around here?" he asked himself. He stood in a vast courtyard bounded by the outer walls and the inner two towers. The courtyard was stark and barren. Paved with gray flagstone, it looked cold and unlovely. No flowers grew, no trees broke the unrelieved monotony of the gray stone. And it was empty, Tas noticed in disappointment. There was absolutely no one around, no one in sight.

Or was there? Tas caught a glimpse of movement out of the corner of his eye, a flutter of white. Turning quickly, however, he was amazed to see it was gone! No one was there. And then, he saw, out of the corner of the other eye, a face and a hand and a red robed sleeve. He looked at it directly—and it was gone! Suddenly, Tas had the impression he was surrounded by people, coming and going, talking, or just sitting and staring, even sleeping! Yet—the courtyard was still silent, still empty.

"These must be mages taking the Test!" Tas said in awe. "Raistlin told me they traveled all over, but I never imagined anything like this! I wonder if they can see me? Do you suppose I could touch one, Caramon, if I—Caramon?"

Tas blinked. Caramon was gone! Bupu was gone! The white-robed figures and Lady Crysania were gone. He was alone!

Not for long. There was a flash of yellow light, a most horrible smell, and a black-robed mage stood towering before him. The mage extended a hand, a woman's hand.

"You have been summoned."

Tas gulped. Slowly, he held out his hand. The woman's fingers closed over his wrist. He shivered at their cold touch. "Perhaps I'm going to be magicked!" he said to himself hopefully.

The courtyard, the black stone walls, the red streaks of sunlight, the gray flagstone, all began to dissolve around Tas, running down the edges of his vision like a rain-soaked painting. Thoroughly delighted, the kender felt the woman's black robes wrap around him. She tucked them up around his chin. . . .

When Tasslehoff came to his senses, he was lying on a very hard, very cold, stone floor. Next to him, Bupu snored blissfully. Caramon was sitting up, shaking his head, trying to clear away the cobwebs.

"Ouch." Tas rubbed the back of his neck. "Funny kind of accommodations, Caramon," he grumbled, getting to his feet. "You'd think they could at least magic up beds. And if they want a fellow to take a nap, why don't they just say so instead of sending—oh—"

Hearing Tas's voice break off in a strange sort of gurgle, Caramon glanced up quickly.

They were not alone.

"I know this place," Caramon whispered.

They were in a vast chamber carved of obsidian. It was so wide that its perimeter was lost in shadow, so high that its ceiling was obscured in shadow. No pillars supported it, no lights lit it. Yet light there was, though none could name its source. It was a pale light, white—not yellow. Cold and cheerless, it gave no warmth.

The last time Caramon had been in this chamber, the light shone upon one old man, dressed in white robes, sitting by himself in a great stone chair. This time, the light shone upon the same old man, but he was no longer alone. A half-circle of stone chairs sat around him—twenty-one to be exact. The white-robed old man sat in the center. To his left were three indistinct figures, whether male or female, human or some other race, it was difficult to tell. Their hoods were pulled low over their faces. They were dressed in red robes. To their left sat six figures, clothed all in black. One chair among them was empty. On the old man's right sat four more red-robed figures, and—to their right, six dressed all in white. Lady Crysania lay on the floor before them, her body on a white pallet, covered with white linen.

Of all the Conclave, only the old man's face was visible.

"Good evening," Tasslehoff said, bowing and backing up and bowing and backing up until he bumped into Caramon. "Who *are* these people?" the kender whispered loudly. "And what are they doing in our bedroom?"

"The old man in the center is Par-Salian," Caramon said softly. "And we're not in a bedroom. This is the central hall, the Hall of Mages or some such thing. You better wake up the gully dwarf."

"Bupu!" Tas kicked the snoring dwarf with his foot.

"Gulphphunger spawn," she snarled, rolling over, her eyes tightly closed. "Go way. Me sleep."

"Bupu!" Tas was desperate; the old man's eyes seemed to go right through him. "Hey, wake up. Dinner."

"Dinner!" Opening her eyes, Bupu jumped to her feet. Glancing around eagerly, she caught sight of the twenty robed figures, sitting silently, their hooded faces invisible.

Bupu let out a scream like a tortured rabbit. With a convulsive leap, she threw herself at Caramon and wrapped her arms around his ankle in a deathlike grip. Aware of the glittering eyes watching him, Caramon tried to shake her loose, but it was impossible. She clung to him like a leech, shivering, peering at the mages in terror. Finally, Caramon gave up.

The old man's face creased in what might have been a smile. Tas saw Caramon look down self-consciously at his smelly clothes. He saw the big man finger his unshaven jowls and run a hand through his tangled hair. Embarrassed, he flushed uncomfortably. Then his expression hardened. When he spoke, it was with simple dignity.

"Par-Salian," Caramon said, the words booming out too loudly in the vast, shadowy hall, "do you remember me?"

"I remember you, warrior," said the mage. His voice was soft, yet it carried in the chamber. A dying whisper would have carried in that chamber.

He said nothing more. None of the other mages spoke. Caramon shifted uncomfortably. Finally he gestured at Lady

Crysania. "I have brought her here, hoping you could help her. Can you? Will she be all right?"

"Whether she will be all right or not is not in our hands," Par-Salian answered. "It is beyond our skill to care for her. In order to protect her from the spell the death knight cast upon her—a spell that surely would have meant her death—Paladine heard her last prayer and sent her soul to dwell in his peaceful realms."

Caramon's head bowed. "It's my fault," he said huskily. "I-I failed her. I might have been able—"

"To protect her?" Par-Salian shook his head. "No, warrior, you could not have protected her from the Knight of the Black Rose. You would have lost your own life trying. Is that not true, kender?"

Tas, suddenly finding the gaze of the old man's blue eyes upon him felt tingling sparks shoot through his body. "Y-Yes," he stammered. "I-I saw him—it," Tasslehoff shuddered.

"This from one who knows no fear," Par-Salian said mildly. "No, warrior, do not blame yourself. And do not give up hope for her. Though we ourselves cannot restore her soul to her body, we know of those who can. But, first, tell me why Lady Crysania sought us out. For we know she was searching for the Forest of Wayreth."

"I'm not sure." Caramon mumbled.

"She came because of Raistlin," Tas chimed in helpfully. But his voice sounded shrill and discordant in the hall. The name rang out eerily. Par-Salian frowned, Caramon turned to glare at him. The mages' hooded heads shifted slightly, as if they were glancing at each other, their robes rustled softly. Tas gulped and fell silent.

"Raistlin," the name hissed softly from Par-Salian's lips. He stared at Caramon intently. "What does a cleric of good have to do with your brother? Why did she undertake this perilous journey for his sake?"

Caramon shook his head, unwilling or unable to talk.

"You know of his evil?" Par-Salian pursued sternly.

Caramon stubbornly refused to answer, his gaze was fixed on the stone floor.

"I know—" Tas began, but Par-Salian made a slight movement with his hand and the kender hushed.

"You know that now we believe he intends to conquer the world?" Par-Salian continued, his relentless words hitting Caramon like darts. Tas could see the big man flinch. "Along with your half-sister, Kitiara—or the Dark Lady, as she is known among her troops—Raistlin has begun to amass armies. He has dragons, flying citadels. And in addition we know—"

A sneering voice rang through the hall. "You know nothing, Great One. You are a fool!"

The words fell like drops of water into a still pond, causing ripples of movement to spread among the mages. Startled, Tas turned, searching for the source of the strange voice, and saw, behind him, a figure emerging from the shadows. Its black robes rustled as it walked past them to face Par-Salian. At that moment, the figure removed its hood.

Tas felt Caramon stiffen. "What is it?" the kender whispered, unable to see.

"A dark elf!" Caramon muttered.

"Really?" Tas said, his eyes brightening. "You know, in all the years I've lived on Krynn, I've never seen a dark elf." The kender started forward only to be caught by the collar of his tunic. Tas squawked in irritation, as Caramon dragged him back, but neither Par-Salian nor the black-robed figure appeared to notice the interruption.

"I think you should explain yourself, Dalamar," Par-Salian said quietly. "Why am I a fool?"

"Conquer the world!" Dalamar sneered. "*He* does not plan to conquer the world! The world means nothing to him. He could have the world tomorrow, tonight, if he wanted it!"

"Then what does he want?" This question came from a red-robed mage seated near Par-Salian.

Tas, peering out around Caramon's arm, saw the delicate, cruel features of the dark elf relax in a smile—a smile that made the kender shiver.

"He wants to become a god," Dalamar answered softly. "He will challenge the Queen of Darkness herself. That is his plan."

The mages said nothing, they did not move, but their

silence seemed to stir among them like shifting currents of air as they stared at Dalamar with glittering, unblinking eyes.

Then Par-Salian sighed. "I think you overestimate him."

There was a ripping, rending sound, the sound of cloth being torn apart. Tas saw the dark elf's arms jerk, tearing open the fabric of his robes.

"Is this overestimating him?" Dalamar cried.

The mages leaned forward, a gasp whispered through the vast hall like a chill wind. Tas struggled to see, but Caramon's hand held him fast. Irritably, Tas glanced up at Caramon's face. Wasn't he curious? But Caramon appeared totally unmoved.

"You see the mark of his hand upon me," Dalamar hissed. "Even now, the pain is almost more than I can bear." The young elf paused, then added through clenched teeth. "He said to give you his regards, Par-Salian!"

The great mage's head bent. The hand rising to support it shook as with a palsy. He seemed old, feeble, weary. For a moment, the mage sat with his eyes covered, then he raised his head and looked intently at Dalamar.

"So—our worst fears are realized." Par-Salian's eyes narrowed questioningly. "He knows, then, that *we* sent you—"

"To spy on him?" Dalamar laughed, bitterly. "Yes, he knows!" The dark elf spit the words. "He's known all along. He's been using me—using all of us—to further his own ends."

"I find this all very difficult to believe," stated the red-robed mage in a mild voice. "We all admit that young Raistlin is certainly powerful, but I find this talk of challenging a goddess quite ridiculous . . . quite ridiculous indeed."

There were murmured assents from both halves of the semi-circle.

"Oh, do you?" Dalamar asked, and there was a lethal softness in his voice. "Then, let me tell you fools that you have no idea of the meaning of the word *power*. Not as it relates to him! You cannot begin to fathom the depths of his power or to soar the heights! I can! I have seen"—for a moment Dalamar paused, his voice lost its anger and was filled with wonder—"I have seen such things as none of you have dared imagine! I have walked the realms of dreams with my eyes open! I have seen beauty to make the heart burst with pain. I have descended into nightmares—I have witnessed horrors"—he shuddered—"horrors so nameless and terrible that I begged to be struck dead rather than look upon them!" Dalamar glanced around the semi-circle, gathering them all together with his flashing, dark-eyed gaze. "And all these wonders *he* summoned, *he* created, *he* brought to life with his magic."

There was no sound, no one moved.

"You are wise to be afraid, Great One," Dalamar's voice sank to a whisper. "But no matter how great your fear, you do not fear him enough. Oh, yes, he lacks power to cross that dread threshold. But that power he goes to find. Even as we speak, he is preparing himself for the long journey. Upon my return tomorrow, he will leave."

Par-Salian raised his head. "Your return?" he asked, shocked. "But he knows you for what you are—a spy, sent by us, the Conclave, his fellows." The great mage's glance went to the chair that stood empty amidst the Black Robes, then he rose to his feet. "No, young Dalamar. You are very courageous, but I cannot allow you to return to what would undoubtedly be tortured death at his hands."

"You cannot stop me," Dalamar said, and there was no emotion in his voice. "I said before—I would give my soul to study with such as he. And now, though it costs me my life, I will stay with him. He expects me back. He leaves me in charge of the Tower of High Sorcery in his absence."

"He leaves you to guard?" the red-robed mage said dubiously. "You, who have betrayed him?"

"He knows me," Dalamar said bitterly. "He knows he has ensnared me. He has stung my body and sucked my soul dry, yet I will return to the web. Nor will I be the first," Dalamar motioned down at the still, white form lying on the pallet before him. Then, half-turning, the dark elf glanced at Caramon. "Will I, *brother*?" he said with a sneer.

At last, Caramon seemed driven to action. Angrily shaking Bupu loose from his foot, the warrior took a step forward, both the kender and the gully dwarf crowding close behind him.

"Who is this?" Caramon demanded, scowling at the dark elf. "What's going on? Who are you talking about?"

Before Par-Salian could answer, Dalamar turned to face the big warrior.

"I am called Dalamar," the dark elf said coldly. "And I speak of your twin brother, Raistlin. He is my master. I am his apprentice. I am, in addition, a spy, sent by this august company you see before you to report on the doings of your brother."

Caramon did not answer. He may not have even heard. His eyes—wide with horror—were fixed on the dark elf's chest. Following Caramon's gaze, Tas saw five burned and bloody holes in Dalamar's flesh. The kender swallowed, feeling suddenly queasy.

"Yes, your brother's hand did this," Dalamar remarked, guessing Caramon's thoughts. Smiling grimly, the dark elf gripped the torn edges of his black robes with his hand and pulled them together, hiding the wounds. "It is no matter," he muttered, "it was no more than I deserved."

Caramon turned away, his face so pale Tas slipped his hand in the big man's hand, fearing he might collapse. Dalamar regarded Caramon with scorn.

"What's the matter?" he asked. "Didn't you believe him capable of this?" The dark elf shook his head in disbelief, his eyes swept the assemblage before him. "No, you are like the rest of them. Fools . . . all of you, fools!"

The mages murmured together, some voices angry, some fearful, most questioning. Finally, Par-Salian raised his hand for silence.

"Tell us, Dalamar, what he plans. Unless, of course, he has forbidden you to speak of it." There was a note of irony in the mage's voice that the dark elf did not miss.

"No," Dalamar smiled grimly. "I know his plans. Enough of them, that is. He even asked that I be certain and report them to you accurately."

There were muttered words and snorts of derision at this. But Par-Salian only looked more concerned, if that were possible. "Continue," he said, almost without voice.

Dalamar drew a breath.

"He journeys back in time, to the days just prior to the Cataclysm, when the great Fistandantilus was at the height of his power. It is my *Shalafi's* intention to meet this great mage, to study with him, and to recover those works of Fistandantilus we know were lost during the Cataclysm. For my *Shalafi* believes, from what he has read in the spellbooks he took from the Great Library at Palanthas, that Fistandantilus learned how to cross the threshold that exists between god and men. Thus, the great wizard was able to prolong his life after the Cataclysm to fight the Dwarven Wars. Thus, he was able to survive the terrible explosion that devastated the lands of Dergoth. Thus, was he able to live until he found a new receptacle for his soul."

"I don't understand any of this! Tell me what's going on!" Caramon demanded, striding forward angrily. "Or I'll tear this place down around your miserable heads! Who is this Fistandantilus? What does he have to do with my brother?"

"Shhh," Tas said, glancing apprehensively at the mages.

"We understand, kenderken," Par-Salian said, smiling at Tas gently. "We understand his anger and his sorrow. And he is right—we owe him an explanation," The old mage sighed. "Perhaps what I did was wrong. And yet—did I have a choice? Where would we be today if I had not made the decision I made?"

Tas saw Par-Salian turn to look at the mages who sat on either side of him, and suddenly the kender realized Par-Salian's answer was for them as much as for Caramon. Many had cast back their hoods and Tas could see their faces now. Anger marked the faces of those wearing the black robes, sadness and fear were reflected in the pale faces of those wearing white. Of the red robes, one man in particular caught Tas's attention, mainly because his face was smooth, impassive, yet the eyes were dark and stirring. It was the mage who had doubted Raistlin's power. It seemed to Tas that it was to this man in particular that Par-Salian directed his words.

"Over seven years ago, Paladine appeared to me," Par-Salian's eyes stared into the shadows. "The great god warned me that a time of terror was going to engulf the world. The Queen of Darkness had awakened the evil dragons and was planning to wage war upon the people in an effort to conquer them. 'One among your Order you will choose to help fight this evil.' Paladine told me. 'Choose well, for this person shall be as a sword to cleave the darkness. You may tell him nothing of what the future holds, for by his decisions, and the decisions of others, will your world stand or fall forever into eternal night.' "

Par-Salian was interrupted by angry voices, coming particularly from those wearing the black robes. Par-Salian glanced at them, his eyes flashing. Within that moment, Tas saw revealed the power and authority that lay within the feeble old mage.

"Yes, perhaps I should have brought the matter before the Conclave," Par-Salian said, his voice sharp. "But I believed then—as I believe now—that it was my decision alone. I knew well the hours that the Conclave would spend bickering, I knew well none of you would agree! I made my decision. Do any of you challenge my right to do so?"

Tas held his breath, feeling Par-Salian's anger roll around the hall like thunder. The Black Robes sank back into their stone seats, muttering. Par-Salian was silent for a moment, then his eyes went back to Caramon, and their stern glance softened.

"I chose Raistlin," he said.

Caramon scowled. "Why?" he demanded.

"I had my reasons," Par-Salian said gently. "Some of them I cannot explain to you, not even now. But I can tell you this—he was born with the gift. And that is most important. The magic dwells deep within your brother. Did you know that, from the first day Raistlin attended school, his own master held him in fear and awe. How does one teach a pupil who knows more than the teacher? And combined with the gift of magic is intelligence. Raistlin's mind is never at rest. It seeks knowledge, demands answers. And he is courageous—perhaps more courageous than you are, warrior. He fights pain every day of his life. He has faced death more than once and defeated it. He fears nothing—neither the darkness nor the light. And his soul . . ." Par-Salian paused. "His soul burns with ambition, the desire for power, the desire for more knowledge. I knew that nothing, not even the fear of death itself, would stop him from attaining his goals. And I knew that the goals he sought to attain might well benefit the world, even if he, himself, should choose to turn his back upon it."

Par-Salian paused. When he spoke, it was with sorrow. "But first he had to take the Test."

"You should have foreseen the outcome," the red-robed mage said, speaking in the same mild tone. "We all knew *he* was waiting, biding his time...."

"I had no choice!" Par-Salian snapped, his blue eyes flashing. "Our time was running out. The world's time was running out. The young man had to take the Test and assimilate what he had learned. I could delay no longer."

Caramon stared from one to the other. "You knew Raist was in some kind of danger when you brought him here?"

"There is always danger," Par-Salian answered. "The Test is designed to weed out those who might be harmful to themselves, to the Order, to the innocents in the world." He put his hand to his head, rubbing his brows. "Remember, too, that the Test is designed to teach as well. We hoped to teach your brother compassion to temper his selfish ambition, we hoped to teach him mercy, pity. And, it was, perhaps, in my eagerness to teach that I made a mistake. I forgot Fistandantilus."

"Fistandantilus?" Caramon said in confusion. "What do you mean—forgot him? From what you've said, that old mage is dead."

"Dead? No," Par-Salian's face darkened. "The blast that killed thousands in the Dwarven Wars and laid waste a land that is still devastated and barren did not kill Fistandantilus. His magic was powerful enough to defeat death itself. He moved to another plane of existence, a plane far from here, yet not far enough. Constantly he watched, biding his time, searching for a body to accept his soul. And he found that body—your brother's."

Caramon listened in tense silence, his face deathly white. Out of the corner of his eye, Tas saw Bupu start edging backward. He grabbed her hand and held onto her tightly, keeping the terrified gully dwarf from turning and fleeing headlong out of the hall.

"Who knows what deal the two made during the Test? None of us, probably," Par-Salian smiled slightly. "I know this. Raistlin did superbly, yet his frail health was failing him.

Perhaps he could have survived the final test—the confrontation with the dark elf—if Fistandantilus had not aided him. Perhaps not."

"Aided him? He saved his life?"

Par-Salian shrugged. "We know only this, warrior—it was not any of us who left your brother with that gold-tinted skin. The dark elf cast a fireball at him, and Raistlin survived. Impossible, of course—"

"Not for Fistandantilus," interrupted the red-robed mage.

"No," Par-Salian agreed sadly, "not for Fistandantilus. I wondered at the time, but I was not able to investigate. Events in the world were rushing to a climax. Your brother was himself when he came out of the Test. More frail, of course, but that was only to be expected. And I was right"—Par-Salian cast a swift, triumphant glance around the semicircle—"*he was strong in his magic!* Who else could have gained power over a dragon orb without years of study?"

"Of course," the red-robed mage said, "he had help from one who'd *had* years of study."

Par-Salian frowned and did not answer.

"Let me get this straight," Caramon said, glowering at the white-robed mage. "This Fistandantilus . . . took over Raistlin's soul? *He's* the one that made Raistlin take the Black Robes."

"Your brother made his own choice," Par-Salian spoke sharply. "As did we all."

"I don't believe it!" Caramon shouted. "Raistlin didn't make this decision. You're lying—all of you! You tortured my brother, and then one of your old wizards claimed what was left of his body!" Caramon's words boomed through the chamber and sent the shadows dancing in alarm.

Tas saw Par-Salian regard the warrior grimly, and the kender cringed, waiting for the spell that would sizzle Caramon like a spitted chicken. It never came. The only sound was Caramon's ragged breathing.

"I'm going to get him back," Caramon said finally, tears gleaming in his eyes. "If he can go back in time to meet this old wizard, so can I. You can send me back. And when I find Fistandantilus, I'll kill him. Then Raist will be . . ." He choked back a sob, fighting for control. "He'll be Raist again. And he'll forget all this nonsense about challenging th-the Queen of Darkness and . . . becoming a god."

The semi-circle broke into chaos. Voices raised, clamboring in anger. "Impossible! He'll change history! You've gone too far, Par-Salian—"

The white-robed mage rose to his feet and, turning, stared at every mage in the semi-circle, his eyes going to each individually. Tas could sense the silent communication, swift and searing as lightning.

Caramon wiped his hand across his eyes, staring at the mages defiantly. Slowly, they all sank back into their seats. But Tas saw hands clench, he saw faces that were unconvinced, faces filled with anger. The red-robed mage stared at Par-Salian speculatively, one eyebrow raised. Then he, too, sat back. Par-Salian cast a final, quick glance around the Conclave before he turned to face Caramon.

"We will consider your offer," Par-Salian said. "It might work. Certainly, it is not something he would expect—"

Dalamar began to laugh.

Chapter 13

"Expects?" Dalamar laughed until he could scarcely breathe. "He *planned* all of this! Do you think this great idiot"—he waved at Caramon—"could have found his way here by himself? When creatures of darkness pursued Tanis Half-Elven and Lady Crysania—pursued but never caught them—who do you think sent them? Even the encounter with the death knight, an encounter plotted by his sister, an encounter that could have wrecked his plans—my *Shalafi* has turned to his own advantage. For, undoubtedly you fools will send this woman, Lady Crysania, back in time to the only ones who can heal her—the Kingpriest and his followers. You will send her back in time to meet Raistlin! Not only that, you'll even provide her with this man—his brother—as bodyguard. Just what the *Shalafi* wants."

Tas saw Par-Salian's clawlike fingers clench over the cold stone arms of his chair, the old man's blue eyes gleamed dangerously.

"We have suffered enough of your insults, Dalamar," Par-Salian said. "I begin to think your loyalty to your *Shalafi* is too great. If that is true, your usefulness to this Conclave is ended."

Ignoring the threat, Dalamar smiled bitterly. "My *Shalafi*—" he repeated softly, then sighed. A shudder convulsed his slender body, he gripped the torn robes in his hand and bowed his head. "I am caught in the middle, as he intended," the dark elf whispered. "I don't know who I serve anymore, if anyone." He raised his dark eyes, and their haunted look made Tas's heart ache. "But I know this—if any of you came and tried to enter the Tower while he was gone, I would kill you. That much loyalty I owe him. Yet, I am just as frightened of him as you are. I'll help you, if I can."

Par-Salian's hands relaxed, though he still continued to regard Dalamar sternly. "I fail to understand why Raistlin told you of his plans? Surely he must know we will move to prevent him from succeeding in his terrifying ambitions."

"Because—like me—he has you where he wants you," Dalamar said. Suddenly he staggered, his face pale with pain and exhaustion. Par-Salian made a motion, and a chair materialized out of the shadows. The dark elf slumped into it. "You must go along with his plans. You must send this man back into time"—he gestured at Caramon—"along with the woman. It is the only way he can succeed—"

"And it is the only way we can stop him," Par-Salian said, his voice low. "But why Lady Crysania? What possible interest could he have in one so good, so pure—"

"So powerful," Dalamar said with a grim smile. "From what he has been able to gather from the writings of Fistandantilus that still survive, he will need a cleric to go with him to face the dread Queen. And only a cleric of good has power enough to defy the Queen and open the Dark Door. Oh, Lady Crysania was not the *Shalafi's* first choice. He had vague plans to use the dying Elistan—but I won't relate that. As it turned out, however, Lady Crysania fell into his hands—one might say literally. She is good, strong in her faith, powerful—"

"And drawn to evil as a moth is drawn to the flame," Par-Salian murmured, looking at Crysania with deep pity.

Tas, watching Caramon, wondered if the big man was even absorbing half of this. He had a vague, dull-witted look about him, as if he wasn't quite certain where—or who—he was. Tas shook his head dubiously. They're going to send *him* back in time? the kender thought.

"Raistlin has other reasons for wanting both this woman and his brother back in time with him, of that you may be certain," the red-robed mage said to Par-Salian. "He has not revealed his game, not by any means. He has told us—through our agent—just enough to leave us confused. I say we thwart his plans!"

Par-Salian did not reply. But, lifting his head, he stared at Caramon for long moments and in his eyes was a sadness that pierced Tas's heart. Then, shaking his head, he lowered his gaze, looking fixedly at the hem of his robes. Bupu whimpered, and Tas patted her absently. Why that strange look at Caramon? the kender wondered uneasily. Surely they wouldn't send him off to certain death? Yet, wasn't that what they'd be doing if they sent him back the way he was now—sick, depressed, confused? Tas shifted from one foot to the other, then yawned. No one was paying any attention to him. All this talk was boring. He was hungry, too. If they were going to send Caramon back in time, he wished they'd just *do* it.

Suddenly, he felt one part of his mind (the part that was listening to Par-Salian) tug at the other part. Hurriedly, Tas brought both parts together to listen to what was being said.

Dalamar was talking. "She spent the night in his study. I do not know what was discussed, but I know that when she left in the morning, she appeared distraught and shaken. His last words to her were these, 'Has it occurred to you that Paladine did not send you to stop me but to help me?' "

"And what answer did she make?"

"She did not answer him," Dalamar replied. "She walked back through the Tower and then through the Grove like one who can neither see nor hear."

"What I do not understand is why Lady Crysania was traveling here to seek our help in sending her back? Surely she must have known we would refuse such a request!" the red-robed mage stated.

"I can answer that!" Tasslehoff said, speaking before he thought.

Now Par-Salian was paying attention to him, now all the mages in the semi-circle were paying attention to him. Every head turned in his direction. Tas had talked to spirits in Darken Wood, he had spoken at the Council of White Stone but, for a moment, he was awed at this silent, solemn audience. Especially when it occurred to him what he had to say.

"Please, Tasslehoff Burrfoot," Par-Salian spoke with great courtesy, "tell us what you know." The mage smiled. "Then, perhaps, we can bring this meeting to a close and you can have your dinner."

Tas blushed, wondering if Par-Salian could, perhaps, see through his head and read his thoughts printed on his brain like he read words printed on a sheet of parchment.

"Oh! Yes, dinner would be great. But, now, um—about Lady Crysania." Tas paused to collect his thoughts, then launched into his tale. "Well, I'm not certain about this, mind you. I just know from what little I was able to pick up here and there. To begin at the beginning, I met Lady Crysania when I was in Palanthas visiting my friend, Tanis Half-Elven. You know him? And Laurana, the Golden General? I fought with them in the War of the Lance. I helped save Laurana from the Queen of Darkness." The kender spoke with pride. "Have you ever heard that story? I was in the Temple at Neraka—"

Par-Salian's eyebrows raised ever so slightly, and Tas stuttered.

"Uh, w-well, I'll tell that later. Anyway, I met Lady Crysania at Tanis's home and I heard their plans to travel to Solace to see Caramon. As it happened, I-I sort of . . . well, found a letter Lady Crysania had written to Elistan. I think it must have fallen out of her pocket."

The kender paused for breath. Par-Salian's lips twitched, but he refrained from smiling.

"I read it," Tas continued, now enjoying the attention of his audience, "just to see if it was important. After all, she might have thrown it away. In the letter, she said she was more—uh, how did it go—'firmly convinced than ever, after my talk with Tanis, that there was good in Raistlin' and that he could be 'turned from his evil path. I must convince the mages of this—' Anyhow, I saw that the letter was important, so I took it to her. She was *very* grateful to get it back," Tas said solemnly. "She hadn't realized she'd lost it."

Par-Salian put his fingers on his lips to control them.

"I said I could tell her lots of stories about Raistlin, if she wanted to hear them. She said she'd like that a lot, so I told her all the stories I could think of. She was particularly interested in the ones I told her about Bupu—

" 'If only I could find the gully dwarf!' she said to me one night. 'I'm certain I could convince Par-Salian that there is hope, that he may be reclaimed!' "

At this, one of the Black Robes snorted loudly. Par-Salian glanced sharply in that direction, the wizards hushed. But Tas saw many of them—particularly the Black Robes—fold their arms across their chests in anger. He could see their eyes glittering from the shadows of their hoods.

"Uh, I'm s-sure I didn't mean to offend," Tas stuttered. "I know I always thought Raistlin looked much better in black—with that golden skin of his and all. *I* certainly don't believe everyone has to be good, of course. Fizban—he's really Paladine—we're great *personal* friends, Paladine and I—Anyway, Fizban said that there had to be a balance in the world, that we were fighting to restore the balance. So that means that there has to be Black Robes as well as White, doesn't it?"

"We know what you mean, kenderken," Par-Salian said gently. "Our brethren take no offense at your words. Their anger is directed elsewhere. Not everyone in the world is as wise as the great Fizban the Fabulous."

Tas sighed. "I miss him, sometimes. But, where was I? Oh, yes, Bupu. That's when I had my idea. Maybe if Bupu told her story, the mages would believe her, I said Lady Crysania. She agreed and I offered to go and find Bupu. I hadn't been to Xak Tsaroth since Goldmoon killed the black dragon and it was just a short hop from where we were and Tanis said it would be fine with him. He seemed quite pleased to see me off, actually.

"The Highpulp let me take Bupu, after a—uh—small bit of discussion and some interesting items that I had in my pouch. I took Bupu to Solace, but Tanis had already gone and so had Lady Crysania. Caramon was—" Tas stopped, hearing Caramon clear his throat behind him. "Caramon was—wasn't feeling too good, but Tika—that's Caramon's wife and a great friend of mine—anyway, Tika said we had to go after Lady Crysania, because the Forest of Wayreth was a terrible place and—No offense meant, I'm certain, but did you ever stop to think that your Forest is really nasty? I mean, it is *not* friendly"— Tas glared at the mages sternly—"and I don't know why you let it wander around loose! I think it's irresponsible!"

Par-Salian's shoulders quivered.

"Well, that's all I know," Tas said. "And, there's Bupu, and she can—" Tas stopped, looking around. "Where'd she go?"

"Here," Caramon said grimly, dragging the gully dwarf out from behind his back where she had been cowering in abject terror. Seeing the mages staring at her, the gully dwarf gave a shriek and collapsed onto the floor, a quivering bundle of ragged clothes.

"I think you had better tell us her story," Par-Salian said to Tas. "If you can, that is."

"Yes," Tas replied, suddenly subdued. "I know what it was Lady Crysania wanted me to tell. It happened back during the war, when we were in Xak Tsaroth. The only ones who knew anything about that city were gully dwarves. But most wouldn't help us. Raistlin cast a charm spell on one of them—Bupu. Charmed wasn't exactly the word for what it did to her. She fell in love with him," Tas paused, sighing, then continued in a remorseful tone. "Some of us thought it was funny, I guess. But Raistlin didn't. He was really kind to her, and he even saved her life, once, when draconians attacked us. Well, after we left Xak Tsaroth, Bupu came with us. She couldn't bear to leave Raistlin."

Tas's voice dropped. "One night, I woke up. I heard Bupu crying. I started to go to her, but I saw Raistlin had heard her, too. She was homesick. She wanted to go back to her people, but she couldn't leave him. I don't know what he said, but I saw him lay his hand on her head. And it seemed that I could see a light shining all around Bupu. And, then, he sent her home. She had to travel through a land filled with terrible creatures but, somehow, I *knew* she would be safe. And she was," Tas finished solemnly.

There was a moment's silence, then it seemed that all the mages began to talk at once. Those of the Black Robes shook their heads. Dalamar sneered.

"The kender was dreaming," he said scornfully.

"Who believes kender anyway?" said one.

Those of the Red Robes and the White Robes appeared thoughtful and perplexed.

"If this is true," said one, "perhaps we have misjudged him. Perhaps we should take this chance, however slim."

Finally Par-Salian raised a hand for silence.

"I admit I find this difficult to believe," he said at last. "I mean no disparagement to you, Tasslehoff Burrfoot," he added gently, smiling at the indignant kender. "But all know your race has a most lamentable tendency to, uh, exaggerate. It is obvious to me that Raistlin simply charmed this—this *creature*"—Par-Salian spoke with disgust—"to use her and—"

"Me no creature!"

Bupu lifted her tear-stained, mud-streaked face from the floor, her hair frizzed up like an angry cat's. Glaring at Par-Salian, she stood up and started forward, tripped over the bag she carried, and sprawled flat on the floor. Undaunted, the gully dwarf picked herself up and faced Par-Salian.

"Me know nothing 'bout big, powerful wizards." Bupu waved a grubby hand. "Me know nothing 'bout no charm spell. Me know magic is in this"—she scrabbled around in the bag, then drew forth the dead rat and waved it in Par-Salian's direction—"and me know that man you talk 'bout here is nice man. Him nice to me." Clutching the dead rat to her chest, Bupu stared tearfully at Par-Salian. "The others—the big man, the kender—they laugh at Bupu. They look at me like me some sort of bug."

Bupu rubbed her eyes. There was a lump in Tas's throat, and he felt lower than a bug himself.

Bupu continued, speaking softly. "Me know how me look." Her filthy hands tried in vain to smooth her dress, leaving streaks of dirt down it. "Me know me not pretty, like lady lying there." The gully dwarf snuffled, but then she wiped her hand across her nose and—raising her head—

looked at Par-Salian defiantly. "But him not call me 'creature!' Him call me 'little one.' Little one," she repeated.

For a moment, she was quiet, remembering. Then she heaved a gusty sigh. "I-I want to stay with him. But him tell me, 'no.' Him say he must walk roads that be dark. Him tell me, he want me to be safe. Him lay his hand on my head"— Bupu bowed her head, as if in memory— "and I feel warm inside. Then him tell me, 'Farewell, Bupu.' Him call me 'little one.'" Looking up, Bupu glanced around at the semicircle. "Him never laugh at me," she said, choking. "Never!" She began to cry.

The only sounds in the room, for a moment, were the gully dwarf's sobs. Caramon put his hands over his face, overcome. Tas drew a shuddering breath and fished around for a handkerchief. After a few moments, Par-Salian rose from his stone chair and came to stand in front of the gully dwarf, who was regarding him with suspicion and hiccuping at the same time.

The great mage extended his hand. "Forgive me, Bupu," he said gravely, "if I offended you. I must confess that I spoke those cruel words on purpose, hoping to make you angry enough to tell your story. For, only then, could we be certain of the truth." Par-Salian laid his hand on Bupu's head, his face was drawn and tired, but he appeared exultant. "Maybe we did not fail, maybe he did learn some compassion," he murmured. Gently he stroked the gully dwarf's rough hair. "No, Raistlin would never laugh at you, little one. He knew, he remembered. There were too many who had laughed at him."

Tas couldn't see through his tears, and he heard Caramon weeping quietly beside him. The kender blew his nose on his handkerchief, then went up to retrieve Bupu, who was blubbering into the hem of Par-Salian's white robe.

"So this is the reason Lady Crysania made this journey?" Par-Salian asked Tas as the kender came near. The mage glanced at the still, white, cold form lying beneath the linen, her eyes staring sightlessly into the shadowy darkness. "She believes that she can rekindle the spark of goodness that we tried to light and failed?"

"Yes," Tas answered, suddenly uncomfortable beneath the gaze of the mage's penetrating blue eyes.

"And why does she want to attempt this?" Par-Salian persisted.

Tas dragged Bupu to her feet and handed her his handkerchief, trying to ignore the fact that she stared at it in wonder, obviously having no idea what she was supposed to do with it. She blew her nose on the hem of her dress.

"Uh, well, Tika said—" Tas stopped, flushing.

"What did Tika say?" Par-Salian asked softly.

"Tika said"—Tas swallowed—"Tika said she was doing it . . . because she l-loved him—Raistlin."

Par-Salian nodded. His gaze went to Caramon. "What about you, twin?" he asked suddenly. Caramon's head lifted, he stared at Par-Salian with haunted eyes.

"Do you love him still? You have said you would go back to destroy Fistandantilus. The danger you face will be great. Do you love your brother enough to undertake this perilous journey? To risk your life for him, as this lady has done? Remember, before you answer, you do not go back on a quest to save the world. You go back on a quest to save a soul, nothing more. Nothing less."

Caramon's lips moved, but no sound came from them. His face was lighted by joy, however, a happiness that sprang from deep within him. He could only nod his head.

Par-Salian turned to face the assembled Conclave.

"I have made my decision," he began.

One of the Black Robes rose and cast her hood back. Tas saw that it was the woman who had brought him here. Anger burned in her eyes. She made a swift, slashing motion with her hand.

"We challenge this decision, Par-Salian," she said in a low voice. "And you know that means you cannot cast the spell."

"The Master of the Tower may cast the spell alone, Ladonna," Par-Salian replied grimly. "That power is given to all the Masters. Thus did Raistlin discover the secret when he became Master of the Tower in Palanthas. I do not need the help of either Red or Black."

There was a murmur from the Red Robes, as well; many looking at the Black Robes and nodding in agreement with them. Ladonna smiled.

"Indeed, Great One," she said, "I know this. You do not need us for the casting of the spell, but you need us nonetheless. You need our cooperation, Par-Salian, our silent cooperation—else the shadows of our magic will rise and blot out the light of the silver moon. And you will fail."

Par-Salian's face grew cold and gray. "What of the life of this woman?" he demanded, gesturing at Crysania.

"What is the life of a cleric of Paladine to us?" Ladonna sneered. "Our concerns are far greater and not to be discussed among outsiders. Send these away"—she motioned at Caramon—"and we will meet privately."

"I believe that is wise, Par-Salian," said the red-robed mage mildly. "Our guests are tired and hungry, and they would find our family disagreements most boring."

"Very well," Par-Salian said abruptly. But Tas could see the white-robed mage's anger as he turned to face them. "You will be summoned."

"Wait!" Caramon shouted, "I demand to be present! I—"

The big man stopped, nearly strangling himself. The Hall was gone, the mages were gone, the stone chairs were gone. Caramon was yelling at a hat stand.

Dizzily, Tas looked around. He and Caramon and Bupu were in a cozy room that might have come straight from the Inn of the Last Home. A fire burned in the grate, comfortable beds stood at one end. A table laden with food was near the fire, the smells of fresh-baked bread and roasted meat made his mouth water. Tas sighed in delight.

"I think this is the most wonderful place in the whole world," he said.

Chapter 14

The old, white-robed mage sat in a study that was much like Raistlin's in the Tower of Palanthas, except that the books which lined Par-Salian's shelves were bound in white leather. The silver runes traced upon their spines and covers glinted in the light of a crackling fire. To anyone entering, the room seemed hot and stuffy. But Par-Salian was feeling the chill of age enter his bones. To him, the room was quite comfortable.

He sat at his desk, his eyes staring into the flames. He started slightly at a soft knock upon his door, then, sighing, he called softly, "Enter."

A young, white-robed mage opened the door, bowing to the black-robed mage who walked past him—as was proper to one of her standing. She accepted the homage without comment. Casting her hood aside, she swept past him into Par-Salian's chamber and stopped, just inside the doorway. The white-robed mage gently shut the door behind her, leaving the two heads of their Orders alone together.

Ladonna cast a quick, penetrating glance about the room. Much of it was lost in shadow, the fire casting the only light. Even the drapes had been closed, blotting out the moons' eerie glow. Raising her hand, Ladonna murmured a few, soft words. Several items in the room began to gleam with a weird, reddish light indicating that they had magical properties—a staff leaning up against the wall, a crystal prism on Par-Salian's desk, a branched candelabra, a gigantic hourglass, and several rings on the old man's fingers among others. These did not seem to alarm Ladonna, she simply looked at each and nodded. Then, satisfied, she sat down in a chair near the desk. Par-Salian watched her with a slight smile on his lined face.

"There are no Creatures from Beyond lurking in the corners, Ladonna, I assure you," the old mage said dryly. "Had I wanted to banish you from this plane, I could have done so long ago, my dear."

"When we were young?" Ladonna cast aside her hood. Iron-gray hair, woven into an intricate braid coiled about her head, framed a face whose beauty seemed enhanced by the lines of age that appeared to have been drawn by a masterful artist, so well did they highlight her intelligence and dark wisdom. "That would have been a contest indeed, Great One."

"Drop the title, Ladonna," Par-Salian said. "We have known each other too long for that."

"Known each other long and well, Par-Salian," Ladonna said with a smile. "Quite well," she murmured softly, her eyes going to the fire.

"Would you go back to our youth, Ladonna?" Par-Salian asked.

She did not answer for a moment, then she looked up at him and shrugged. "To trade power and wisdom and skill for what? Hot blood? Not likely, my dear. What about you?"

"I would have answered the same twenty years ago," Par-Salian said, rubbing his temples. "But now . . . I wonder."

"I did not come to relive old times, no matter how pleasant," Ladonna said, clearing her throat, her voice suddenly stern and cold. "I have come to oppose this madness." She leaned forward, her dark eyes flashing. "You are not serious, I hope, Par-Salian? Even you cannot be soft-hearted or soft-headed enough to send that stupid human back in time to try and stop Fistandantilus? Think of the danger! He could change history! We could all cease to exist!"

"Bah! Ladonna, *you* think!" Par-Salian snapped. "Time is a great flowing river, vaster and wider than any river we know. Throw a pebble into the rushing water—does the water suddenly stop? Does it begin to flow backward? Does it turn in its course and flow another direction? Of course not! The pebble creates a few ripples on the surface, perhaps, but then it sinks. The river flows onward, as it has ever done."

"What are you saying?" Ladonna asked, regarding Par-Salian warily.

"That Caramon and Crysania are pebbles, my dear. They will no more affect the flow of time than two rocks thrown into the Thon-Tsalarian would affect its course. They are pebbles—" he repeated.

"We underestimate Raistlin, Dalamar says," Ladonna interrupted. "He must be fairly certain of his success, or he would not take this risk. He is no fool, Par-Salian."

"He is certain of acquiring the magic. In that we cannot stop him. But that magic will be meaningless to him without the cleric. He needs Crysania." The white-robed mage sighed. "And that is why we must send her back in time."

"I fail to see—"

"She must die, Ladonna!" Par-Salian snarled. "Must I conjure a vision for you? She must be sent back to a time when *all* clerics passed from this land. Raistlin said that we would have to send her back. We would have no choice. As he himself said—this is the one way we can thwart his plans! It is his greatest hope—and his greatest fear. He needs to take her with him to the Gate, but he needs her to come willingly! Thus he plans to shake her faith, disillusion her enough so that she will work with him." Par-Salian waved his hand irritably. "We are wasting time. He leaves in the morning. We must act at once."

"Then keep her here!" Ladonna said scornfully. "That seems simple enough."

Par-Salian shook his head. "He would simply return for her. And—by then he will have the magic. He will have the power to do what he chooses."

"Kill her."

"That has been tried and failed. Besides, could even you, with your arts, kill her while she is under Paladine's protection?"

"Perhaps the god will prevent her going, then?"

"No. The augury I cast was neutral. Paladine has left the matter in our hands. Crysania is nothing but a vegetable here, nor will ever be anything more, since none alive today have the power to restore her. Perhaps Paladine intends her to die in a place and time where her death will have meaning so that she may fulfill her life's cycle."

"So you will send her to her death," Ladonna murmured, looking at Par-Salian in amazement. "Your white robes will be stained red with blood, my old friend."

Par-Salian slammed his hands upon the table, his face contorted in agony. "I don't enjoy this, damn it! But what can I do? Can't you see the position I'm in? Who sits now as the Head of the Black Robes?"

"I do," Ladonna replied.

"Who sits as the Head if *he* returns victorious?"

Ladonna frowned and did not answer.

"Precisely. My days are numbered, Ladonna. I know that." "Oh"—he gestured—"my powers are still great. Perhaps they have never been greater. But every morning when I awake, I feel the fear. Will today be the day it fails? Every time I have trouble recalling a spell, I shiver. Someday, I know, I will not be able to remember the correct words." He closed his eyes. "I am tired, Ladonna, very tired. I want to do nothing more than stay in this room, near this warm fire, and record in these books the knowledge I have acquired through the years. Yet I dare not step down now, for I know who would take my place."

The old mage sighed. "I will choose my successor, Ladonna," he said softly. "I will not have my position wrested from my hands. My stake in this is greater than any of yours."

"Perhaps not," Ladonna said, staring at the flames. "If he returns victorious, there will no longer be a Conclave. We shall all be his servants." Her hand clenched. "I still oppose this, Par-Salian! The danger is too great! Let her remain here, let Raistlin learn what he can from Fistandantilus. We can deal with him when he returns! He is powerful, of course, but it will take him years to master the arts that Fistandantilus knew when he died! We can use that time to arm ourselves against him! We can—"

There was rustling in the shadows of the room. Ladonna started and turned, her hand darting immediately to a hidden pocket in her robe.

"Hold, Ladonna," said a mild voice. "You need not waste your energies on a shield spell. I am no Creature from Beyond, as Par-Salian has already stated." The figure stepped into the light of the fire, its red robes gleaming softly.

Ladonna settled back with a sigh, but there was a glint of anger in her eyes that would have made an apprentice start back in alarm. "No, Justarius" she said coolly, "you are no Creature from Beyond. So you managed to hide yourself from me? How clever you have become, Red Robe." Twisting around in her chair, she regarded Par-Salian with scorn. "You *are* getting old, my friend, if you required help to deal with me!"

"Oh, I'm sure Par-Salian is just as surprised to see me here as you are, Ladonna," Justarius stated. Wrapping his red robes around him, he walked slowly forward to sit down in another chair before Par-Salian's desk. He limped as he walked, his left foot dragging the ground. Raistlin was not the only mage ever injured in the Test.

Justarius smiled. "Though the Great One has become quite adept at hiding his feelings," he added.

"I was aware of you," Par-Salian said softly. "You know me better than that, my friend."

Justarius shrugged. "It doesn't really matter. I was interested in hearing what you had to say to Ladonna—"

"I would have said the same to you."

"Probably less, for I would not have argued as she has. I agree with you, I have from the beginning. But that is because we know the truth, you and I."

"What truth?" Ladonna repeated. Her gaze went from Justarius to Par-Salian, her eyes dilating with anger.

"You will have to show her," Justarius said, still in the same mild voice. "She will not be convinced otherwise. Prove to her how great the danger is."

"You will show me nothing!" Ladonna said, her voice shaking. "I would believe nothing you two devised—"

"Then let her do it herself," Justarius suggested, shrugging.

Par-Salian frowned, then—scowling—he shoved the crystal prism upon the desk toward her. He pointed. "The staff in the corner belonged to Fistandantilus—the greatest, most powerful wizard who has ever lived. Cast a Spell of Seeing, Ladonna. Look at the staff."

Ladonna touched the prism hesitantly, her glance moving suspiciously once more from Par-Salian to Justarius, then back.

"Go ahead!" Par-Salian snapped. "I have not tampered with it." His gray eyebrows came together. "You know I cannot lie to you, Ladonna."

"Though you may lie to others," Justarius said softly.

Par-Salian cast the red-robed mage an angry look but did not reply.

Ladonna picked up the crystal with sudden resolution. Holding it in her hand, she raised it to her eyes, chanting words that sounded harsh and sharp. A rainbow of light beamed from the prism to the plain wooden staff that leaned up against the wall in a dark corner of the study. The rainbow expanded as it welled out from the crystal to encompass the entire staff. Then it wavered and coalesced, forming into the shimmering image of the owner of the staff.

Ladonna stared at the image for long moments, then slowly lowered the prism from her eye. The moment she withdrew her concentration from it, the image vanished, the rainbow light winked out. Her face was pale.

"Well, Ladonna," Par-Salian asked quietly, after a moment. "Do we go ahead?"

"Let me see the Time Travel spell," she said, her voice taut.

Par-Salian made an impatient gesture. "You know that is not possible, Ladonna! Only the Masters of the Tower may know this spell—"

"I am within my rights to see the description, at least," Ladonna returned coldly. "Hide the components and the words from my sight, if you will. But I demand to see the expected results." Her expression hardened. "Forgive me if I do not trust you, old friend, as I might once have done. But your robes seem to be turning as gray as your hair."

Justarius smiled, as if this amused him.

Par-Salian sat for a moment, irresolute.

"Tomorrow morning, friend," Justarius murmured.

Angrily, Par-Salian rose to his feet. Reaching beneath his robes, he drew forth a silver key that he wore around his neck on a silver chain—the key that only the Master of a Tower of High Sorcery may use. Once there were five, now only two remained. As Par-Salian took the key from around his neck and inserted it into an ornately carved wooden chest standing near his desk, all three mages present were wondering silently if Raistlin was—even now—doing the same thing with the key *he* possessed, perhaps even drawing out the same spellbook, bound in silver. Perhaps even turning slowly and reverently through the same pages, casting his gaze upon the spells known only to the Masters of the Towers.

Par-Salian opened the book, first muttering the prescribed words that only the Masters know. If he had not, the book would have vanished from beneath his hand. Arriving at the correct page, he lifted the prism from where Ladonna had set it, then held it above the page, repeating the same harsh, sharp words Ladonna had used.

The rainbow light streamed down from the prism, brightening the page. At a command from Par-Salian, the light from the prism beamed out to strike a bare wall opposite them.

"Look," Par-Salian said, his anger still apparent in his voice. "There, upon the wall. Read the description of the spell."

Ladonna and Justarius turned to face the wall where they could read the words as the prism presented them. Neither Ladonna nor Justarius could read the components needed or the words required. Those appeared as gibberish, either through Par-Salian's art or the conditions imposed by the spell itself. But the description of the spell was clear.

The ability to travel back in time is available to elves, humans, and ogres, since these were the races created by the gods at the beginning of time and so travel within its flow. The spell may not be used by dwarves, gnomes, or kender, since the creation of these races was an accident, unforeseen by the gods. (Refer to the Gray Stone of Gargarth, see Appendix G.) The introduction of any of these races into a previous time span could have serious repercussions on the present, although what these might be is unknown. (A note in Par-Salian's wavering handwriting had the word 'draconian' inked in among the forbidden races.

There are dangers, however, that the spellcaster needs to be fully aware of before proceeding. If the spellcaster dies while back in time, this will affect nothing in the future, for it will be as if the spellcaster died this day in the present. His other death will affect neither the past nor the present nor the future, except as it would have normally affected those. Therefore, we do not waste power on any type of protection spell.

The spellcaster will not be able to change or affect what has occurred previously in any way. That is an obvious precaution. Thus this spell is really useful only for study. That was the purpose for which it was designed. (Another note, this time in a handwriting much older than Par-Salian's adds on the margin—*"It is not possible to prevent the Cataclysm. So we have learned to our great sorrow and at a great cost. May his soul rest with Paladine."*)

"So *that's* what happened to him," Justarius said with a low whistle of surprise. "That was a well-kept secret."

"They were fools to even try it," Par-Salian said, "but they were desperate."

"As are we," Ladonna added bitterly. "Well, is there more?"

"Yes, the next page," Par-Salian replied.

If the spellcaster is not going himself but is sending back another (please note racial precaution on previous page), he or she should equip the one traveling with a device that can be activated at will and so return the traveler to his own time. Descriptions of such devices and their making will be found following—

"And so forth," Par-Salian said. The rainbow light disappeared, swallowed in the mage's hand as Par-Salian wrapped his fingers around it. "The rest is devoted to the technical details of making such a device. I have an ancient one. I will give it to Caramon."

His emphasis on the man's name was unconscious, but everyone in the room noticed it. Ladonna smiled wryly, her hands softly caressing her black robes. Justarius shook his head. Par-Salian himself, realizing the implications, sank down in his chair, his face lined with sorrow.

"So Caramon will use it alone," Justarius said. "I understand why we send Crysania, Par-Salian. She must go back, never to return. But Caramon?"

"Caramon is my redemption," Par-Salian said without looking up. The old mage stared at his hands that lay, trembling, on the open spellbook. "He is going on a journey to save a soul, as I told him. But it will not be his brother's." Par-Salian looked up, his eyes filled with pain. His gaze went first to Justarius, then to Ladonna. Both met that gaze with complete understanding.

"The truth could destroy him," Justarius said.

"There is very little left to destroy, if you ask me," Ladonna remarked coldly. She rose to her feet. Justarius rose with her, staggering a little until he obtained his balance on his crippled leg. "As long as you get rid of the woman, I care little what you do about the man, Par-Salian. If you believe it will wash the blood from your robes, then help him, by all means," She smiled grimly. "In a way, I find this quite funny. Maybe—as we get older—we aren't so different after all, are we, my dear?"

"The differences are there, Ladonna," Par-Salian said, smiling wearily. "It is the crisp, clear outlines that begin to fade and blur in our sight. Does this mean the Black Robes will go along with my decision?"

"It seems we have no choice," Ladonna said without emotion. "If you fail—"

"Enjoy my downfall," Par-Salian said wryly.

"I will," the woman answered softly, "the more so as it will probably be the last thing I enjoy in this life. Farewell, Par-Salian."

"Farewell, Ladonna," he said.

"A wise woman," Justarius remarked as the door shut behind her.

"A rival worthy of you, my friend." Par-Salian returned to his seat behind the desk. "I will enjoy watching you two do battle for my position."

"I sincerely hope you have the opportunity to do so," Justarius said, his hand on the door. "When will you cast the spell?"

"Early morning," Par-Salian said, speaking heavily. "It takes days of preparation. I have already spent long hours working on it."

"What about assistance?"

"No one, not even an apprentice. I will be exhausted at the end. See to the disbanding of the Conclave, will you, my friend?"

"Certainly. And the kender and the gully dwarf?"

"Return the gully dwarf to her home with whatever small treasures you think she would like. As for the kender"—Par-Salian smiled—"you may send him wherever he would like to go—barring the moons, of course. As for treasure, I'm certain *he* will have acquired a sufficient amount before he leaves. Do a surreptitious check on his pouches, but, if it's nothing important, let him keep what he finds."

Justarius nodded. "And Dalamar?"

Par-Salian's face grew grim. "The dark elf has undoubtedly left already. He would not want to keep his *Shalafi* waiting." Par-Salian's fingers drummed on the desk, his brow furrowed in frustration. "It is a strange charm Raistlin possesses! You never met him, did you? No. I felt it myself and I cannot understand. . . ."

"Perhaps I can," Justarius said. "We've all been laughed at one time in our lives. We've all been jealous of a sibling. We have felt pain and suffered, just as he has suffered. And we've all longed—just once—for the power to crush our enemies! We pity him. We hate him. We fear him—all because there is a little of him in each of us, though we admit it to ourselves only in the darkest part of the night."

"If we admit it to ourselves at all. That wretched cleric! Why did she have to get involved!" Par-Salian clasped his head in his shaking hands.

"Farewell, my friend," Justarius said gently. "I will wait for you outside the laboratory should you need help when it is all over."

"Thank you," Par-Salian whispered without raising his head.

Justarius limped from the study. Shutting the door too hastily, he caught the hem of his red robe and was forced to open it again to free himself. Before he closed the door again, he heard the sound of weeping.

Chapter 15

asslehoff Burrfoot was bored.

And, as everyone knows, there is nothing more dangerous on Krynn than a bored kender.

Tas and Bupu and Caramon had finished their meal—a very dull one. Caramon, lost in his thoughts, never said a word but sat wrapped in bleak silence while absent-mindedly devouring nearly everything in sight. Bupu did not even sit. Grabbing a bowl, she scooped out the contents with her hands, shoveling it into her mouth with a rapidity learned long ago at gully dwarf dining tables. Putting that one down, she started on another and polished off a dish of gravy, the butter, the sugar and cream, and finally half a dish of milk potatoes before Tas realized what she was doing. He just barely saved a salt cellar.

"Well," said Tas brightly. Pushing back his empty plate, he tried to ignore the sight of Bupu grabbing it and licking it clean. "I'm feeling much better. How about you, Caramon? Let's go explore!"

"Explore!" Caramon gave him such a horrified look that Tas was momentarily taken aback. "Are you mad? I wouldn't set foot outside that door for all the wealth in Krynn!"

"Really?" Tas asked eagerly. "Why not? Oh, tell me, Caramon! What's out there?"

"I don't know." The big man shuddered. "But it's bound to be awful."

"I didn't see any guards—"

"No, and there's a damn good reason for that," Caramon snarled. "Guards aren't needed around here. I can see that look in your eye, Tasslehoff, and you just forget about it right now! Even if you could get out"—Caramon gave the door to the room a haunted look—"which I doubt, you'd probably walk into the arms of a lich or worse!"

Tas's eyes opened wide. He managed, however, to squelch an exclamation of delight. Looking down at his shoes, he muttered, "Yeah, I guess you're right, Caramon. I'd forgotten where we were."

"I guess you did," Caramon said severely. Rubbing his aching shoulders, the big man groaned. "I'm dead tired. I've got to get some sleep. You and what's-er-name there turn in, too. All right?"

"Sure, Caramon," Tasslehoff said.

Bupu, belching contently, had already wrapped herself up in a rug before the fire, using the remainder of the bowl of milk potatoes for a pillow.

Caramon eyed the kender suspiciously. Tas assumed the most innocent look a kender could possibly assume, the result of which was that Caramon shook his finger at him sternly.

"Promise me you won't leave this room, Tasslehoff Burrfoot. Promise just like you'd promise . . . say, Tanis, if he were here."

"I promise," Tas said solemnly, "just like I'd promise Tanis—if he were here."

"Good." Caramon sighed and collapsed onto a bed that creaked in protest, the mattress sagging clear to the floor beneath the big man's weight. "I guess someone'll wake us up when they decide what they're going to do."

"Will you really go back in time, Caramon?" Tas asked

wistfully, sitting down on his own bed and pretending to unlace his boots.

"Yeah, sure. 'S no big thing," Caramon murmured sleepily. "Now get some sleep and . . . thanks, Tas. You've been . . . you've been . . . a big help. . . ." His words trailed off into a snore.

Tas held perfectly still, waiting until Caramon's breathing became even and regular. That didn't take long because the big man was emotionally and physically exhausted. Looking at Caramon's pale, careworn, and tear-streaked face, the kender felt a moment's twinge of conscience. But kender are accustomed to dealing with twinges of conscience—just as humans are accustomed to dealing with mosquito bites.

"He'll never know I've been gone," Tas said to himself as he sneaked across the floor past Caramon's bed. "And I really didn't promise *him* I wouldn't go anywhere. I promised Tanis. And Tanis isn't here, so the promise doesn't count. Besides, I'm certain he would have wanted to explore, if he hadn't been so tired."

By the time Tas crept past Bupu's grubby little body, he had firmly convinced himself that Caramon had ordered him to look around before going to bed. He tried the door handle with misgivings, remembering Caramon's warning. But it opened easily. We *are* guests then, not prisoners. Unless there was a lich standing guard outside. Tas poked his head around the door frame. He looked up the hall, then down the hall. Nothing. Not a lich in sight. Sighing a bit in disappointment, Tas slipped out the door, then shut it softly behind him.

The hallway ran to his left and to his right, vanishing around shadowy corners at either end. It was barren, cold, and empty. Other doors branched off from the hallway, all of them dark, all of them closed. There were no decorations of any kind, no tapestries hung on the walls, no carpets covered the stone floor. There weren't even any lights, no torches, no candles. Apparently the mages were supposed to provide their own if they did any wandering about after dark.

A window at one end did allow the light of Solinari, the silver moon, to filter through its glass panes, but that was all. The rest of the hallway was completely dark. Too late Tas thought of sneaking back into the room for a candle. No. If

Caramon woke up, he might not remember he had told the kender to go exploring.

"I'll just pop into one of these other rooms and borrow a candle," Tas said to himself. "Besides, that's a good way to meet people."

Gliding down the hall quieter than the moonbeams that danced on the floor, Tas reached the next door. "I won't knock, in case they're asleep," he reasoned and carefully turned the doorknob. "Ah, locked!" he said, feeling immensely cheered.

This would give him something to do for a few minutes at least. Pulling out his lock-picking tools, he held them up to the moonlight to select the proper size wire for this particular lock.

"I hope it's not magically locked," he muttered, the sudden thought making him grow cold. Magicians did that sometimes, he knew—a habit kender consider highly unethical. But maybe in the Tower of High Sorcery, surrounded by mages, they wouldn't figure it would be worthwhile. "I mean, anyone could just come along and *blow* the door down," Tas reasoned.

Sure enough, the lock opened easily. His heart beating with excitement, Tas shoved the door open quietly and peered inside. The room was lit only by the faint glow of a dying fire. He listened. He couldn't hear anyone in it, no sounds of snoring or breathing, so he walked in, padding softly. His sharp eyes found the bed. It was empty. No one home.

"Then they won't mind if I borrow their candle," the kender said to himself happily. Finding a candlestick, he lit the wick with a glowing coal. Then he gave himself up to the delights of examining the occupant's belongings, noticing as he did so that whoever resided in this room was *not* a very tidy person.

About two hours and many rooms later, Tas was wearily returning to his own room, his pouches bulging with the most fascinating items—all of which he was fully determined to return to their owners in the morning. He had picked most of them up off the tops of tables where they had obviously been carelessly tossed. He found more than a few on the floor (he was certain the owners had lost them) and had even rescued several from the pockets of robes that were probably destined to be laundered, in which case these items would certainly have been misplaced.

Looking down the hall, he received a severe shock, however, when he saw light streaming out from under their door!

"Caramon!" He gulped, but at that moment a hundred plausible excuses for being out of the room entered his brain. Or perhaps Caramon might not even have missed him yet. Maybe he was into the dwarf spirits. Considering this possibility, Tas tiptoed up to the closed door of their room and pressed his ear against it, listening.

He heard voices. One he recognized immediately—Bupu's. The other . . . he frowned. It seemed familiar . . . where had he heard it?

"Yes, I am going to send you back to the Highpulp, if that is where you want to go? But first you must tell where the Highpulp is."

The voice sound faintly exasperated. Apparently, this had been going on for some time. Tas put his eye to the keyhole. He could see Bupu, her hair clotted with milk potatoes, glaring suspiciously at a red-robed figure. Now Tas remembered where he'd heard the voice—that was the man at the Conclave, who kept questioning Par-Salian!

"High*bulp*!" Bupu repeated indignantly. "Not Highpulp! And Highbulp is home. You send me home."

"Yes, of course. Now where is home?"

"Where Highbulp is."

"And where is the Highpul-bulp?" the red-robed mage asked in hopeless tones.

"Home," Bupu stated succinctly. "I tell you that before. You got ears under that hood? Maybe you deaf." The gully dwarf disappeared from Tas's sight for a moment, diving into her bag. When she reappeared, she held another dead lizard, a leather thong wrapped around its tail. "Me cure. You stick tail in ear and—"

"Thank you," said the mage hastily, "but my hearing is quite perfect, I assure you. Uh, what do you call your home? What is the name?"

"The Pitt. Two Ts. Some fancy name, huh?" Bupu said proudly. "That Highbulp's idea. Him ate book once. Learned lots. All right here." She patted her stomach.

Tas clapped his hand over his mouth to keep from giggling. The red-robed mage was experiencing similar problems as well. Tas saw the man's shoulders shake beneath his red robes, and it took him a while to respond. When he did, his voice had a faint quiver.

"What . . . what do humans call the name of your—the—uh—Pitt?"

Tas saw Bupu scowl. "Dumb name. Sound like someone spit up. Skroth."

"Skroth," the red-robed mage repeated, mystified. "Skroth," he muttered. Then he snapped his fingers. "I remember. The kender said it in the Conclave. Xak Tsaroth?"

"Me say that once already. You sure you not want lizard cure for ears? You put tail—"

Heaving a sigh of relief, the red-robed mage held his hand out over Bupu's head. Sprinkling what looked like dust down over her (Bupu sneezed violently), Tas heard the mage chant strange words.

"Me go home now?" Bupu asked hopefully.

The mage did not answer, he kept chanting.

"Him not nice," she muttered to herself, sneezing again as the dust slowly coated her hair and body. "None of them nice. Not like my pretty man." She wiped her nose, snuffling. "Him not laugh . . . him call me 'little one.' "

The dust on the gully dwarf began to glow a faint yellow. Tas gasped softly. The glow grew brighter and brighter, changing color, turning yellow-green, then green, then green-blue, then blue and suddenly—

"Bupu!" Tas whispered.

The gully dwarf was gone!

"And I'm next!" Tas realized in horror. Sure enough, the red-robed mage was limping across the room to the bed where the thoughtful kender had made up a dummy of himself so that Caramon wouldn't be worried in case he woke up.

"Tasslehoff Burrfoot" the red-robed mage called softly. He had passed beyond Tas's sight. The kender stood frozen, waiting for the mage to discover he was missing. Not that he was afraid of getting caught. He was used to getting caught and was fairly certain he could talk his way out of it. But he *was* afraid of being sent home! They didn't really expect Caramon to go anywhere without him, did they?

"Caramon *needs* me!" Tas whispered to himself in agony. "They don't know what bad shape he's in. Why, what would happen if he didn't have me along to drag him out of bars?"

"Tasslehoff," the red-robed mage's voice repeated. He must be nearing the bed.

Hurriedly, Tas's hand dove into his pouch. Pulling out a fistful of junk, he hoped against hope he'd found something useful. Opening his small hand, he held it up to the candlelight. He had come up with a ring, a grape, and a lump of mustache wax. The wax and the grape were obviously out. He tossed them to the floor.

"Caramon!" Tas heard the red-robed mage say sternly. He could hear Caramon grunt and groan and pictured the mage shaking him. "Caramon, wake up. Where's the kender?"

Trying to ignore what was happening in the room, Tas concentrated on examining the ring. It was probably magical. He'd picked it up in the third room to the left. Or was it the fourth? And magical rings *usually* worked just by being worn. Tas was an expert on the subject. He'd accidentally put on a magical ring once that had teleported him right into the heart of an evil wizard's palace. There was every possibility this might do the same. He had no idea what it did.

Maybe there was some sort of clue on the ring?

Tas turned it over, nearly dropping it in his haste. Thank the gods Caramon was so hard to wake up!

It was a plain ring, carved out of ivory, with two small pink stones. There were some runes traced on the inside. Tas recalled his magical Glasses of Seeing with a pang, but they were lost in Neraka, unless some draconian was wearing them.

"Wha . . . wha . . ." Caramon was babbling. "Kender? I told him . . . don't go out there . . . liches. . . ."

"Damn!" The red-robed mage was heading for the door.

Please, Fizban! the kender whispered, if you remember me at all, which I don't suppose you do, although you might—I was the one who kept finding your hat. Please, Fizban! Don't let them send Caramon off without me. Make this a Ring of Invisibility. Or at least a Ring of Something that will keep them from catching me!

Closing his eyes tightly so he wouldn't see anything Horrible he might accidentally conjure up, Tas thrust the ring over his thumb. (At the last moment he opened his eyes, so that he wouldn't miss seeing anything Horrible he might conjure up.)

At first, nothing happened. He could hear the red-robed mage's halting footsteps coming nearer and nearer the door.

Then—something *was* happening, although not quite what Tas expected. The hall was growing! There was a rushing sound in the kender's ears as the walls swooped past him and the ceiling soared away from him. Open-mouthed, he watched as the door grew larger and larger, until it was an immense size.

What have I done? Tas wondered in alarm. Have I made the Tower grow? Do you suppose anyone'll notice? If they do, will they be *very* upset?

The huge door opened with a gust of wind that nearly flattened the kender. An enormous red-robed figure filled the doorway.

A giant! Tas gasped. I've not only made the Tower grow! I've made the mages grow, too! Oh, dear. I guess they'll notice *that!* At least they will the first time they try to put on their shoes! And I'm sure they'll be upset. I would be if I was twenty feet tall and none of my clothes fit.

But the red-robed mage didn't seem at all perturbed about suddenly shooting up in height, much to Tas's astonishment. He just peered up and down the hall, yelling, "Tasslehoff Burrfoot!"

He even looked right at where Tas was standing—and didn't see him!

"Oh, thank you, Fizban!" the kender squeaked. Then he coughed. His voice certainly did sound funny. Experimentally, he said, "Fizban?" again. Again, he squeaked.

At that moment, the red-robed mage glanced down.

"Ah, ha! And whose room have you escaped from, my little friend?" the mage said.

As Tasslehoff watched in awe, a giant hand reached down—it was reaching down for him! The fingers got nearer and nearer. Tas was so startled he couldn't run or do anything except wait for that gigantic hand to grab him. Then it would be all over! They'd send him home instantly, if they didn't inflict a worse punishment on him for enlarging their Tower when he wasn't at all certain that they wanted it enlarged.

The hand hovered over him and then picked him up by his tail.

"My tail!" Tas thought wildly, squirming in midair as the hand lifted him off the floor. "I haven't got a tail! But I must! The hand's got hold of me by something!"

Twisting his head around. Tas saw that indeed, he did have a tail! Not only a tail, but four pink feet! Four! And instead of bright blue leggings, he was wearing white fur!

"Now, then," boomed a stern voice right in one of his ears, "answer me, little rodent! Whose familiar are you?"

Chapter 16

F amiliar! Tasslehoff clutched at the word. Familiar.... Talks with Raistlin came back to his fevered mind.

"Some magi have animals that are bound to do their bidding," Raistlin had told him once. "These animals, or *familiars* as they are called, can act as an extension of a mage's own senses. They can go places he cannot, see things he is unable to see, hear conversations he has not been invited to share."

At the time, Tasslehoff had thought it a wonderful idea, although he recalled Raistlin had not been impressed. He seemed to consider it a weakness, to be so heavily dependent upon another living being.

"Well, answer me?" the red-robed mage demanded, shaking Tasslehoff by the tail. Blood rushed to the kender's head, making him dizzy, plus being held by the tail was quite painful, to say nothing of the indignity! All he could do, for a moment, was to give thanks that Flint couldn't see him.

I suppose, he thought bleakly, that familiars can talk. I hope they speak Common, not something strange—like Mouse, for example.

"I'm—I—uh—belong to"—what was a good name for a mage?—"Fa—Faikus," Tas squeaked, remembering hearing Raistlin use this name in connection with a fellow student long ago.

"Ah," the red-robed mage said with a frown, "I might have known. Were you out upon some errand for your master or simply roaming around loose?"

Fortunately for Tas, the mage changed his hold upon the kender, releasing his tail to grasp him firmly in his hand. The kender's front paws rested quivering on the red-robed mage's thumb, his now beady, bright-red eyes stared into the mage's cool, dark ones.

What shall I answer? Tas wondered frantically. Neither choice sounded very good.

"It—it's my n-night off," Tas said in what he hoped was an indignant tone of squeak.

"Humpf!" The mage sniffed. "You've been around that lazy Faikus too long, that's for certain. I'll have a talk with that young man in the morning. As for you, no, you needn't start squirming! Have you forgotten that Sudora's familiar prowls the halls at night? You could have been Marigold's dessert! Come along with me. After I'm finished with this evening's business, I'll return you to your master."

Tas, who had just been ready to sink his sharp little teeth into the mage's thumb, suddenly thought better of the idea. "Finished with this evening's business!" Of course, that had to be Caramon! This was better than being invisible! He would just go along for the ride!

The kender hung his head in what he imagined was a mousy expression of meekness and contrition. It seemed to satisfy the red-robed mage, for he smiled in a preoccupied manner and began to search the pocket of his robes for something.

"What is it, Justarius?" There was Caramon, looking befuddled and still half asleep, He peered vaguely up and down the hallway. "You find Tas?"

"The kender? No." The mage smiled again, this time rather ruefully. "It may be a while before we find him, I'm afraid—kender being very adept at hiding."

"You won't hurt him?" Caramon asked anxiously, so anxiously Tas felt sorry for the big man and longed to reassure him.

"No, of course not," Justarius replied soothingly, still searching through his robes. "Though," he added as an afterthought, "he might inadvertently hurt himself. There are objects lying around here it wouldn't be advisable to play with. Well, now, are you ready?"

"I really don't want to go until Tas is back and I know he's all right," Caramon said stubbornly.

"I'm afraid you haven't any choice," the mage said, and Tas heard the man's voice grow cool. "Your brother travels in the morning. You must be prepared to go then as well. It takes hours for Par-Salian to memorize and cast this complex spell. Already he has started. I have stayed too long searching for the kender, in fact. We are late. Come along."

"Wait . . . my things. . . ." Caramon said pathetically. "My sword . . ."

"You need not worry about any of that," Justarius answered. Apparently finding what he had been searching for, he drew a silken bag out of the pocket of his robes. "You may not go back in time with any weapon or any device from this time period. Part of the spell will see to it that you are suitably dressed for the period you journey within."

Caramon looked down at his body, bewildered. "Y-you mean, I'll have to change clothes? I won't have a sword? What—"

And you're sending this man back in time *by himself*! Tas thought indignantly. He'll last five minutes. Five minutes, if that long! No, by all the gods, I'm—

Just exactly what the kender was going to do was lost as he suddenly found himself popped headfirst into the silken bag!

Everything went inky black. He tumbled down to the bottom of the bag, feet over tail, landing on his head. From somewhere inside of him came a horrifying fear of being on his back in a vulnerable position. Frantically, he fought to right himself, scrabbling wildly at the slick sides of the bag with his clawed feet. Finally he was right side up, and the terrible feeling subsided.

So *that's* what it's like to be panic-stricken, Tas thought with a sigh. I don't think much of it, that's certain. And I'm very glad kender don't get that way, as a general rule. Now what?

Forcing himself to calm down and his little heart to stop racing, Tas crouched in the bottom of the silken bag and tried to think what to do next. He appeared to have lost track of what was going on in his wild scrambling, for—by listening—he could hear two pairs of footsteps walking down a stone hall; Caramon's heavy, booted feet and the mage's shuffling tread.

He also experienced a slight swaying motion, and he could hear the soft sounds of cloth rubbing against cloth. It suddenly occurred to him that the red-robed mage had undoubtedly suspended the sack he was in from his belt!

"What am I supposed to do back there? How'm I supposed to get back here afterwards—"

That was Caramon's voice, muffled a bit by the cloth bag but still fairly clear.

"All that will be explained to you." The mage's voice sounded overly patient. "I wonder—Are you having doubts, second thoughts perhaps. If so, you should tell us now—"

"No," Caramon's voice sounded firm, firmer than it had in a long time. "No, I'm not having doubts. I'll go. I'll take Lady Crysania back. It's my fault she's hurt, no matter what that old man says. I'll see that she gets the help she needs and I'll take care of this Fistandantilus for you."

"M-m-m-m."

Tas heard that "m-m-m-m," though he doubted Caramon could. The big man was rambling on about what he would do to Fistandantilus when he caught up with him. But Tas felt chilled, as he had when Par-Salian gave Caramon that strange, sad look in the Hall. The kender, forgetting where he was, squeaked in frustration.

"Shhhh," Justarius murmured absently, patting the bag with his hand. "This is only for a short while, then you'll be back in your cage, eating corn."

"Huh?" Caramon said. Tas could almost see the big man's startled look. The kender gnashed his small teeth. The word "cage" called up a dreadful picture in his mind and a truly alarming thought occurred to him—what if I can't get back to being myself?

"Oh, not you!" the mage said hastily. "I was talking to my little furry friend here. He's getting restless. If we weren't late, I'd take him back right now." Tas froze. "There, he seems to have settled down. Now, what were you saying?"

Tas didn't pay any more attention. Miserably, he clung to the bag with his small feet as it swayed back and forth, bumping gently against the mage's thigh as he limped along. Surely the spell could be reversed by simply taking off the ring?

Tas's fingers itched to try it and see The last magic ring he'd put on he hadn't been able to get off! What if this was the same? Was he doomed to a life of white fur and pink feet forever? At the thought, Tas wrapped one foot around the ring that was still stuck to a toe (or whatever) and almost pulled it off, just to make sure.

But the thought of suddenly bursting out of a silk bag, a full-grown kender, and landing at the mage's feet came to his mind. He forced his quivering little paw to stop. No. At least this way he was being taken to wherever Caramon was being taken. If nothing else, maybe he could go back with him in mouse shape. There might be worse things. . . .

How was he going to get out of the bag!

The kender's heart sank to his hind feet. Of course, getting out was easy if he turned back into himself. Only then they'd catch him and send him home! But if he stayed a mouse, he'd end up eating corn with Faikus! The kender groaned and hunkered down, his nose between his paws. This was by far the worst predicament he'd ever been in in his entire life, even counting the time the two wizards caught him running off with their woolly mammoth. To top it off, he was beginning to feel queasy, what with the swaying motion of the bag, being cooped up, the funny smell inside the bag, and the bumping around and all.

"The whole mistake lay in saying a prayer to Fizban," the kender told himself gloomily. "He may be Paladine in reality, but I bet somewhere that wacky old mage is getting a real chuckle out of this."

Thinking about Fizban and how much he missed the crazy old mage wasn't making Tas feel any better, so he put the thought out of his mind and tried once more to concentrate on his surroundings, hoping to figure a way out. He stared into the silky darkness and suddenly—

"You idiot!" he told himself excitedly. "You lamebrained doorknob of a kender, as Flint would say! Or lamebrained mouse, because I'm not a kender anymore! I'm a mouse . . . and I have teeth!"

Hurriedly Tas took an experimental nibble. At first he couldn't get a grip on the slick fabric and he despaired once more.

"Try the seam, fool," he scolded himself severely, and sank his teeth into the thread that held the fabric together. It gave way almost instantly as his sharp little teeth sheared right through. Tas quickly nibbled away several more stitches and soon he could see something red—the mage's red robes! He caught a whiff of fresh air (what *had* that man been keeping in here!) and was so elated he quickly started to chew through some more.

Then he stopped. If he enlarged the hole anymore, he'd fall out. And he wasn't ready to, at least not yet. Not until they got to wherever it was they were going. Apparently that wasn't far off. It occurred to Tas that they had been climbing a series of stairs for some time now. He could hear Caramon wheezing from the unaccustomed exercise and even the red-robed mage appeared a bit winded.

"Why can't you just magic us up to this laboratory place?" Caramon grumbled, panting.

"No!" Justarius answered softly, his voice tinged with awe. "I can feel the very air tingle and crackle with the power Par-Salian extends to perform this spell. I would have no minor spell of mine disturb the forces that are at work here this night!"

Tas shivered at this beneath his fur, and he thought Caramon might have done the same, for he heard the big man clear his throat nervously and then continue to climb in silence. Suddenly, they came to a halt.

"Are we here?" Caramon asked, trying to keep his voice steady.

"Yes," came the whispered answer. Tas strained to hear. "I will take you up these last few stairs, then—when we come to the door at the top—I will open it very softly and allow you to enter. Speak no word! Say nothing that might disturb Par-Salian in his concentration. This spell takes days of preparation—"

"You mean he knew days ago he was going to be doing this?" Caramon interrupted harshly.

"Hush!" Justarius ordered, and his voice was tinged with anger. "Of course, he knew this was a possibility. He had to be prepared. It was well he did so, for we had no idea your brother intended to move this fast!" Tas heard the man draw a deep breath. When he spoke again, it was in calmer tones. "Now, I repeat, when we climb these last few stairs—speak no word! Is that understood?"

"Yes," Caramon sounded subdued.

"Do exactly as Par-Salian commands you to do. Ask no questions! Just obey. Can you do that?"

"Yes," Caramon sounded more subdued still. Tas heard a small tremor in the big man's reply.

He's scared, Tas realized. Poor Caramon. Why are they doing this to him? I don't understand. There's more going on here than meets the eye. Well, that makes it final. I don't care if I *do* break Par-Salian's concentration. I'll just have to risk it. Somehow, someway—I'm going to go with Caramon! He needs me. Besides—the kender sighed—to travel back in time! How wonderful. . . .

"Very well." Justarius hesitated, and Tas could feel his body grow tense and rigid. "I will say my farewells here, Caramon. May the gods go with you. What you are doing is dangerous . . . for us all. You cannot begin to comprehend the danger." This last was spoken so softly only Tas heard it, and the kender's ears twitched in alarm. Then the red-robed mage sighed. "I wish I could say I thought your brother was worth it."

"He is," Caramon said firmly. "You will see."

"I pray Gilean you are right. . . . Now, are you ready?"

"Yes."

Tas heard a rustling sound, as if the hooded mage nodded his head. Then they began to move again, climbing the stairs slowly. The kender peered out of the hole in the bottom of the sack, watching the shadowy steps slide by underneath him. He would have seconds only, he knew.

The stairs came to an end. He could see a broad stone landing beneath him. This is it! he told himself with a gulp. He could hear the rustling sound again and feel the mage's body move. A door creaked. Quickly, Tas's sharp teeth sliced through the remaining threads that held the seam together. He heard Caramon's slow steps, entering the door. He heard the door starting to close. . . .

The seam gave way. Tas fell out of the sack. He had a passing moment to wonder if mice always landed on their feet—like cats. (He had once dropped a cat off the roof of his house to see if that old saying was true. It is.) And then he hit the stone floor running. The door was shut, the red-robed mage had turned away. Without stopping to look around, the kender darted swiftly and silently across the floor. Flattening his small body, he wriggled through the crack between the door and the floor and dove beneath a bookcase that was standing near the wall.

Tas paused to catch his breath and listen.

What if Justarius discovered him missing? Would he come back and look for him?

Stop this, Tas told himself sternly. He won't know where I fell out. And he probably wouldn't come back here, anyway. Might disturb the spell.

After a few moments, the kender's tiny heart slowed down its pace so that he could hear over the blood pounding in his ears. Unfortunately, his ears told him very little. He could hear a soft murmuring, as if someone were rehearsing lines for a street play. He could hear Caramon try to catch his breath from the long climb and still keep his breathing muffled so as not to disturb the mage. The big man's leather boots creaked as he shifted nervously from one foot to the other.

But that was all.

"I have to see!" Tas said to himself. "Otherwise I won't know what's going on."

Creeping out from underneath the bookcase, the kender truly began to experience this tiny, unique world he had tumbled into. It was a world of crumbs, a world of dust balls and thread, of pins and ash, of dried rose petals and damp tea leaves. The insignificant was suddenly a world in itself. Furniture soared above him, like trees in a forest, and served about the same purpose—it provided cover. A candle flame was the sun, Caramon a monstrous giant.

Tas circled the man's huge feet warily. Catching a glimpse of movement out of one corner of his eye, he saw a slippered foot beneath a white robe. Par-Salian. Swiftly, Tas made a dart for the opposite end of the room, which was, fortunately, lit only by candles.

Then Tas skidded to a stop. He had been in a mage's laboratory once before this, when he'd been wearing that cursed teleporting ring. The strange and wonderful sights he'd seen there remained with him, and now he halted just before he stepped inside a circle drawn on the stone floor with silver powder. Within the center of the circle that glistened in the candlelight lay Lady Crysania, her sightless eyes still staring up at nothing, her face as white as the linen that shrouded her.

This was where the magic would be performed!

The fur rising on the back of his neck, Tas hastily scrambled back, out of the way, cowering beneath an overturned chamber pot. On the outside of the circle stood Par-Salian, his white robes glowing with an eerie light. In his hands, he held an object encrusted with jewels that sparkled and flashed as he turned it. It looked like a sceptre Tas had seen a Nordmaar king holding once, yet this device looked far more fascinating. It was faceted and jointed in the most unique fashion. Parts of it moved, Tas saw, while—more amazing still—other parts moved without moving! Even as he watched, Par-Salian deftly manipulated the object, folding and bending and twisting, until it was no bigger than an egg. Muttering strange words over it, the archmage dropped it into the pocket of his robe.

Then, though Tas could have sworn Par-Salian never took a step, he was suddenly standing inside the silver circle, next to Crysania's inert figure. The mage bent over her, and Tas saw him place something in the folds of her robes. Then Par-Salian began to chant the language of magic, moving his gnarled hands above her in ever-widening circles. Glancing quickly at Caramon, Tas saw him standing near the circle, a strange expression on his face. It was the expression of one who is somewhere unfamiliar, yet who feels completely at home.

Of course, Tas thought wistfully, he grew up with magic. Maybe this is just like being back with his brother again.

Par-Salian rose to his feet, and the kender was shocked at the change that had come over the man. His face had aged years, it was gray in color, and he staggered as he stood. He made a beckoning motion to Caramon and the man came forward, walking slowly, stepping carefully over the silver powder. His face fixed in a dreamlike trance, he stood silently beside the still form of Crysania.

Par-Salian removed the device from his pocket and held it out to Caramon. The big man placed his hand on it and, for a moment, the two stood holding it together. Tas saw Caramon's lips move, though he heard no sound. It was as if the warrior were reading to himself, memorizing some magically communicated information. Then Caramon ceased to speak. Par-Salian raised his hands and, with the motion, lifted himself from the floor and floated backward out of the circle into the shadowy darkness of the laboratory.

Tas could no longer see him, but he could hear his voice. The chanting grew louder and louder and suddenly a wall of silver light sprang from the circle traced upon the floor. It was so bright it made Tas's red mouse eyes burn, but the kender could not look away. Par-Salian cried out now with such a loud voice that the very stones of the chamber themselves began to answer in a chorus of voices that rose from the depths of the ground.

Tas's gaze was fixed upon that shimmering curtain of power. Within it, he could see Caramon standing near Crysania, still holding the device in his hand. Then Tas gasped a tiny gasp that made no more sound in the chamber than a mouse's breath. He could still see the laboratory itself through that shimmering curtain, but now it seemed to wink on and off, as if fighting for its own existence. And—when it winked out—the kender caught a glimpse of somewhere else! Forests, cities, lakes, and oceans blurred in his vision, coming and going, people seen for an instant than vanishing, replaced by others.

Caramon's body began to pulse with the same regularity as the strange visions as he stood within the column of light. Crysania, too, was there and then she wasn't.

Tears streaked down past Tas's quivering nose, sliding down his whiskers. "Caramon's going on the greatest adventure of all time!" the kender thought bleakly. "And he's leaving *me* behind!"

For one wild moment, Tas fought with himself. Everything inside of him that was logical and conscientious and Tanis-like told him—Tasslehoff, don't be a fool. This is Big Magic. You're likely to really Mess Things Up! Tas heard that voice, but it was being drowned out by all the chanting and the stones singing and, soon, it vanished altogether. . . .

Par-Salian never heard the small squeak. Lost in his casting of the spell, he caught only the barest glimpse of movement out of the corner of his eye. Too late, he saw the mouse streak out of its hiding place, heading straight for the silvery wall of light! Horrified, Par-Salian ceased his chant, the voices of the stones rang hollow and died. In the silence he could now hear the tiny voice, "Don't leave me, Caramon! Don't leave me! You know what trouble you'll get into without me!"

The mouse ran through the silver powder, scattering a sparkling trail behind it, and burst into the lighted circle. Par-Salian heard a small, tinging sound and saw a ring roll round and round on the stone floor. He saw a third figure materialize in the circle, and he gasped in horror. Then the pulsing figures were gone. The light of the circle was sucked into a great vortex, the laboratory was plunged into darkness.

Weak and exhausted, Par-Salian collapsed onto the floor. His last thought, before he lost consciousness, was a terrible one.

He had sent a kender back in time.

BOOK 2

Chapter 1

Denubis walked with slow steps through the wide, airy halls of the light-filled Temple of the Gods in Istar. His thoughts were abstracted, his gaze on the marble floor's intricate patterns. One might have supposed, seeing him walk thus aimlessly and preoccupied, the cleric was insensible of the fact that he was walking in the heart of the universe. But Denubis was not insensible of this fact, nor was it one he was likely to forget. Lest he should, the Kingpriest reminded him of it daily in his morning call to prayers.

"We are the heart of the universe," the Kingpriest would say in the voice whose music was so beautiful one occasionally forgot to listen to the words. "Istar, city beloved of the gods, is the center of the universe and we—being at the heart of the city—are therefore the heart of the universe. As the blood flows from the heart, bringing nourishment to even the smallest toe, so our faith and our teachings flow from this great temple to the smallest, most insignificant among us. Remember this as you go about your daily duties, for you who work here are favored of the gods. As one touch upon the tiniest strand of the silken web will send tremors through the entire web, so your least action could spread tremors throughout Krynn."

Denubis shivered. He wished the Kingpriest would not use that particular metaphor. Denubis detested spiders. He hated all insects, in fact; something he never admitted and, indeed, felt guilty about. Was he not commanded to love all creatures, except, of course, those created by the Queen of Darkness? That included ogres, goblins, trolls, and other evil races, but Denubis was not certain about spiders. He kept meaning to ask, but he knew this would entail an hour-long philosophical argument among the Revered Sons, and he simply didn't think it was worth it. Secretly, he would continue to hate spiders.

Denubis slapped himself gently on his balding head. How had his mind wandered to spiders? I'm getting old, he thought with a sigh. I'll soon be like poor Arabacus, doing nothing all day but sitting in the garden and sleeping until someone wakens me for dinner. At this, Denubis sighed again, but it was nearer a sigh of envy than one of pity. Poor Arabacus, indeed! At least he is spared—

"Denubis. . ."

Denubis paused. Glancing this way and that around the large corridor, he saw no one. The cleric shuddered. Had he heard that soft voice, or just imagined it?

"Denubis," came the voice again.

This time the cleric looked more closely into the shadows formed by the huge marble columns supporting the gilded ceiling. A darker shadow, a patch of blackness within the darkness was now discernible. Denubis checked an exclamation of irritation. Suppressing the second shudder that swept over his body, he halted in his course and moved slowly over to the figure that stood in the shadows, knowing that the figure would never move out of the shadows to meet him. It was not that light was harmful to the one who awaited Denubis, as light is harmful to some of the creatures of darkness. In fact, Denubis wondered if anything on the face of this world could be harmful to this man. No, it was simply that he preferred shadows. Theatrics, Denubis thought sarcastically.

"You called me, Dark One?" Denubis asked in a voice he tried hard to make sound pleasant.

He saw the face in the shadows smile, and Denubis knew at once that all of his thoughts were well-known to this man.

"Damn it!" Denubis cursed (a habit frowned upon by the Kingpriest but one which Denubis, a simple man, had never been able to overcome). "Why does the Kingpriest keep him around the court? Why not send him away, as the others were banished?"

He said this to himself, of course, because—deep within his soul—Denubis knew the answer. This one was too dangerous, too powerful. This one was not like the others. The Kingpriest kept him as a man keeps a ferocious dog to protect his house; he knows the dog will attack when ordered, but he must constantly make certain that the dog's leash is secure. If the leash ever broke, the animal would go for his throat.

"I am sorry to disturb you, Denubis," said the man in his soft voice, "especially when I see you absorbed in such weighty thought. But an event of great importance is happening, even as we speak. Take a squadron of the Temple guards and go to the marketplace. There, at the crossroads, you will find a Revered Daughter of Paladine. She is near death. And there, also, you will find the man who assaulted her."

Denubis's eyes opened wide, then narrowed in sudden suspicion.

"How do you know this?" he demanded.

The figure within the shadows stirred, the dark line formed by the thin lips widened—the figure's approximation of a laugh.

"Denubis," the figure chided, "you have known me many years. Do you ask the wind how it blows? Do you question the stars to find out why they shine? I *know*, Denubis. Let that be enough for you."

"But—" Denubis put his hand to his head in confusion. This would entail explanations, reports to the proper authorities. One did not simply conjure up a squadron of Temple guards!

"Hurry, Denubis," the man said gently. "She will not live long. . . ."

Denubis swallowed. A Revered Daughter of Paladine, assaulted! Dying—in the marketplace! Probably surrounded by gaping crowds. The scandal! The Kingpriest would be highly displeased—

The cleric opened his mouth, then shut it again. He looked for a moment at the figure in the shadows, then, finding no help there, Denubis whirled about and, in a flurry of robes, ran back down the corridor the way he had come, his leather sandals slapping on the marble floor.

Reaching the central headquarters of the Captain of the Guard, Denubis managed to gasp out his request to the lieutenant on duty. As he had foreseen, this caused all sorts of commotion. Waiting for the Captain himself to appear, Denubis collapsed in a chair and tried to catch his breath.

The identity of the creator of spiders might be open to question, Denubis thought sourly, but there was no doubt in his mind at all about the creator of *that* creature of darkness who, no doubt, was standing back there in the shadows laughing at him.

"Tasslehoff!"

The kender opened his eyes. For a moment, he had no idea where he was or even who he was. He had heard a voice speaking a name that sounded vaguely familiar. Confused, the kender looked around. He was lying on top of a big man, who was flat on his back in the middle of a street. The big man was regarding him with utter astonishment, perhaps because Tas was perched upon his broad stomach.

"Tas?" the big man repeated, and this time his face grew puzzled. "Are you supposed to be here?"

"I-I'm really not sure," the kender said, wondering who "Tas" was. Then it all came back to him—hearing Par-Salian chanting, ripping the ring off his thumb, the blinding light, the singing stones, the mage's horrified shriek. . . .

"Of course, I'm supposed to be here," Tas snapped irritably, blocking out the memory of Par-Salian's fearful yell. "You don't think they'd let you come back here by yourself, do you?" The kender was practically nose to nose with the big man.

Caramon's puzzled look darkened to a frown. "I'm not sure," he muttered, "but I don't think you—"

"Well, I'm here." Tas rolled off Caramon's rotund body to land on the cobblestones beneath them. "Wherever 'here' is," he muttered beneath his breath. "Let me help you up," he said to Caramon, extending his small hand, hoping this action would take Caramon's mind off him. Tas didn't know whether or not he could be sent back, but he didn't intend to find out.

Caramon struggled to sit up, looking for all the world like an overturned turtle, Tas thought with a giggle. And it was then the kender noticed that Caramon was dressed much differently than he had been when they left the Tower. He had been wearing his own armor (as much of it that fit), a loose-fitting tunic made of fine cloth, sewn together with Tika's loving care.

But, now, he was wearing coarse cloth, slovenly stitched together. A crude leather vest hung from his shoulders. The vest might have had buttons once, but, if so, they were gone now. Buttons weren't needed anyway, Tas thought, for there was no way the vest would have stretched to fit over Caramon's sagging gut. Baggy leather breeches and patched leather boots with a big hole over one toe completed the unsavory picture.

"Whew!" Caramon muttered, sniffing. "What's that horrible smell?"

"You," Tas said, holding his nose and waving his hand as though this might dissipate the odor. Caramon reeked of dwarf spirits! The kender regarded him closely. Caramon had been sober when they'd left, and he certainly looked sober now. His eyes, if confused, were clear and he was standing straight, without weaving.

The big man looked down and, for the first time, saw himself.

"What? How?" he asked, bewildered.

"You'd think," Tas said sternly, regarding Caramon's clothes in disgust, "that the mages could afford something better than this! I mean, I know this spell must be hard on clothes, but surely—"

A sudden thought occurred to him. Fearfully, Tas looked down at his clothes, then breathed a sigh of relief. Nothing had happened to him. Even his pouches were with him, all perfectly intact. A nagging voice inside him mentioned that this was probably because he wasn't supposed to have come along, but the kender conveniently ignored it.

"Well, let's have a look around," Tas said cheerfully, suiting his action to his words. He'd already been able to guess where they were by the odor—in a alley. The kender wrinkled his nose. He'd thought Caramon smelled bad! Filled with garbage and refuse of every kind, the alley was dark, overshadowed by a huge stone building. But it was daylight, Tas could tell, glancing down at the end of the alley where he could see what appeared to a busy street, thronged with people who were coming and going.

"I think that's a market," Tas said with interest, starting to walk nearer the end of the alley to investigate. "What city did you say they sent us to?"

"Istar," he heard Caramon mumble from behind him. Then, "Tas!"

Hearing a frightened tone in Caramon's voice, the kender turned around hurriedly, his hand going immediately to the little knife he carried in his belt. Caramon was kneeling by something lying the alley.

"What is it?" Tas called, running back.

"Lady Crysania," Caramon said, lifting a dark cloak.

"Caramon!" Tas drew a horrified breath. "What did they do to her? Did their magic go wrong?"

"I don't know," Caramon said softly, "but we've got to get help." He carefully covered the woman's bruised and bloody face with the cloak.

"I'll go," Tas offered, "you stay here with her. This doesn't look like a really good part of town, if you take my meaning."

"Yeah," Caramon said, sighing heavily.

"It'll be all right," Tas said, patting the big man on his shoulder reassuringly. Caramon nodded but said nothing. With a final pat, Tas turned and ran back down the alley toward the street. Reaching the end, he darted out onto the sidewalk.

"Hel—" he began, but just then a hand closed over his arm in a grip of iron, hoisting him clear up off the sidewalk.

"Here, now," said a stern voice, "where are you going?"

Tas twisted around to see a bearded man, his face partially covered by the shining visor of his helm, staring at him with dark, cold eyes.

Townguard, the kender realized quickly, having had a great deal of experience with this type of official personage.

"Why, I was coming to look for you," Tas said, trying to wriggle free and assume an innocent air at the same time.

"*That's* a likely story from a kender!" The guard snorted, getting an even firmer grasp on Tas. "It'd be a history-making event in Krynn, if it was true, that's for certain."

"But it *is* true," Tas said, glaring at the man indignantly. "A friend of ours is hurt, down there."

He saw the guard glance over at a man he had not noticed before—a cleric, dressed in white robes. Tas brightened. "Oh? A cleric? How—"

The guard clapped his hand over the kender's mouth.

"What do you think, Denubis? That's Beggar's Alley down there. Probably a knifing, nothing more than thieves falling out."

The cleric was a middle-aged man with thinning hair and a rather melancholy, serious face. Tas saw him look around the marketplace and shake his head. "The Dark One said the crossroads, and this is it—or near enough. We should investigate."

"Very well." The guardsman shrugged. Detailing two of his men, he watched them advance cautiously down the filthy alleyway. He kept his hand over the kender's mouth, and Tas, slowly being smothered, made a pathetic, squeaking sound.

The cleric, gazing anxiously after the guards, glanced around. "Let him breathe, Captain," he said.

"We'll have to listen to him chatter," the captain grumbled irritably, but he removed his hand from Tas's mouth.

"He'll be quiet, won't you?" the cleric asked, looking at Tas with eyes that were kind in a preoccupied fashion. "He realizes how serious this is, don't you?"

Not quite certain whether the cleric was addressing him or the captain or both, Tas thought it best simply to nod in agreement. Satisfied, the cleric turned back to watch the guards. Tas twisted enough in the captain's grasp so that he, too, was able to see. He saw Caramon stand up, gesturing at the dark, shapeless bundle lying beside him. One of the guards knelt down and drew aside the cloak.

"Captain!" he shouted as the other guard immediately grabbed hold of Caramon. Startled and angry at the rough treatment, the big man jerked out of the guard's grasp. The guard shouted, his companion rose to his feet. There was a flash of steel.

"Damn!" swore the captain. "Here, watch this little bastard, Denubis!" He thrust Tasslehoff in the cleric's direction.

"Shouldn't I go?" Denubis protested, catching hold of Tas as the kender stumbled into him.

"No!" The captain was already running down the alley, his own shortsword drawn. Tas heard him mutter something about "big brute . . . dangerous."

"Caramon isn't dangerous," Tas protested, looking up at the cleric called Denubis in concern. "They won't hurt him, will they? What's wrong?"

"I'm afraid we'll find out soon enough," Denubis said in a stern voice, but holding Tas in such a gentle grip that the kender could easily have broken free. At first Tas considered escape—there was no better place in the world to hide than in a large city market. But the thought was a reflexive one, just like Caramon's breaking away from the guard. Tas couldn't leave his friend.

"They won't hurt him, if he comes peacefully." Denubis sighed. "Though if he's done—" The cleric shivered and for a moment paused. "Well, if he's done *that*, he might find an easier death here."

"Done what?" Tas was growing more and more confused. Caramon, too, appeared confused, for Tas saw him raise his hands in a protestation of innocence.

But even as he argued, one of the guards came up behind the big man and struck him in the back of his knees with the shaft of his spear. Caramon's legs buckled. As he staggered, the guard in front of him knocked the big man to the ground with an almost nonchalant blow to the chest.

Caramon hadn't even hit the pavement before the point of the spear was at his throat. He lifted his hands feebly in a gesture of surrender. Quickly, the guards rolled him over onto his stomach and, grasping his hands, tied them behind his back with rapid expertise.

"Make them stop!" Tas cried, straining forward. "They can't do that—"

The cleric caught him. "No, little friend, it would be best for you to stay with me. Please," Denubis said, gently gripping Tas by the shoulders. "You cannot help him, and trying will only make things worse for you."

The guards dragged Caramon to his feet and began to search him thoroughly, even reaching their hands down into his leather breeches. They found a dagger at his belt—this they handed to their captain—and a flagon of some sort. Opening the top, they sniffed and then tossed it away in disgust.

One of the guards motioned to the dark bundle on the pavement. The captain knelt down and lifted the cloak. Tas saw him shake his head. Then the captain, with the other guard's help, carefully lifted the bundle and turned to walk out of the alley. He said something to Caramon as he passed. Tas heard the filthy word with riveting shock, as did Caramon, apparently, for the big man's face went deathly white.

Glancing up at Denubis, Tas saw the cleric's lips tighten, the fingers on Tas's shoulder trembled.

Then Tas understood.

"No," he whispered softly in agony, "oh, no! They can't think that! Caramon wouldn't harm a mouse! He didn't hurt Lady Crysania! He was only trying to help her! That's why we came here. Well, one reason anyway. Please!" Tas whirled around to face Denubis, clasping his hands together. "Please, you've got to believe me! Caramon's a soldier. He's killed things—sure. But only nasty things like draconians and goblins. Please, please believe me!"

But Denubis only looked at him sternly.

"No! How could you think that? I hate this place! I want to go back home!" Tas cried miserably, seeing Caramon's stricken, confused expression. Bursting into tears, the kender buried his face in his hands and sobbed bitterly.

Then Tas felt a hand touch him, hesitate, then pat him gently.

"There, there, now," Denubis said. "You'll have a chance to tell your story. Your friend will, too. And, if you're innocent, no harm will come to you." But Tas heard the cleric sigh. "Your friend had been drinking, hadn't he?"

"No!" Tas snuffled, looking up at Denubis pleadingly. "Not a drop, I swear. . . ."

The kender's voice died, however, at the sight of Caramon as the guards led him out of the alley into the street where Tas and the cleric stood. Caramon's face was covered with muck and filth from the alley, blood dribbled from a cut on his lip. His eyes were wild and blood-shot, the expression on his face vacant and filled with fear. The legacy of past drinking bouts was marked plainly in his puffy, red cheeks and shaking limbs. A crowd, which had begun to form at the sight of the guards, began to jeer.

Tas hung his head. What was Par-Salian doing? he wondered in confusion. Had something gone wrong? Were they even in Istar? Were they lost somewhere? Or maybe this was some terrible nightmare. . . .

"Who—What happened?" Denubis asked the captain. "Was the Dark One right?"

"Right? Of course, he was right. Have you ever known him to be wrong?" the captain snapped. "As for who—I don't know who she is, but she's a member of your order. Wears the medallion of Paladine around her neck. She's hurt pretty bad, too. I thought she was dead, in fact, but there's a faint lifebeat in her neck."

"Do you think she was . . . she was . . ." Denubis faltered.

"I don't know," the captain said grimly. "But she's been beaten up. She's had some kind of fit, I guess. Her eyes are wide open, but she doesn't seem to see or hear anything."

"We must convey her to the Temple at once," Denubis said briskly, though Tas heard a tremor in the man's voice. The guards were dispersing the crowd, holding their spears in front of them and pushing back the curious.

"Everything's in hand. Move along, move along. Market's about to close for the day. You best finish your shopping while there's still time."

"I didn't hurt her!" Caramon said bleakly. He was shivering in terror. "I didn't hurt her," he repeated, tears streaking down his face.

"Yeah!" the captain said bitterly. "Take these two to the prisons," he ordered his guards.

Tas whimpered. One of the guards grabbed him roughly, but the kender—confused and stunned—caught hold of Denubis's robes and refused to let go. The cleric, his hand resting on Lady Crysania's lifeless form, turned around when he felt the kender's clinging hands.

"Please," Tas begged, "please, he's telling the truth."

Denubis's stern face softened. "You are a loyal friend," he said gently. "A rather unusual trait to find in a kender. I hope your faith in this man is justified." Absently, the cleric stroked Tas's topknot of hair, his expression sad. "But, you must realize that sometimes, when a man has been drinking, the liquor makes him do things—"

"Come along, you!" the guard snarled, jerking Tas backward. "Quit your little act. It won't work."

"Don't let this upset you, Revered Son," the captain said. "You know kender!"

"Yes," Denubis replied, his eyes on Tas as the two guards led the kender and Caramon away through the rapidly thinning crowd in the marketplace. "I do know kender. And that's a remarkable one." Then, shaking his head, the cleric turned his attention back to Lady Crysania. "If you will continue holding her, Captain," he said softly, "I will ask Paladine to convey us to the Temple with all speed."

Tas, twisting around in the guard's grip, saw the cleric and the Captain of the Guard standing alone in the marketplace. There was a shimmer of white light, and they were gone.

Tas blinked and, forgetting to look where he was going stumbled over his feet. He tumbled to the cobblestone pavement, skinning his knees and his hands painfully. A firm grip on his collar jerked him upright, and a firm hand gave him a shove in the back.

"Come along. None of your tricks."

Tas moved forward, too miserable and upset to even look around at his surroundings. His gaze went to Caramon, and the kender felt his heart ache. Overwhelmed by shame and fear, Caramon plodded down the street blindly, his steps unsteady.

"I didn't hurt her!" Tas heard him mumble. "There must be some sort of mistake. . . ."

Chapter 2

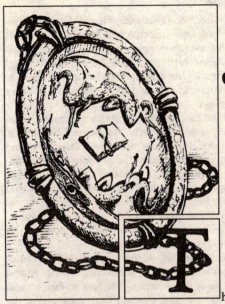

The beautiful elven voices rose higher and higher, their sweet notes spiraling up the octaves as though they would carry their prayers to the heavens simply by ascending the scales. The faces of the elven women, touched by the rays of the setting sun slanting through the tall crystal windows, were tinged a delicate pink, their eyes shone with fervent inspiration.

The listening pilgrims wept for the beauty, causing the choir's white and blue robes—white robes for the Revered Daughters of Paladine, blue robes for the Daughters of Mishakal—to blur in their sight. Many would swear later that they had seen the elven women transported skyward, swathed in fluffy clouds.

When their song reached a crescendo of sweetness, a chorus of deep, male voices joined in, keeping the prayers that had been sweeping upward like freed birds tied to the ground—clipping the wings, so to speak, Denubis thought sourly. He supposed he was jaded. As a young man, he, too, had cleansed his soul with tears when he first heard the Evening Hymn.

Then, years later, it had become routine. He could well remember the shock he had experienced when he first realized his thoughts had wandered to some pressing piece of church business during the singing. Now it was worse than routine. It had become an irritant, cloying and annoying. He had come to dread this time of day, in fact, and took advantage of every opportunity to escape.

Why? He blamed much of it on the elven women. Racial prejudice, he told himself morosely. Yet, he couldn't help it. Every year a party of elven women, Revered Daughters and those in training, journeyed from the glorious lands of Silvanesti to spend a year in Istar, devoting themselves to the church. This meant they sang the Evening Hymn nightly and spent their days reminding all around them that the elves were the favored of the gods—created first of all the races, granted a lifespan of hundreds of years. Yet nobody but Denubis seemed to take offense at this.

Tonight, in particular, the singing was irritating to Denubis because he was worried about the young woman he had brought to the Temple that morning. He had, in fact, almost avoided coming this evening but had been captured at the last moment by Gerald, an elderly human cleric whose days on Krynn were numbered and who found his greatest comfort in attending Evening Prayers. Probably, Denubis reflected, because the old man was almost totally deaf. This being the case, it had been completely impossible to explain to Gerald that he—Denubis—had somewhere else to go. Finally Denubis gave up and gave the old cleric his arm in support. Now Gerald stood next to him, his face rapt, picturing in his mind, no doubt, the beautiful plane to which he, someday, would ascend.

Denubis was thinking about this and about the young woman, whom he had not seen or heard anything about since he had brought her to the Temple that morning, when he felt a gentle touch upon his arm. The cleric jumped and glanced about guiltily, wondering if his inattention had been observed and would be reported. At first he couldn't figure out who had touched him, both of his neighbors apparently lost in their prayers. Then he felt the touch again and realized it came from behind. Glancing in back of him, he saw a hand had slipped unobtrusively through the curtain that separated the balcony on which the Revered Sons stood from the antechambers around the balcony.

The hand beckoned, and Denubis, puzzled, left his place in line and fumbled awkwardly with the curtain, trying to leave without calling undue attention to himself. The hand had withdrawn and Denubis couldn't find the separation in the folds of the heavy velvet curtains. Finally, after he was certain every pilgrim in the place must have his eyes fixed on him in disgust, he found the opening and stumbled through it.

A young acolyte, his face smooth and placid, bowed to the flushed and perspiring cleric as if nothing were amiss.

"My apologies for interrupting your Evening Prayers, Revered Son, but the Kingpriest requests that you honor him with a few moments of your time, if it is convenient." The acolyte spoke the prescribed words with such casual courtesy that it would not have seemed unusual to any observer if Denubis had replied, "No, not now. I have other matters I must attend to directly. Perhaps later?"

Denubis, however, said nothing of the sort. Paling visibly, he mumbled something about "being much honored," his voice dying off at the end. The acolyte was accustomed to this, however, and—nodding acknowledgment—turned and led the way through the vast, airy, winding halls of the Temple to the quarters of the Kingpriest of Istar.

Hurrying behind the youth, Denubis had no need to wonder what this could be about. The young woman, of course. He had not been in the Kingpriest's presence for well over two years, and it could not be coincidence that brought him this summons on the very day he had found a Revered Daughter lying near death in an alley.

Perhaps she has died, Denubis thought sadly. The Kingpriest is going to tell me in person. It would certainly be kind of the man. Out of character, perhaps, in one who had such weighty affairs as the fate of nations on his mind, but certainly kind.

He hoped she hadn't died. Not just for her sake, but for the sake of the human and the kender. Denubis had been thinking a lot about them, too. Particularly the kender. Like others on Krynn, Denubis hadn't much use for kender, who had no respect at all for rules or personal property—either their own or other people's. But this kender seemed different. Most kender Denubis knew (or thought he knew) would have run off at the first sign of trouble. This one had stayed by his big friend with touching loyalty and had even spoken up in his friend's defense.

Denubis shook his head sadly. If the girl died, they would face—No, he couldn't think about it. Murmuring a sincere prayer to Paladine to protect everyone concerned (if they were worthy), Denubis wrenched his mind from its depressing thoughts and forced it to admire the splendors of the Kingpriest's private residence in the Temple.

He had forgotten the beauty—the milky white walls, glowing with a soft light of their own that came—so legend had it—from the very stones themselves. So delicately shaped and carved were they, that they glistened like great white rose petals springing up from the polished white floor. Running through them were faint veins of light blue, softening the harshness of the stark white.

The wonders of the hallway gave way to the beauties of the antechamber. Here the walls flowed upward to support the dome overhead, like a mortal's prayer ascended to the gods. Frescoes of the gods were painted in soft colors. They, too, seemed to glow with their own light—Paladine, the Platinum Dragon, God of Good; Gilean of the Book, God of Neutrality; even the Queen of Darkness was represented here—for the Kingpriest would offend no god overtly. She was portrayed as the five-headed dragon, but such a meek and inoffensive dragon Denubis wondered she didn't roll over and lick Paladine's foot.

He thought that only later, however, upon reflection. Right now, he was much too nervous to even look at the wonderful paintings. His gaze was fixed on the carefully wrought platinum doors that opened into the heart of the Temple itself.

The doors swung open, emitting a glorious light. His time of audience had come.

The Hall of Audience first gave those who came here a sense of their own meekness and humility. This was the heart of goodness. Here was represented the glory and power of the church. The doors opened onto a huge circular room with a floor of polished white granite. The floor continued upward to form the walls into the petals of a gigantic rose, soaring skyward to support a great dome. The dome itself was of frosted crystal that absorbed the glow of the sun and the moons. Their radiance filled every part of the room.

A great arching wave of seafoam blue swept up from the center of the floor into an alcove that stood opposite the door. Here stood a single throne. More brilliant than the light streaming down from the dome was the light and warmth that flowed from this throne.

Denubis entered the room with his head bowed and his hands folded before him as was proper. It was evening and the sun had now set. The Hall Denubis walked into was lit only by candles. Yet, as always, Denubis had the distinct impression he had stepped into an open-air courtyard bathed in sunlight.

Indeed, for a moment his eyes were dazzled by the brilliance. Keeping his gaze lowered, as was proper until he was given leave to raise it, he caught glimpses of the floor and objects and people present in the Hall. He saw the stairs as he ascended them. But the radiance welling from the front of the room was so splendid that he literally noticed nothing else.

"Raise your eyes, Revered Son of Paladine," spoke a voice whose music brought tears to Denubis's eyes when the lovely music of the elven women could move him no longer.

Denubis looked up, and his soul trembled in awe. It had been two years since he had been this near the Kingpriest, and time had dulled his memory. How different it was to observe him every morning from a distance—seeing him as one sees the sun appearing on the horizon, basking in its warmth, feeling cheered at its light. How different to be summoned into the presence of the sun, to stand before it and feel one's soul burned by the purity and clarity of its brilliance.

This time, I'll remember, thought Denubis sternly. But no one, returning from an audience with the Kingpriest, could ever recall exactly what he looked like. It seemed sacrilegious to attempt to do so, in fact—as though thinking of him in terms of mere flesh was a desecration. All anyone ever remembered was that they had been in the presence of someone incredibly beautiful.

The aura of light surrounded Denubis, and he was immediately rent by the most terrible guilt for his doubts and misgivings and questionings. In contrast to the Kingpriest, Denubis saw himself as the most wretched creature on Krynn. He fell to his knees, begging forgiveness, almost totally unaware of what he was doing, knowing only that it was the right thing to do.

And forgiveness was granted. The musical voice spoke, and Denubis was immediately filled with a sense of peace and sweet calm. Rising to his feet, he faced the Kingpriest in reverent humility and begged to know how he could serve him.

"You brought a young woman, a Revered Daughter of Paladine, to the Temple this morning," said the voice, "and we understand you have been concerned about her—as is only natural and most proper. We thought it would give you comfort to know that she is well and fully recovered from her terrible ordeal. It may also ease your mind, Denubis, beloved son of Paladine, to know that she was not physically injured."

Denubis offered his thanks to Paladine for the young woman's recovery and was just preparing to stand aside and bask for a few moments in the glorious light when the full import of the Kingpriest's words struck him.

"She-she was not assaulted?" Denubis managed to stammer.

"No, my son," answered the voice, sounding a joyous anthem. "Paladine in his infinite wisdom had gathered her soul to himself, and I was able, after many long hours of prayer, to prevail upon him to return such a treasure to us, since it had been snatched untimely from its body. The young woman now finds rest in a life-giving sleep."

"But the marks on her face?" Denubis protested, confused. "The blood—"

"There were no marks," the Kingpriest said mildly, but with a hint of reproof that made Denubis feel unaccountably miserable. "I told you, she was not physically injured."

"I-I am delighted I was mistaken," Denubis answered sincerely. "All the more so because it means that young man who was arrested is innocent as he claimed and may now go free."

"I am truly thankful, even as you are thankful, Revered Son, to know that a fellow creature in this world did not commit a crime as foul as was first feared. Yet who among us is truly innocent?"

The musical voice paused and seemed to be awaiting an answer. And answers were forthcoming. The cleric heard murmured voices all around him give the proper response, and Denubis became consciously aware for the first time that there were others present near the throne. Such was the influence of the Kingpriest that he had almost believed himself alone with the man.

Denubis mumbled the response to this question along with the rest and suddenly knew without being told that he was dismissed from the august presence. The light no longer beat upon him directly, it had turned from him to another. Feeling as if he had stepped from brilliant sun into the shade, he stumbled, half-blind, back down the stairs. Here, on the main floor, he was able to catch his breath, relax, and look around.

The Kingpriest sat at one end, surrounded by light. But, it seemed to Denubis that his eyes were becoming accustomed to the light, so to speak, for he could at last begin to recognize others with him. Here were the heads of the various orders—the Revered Sons and Revered Daughters. Known almost jokingly as "the hands and feet of the sun," it was these who handled the mundane, day-to-day affairs of the church. It was these who ruled Krynn. But there were others here, besides high church officials. Denubis felt his gaze drawn to a corner of the Hall, the only corner, it seemed, that was in shadow.

There sat a figure robed in black, his darkness outshone by the Kingpriest's light. But Denubis, shuddering, had the distinct impression that the darkness was only waiting, biding its time, knowing that—eventually—the sun must set.

The knowledge that the Dark One, as Fistandantilus was known around the court, was allowed within the Kingpriest's Hall of Audience came as a shock to Denubis. The Kingpriest was trying to rid the world of evil, yet it was here—in his court! And then a comforting thought came to Denubis—perhaps, when the world was totally free of evil, when the last of the ogre races had been eliminated, then Fistandantilus himself would fall.

But even as he thought this and smiled at the thought, Denubis saw the cold glitter of the mage's eyes turn their gaze toward him. Denubis shivered and looked away hurriedly. What a contrast there was between that man and the Kingpriest! When basking in the Kingpriest's light, Denubis felt calm and peaceful. Whenever he happened to look into the eyes of Fistandantilus, he was reminded forcefully of the darkness within himself.

And, under the gaze of those eyes, he suddenly found himself wondering what the Kingpriest had meant by the curious statement, "who of us is truly innocent?"

Feeling uncomfortable, Denubis walked into an antechamber where stood a gigantic banquet table.

The smell of the luscious, exotic foods, brought from all over Ansalon by worshipful pilgrims or purchased in the huge open-air markets of cities as far away as Xak Tsaroth, made Denubis remember that he had not eaten since morning. Taking a plate, he browsed among the wonderful food, selecting this and that until his plate was filled and he had only made it halfway down the table that literally groaned under its aromatic burden.

A servant brought round cups of fragrant, elven wine. Taking one of these and juggling the plate and his eating implements in one hand, the wine in the other, Denubis sank into a chair and began to eat heartily. He was just enjoying the heavenly combination of a mouthful of roast pheasant and the lingering taste of the elven wine when a shadow fell across his plate.

Denubis glanced up, choked, and bolted the remainder of the mouthful, dabbing at the wine dribbling down his chin in embarrassment.

"R-revered Son," he stuttered, making a feeble attempt to rise in the gesture of respect that the Head of the Brethren deserved.

Quarath regarded him with sardonic amusement and waved a hand languidly. "Please, Revered Son, do not let me disturb you. I have no intention of interrupting your dinner. I merely wanted a word with you. Perhaps, when you are finished—"

"Quite . . . quite finished," Denubis said hastily, handing his half-full plate and glass to a passing servant. "I don't seem to be as hungry as I thought." That, at least, was true. He had completely lost his appetite.

Quarath smiled a delicate smile. His thin elven face with its finely sculpted features seemed to be made of fragile porcelain, and he always smiled carefully, as if fearing his face would break.

"Very well, if the desserts do not tempt you?"

"N-no, not in the slightest. Sweets . . . bad for th-the digestion th-this late—"

"Then, come with me, Revered Son. It has been a long time since we talked." Quarath took Denubis's arm with casual familiarity—though it had been months since the cleric had last seen his superior.

First the Kingpriest, now Quarath. Denubis felt a cold lump in the pit of his stomach. As Quarath was leading him out of the Audience Hall, the Kingpriest's musical voice rose. Denubis glanced backward, basking for one more moment in that wondrous light. Then, as he looked away with a sigh, his gaze came to rest upon the black-robed mage. Fistandantilus smiled and nodded. Shuddering, Denubis hurriedly accompanied Quarath out the door.

The two clerics walked through sumptuously decorated corridors until they came to a small chamber, Quarath's own. It, too, was splendidly decorated inside, but Denubis was too nervous to notice any detail.

"Please, sit down, Denubis. I may call you that, since we are comfortably alone."

Denubis didn't know about the comfortably, but they were certainly alone. He sat on the edge of the seat Quarath offered him, accepted a small glass of cordial which he didn't drink, and waited. Quarath talked of inconsequential nothings for a few moments, asking after Denubis's work—he translated passages of the Disks of Mishakal into his native language, Solamnic—and other items in which he obviously wasn't the least bit interested.

Then, after a pause, Quarath said casually, "I couldn't help but hear you questioning the Kingpriest."

Denubis set his cordial down on a table, his hand shaking so he barely avoided spilling it. "I. . . I was . . . simply concerned . . . about—about the young man . . . they arrested erroneously," he stammered faintly.

Quarath nodded gravely. "Very right, too. Very proper. It is written that we should be concerned about our fellows in this world. It becomes you, Denubis, and I shall certainly note that in my yearly report."

"Thank you, Revered Son," Denubis murmured, not certain what else to say.

Quarath said nothing more but sat regarding the cleric opposite with his slanted, elven eyes.

Denubis mopped his face with the sleeve of his robe. It was unbelievably hot in this room. Elves had such thin blood.

"Was there something else?" Quarath asked mildly.

Denubis drew a deep breath. "My lord," he said earnestly, "about that young man. Will he be released? And the kender?" He was suddenly inspired. "I thought perhaps I could be of some help, guide them back to the paths of good. Since the young man is innocent—"

"Who of us is truly innocent?" Quarath questioned, looking at the ceiling as if the gods themselves might write the answer there for him.

"I'm certain that is a very good question," Denubis said meekly, "and one no doubt worthy of study and discussion, but this young man is, apparently innocent—at least as innocent as he's likely to be of anything—" Denubis stopped, slightly confused.

Quarath smiled sadly. "Ah, there, you see?" he said, spreading his hands and turning his gaze upon the cleric. "The fur of the rabbit covers the tooth of the wolf, as the saying goes."

Leaning back in his chair, Quarath once again regarded the ceiling. "The two are being sold in the slave markets tomorrow."

Denubis half rose from his chair. "What? My lord—"

Quarath's gaze instantly fixed itself upon the cleric, freezing the man where he stood.

"Questioning? Again?"

"But . . . he's innocent!" was all Denubis could think of to say.

Quarath smiled again, this time wearily, indulgently.

"You are a good man, Denubis. A good man, a good cleric. A simple man, perhaps, but a good one. This was not a decision we made lightly. We questioned the man. His accounts of where he came from and what he was doing in Istar are confused, to say the least. If he was innocent of the girl's injuries, he undoubtedly has other crimes that are tearing at his soul. That much is visible upon his face. He has no means of support, there was no money on him. He is a vagrant and likely to turn to thievery if left on his own. We are doing him a favor by providing him with a master who will care for him. In time, he can earn his freedom and, hopefully, his soul will have been cleansed of its burden of guilt. As for the kender—" Quarath waved a negligent hand.

"Does the Kingpriest know?" Denubis summoned up courage to ask.

Quarath sighed, and this time the cleric saw a faint wrinkle of irritation appear on the elf's smooth brow. "The Kingpriest has many more pressing issues on his mind, Revered Son Denubis," he said coldly. "He is so good that the pain of this one man's suffering would upset him for days. He did not specifically say the man was to be freed, so we simply removed the burden of this decision from his thoughts."

Seeing Denubis's haggard face fill with doubt, Quarath sat forward, regarding his cleric with a frown. "Very well, Denubis, if you must know—there were some very strange circumstances regarding the young woman's discovery. Not the least of which is that it was instituted, we understand, by the Dark One."

Denubis swallowed and sank back into his seat. The room no longer seemed hot. He shivered. "That is true," he said miserably, passing his hand over his face. "He met me—"

"I know!" Quarath snapped. "He told me. The young woman will stay here with us. She is a Revered Daughter. She wears the medallion of Paladine. She, also, is somewhat confused, but that is to be expected. We can keep an eye on her. But I'm certain you realize how impossible it is that we allow that young man to simply wander off. In the Elder Days, they would have tossed him in a dungeon and thought no more of it. We are more enlightened than that. We will provide a decent home for him and be able to watch over him at the same time."

Quarath makes it sound like a charitable act, selling a man into slavery, Denubis thought in confusion. Perhaps it is. Perhaps I am wrong. As he says, I am a simple man. Dizzily, he rose from his chair. The rich food he had eaten sat in his stomach like a cobblestone. Mumbling an apology to his superior, he started toward the door. Quarath rose, too, a conciliatory smile on his face.

"Come visit with me again, Revered Son," he said, standing by the door. "And do not fear to question us. That is how we learn."

Denubis nodded numbly, then paused. "I—I have one more question, then," he said hesitantly. "You mentioned the Dark One. What do you know of him? I mean, why is he here? He—he frightens me."

Quarath's face was grave, but he did not appear displeased at this question. Perhaps he was relieved that Denubis's mind had turned to another subject. "Who knows anything of the ways of magic-users," he answered, "except that their ways are not our ways, nor yet the ways of the gods. It was for that reason the Kingpriest felt compelled to rid Ansalon of them, as much as was possible. Now they are holed up in their one remaining Tower of High Sorcery in that cast-off Forest of Wayreth. Soon, even that will disappear as their numbers dwindle, since we have closed the schools. You heard about the cursing of the Tower at Palanthas?"

Denubis nodded silently.

"That terrible incident!" Quarath frowned. "It just goes to show you how the gods have cursed these wizards, driving that one poor soul to such madness that he impaled himself upon the gates, bringing down the wrath of the gods and sealing the Tower forever, we suppose. But, what were we discussing?"

"Fistandantilus," Denubis murmured, sorry he had brought it up. Now he wanted only to get back to his room and take his stomach powder.

Quarath raised his feathery eyebrows. "All I know of him is that he was here when I came, some one hundred years ago. He is old—older even than many of my kindred, for there are few even of the eldest of my race who can remember a time when his name was not whispered. But he is human and therefore must use his magic arts to sustain his life. How, I dare not imagine." Quarath looked at Denubis intently. "You understand now, of course, why the Kingpriest keeps him at court?"

"He fears him?" Denubis asked innocently.

Quarath's porcelain smile became fixed for a moment, then it was the smile of a parent explaining a simple matter to a dull child. "No, Revered Son," he said patiently. "Fistandantilus is of great use to us. Who knows the world better? He has traveled its width and breadth. He knows the languages, the customs, the lore of every race on Krynn. His knowledge is vast. He is useful to the Kingpriest, and so we allow him to remain here, rather than banish him to Wayreth, as we have banished his fellows."

Denubis nodded. "I understand," he said, smiling weakly. "And . . . and now, I must go. Thank you for your hospitality, Revered Son, and for clearing up my doubts. I-I feel much better now."

"I am glad to have been able to help," Quarath said gently. "May the gods grant you restful sleep, my son."

"And you as well," Denubis murmured the reply, then left, hearing, with relief, the door shut behind him.

The cleric walked hurriedly past the Kingpriest's audience chamber. Light welled from the door, the sound of the sweet, musical voice tugged at his heart as he went by, but he feared he might be sick and so resisted the temptation to return.

Longing for the peace of his quiet room, Denubis walked quickly through the Temple. He became lost once, taking a wrong turn in the crisscrossing corridors. But a kindly servant led him back the direction he needed to take to reach the part of the Temple where he lived.

This part was austere, compared to that where the Kingpriest and the court resided, although still filled with every conceivable luxury by Krynnish standards. But as Denubis walked the halls, he thought how homey and comforting the soft candlelight appeared. Other clerics passed him with smiles and whispered evening greetings. This was where he belonged. It was simple, like himself.

Heaving another sigh of relief, Denubis reached his own small room and opened the door (nothing was ever locked in the Temple—it showed a distrust of one's fellows) and started to enter. Then he stopped. Out of the corner of his eye he had glimpsed movement, a dark shadow within darker shadows. He stared intently down the corridor. There was nothing there. It was empty.

I *am* getting old. My eyes are playing tricks, Denubis told himself, shaking his head wearily. Walking into the room, his white robes whispering around his ankles, he shut the door firmly, then reached for his stomach powder.

Chapter 3

key rattled in the lock of the cell door.

Tasslehoff sat bolt upright. Pale light crept into the cell through a tiny, barred window set high in the thick, stone wall. Dawn, he thought sleepily. The key rattled again, as if the jailer was having trouble opening the lock. Tas cast an uneasy glance at Caramon on the opposite side of the cell. The big man lay on the stone slab that was his bed without moving or giving any sign that he heard the racket.

A bad sign, Tas thought anxiously, knowing the well-trained warrior (when he wasn't drunk) would once have awakened at the sound of footsteps outside the room. But Caramon had neither moved nor spoken since the guards brought them here yesterday. He had refused food and water (although Tas had assured him it was a cut above most prison food). He lay on the stone slab and stared up at the ceiling until nightfall. Then he had moved, a little at least—he had shut his eyes.

The key was rattling louder than ever, and added to its noise was the sound of the jailer swearing. Hurriedly Tas stood up and crossed the stone floor, plucking straw out of his hair and smoothing his clothes as he went. Spotting a battered stool in the corner, the kender dragged it over to the door, stood upon it, and peered through the barred window in the door down at the jailer on the other side.

"Good morning," Tas said cheerfully. "Having some trouble?"

The jailer jumped three feet at the unexpected sound and nearly dropped his keys. He was small man, wizened and gray as the walls. Glaring up at the kender's face through the bars the jailer snarled and, inserting the key in the lock once more poked and shook it vigorously. A man standing behind the jailer scowled. He was a large, well-built man, dressed in fine clothes and wrapped against the morning chill in a bear-skin cape. In his hand, he held a piece of slate, a bit of chalkrock dangling from it by a leather thong.

"Hurry up," the man snarled at the jailer. "The market opens at midday and I've got to get this lot cleaned up and decent-looking by then."

"Must be broken," muttered the jailer.

"Oh, no, it's not broken," Tas said helpfully. "Actually, in fact, I think your key would fit just fine if my lockpick wasn't in the way."

The jailer slowly lowered the keys and raised his eyes to look balefully at the kender.

"It was the oddest accident," Tas continued. "You see, I was rather bored last night—Caramon fell asleep early—and you had taken away all my things, so, when I just happened to discover that you'd missed a lockpick I keep in my sock, I decided to try it on this door, just to keep my hand in, so to speak, and to see what kind of jails you built back here. You do build a very nice jail, by the way," Tas said solemnly. "One of the nicest I've ever been in—er, one of the nicest I've ever seen. By the way, my name is Tasslehoff Burrfoot." The kender squeezed his hand through the bar in case either of them wanted to shake it. They didn't. "And I'm from Solace. So's my friend. We're here on a sort of mission you might say and—Oh, yes, the lock. Well, you needn't glare at me so, it wasn't *my* fault. In fact, it was your stupid lock that broke my lockpick! One of my best too. My father's," the kender said sadly. "He gave it to me on the day I came of age. I really think," Tas added in a stern voice, "that you could at least apologize."

At this, the jailer made a strange sound, sort of a snort and an explosion. Shaking his ring of keys at the kender, he snapped something incoherent about "rotting in that cell forever" and started walking off, but the man in the bear-skin cape grabbed hold of him.

"Not so fast. I need the one in here."

"I know, I know," the jailer whined in a thin voice, "but you'll have to wait for the locksmith—"

"Impossible. My orders are to put 'im on the block today"

"Well, then you come up with some way to get them outta there." The jailer sneered. "Get the kender a new lockpick. Now, do you want the rest of the lot or not?"

He started to totter off, leaving the bear-skin man staring grimly at the door. "You know where my orders come from," he said in ominous tones.

"My orders come from the same place," the jailer said over his bony shoulder, "and if *they* don't like it they can come *pray* the door open. If that don't work, they can wait for the locksmith, same as everyone else."

"Are you going to let us out?" Tas asked eagerly. "If you are, we might be able to help—" Then a sudden thought crossed his mind. "You're not going to execute us, are you? Because, in that case, I think we'd just as soon wait for the locksmith. . . ."

"Execute!" the bear-skin man growled. "Hasn't been an execution in Istar in ten years. Church forbade it."

"Aye, a quick, clean death was too good for a man," cackled the jailer, who had turned around again. "Now, what do you mean about helping, you little beast?"

"Well," Tas faltered, "if you're not going to execute us, what are you going to do with us, then? I don't suppose you're letting us go? We are innocent, after all. I mean, we didn't—"

"I'm not going to do anything with *you*," the bear-skin man said sarcastically. "It's your friend I want. And, no, they're not letting him go."

"Quick, clean death," the old jailer muttered, grinning toothlessly. "Always a nice crowd gathered to watch, too.

Made a man feel his going out meant something, which is just what Harry Snaggle said to me as they was marching him off to be hung. He hoped there would be a good crowd and there was. Brought a tear to his eye. 'All these people,' he says to me, 'giving up their holiday just to come give me a sendoff.' A gentleman to the end."

"He's going on the block!" the bear-skin man said loudly, ignoring the jailer.

"Quick, clean." The jailer shook his head.

"Well," Tas said dubiously, "I'm not sure what that means, but if you're truly letting us out, perhaps Caramon can help."

The kender disappeared from the window, and they heard him yelling, "Caramon, wake up! They're wanting to let us out and they can't get the door open and I'm afraid it's my fault, well, partly—"

"You realize you've got to take them both," the jailer said cunningly.

"What?" The bear-skin man turned to glare at the jailer. "That was never mentioned—"

"They're to be sold together. Those are my orders and since your orders and my orders come from the same place—"

"Is this in writing?" The man scowled.

"Of course." The jailer was smug.

"I'll lose money! Who'll buy a kender?"

The jailer shrugged. It was none of his concern.

The bear-skin man opened his mouth again, then shut it as another face appeared framed in the cell door. It wasn't the kender's this time. It was the face of a human, a young man, around twenty-eight. The face might once have been handsome, but now the strong jawline was blurred with fat, the brown eyes were lackluster, the curly hair tangled and matted.

"How is Lady Crysania?" Caramon asked.

The bear-skin man blinked in confusion.

"Lady Crysania. They took her to the Temple," Caramon repeated.

The jailer prodded the bear-skin man in the ribs. "You know—the woman he beat up."

"I didn't touch her," Caramon said evenly. "Now, how is she?"

"That's none of your concern," the bear-skin man snapped, suddenly remembering what time it was, "Are you a locksmith? The kender said something about you being able to open the door."

"I'm not a locksmith," Caramon said, "but maybe I can open it." His eyes went to the jailer. "If you don't mind it breaking?"

"Lock's broken now!" the jailer said shrilly. "Can't see as you could hurt it much worse unless you broke the door down."

"That's what I intend to do," Caramon said coolly.

"Break the door down?" the jailer's shrieked. "You're daft! Why—"

"Wait." The bear-skin man had caught a glimpse of Caramon's shoulders and bull-like neck through the bars in the door. "Let's see this. If he does, I'll pay damages."

"You bet you will!" the jailer jabbered. The bear-skin man glanced at him out of the corner of his eye, and the jailer fell silent.

Caramon closed his eyes and drew several deep breaths, letting each out slowly. The bear-skin man and the jailer backed away from the door. Caramon disappeared from sight. They heard a grunt and then the sound of a tremendous blow hitting the solid wooden door. The door shuddered on its hinges, indeed, even the stone walls seemed to shake with the force of the blow. But the door held. The jailer, however, backed up another step, his mouth wide open.

There was another grunt from inside the cell, then another blow. The door exploded with such force that the only remaining, recognizable pieces were the twisted hinges and the lock—still fastened securely to the doorframe. The force of Caramon's momentum sent him flying into the corridor. Muffled sounds of cheering could be heard from surrounding cells where other prisoners had their faces pressed to the bars.

"You'll pay for this!" the jailer squeaked at the bear-skin man.

"It's worth every penny," the man said, helping Caramon to his feet and dusting him off, eyeing him critically at the same time. "Been eating a bit too well, huh? Enjoy your liquor, too, I'll bet? Probably what got you in here. Well, never mind. That's soon mended. Name's—Caramon?"

The big man nodded morosely.

"And I'm Tasslehoff Burrfoot," said the kender, stepping out through the broken door and extending his hand again. "I go everywhere with him, absolutely everywhere. I promised Tika I would and—"

The bear-skin man was writing something down on his slate and only glanced at the kender absently. "Mmmmm, I see."

"Well, now," the kender continued, putting his hand into his pocket with a sigh, "if you'd take these chains off our feet, it would certainly be easier to walk."

"Wouldn't it," the bear-skin man murmured, jotting down some figures on the slate. Adding them up, he smiled. "Go ahead," he instructed the jailer. "Get any others you've got for me today."

The old man shuffled off, first casting a vicious glance at Tas and Caramon.

"You two, sit over there by the wall until we're ready to go," the bear-skin man ordered.

Caramon crouched down on the floor, rubbing his shoulder. Tas sat next to him with a happy sigh. The world outside the jail cell looked brighter already. Just like he'd told Caramon—"Once we're out, we'll have a chance! We've got no chance at all, cooped up in here."

"Oh, by the way," Tas called after the retreating figure of the jailer, "would you please see that my lockpick's returned to me? Sentimental value, you know."

"A chance, huh?" Caramon said to Tas as the blacksmith prepared to bolt on the iron collar. It had taken a while to find one big enough, and Caramon was the last of the slaves to have this sign of his bondage fastened around his neck. The big man winced in pain as the smith soldered the bolt with a red-hot iron. There was a smell of burning flesh.

Tas tugged miserably at his collar and winced in sympathy for Caramon's suffering. "I'm sorry," he said, snuffling. "I didn't know he meant '*on* the block'! I thought he said '*down* the block.' Like, we're going to take a walk 'down the block.' They talk kinda funny back here. Honestly, Caramon . . ."

"That's all right," Caramon said with a sigh. "It's not your fault."

"But it's somebody's fault," Tas said reflectively, watching with interest as the smith slapped grease over Caramon's burn, then inspected his work with a critical eye. More than one blacksmith in Istar had lost his job when a slave-owner turned up, demanding retribution for a runaway slave who had slipped his collar.

"What do you mean?" Caramon muttered dully, his face settling into its resigned, vacant look.

"Well," Tas whispered, with a glance at the smith, "stop and think. Look how you were dressed when we got here. You looked just like a ruffian. Then there was that cleric and those guards turning up, just like they were expecting us. And Lady Crysania, looking like she did."

"You're right," Caramon said, a gleam of life flickering in his dull eyes. The gleam became a flash, igniting a smoldering fire. "Raistlin," he murmured. "He knows I'm going to try and stop him. *He's* done this!"

"I'm not so sure," Tas said after some thought. "I mean, wouldn't he be more likely to just burn you to a crisp or make you into a wall hanging or something like that?"

"No!" Caramon said, and Tas saw excitement in his eyes. "Don't you see? He *wants* me back here . . . to do something. He wouldn't murder us. That . . . that dark elf who works for him told us, remember?"

Tas looked dubious and started to say something, but just then the blacksmith pushed the warrior to his feet. The bearskin man, who had been peering in at them impatiently from the doorway of the smith's shop, motioned to two of his own personal slaves. Hurrying inside, they roughly grabbed hold of Caramon and Tas, shoving them into line with the other slaves. Two more slaves came up and began attaching the leg chains of all the slaves together until they were strung out in a line. Then—at a gesture from the bear-skin man—the wretched living chain of humans, half-elves, and two goblins shuffled forward.

They hadn't taken more than three steps before they were all immediately tangled up by Tasslehoff, who had mistakenly started off in the wrong direction.

After much swearing and a few lashes with a willow stick (first looking to see if any clerics were about), the bear-skin man got the line moving. Tas hopped about trying to get into step. It was only after the kender was twice dragged to his knees, imperiling the entire line again, that Caramon finally wrapped his big arm around his waist, lifted him up—chain and all—and carried him.

"That was kind of fun," Tas commented breathlessly. "Especially where I fell over. Did you see that man's face? I—"

"What did you mean, back there?" Caramon interrupted. "What makes you think Raistlin's not behind this?"

Tas's face grew unusually serious and thoughtful. "Caramon," he said after a moment, putting his arms around Caramon's neck and speaking into his ear to be heard above the rattling of chains and the sounds of the city streets. "Raistlin must have been awfully busy, what with traveling back here and all. Why, it took Par-Salian days to cast that time-traveling spell and he's a really powerful mage. So it must have taken a lot of Raistlin's energy. How could he have possibly done that and done this to us at the same time?"

"Well," Caramon said, frowning. "If he didn't, who did?"

"What about—Fistandantilus?" Tas whispered dramatically.

Caramon sucked in his breath, his face grew dark.

"He—he's a really powerful wizard," Tas reminded him, "and, well, you didn't make any secret of the fact that you've come back here to—uh—well, do him in, so to speak. I mean, you even said that right in the Tower of High Sorcery. And we *know* Fistandantilus can hang around in the Tower. That's where he met Raistlin, wasn't it? What if he was standing there and heard you? I guess he'd be pretty mad."

"Bah! If he's that powerful, he would have just killed me on the spot!" Caramon scowled.

"No, he can't," Tas said firmly. "Look, I've got this all figured out. He can't murder his own pupil's brother. Especially if Raistlin's brought you back here for a reason. Why, for all Fistandantilus knows, Raistlin may love you, deep down inside."

Caramon's face paled, and Tas immediately felt like biting off his tongue. "Anyway," he went on hurriedly, "he can't get rid of you right away. He's got to make it look good."

"So?"

"So—" Tas drew a deep breath. "Well, they don't execute people around here, but they apparently have other ways of dealing with those no one wants hanging around. That cleric and the jailer both talked about executions being 'easy' death compared to what was going on now."

The lash of a whip across Caramon's back ended further conversation. Glaring furiously at the slave who had struck him—an ingratiating, sniveling fellow, who obviously enjoyed his work—Caramon lapsed into gloomy silence, thinking over what Tas had told him. It certainly made sense. He had seen how much power and concentration Par-Salian had exerted casting this difficult spell. Raistlin may be powerful, but not like that! Plus, he was still weak physically.

Caramon suddenly saw everything quite clearly. Tasslehoff's right! We're being set up. Fistandantilus will do away with me somehow and then explain my death to Raistlin as an accident.

Somewhere, in the back of Caramon's mind, he heard a gruff old dwarvish voice say, "I don't know who's the bigger ninny—you or that doorknob of a kender! If either of you make it out of this alive, *I'll* be surprised!" Caramon smiled sadly at the thought of his old friend. But Flint wasn't here, neither was Tanis or anyone else who could advise him. He and Tas were on their own and, if it hadn't been for the kender's impetuous leap into the spell, he might very well have been back here by himself, without anyone! That thought appalled him. Caramon shivered.

"All this means is that I've got to get to this Fistandantilus before he gets to me," he said to himself softly.

The great spires of the Temple looked down on city streets kept scrupulously clean—all except the back alleys. The streets were thronged with people. Temple guards roamed about, keeping order, standing out from the crowd in their colorful mantles and plumed helms. Beautiful women cast admiring glances at the guards from the corners of their eyes as they strolled among the bazaars and shops, their fine gowns sweeping the pavement as they moved. There was one place in the city the women didn't go near, however, though many cast curious glances toward it—the part of the square where the slave market stood.

The slave market was crowded, as usual. Auctions were held once a week—one reason the bear-skin man, who was the manager, had been so eager to get his weekly quotient of slaves from the prisons. Though the money from the sales of prisoners went into the public coffers, the manager got his cut, of course. This week looked particularly promising.

As he had told Tas, there were no longer executions in Istar or parts of Krynn that it controlled. Well, few. The Knights of Solamnia still insisted on punishing knights who betrayed their Order in the old barbaric fashion—slitting the knight's throat with his own sword. But the Kingpriest was counseling with the Knights, and there was hope that soon even that heinous practice would be stopped.

Of course, the halting of executions in Istar had created another problem—what to do with the prisoners, who were increasing in number and becoming a drain on the public coffers. The church, therefore, conducted a study. It was discovered that most prisoners were indigent, homeless, and penniless. The crimes they had committed—thievery, burglary, prostitution, and the like—grew out of this.

"Isn't it logical, therefore," said the Kingpriest to his ministers on the day he made the official pronouncement, "that slavery is not only the answer to the problem of overcrowding in our prisons but is a most kind and beneficent way of dealing with these poor people, whose only crime is that they have been caught in a web of poverty from which they cannot escape?

"Of course it is. It is our duty, therefore, to help them. As slaves, they will be fed and clothed and housed. They will be given everything they lacked that forced them to turn to a life of crime. We will see to it that they are well-treated, of course, and provide that after a certain period of servitude—if they have done well—they may purchase their own freedom. They will then return to us as productive members of society."

The idea was put into effect at once and had been practiced for about ten years now. There had been problems. But these had never reached the attention of the Kingpriest—they had not been serious enough to demand his concern.

Underministers had dealt efficiently with them, and now the system ran quite smoothly. The church had a steady income from the money received for the prison slaves (to keep them separate from slaves sold by private concerns), and slavery even appeared to act as a deterrent from crime.

The problems that had arisen concerned two groups of criminals—kenders and those criminals whose crimes were particularly unsavory. It was discovered that it was impossible to sell a kender to anyone, and it was also difficult to sell a murderer, rapist, the insane, etc. The solutions were simple. Kender were locked up overnight and then escorted to the city gates (this resulted in a small procession every morning). Institutions had been created to handle the more obdurate type of criminal.

It was to the dwarven head of one of these institutions that the bear-skin man stood talking animatedly that morning, pointing at Caramon as he stood with the other prisoners in the filthy, foul-smelling pen behind the block, and making a dramatic motion of knocking a door down with his shoulder.

The head of the institution did not seem impressed. This was not unusual, however. He had learned, long ago, that to seem impressed over a prisoner resulted in the asking price doubling on the spot. Therefore, the dwarf scowled at Caramon, spit on the ground, crossed his arms and, planting his feet firmly on the pavement, glared up at the bear-skin man.

"He's out of shape, too fat. Plus he's a drunk, look at his nose." The dwarf shook his head. "And he doesn't look mean. What did you say he did? Assaulted a cleric? Humpf!" The dwarf snorted. "The only thing it looks like he could assault'd be a wine jug!"

The bear-skin man was accustomed to this, of course.

"You'd be passing up the chance of a lifetime, Rockbreaker" he said smoothly. "You should have seen him bash that door down. I've never seen such strength in any man. Perhaps he is overweight, but that's easily cured. Fix him up and he'll be a heartthrob. The ladies'll adore him. Look at those melting brown eyes and that wavy hair." The bearskin man lowered his voice. "It would be a real shame to lose him to the mines. . . . I tried to keep word of what he had done quiet, but Haarold got wind of it, I'm afraid."

Both the bear-skin man and the dwarf glanced at a human standing some distance away, talking and laughing with several of his burly guards. The dwarf stroked his beard, keeping his face impassive.

The bear-skin man went on, "Haarold's sworn to have him at all costs. Says he'll get the work of two ordinary humans out of him. Now, you being a preferred customer, I'll try to swing things your direction."

"Let Haarold have him," growled the dwarf. "Fat slob."

But the bear-skin man saw the dwarf regarding Caramon with a speculative eye. Knowing from long experience when to talk and when to keep quiet, the bear-skin man bowed to the dwarf and went on his way, rubbing his hands.

Overhearing this conversation, and seeing the dwarf's gaze run over him like a man looks at a prize pig, Caramon felt the sudden, wild desire to break out of his bonds, crash through the pen where he stood caged, and throttle both the bear-skin man and the dwarf. Blood hammered in his brain, he strained against his bonds, the muscles in his arms rippled—a sight that caused the dwarf to open his eyes wide and caused the guards standing around the pen to draw their swords from their scabbards. But Tasslehoff suddenly jabbed him in the ribs with his elbow.

"Caramon, look!" the kender said in excitement.

For a moment, Caramon couldn't hear over the throbbing in his ears. Tas poked him again.

"Look, Caramon. Over there, at the edge of the crowd, standing by himself. See?"

Caramon drew a shaking breath and forced himself to calm down. He looked over to where the kender was pointing, and suddenly the hot blood in his veins ran cold.

Standing on the fringes of the crowd was a black-robed figure. He stood alone. Indeed, there was even a wide, empty circle around him. None in the crowd came near him. Many made detours, going out of their way to avoid coming close to him. No one spoke to him, but all were aware of his presence. Those near him, who had been talking animatedly, fell into uncomfortable silence, casting nervous glances his direction.

The man's robes were a deep black, without ornamentation. No silver thread glittered on his sleeves, no border surrounded the black hood he wore pulled low over his face. He carried no staff, no familiar walked by his side. Let other mages wear runes of warding and protection, let other mages carry staves of power or have animals do their bidding. This man needed none. His power sprang from within—so great, it had spanned the centuries, spanned even planes of existence. It could be felt, it shimmered around him like the heat from the smith's furnace.

He was tall and well-built, the black robes fell from shoulders that were slender but muscular. His white hands—the only parts of his body that were visible—were strong and delicate and supple. Though so old that few on Krynn could venture even to guess his age, he had the body of one young and strong. Dark rumors told how he used his magic arts to overcome the debilities of age.

And so he stood alone, as if a black sun had been dropped into the courtyard. Not even the glitter of his eyes could be seen within the dark depths of his hood.

"Who's that?" Tas asked a fellow prisoner conversationally, nodding at the black-robed figure.

"Don't you know?" the prisoner said nervously, as if reluctant to reply.

"I'm from out of town," Tas apologized.

"Why, that's the Dark One—Fistandantilus. You've heard of him, I suppose?"

"Yes," Tas said, glancing at Caramon as much as to say *I told you so!* "We've heard of him."

Chapter 4

When Crysania first awakened from the spell Paladine had cast upon her, she was in such a state of bewilderment and confusion that the clerics were greatly concerned, fearing her ordeal had unbalanced her mind.

She spoke of Palanthas, so they assumed she must come from there. But she called continually for the Head of her Order—someone named Elistan. The clerics were familiar with the Heads of all the Orders on Krynn and this Elistan was not known. But she was so insistent that there was, at first, some fear that something might have happened to the current Head in Palanthas. Messengers were hastily dispatched.

Then, too, Crysania spoke of a Temple in Palanthas, where no Temple existed. Finally she talked quite wildly of dragons and the "return of the gods," which caused those in the room—Quarath and Elsa, head of the Revered Daughters—to look at each other in horror and make the signs of protection against blasphemy. Crysania was given an herbal potion, which calmed her, and eventually she fell asleep. The two stayed with her for long moments after she slept, discussing her case in low voices. Then the Kingpriest entered the room, coming to allay their fears.

"I cast an augury," said the musical voice, "and was told that Paladine called her to him to protect her from a spell of evil magic that had been used upon her. I don't believe any of us find that difficult to doubt."

Quarath and Elsa shook their head, exchanging knowing glances. The Kingpriest's hatred of magic-users was well known.

"She has been with Paladine, therefore, living in that wondrous realm which we seek to recreate upon this soil. Undoubtedly, while there, she was given knowledge of the future. She speaks of a beautiful Temple being built in Palanthas. Have we not plans to build such a Temple? She talks of this Elistan, who is probably some cleric destined to rule there."

"But . . . dragons, return of the gods?" murmured Elsa.

"As to the dragons," the Kingpriest said in a voice radiating warmth and amusement, "that is probably some tale of her childhood that haunted her in her illness, or perhaps had something to do with the spell cast upon her by the magic-user." His voice became stern. "It is said, you know, that the wizards have the power to make people see that which does not exist. As for her talk of the 'return of the gods'. . ."

The Kingpriest was silent for a moment. When he spoke again, it was with a hushed and breathless quality. "You two, my closest advisors, know of the dream in my heart. You know that someday—and that day is fast approaching—I will go to the gods and demand their help to fight the evil that is still present among us. On that day, Paladine himself will heed my prayers. He will come to stand at my side, and together we will battle the darkness until it is forever vanquished! This is what she has foreseen! This is what she means by the 'return of the gods!'"

Light filled the room, Elsa whispered a prayer, and even Quarath lowered his eyes.

"Let her sleep," said the Kingpriest. "She will be better by morning. I will mention her in my prayers to Paladine."

He left the room and it grew darker with his passing. Elsa stood looking after him in silence. Then, as the door shut to Crysania's chamber, the elven woman turned to Quarath.

"Does he have the power?" Elsa asked her male counterpart as he stood staring thoughtfully at Crysania. "Does he truly intend to do . . . what he spoke of doing?"

"What?" Quarath's thoughts had been far away. He glanced after the Kingpriest. "Oh, that? Of course he has the power. You saw how he healed this young woman. And the gods speak to him through the augury, or so he claims. When was the last time you healed someone, Revered Daughter?"

"Then you believe all that about Paladine taking her soul and letting her see the future?" Elsa appeared amazed. "You believe he truly healed her?"

"I believe there is something very strange about this young woman and about those two who came with her," Quarath said gravely. "I will take care of *them*. You keep an eye on her. As for the Kingpriest"—Quarath shrugged—"let him call down the power of the gods. If they come down to fight for him, fine. If not, it doesn't matter to us. We know who does the work of the gods on Krynn."

"I wonder," remarked Elsa, smoothing Crysania's dark hair back from her slumbering face. "There was a young girl in our Order who had the power of true healing. That young girl who was seduced by the Solamnic knight. What was his name?"

"Soth," said Quarath. "Lord Soth, of Dargaard Keep. Oh, I don't doubt it. You occasionally find some, particularly among the very young or the very old, who have the power. Or think they do. Frankly, I am convinced most of it is simply a result of people wanting to believe in something so badly that they convince themselves it is true. Which doesn't hurt any of us. Watch this young woman closely, Elsa. If she continues to talk about such things in the morning, after she is recovered, we may need to take drastic measures. But, for now—"

He fell silent. Elsa nodded. Knowing that the young woman would sleep soundly under the influence of the potion, the two of them left Crysania alone, asleep in a room in the great Temple of Istar.

Crysania woke the next morning feeling as if her head were stuffed with cotton. There was a bitter taste in her mouth and she was terribly thirsty. Dizzily, she sat up, trying to piece together her thoughts. Nothing made any sense. She had a vague, horrifying memory of a ghastly creature from beyond the grave approaching her. Then she had been with Raistlin in the Tower of High Sorcery, and then a dim memory of being surrounded by mages dressed in white, red, and black, an impression of singing stones, and a feeling of having taken a long journey.

She also had a memory of awakening and finding herself in the presence of a man whose beauty had been overpowering, whose voice filled her mind and her soul with peace. But he said he was the Kingpriest and that she was in the Temple of the Gods in Istar. That made no sense at all. She remembered calling for Elistan, but no one seemed to have heard of him. She told them about him—how he was healed by Goldmoon, cleric of Mishakal, how he led the fight against the evil dragons, and how he was telling the people about the return of the gods. But her words only made the clerics regard her with pity and alarm. Finally, they gave her an odd-tasting potion to drink, and she had fallen asleep.

Now she was still confused but determined to find out where she was and what was happening. Getting out of bed, she forced herself to wash as she did every morning, then she sat down at the strange-looking dressing table and calmly brushed and braided her long, dark hair. The familiar routine made her feel more relaxed.

She even took time to look around the bedroom, and she couldn't help but admire its beauty and splendor. But she did think, however, that it seemed rather out of place in a Temple devoted to the gods, if that was truly where she was. Her bedroom in her parent's home in Palanthas had not been half so splendid, and it had been furnished with every luxury money could buy.

Her mind went suddenly to what Raistlin had shown her—the poverty and want so near the Temple—and she flushed uncomfortably.

"Perhaps this is a guest room," Crysania said to herself, speaking out loud, finding the familiar sound of her own voice comforting. "After all, the guest rooms in our new Temple are certainly designed to make our guests comfortable. Still"—she frowned, her gaze going to a costly golden statue of a dryad, holding a candle in her golden hands—"that is extravagant. It would feed a family for months."

How thankful she was he couldn't see this! She would speak to the Head of this Order, whoever he was. (Surely she must have been mistaken, thinking he said he was the Kingpriest!)

Having made up her mind to action, feeling her head clear, Crysania removed the night clothes she had been wearing and put on the white robes she found laid out neatly at the foot of her bed.

What quaint, old-fashioned robes, she noticed, slipping them over her head. Not at all like the plain, austere white robes worn by those of her Order in Palanthas. These were heavily decorated. Golden thread sparkled on the sleeves and hem, crimson and purple ribbon ornamented the front, and a heavy golden belt gathered the folds around her slender waist. More extravagance. Crysania bit her lip in displeasure, but she also took a peep at herself in a gilt-framed mirror. It certainly was becoming, she had to admit, smoothing the folds of the gown.

It was then that she felt the note in her pocket.

Reaching inside, she pulled out a piece of rice paper that had been folded into quarters. Staring at it curiously, wondering idly if the owner of the robes had left it by accident, she was startled to see it addressed to herself. Puzzled, she opened it.

Lady Crysania,

I knew you intended to seek my help in returning to the past in an effort to prevent the young mage, Raistlin, from carrying out the evil he plots. Upon your way to us, however, you were atacked by a death knight. To save you, Paladine took your soul to his heavenly dwelling. There are none among us now, even Elistan himself, who can bring you back. Only those clerics living at the time of the Kingpriest have this power. So we have sent you back in time to Istar, right before the Cataclysm, in the company of Raistlin's brother, Caramon. We send you to fulfill a twofold purpose. First, to heal you of your grievous wound and, second, to allow you to try to succeed in your efforts to save the young mage from himself.

If, in this, you see the workings of the gods, perhaps then you may consider your efforts blessed. I would counsel only this—that the gods work in ways strange to mortal men, since we see only that part of the picture being painted around us. I had hoped to discuss this with you personally, before you left, but that proved impossible. I can only caution you of one thing—beware of Raistlin.

You are virtuous, steadfast in your faith, and proud of both your virtue and your faith. This is a deadly combination, my dear. He will take full advantage of it.

Remember this, too. You and Caramon have gone back in dangerous times. The days of the Kingpriest are numbered. Caramon is on a mission that could prove dangerous to his life.

But you, Crysania, are in danger of both your life and your soul. I foresee that you will be forced to choose—to save one, you must give up the other. There are many ways for you to leave this time period, one of which is through Caramon. May Paladine be with you.

Par-Salian
Order of the White Robes
The Tower of High Sorcery
Wayreth

Crysania sank down on the bed, her knees giving way beneath her. The hand that held the letter trembled. Dazedly, she stared at it, reading it over and over without comprehending the words. After a few moments, however, she grew calmer and forced herself to go over each word, reading one sentence at a time until she was certain she had grasped the meaning.

This took nearly a half hour of reading and pondering. At last she believed she understood. Or at least most of it. The memory of why she had been journeying to the Forest of Wayreft returned. So, Par-Salian had known. He had been expecting her. All the better. And he was right—the attack by the death knight had obviously been an example of Paladine's intervention, insuring that she come back here to the past. As for that remark about her faith and her virtue—!

Crysania rose to her feet. Her pale face was fixed in firm resolve, there was a faint spot of color in each cheek, and her eyes glittered in anger. She was only sorry she had *not* been able to confront him with that in person! How dare he?

Her lips drawn into a tight, straight line, Crysania refolded the note, drawing her fingers across it swiftly, as though she would like to tear it apart. A small golden box—the kind of box used by ladies of the court to hold their jewelry—stood on the dressing table beside the gilt-edged mirror and the brush. Picking up the box, Crysania withdrew the small key from the lock, thrust the letter inside, and snapped the lid shut. She inserted the key, twisted it, and heard the lock click. Dropping the key into the pocket where she had found the note, Crysania looked once more into the mirror.

She smoothed the black hair back from her face, drew up the hood of her robe, and draped it over her head. Noticing the flush on her cheeks, Crysania forced herself to relax, allow her anger to seep away. The old mage meant well, after all, she reminded herself. And how could one of magic possibly understand one of faith? She could rise above petty anger. She was, after all, hovering on the edge of her moment of greatness. Paladine was with her. She could almost sense his presence. And the man she had met was truly the Kingpriest!

She smiled, remembering the feeling of goodness he had inspired. How could he have been responsible for the Cataclysm? No, her soul refused to believe it. History must have maligned him. True, she had been with him for only a few seconds, but a man so beautiful, so good and holy—responsible for such death and destruction? It was impossible! Perhaps she would be able to vindicate him. Perhaps that was another reason Paladine had sent her back here—to discover the truth!

Joy filled Crysania's soul. And, at that moment, she heard her joy answered, it seemed, in the pealing of the bells ringing for Morning Prayers. The beauty of the music brought tears to her eyes. Her heart bursting with excitement and happiness, Crysania left her room and hurried out into the magnificent corridors, nearly running into Elsa.

"In the name of the gods," exclaimed Elsa in astonishment, "can it be possible? How are you feeling?"

"I am feeling much better, Revered Daughter," Crysania said in some confusion, remembering that what they had heard her say earlier must have seemed to be wild and incoherent ramblings. "As-as though I had awakened from a strange and vivid dream."

"Paladine be praised," murmured Elsa, regarding Crysania with narrowed eyes and a sharp, penetrating gaze.

"I have not neglected to do so, you may be certain," said Crysania sincerely. In her own joy, she did not notice the elf woman's odd look. "Were you going to Morning Prayers? If so, may I accompany you?" She looked around the splendid building in awe. "I fear it will be some time before I learn my way around."

"Of course," Elsa said, recovering herself. "This way." They started back down the corridor.

"I was also concerned about the—the young man who was . . . was found with me" Crysania stammered, suddenly remembering she knew very little about the circumstances regarding her appearance in this time.

Elsa's face grew cold and stern. "He is where he will be well cared for, my dear. Is he a friend of yours?"

"No, of course not," Crysania said quickly, remembering her last encounter with the drunken Caramon. "He—he was my escort. Hired escort," she stammered, realizing suddenly that she was very poor at lying.

"He is at the School of the Games," Elsa replied. "It would be possible to send him a message, if you are concerned."

Crysania had no idea what this school was, and she was afraid to ask too many more questions. Thanking Elsa, therefore, she let the matter drop, her mind at ease. At least now she knew where Caramon was and that he was safe. Feeling reassured, knowing that she had a way back to her own time, she allowed herself to relax completely.

"Ah, look, my dear," Elsa said, "here comes another to inquire after your health."

"Revered Son," Crysania bowed in reverence as Quarath came up to the two women. Thus she missed his swift glance of inquiry at Elsa and the elfwoman's slight nod.

"I am overjoyed to see you up and around," Quarath said, taking Crysania's hand and speaking with such feeling and warmth that the young woman flushed with pleasure. "The Kingpriest spent the night in prayer for your recovery. This proof of his faith and power will be extremely gratifying. We will present you to him formally this evening. But, now"—he interrupted whatever Crysania had been about to say—"I am keeping you from Prayers. Please, do not let me detain you further."

Bowing to them both with exquisite grace, Quarath walked past, heading down the corridor.

"Isn't he attending services?" Crysania asked, her gaze following the cleric.

"No, my dear," Elsa said, smiling at Crysania's naiveté, "he attends the Kingpriest in his own private ceremonies early each morning. Quarath is, after all, second only to the Kingpriest and has matters of great importance to deal with each day. One might say that, if the Kingpriest is the heart and soul of the church, Quarath is the brain."

"My, how odd," murmured Crysania, her thoughts on Elistan.

"Odd, my dear?" Elsa said, with a slightly reproving air. "The Kingpriest's thoughts are with the gods. He cannot be expected to deal with such mundane matters as the day-to-day business of the church, can he?"

"Oh, of course not." Crysania flushed in embarrassment.

How provincial she must seem to these people; how simple and backward. As she followed Elsa down the bright and airy halls, the beautiful music of the bells and the glorious sound of a children's choir filled her very soul with ecstasy. Crysania remembered the simple service Elistan held every morning. And he still did most of the work of the church himself!

That simple service seemed shabby to her now, Elistan's work demeaning. Certainly it had taken a toll on his health. Perhaps, she thought with a pang of regret, he might not have shortened his own life if he had been surrounded by people like these to help him.

Well, that would change, Crysania resolved suddenly, realizing that this must be another reason why she had been sent back—she had been chosen to restore the glory of the church! Trembling in excitement, her mind already busy with plans for change, Crysania asked Elsa to describe the inner workings of the church hierarchy. Elsa was only too glad to expand upon it as the two continued down the corridor.

Lost in her interest in the conversation, attentive to Elsa's every word, Crysania thought no more of Quarath, who was—at that moment—quietly opening the door to her bedroom and slipping inside.

Chapter 5

Quarath found the letter from Par-Salian within a matter of moments. He had noticed, almost immediately on entering, that the golden box that stood on top of the dressing table had been moved. A quick search of the drawers revealed it and, since he had the master key to the locks of every box and drawer and door in the Temple, he opened it easily.

The letter itself, however, was not so easily understood by the cleric. It took him only seconds to absorb its contents. These would remain imprinted on his mind; Quarath's phenomenal ability to memorize instantly anything he saw being one of his greatest gifts. So it was that he had the complete text of the letter locked in his mind within seconds. But, he realized, it would take hours of pondering to make sense of it.

Absently, Quarath folded the parchment and put it back into the box, then returned the box to its exact position within the drawer. He locked it with the key, glanced through the other drawers without much interest, and—finding nothing—left the young woman's room, lost in thought.

So perplexing and disturbing were the contents of the letter that he canceled his appointments for that morning or shifted them onto the shoulders of underlings. Then he went to his study. Here he sat, recalling each word, each phrase.

At last, he had it figured out—if not to his complete satisfaction, then, at least, enough to allow him to determine a course of action. Three things were apparent. One, the young woman might be a cleric, but she was involved with magic-users and was, therefore, suspect. Two, the Kingpriest was in danger. That was not surprising, the magic-users had good reason to hate and fear the man. Three, the young man who had been found with Crysania was, undoubtedly, an assassin. Crysania, herself might be an accomplice.

Quarath smiled grimly, congratulating himself on having already taken appropriate measures to deal with the threat. He had seen to it that the young man—Caramon was his name apparently—was serving his time in a place where unfortunate accidents occurred from time to time.

As for Crysania, she was safely within the walls of the Temple where she could be watched and subtly interrogated.

Breathing easier, his mind clearing, the cleric rang for the servant to bring his lunch, thankful to know that, for the moment at least, the Kingpriest was safe.

Quarath was an unusual man in many respects, not the least of which was that, though highly ambitious, he knew the limits of his own abilities. He needed the Kingpriest, he had no desire to take his place. Quarath was content to bask in the light of his master, all the while extending his own control and authority and power over the world—all in the name of the church.

And, as he extended his own authority, so he extended the power of his race. Imbued with a sense of their superiority over all others, as well as with a sense of their own innate goodness, the elves were a moving force behind the church.

It was unfortunate, Quarath felt, that the gods had seen fit to create other, weaker races. Races such as humans, who—with their short and frantic lives—were easy targets for the temptations of evil. But the elves were learning to deal with this. If they could not completely wipe out the evil in the world (and they were working on it), then they could at least bring it under control. It was freedom that brought about evil—freedom of choice. Especially to humans, who continually abused this gift. Give them strict rules to follow, make it clear what was right and what was wrong in no uncertain terms, restrict this wild freedom that they misused. Thus, Quarath believed, the humans would fall in line. They would be content.

As for the other races on Krynn, gnomes and dwarves and (sigh) kender, Quarath (and the church) was rapidly forcing them into small, isolated territories where they could cause little trouble and would, in time, probably die out. (This plan was working well with the gnomes and the dwarves, who hadn't much use for the rest of Krynn anyhow. Unfortunately, however, the kender didn't take to it at all and were still happily wandering about the world, causing no end of trouble and enjoying life thoroughly.)

All of this passed through Quarath's mind as he ate his lunch and began to make his plans. He would do nothing in haste about this Lady Crysania. That was not his way, nor the way of the elves, for that matter. Patience in all things. Watch. Wait. He needed only one thing now, and that was more information. To this end, he rang a small golden bell. The young acolyte who had taken Denubis to the Kingpriest appeared so swiftly and quietly at the summons that he might have slipped beneath the door instead of opening it.

"What is your bidding, Revered Son?"

"Two small tasks," Quarath said without looking up, being engaged in writing a note. "Take this to Fistandantilus. It has been some time since he was my guest at dinner, and I desire to talk with him."

"Fistandantilus is not here, my lord," said the acolyte. "In fact, I was on my way to report this to you."

Quarath raised his head in astonishment.

"Not here?"

"No, Revered Son. He left last night, or so we suppose. At least that was the last anyone saw of him. His room is empty, his things gone. It is believed, from certain things he said, that he has gone to the Tower of High Sorcery at Wayreth. Rumor has it that the wizards are holding a Conclave there, though none know for certain."

"A Conclave," Quarath repeated, frowning. He was silent a moment, tapping the paper with the tip of the quill. Wayreth was far away . . . still, perhaps it was not far enough. . . . Cataclysm . . . that odd word that had been used in the letter. Could it be possible that the magic-users were plotting some devastating catastrophe? Quarath felt chilled. Slowly, he crumpled the invitation he had been penning.

"Have his movements been traced?"

"Of course, Revered Son. As much as is possible with him. He has not left the Temple for months, apparently. Then, yesterday, he was seen in the slave market."

"The slave market?" Quarath felt the chill spread throughout his body. "What business did he have there?"

"He bought two slaves, Revered Son."

Quarath said nothing, interrogating the cleric with a look.

"He did not purchase the slaves himself, my lord. The purchase was made through one of his agents."

"Which slaves?" Quarath knew the answer.

"The ones that were accused of assaulting the female cleric, Revered Son."

"I gave orders that those two were to be sold either to the dwarf or the mines."

"Barak did his best and, indeed, the dwarf bid for them, my lord. But the Dark One's agents outbid him. There was nothing Barak could do. Think of the scandal. Besides, his agent sent them to the school anyway—"

"Yes," Quarath muttered. So, it was all falling into place. Fistandantilus had even had the temerity to purchase the young man, the assassin! Then he had vanished. Gone to report, undoubtedly. But why should the mages bother with assassins? Fistandantilus himself could have murdered the Kingpriest on countless occasions. Quarath had the unpleasant impression that he had inadvertently walked from a clear, well-lighted path into a dark and treacherous forest.

He sat in troubled silence for so long that the young acolyte cleared his throat as a subtle reminder of his presence three times before the cleric noticed him.

"You had another task for me, Revered Son?"

Quarath nodded slowly. "Yes, and this news makes this task even more important. I wish you to undertake it yourself. I must talk to the dwarf."

The acolyte bowed and left. There was no need to ask who Quarath meant—there was only one dwarf in Istar.

Just who Arack Rockbreaker was or where he came from no one knew. He never made reference to his past and generally scowled so ferociously if this subject came up that it was usually immediately dropped. There were several interesting speculations concerning this, the favorite being that he was an outcast from Thorbardin—ancient home of the mountain dwarves, where he had committed some crime resulting in exile. Just what that might have been, no one knew. Nor did anyone take into account the fact that dwarves never punished any crime by exile; execution being considered more humane.

Other rumors insisted he was actually a Dewar—a race of evil dwarves nearly exterminated by their cousins and now driven to living a wretched, embittered existence in the very bowels of the world. Though Arack didn't particularly look or act like a Dewar, this rumor was popular due to the fact that Arack's favorite (and only) companion was an ogre. Other rumor had it that Arack didn't even come from Ansalon at all, but from somewhere over the sea.

Certainly, he was the meanest looking of his race anyone could remember seeing. The jagged scars that crossed his face vertically gave him a perpetual scowl. He was not fat, there wasn't a wasted ounce on his frame. He moved with the grace of a feline and, when he stood, planted his feet so firmly that they seemed part of the ground itself.

Wherever he came from, Arack had made Istar his home for so many years now that the subject of his origin rarely came up. He and the ogre, whose name was Raag, had come for the Games in the old days when the Games had been real. They immediately became great favorites with the crowds. People in Istar still told how Raag and Arack defeated the mighty minotaur, Darmoork, in three rounds. It started when Darmoork hurled the dwarf clear out of the arena. Raag, in a berserk fit of anger, lifted the minotaur off his feet and—ignoring several terrible stab wounds—impaled him upon the huge Freedom Spire in the center of the ring.

Though neither the dwarf (who survived only by the fact that a cleric had been standing in the street when the dwarf sailed over the arena wall and landed practically at his feet) nor the ogre won his freedom that day, there was no doubt who had been winner of the contest. (Indeed, it was many days before anyone reached the Golden Key on the Spire, since it took that long to remove the remains of the minotaur.)

Arack related the gruesome details of this fight to his two new slaves.

"That's how I got this old cracked face of mine," the dwarf said to Caramon as he led the big man and the kender through the streets of Istar. "And that's how me and Raag made our name in the Games."

"What games?" asked Tas, stumbling over his chains and sprawling flat on his face, to the great delight of the crowd in the market place.

Arack scowled in irritation. "Take those durn things off 'im" he ordered the gigantic, yellow-skinned ogre, who was acting as guard. "I guess you won't run off and leave yer friend behind, will you?" The dwarf studied Tas intently. "No, I didn't think so. They said you had a chance to run away once and you didn't. Just mind you don't run away on me!" Arack's natural scowl deepened. "I'd have never bought a kender, but I didn't have much choice. *They* said you two was to be sold together. Just remember that—as far as I'm concerned—yer worthless. Now, what fool question was you asking?"

"How are you going to get the chains off? Don't you need a key? Oh—" Tas watched in delighted astonishment as the ogre took the chains in either hand and, with a quick jerk, yanked them apart.

"Did you see that, Caramon?" Tas asked as the ogre picked him up and set him on his feet, giving him a push that nearly sent the kender into the dirt again. "He's really strong! I never met an ogre before. What was I saying? Oh, the games. What games?"

"Why, *the Games*," Arack snapped in exasperation.

Tas glanced up at Caramon, but the big man shrugged and shook his head, frowning. This was obviously something everyone knew about here. Asking too many questions would seem suspicious. Tas cast about in his mind, dragging up every memory and every story he had ever heard about the ancient days before the Cataclysm. Suddenly he caught his breath. "The Games!" he said to Caramon, forgetting the dwarf was listening. "The great Games of Istar! Don't you remember?"

Caramon's face grew grim.

"You mean that's where we're going?" Tas turned to the dwarf, his eyes wide. "We're going to be gladiators? And fight in the arena, with the crowd watching and all! Oh, Caramon, think of it! The great Games of Istar! Why I've heard stories—"

"So have I," the big man said slowly, "and you can forget it, dwarf. I've killed men before, I admit—but only when it was my life or theirs. I never enjoyed killing. I can still see their faces, sometimes, at night. I won't murder for sport!"

He said this so sternly that Raag glanced questioningly at the dwarf and raised his club slightly, an eager look on his yellow, warty face. But Arack glared at him and shook his head.

Tas was regarding Caramon with new respect. "I never thought of that," the kender said softly. "I guess you're right, Caramon." He turned to the dwarf again. "I'm really sorry, Arack, but we won't be able to fight for you."

Arack cackled. "You'll fight. Why? Because it's the only way to get that collar off yer neck, that's why."

Caramon shook his head stubbornly. "I won't kill—"

The dwarf snorted. "Where have you two been living? At the bottom of the Sirrion? Or are they all as dumb as you in Solace? No one fights to kill in the arena anymore." Arack's eyes grew misty. He rubbed them with a sigh. "Those days are gone for good, more's the pity. It's all fake."

"Fake?" Tas repeated in astonishment. Caramon glowered at the dwarf and said nothing, obviously not believing a word.

"There hasn't been a real, true fight in the old arena in ten years," Arack avowed. "It all started with the elves"—the dwarf spat on the ground. "Ten years ago, the elven clerics—curse them to the Abyss where they belong—convinced the Kingpriest to put an end to the Games. Called 'em 'barbaric'!

Barbaric, hah!" The dwarf's scowl twisted into a snarl, then—once more—he sighed and shook his head.

"All the great gladiators left," Arack said wistfully, his eyes looking back to that glorious time. "Danark the Hobgoblin—as vicious a fighter as you'll ever come across. And Old Josepf One-Eye. Remember him, Raag?" The ogre nodded sadly. "Claimed he was a Knight of Solamnia, old Josepf did. Always fought in full battle armor. They all left, except me and Raag." A gleam appeared deep in the dwarf's cold eyes. "We didn't have nowhere to go, you see, and besides—I had a kind of feeling that the Games weren't over. Not yet."

Arack and Raag stayed in Istar. Keeping their quarters inside the deserted arena, they became, as it were, unofficial caretakers. Passers-by saw them there daily—Raag lumbering among the stands, sweeping the aisles with a crude broom or just sitting, staring down dully into the arena where Arack worked, the dwarf lovingly tending the machines in the Death Pits, keeping them oiled and running. Those who saw the dwarf sometimes noticed a strange smile on his bearded, broken-nosed face.

Arack was right. The Games hadn't been banned many months before the clerics began noticing that their peaceful city wasn't so peaceful anymore. Fights broke out in bars and taverns with alarming frequency, there were brawls in the streets and once, even, a full-scale riot. There were reports that the Games had gone underground (literally) and were now being held in caves outside of town. The discovery of several mauled and mutilated bodies appeared to bear this out. Finally, in desperation, a group of human and elf lords sent a delegation to the Kingpriest to request that the Games be started again.

"Just as a volcano must erupt to let the steam and poisonous vapors escape from the ground," said one elflord, "so it seems that humans, in particular, use the Games as an outlet for their baser emotions."

While this speech certainly did nothing to endear the elflord to his human counterparts, they were forced to admit there was some justification to it. At first, the Kingpriest wouldn't hear of it. He had always abhorred the brutal contests. Life was a sacred gift of the gods, not something to be taken away just to provide pleasure to a bloodthirsty crowd.

"And then it was me gave 'em their answer," Arack said smugly. "They weren't going to let me in their fine and fancy Temple." The dwarf grinned. "But no one keeps Raag out of wherever he's a mind to go. So they hadn't much choice.

" 'Start the Games again,' I told 'em, and they looked down at their long noses at me. 'But there needn't be no killing,' I says. 'No real killing, that is. Now, listen me out. You've seen the street actors do Huma, ain't you? You've seen the knight fall to the ground, bleedin' and moanin' and floppin' around. Yet five minutes later he's up and drinking ale at the tavern down the block. I've done a bit of street work in my time, and . . . well . . . watch this. Come here, Raag.'

"Raag came over, a big grin on his ugly, yellow face.

" 'Give me your sword, Raag,' I orders. Then, before they could say a word, I plunges the sword in Raag's gut. You shoulda seen him. Blood all over! Running down my hands, spurting from his mouth. He gave a great bellow and fell to the floor, twitchin' and groanin'.

"You shoulda heard 'em yell," the dwarf said gleefully, shaking his head over the memory. "I thought we was gonna have to pick them elflords up off the floor. So, before they could call the guards to come haul me away, I kicked old Raag, here.

" 'You can get up now, Raag,' I says.

"And he sat up, giving them a big grin. Well, they all started talking at once." The dwarf mimicked high-pitched elven voices.

" 'Remarkable! How is it done? This could be the answer—' "

"How *did* you do it?" Tas asked eagerly.

Arack shrugged. "You'll learn. A lot of chicken blood, a sword with a blade that collapses down into the handle—it's simple. That's what I told 'em. Plus, it's easy to teach gladiators how to act like they're hurt, even a dummy like old Raag here."

Tas glanced at the ogre apprehensively, but Raag was only grinning fondly at the dwarf. "Most of 'em beefed up their fights anyway, to make it look good for the gulls—audience, I should say. Well, the Kingpriest, he went for it and"—the dwarf drew himself up proudly— "he even made me Master. And that's my title, now. Master of the Games."

"I don't understand," Caramon said slowly. "You mean people pay to be tricked? Surely they must have figured it out—"

"Oh, sure," Arack sneered. "We've never made no big secret of it. And now it's the most popular sport on Krynn. People travel fer hundreds of miles to see the Games. The elflords come—and even the Kingpriest himself, sometimes. Well, here we are," Arack said, coming to a halt outside a huge stadium and looking up at it with pride.

It was made of stone and was ages old, but what it might have been built for originally, no one remembered. On Game days, bright flags fluttered from the tops of the stone towers and it would have been thronged with people. But there were no Games today, nor would there be until summer's end. It was gray and colorless, except for the garish paintings on the walls portraying great events in the history of the sport. A few children stood around the outside, hoping for a glimpse of one of their heroes. Snarling at them, Arack motioned to Raag to open the massive, wooden doors.

"You mean no one gets killed," Caramon persisted, staring somberly at the arena with its bloody paintings.

The dwarf looked oddly at Caramon, Tas saw. Arack's expression was suddenly cruel and calculating, his dark, tangled eyebrows creased over his small eyes. Caramon didn't notice, he was still inspecting the wall paintings. Tas made a sound, and Caramon suddenly glanced around at the dwarf. But, by that time, Arack's expression had changed.

"No one," the dwarf said with a grin, patting Caramon's big arm. "No one. . . ."

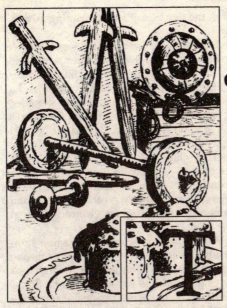

Chapter 6

The ogre led Caramon and Tas into a large room. Caramon had the fevered impression of its being filled with people.

"Him new man," grunted Raag, jerking a yellow, filthy thumb in Caramon's direction as the big man stood next to him. It was Caramon's introduction to the "school." Flushing, acutely conscious of the iron collar around his neck that branded him someone's property, Caramon kept his eyes on the straw-covered, wooden floor. Hearing only a muttered response to Raag's statement, Caramon glanced up. He was in a mess hall, he saw now. Twenty or thirty men of various races and nationalities sat about in small groups, eating dinner.

Some of the men were looking at Caramon with interest, most weren't looking at him at all. A few nodded, the majority continued eating. Caramon wasn't certain what to do next, but Raag solved the problem. Laying a hand on Caramon's shoulder, the ogre shoved him roughly toward a table. Caramon stumbled and nearly fell, managing to catch himself before he smashed into the table. Whirling around, he glared angrily at the ogre. Raag stood grinning at him, his hands twitching.

I'm being baited, Caramon realized, having seen that look too many times in bars where someone was always trying to goad the big man into a fight. And this was one fight he knew he couldn't win. Though Caramon stood almost six and a half feet tall, he didn't even quite come to the ogre's shoulder, while Raag's vast hand could wrap itself around Caramon's thick neck twice. Caramon swallowed, rubbed his bruised leg, and sat down on the long wooden bench.

Casting a sneering glance at the big human, Raag's squinty-eyed gaze took in everyone in the mess hall. With shrugs and low murmurs of disappointment, the men went back to their dinners. From a table in a corner, where sat a group of minotaurs, there was laughter. Grinning back at them, Raag left the room.

Feeling himself blush self-consciously, Caramon hunkered down on the bench and tried to disappear. Someone was sitting across from him, but the big warrior couldn't bear to meet the man's gaze. Tasslehoff had no such inhibitions, however. Clambering up on the bench beside Caramon, the kender regarded their neighbor with interest.

"I'm Tasslehoff Burrfoot," he said, extending his small hand to a large, black-skinned human—also wearing an iron collar—sitting across them. "I'm new, too," the kender added, feeling wounded that he had not been introduced. The black man looked up from his food, glanced at Tas, ignored the kender's hand, then turned his gaze on Caramon.

"You two partners?"

"Yeah," Caramon answered, thankful the man hadn't referred to Raag in any way. He was suddenly aware of the smell of food and sniffed hungrily, his mouth watering. Looking appreciatively at the man's plate, which was stacked high with roast deer meat, potatoes, and slabs of bread, he sighed. "Looks like they feed us well, at any rate."

Caramon saw the black-skinned man glance at his round belly and then exchange amused looks with a tall, extraordinarily beautiful woman who took her seat next to him, her plate loaded with food as well. Looking at her,

Caramon's eyes widened. Clumsily, he attempted to stand up and bow.

"Your servant, ma'am—" he began.

"Sit down, you great oaf!" the woman snapped angrily, her tan skin darkening. "You'll have them all laughing!"

Indeed, several of the men chuckled. The woman turned and glared at them, her hand darting to a dagger she wore in her belt. At the sight of her flashing green eyes, the men swallowed their laughter and went back to their food. The woman waited until she was certain all had been properly cowed, then she, too, turned her attention back to her meal, jabbing at her meat with swift, irritated thrusts of her fork.

"I-I'm sorry," Caramon stammered, his big face flushed. "I didn't mean—"

"Forget it," the woman said in a throaty voice. Her accent was odd, Caramon couldn't place it. She appeared to be human, except for that strange way of talking—stranger even than the other people around here—and the fact that her hair was a most peculiar color—sort of a dull, leaden green. It was thick and straight, and she wore it in a long braid down her back. "You're new here, I take it. You'll soon understand—you don't treat me any different than the others. Either in or out of the arena. Got that?"

"The arena?" Caramon said in blank astonishment. "You—you're a gladiator?"

"One of the best, too," the black-skinned man across from them said, grinning. "I am Pheragas of Northern Ergoth and this is Kiiri the Sirine—"

"A Sirine! From below the sea?" Tas asked in excitement. "One of those women who can change shapes and—"

The woman flashed the kender a glance of such fury that Tas blinked and fell silent. Then her gaze went swiftly to Caramon. "Do you find that funny, *slave*?" Kiiri asked, her eyes on Caramon's new collar.

Caramon put his hand over it, flushing again. Kiiri gave a short, bitter laugh, but Pheragas regarded him with pity.

"You'll get used to it, in time," he said with a shrug.

"I'll never get used to it!" Caramon said, clenching his big fist.

Kiiri glanced at him. "You will, or your heart will break and you will die," she said coolly. So beautiful was she, and so proud her bearing, that her own iron collar might have been a necklace of finest gold, Caramon thought. He started to reply but was interrupted by a fat man in a white, greasy apron who slammed a plate of food down in front of Tasslehoff.

"Thank you," said the kender politely.

"Don't get used to the service," the cook snarled. "After this, you pick up yer own plate, like everyone else. Here"— he tossed a wooden disk down in front of the kender— "there's your meal chit. Show that, or you don't eat. And here's yours," he added, flipping one to Caramon.

"Where's my food?" Caramon asked, pocketing the wooden disk.

Plopping a bowl down in front of the big man, the cook turned to leave.

"What's this?" Caramon growled, staring at the bowl.

Tas leaned over to look. "Chicken broth," he said helpfully.

"I know *what* it is," Caramon said, his voice deep. "I mean, what is this, some kind of joke? Because it's not funny," he added, scowling at Pheragas and Kiiri, who were both grinning at him. Twisting around on the bench, Caramon reached out and grabbed hold of the cook, jerking him backward. "Get rid of this dishwater and bring me something to eat!"

With surprising quickness and dexterity, the cook broke free of Caramon's grip, twisted the big man's arm behind his back and shoved his head face-first into the bowl of soup.

"Eat it and like it," the cook snarled, dragging Caramon's dripping head up out of the soup by the hair. "Because—as far as food goes—that's all you're gonna be seeing for about a month."

Tasslehoff stopped eating, his face lighting up. The kender noticed that everyone else in the room had stopped eating again, too, certain that—this time—there would be a fight.

Caramon's face, dripping with soup, was deathly white. There were red splotches in the cheeks, and his eyes glinted dangerously.

The cook was watching him smugly, his own fists clenched.

Eagerly, Tas waited to see the cook splattered all over the room. Caramon's big fists clenched, the knuckles turned white. One of the big hands lifted and—slowly—Caramon began to wipe the soup from his face.

With a snort of derision, the cook turned and swaggered off.

Tas sighed. That certainly wasn't the old Caramon, he thought sadly, remembering the man who had killed two draconians by bashing their heads together with his bare hands, the Caramon who had once left fifteen ruffians in various stages of hurt when they made the mistake of trying to rob the big man. Glancing at Caramon out of the corner of his eye, Tas swallowed the sharp words that had been on his tongue and went back to his dinner, his heart aching.

Caramon ate slowly, spooning up the soup and gulping it down without seeming to taste it. Tas saw the woman and the black-skinned man exchange glances again and, for a moment, the kender feared they would laugh at Caramon. Kiiri, in fact, started to say something, but—on looking up toward the front of the room—she shut her mouth abruptly and went back to her meal. Tas saw Raag enter the mess hall again, two burly humans trundling along behind him.

Walking over, they came to a halt behind Caramon. Raag poked the big warrior.

Caramon glanced around slowly. "What is it?" he asked in a dull voice that Tas didn't recognize.

"You come now," Raag said.

"I'm eating," Caramon began, but the two humans grabbed the big man by the arms and dragged him off the bench before he could even finish his sentence. Then Tas saw a glimmer of Caramon's old spirit. His face an ugly, dark red, Caramon aimed a clumsy blow at one. But the man, grinning derisively, dodged it easily. His partner kicked Caramon savagely in the gut. Caramon collapsed with a groan, falling to the floor on all fours. The two humans hauled him to his feet. His head hanging, Caramon allowed himself to be led away.

"Wait! Where—" Tas stood up, but felt a strong hand close over his own.

Kiiri shook her head warningly, and Tas sat back down.

"What are they going to do to him?" he asked.

The woman shrugged. "Finish your meal," she said in a stern voice.

Tas set his fork down. "I'm not very hungry," he mumbled despondently, his mind going back to the dwarf's strange, cruel look at Caramon outside the arena.

The black-skinned man smiled at the kender, who sat across from him. "Come on," he said, standing up and holding out his hand to Tas in a friendly manner, "I'll show you to your room. We all go through it the first day. Your friend will be all right—in time."

"In time," Kiiri snorted, shoving her plate away.

Tas lay all alone in the room he had been told he would share with Caramon. It wasn't much. Located beneath the arena, it looked more like a prison cell than a room. But Kiiri told him that all the gladiators lived in rooms like these.

"They are clean and warm," she said. "There are not many in this world who can say that of where they sleep. Besides, if we lived in luxury, we would grow soft."

Well, there was certainly no danger of that, as far as the kender could see, glancing around at the bare, stone walls, the straw-covered floor, a table with a water pitcher and a bowl, and the two small chests that were supposed to hold their possessions. A single window, high up in the ceiling right at ground level, let in a shaft of sunlight. Lying on the hard bed, Tas watched the sun travel across the room. The kender might have gone exploring, but he had the feeling he wouldn't enjoy himself much until he found out what they had done to Caramon.

The sun's line on the floor grew longer and longer. A door opened and Tas leaped up eagerly, but it was only another slave, tossing a sack in onto the floor, then shutting the door again. Tas inspected the sack and his heart sank. It was Caramon's belongings! Everything he'd had on him— including his clothes! Tas studied them anxiously, looking for bloodstains. Nothing. They appeared all right. . . . His hand closed over something hard in an inner, secret pocket.

Quickly, Tas pulled it out. The kender caught his breath.

The magical device from Par-Salian! How had they missed it, he wondered, marveling at the beautiful jeweled pendant as he turned it over in his hand. Of course, it was magical, he reminded himself. It looked like nothing more than a bauble now, but he had himself seen Par-Salian transform it from a sceptre-like object. Undoubtedly it had the power to avoid discovery if it didn't *want* to be discovered.

Feeling it, holding it, watching the sunlight sparkle on its radiant jewels, Tas sighed with longing. This was the most exquisite, marvelous, fantastic thing he'd ever seen in his life. He wanted it most desperately. Without thinking, his little body rose and was heading for his pouches when he caught himself.

Tasslehoff Burrfoot, said a voice that sounded uncomfortably like Flint's, this is Serious Business you're meddling with. This is the Way Home. Par-Salian himself, the Great Par-Salian gave it to Caramon in a solemn ceremony. It belongs to Caramon. It's his, you have no right to it!

Tas shivered. He had certainly never thought thoughts like these before in his life. Dubiously, he glanced at the device. Perhaps *it* was putting these uncomfortable thoughts in his head!

He decided he didn't want any part of them. Hurriedly, he carried the device over and put it in Caramon's chest. Then, as an extra precaution, he locked the chest and stuffed the key in Caramon's clothes. Even more miserable, he returned to his bed.

The sunlight had just about disappeared and the kender was growing more and more anxious when he heard a noise outside. The door was kicked open violently.

"Caramon!" Tas cried in horror, springing to his feet.

The two burly humans dragged the big man in over the doorstep and flung him down on the bed. Then, grinning, they left, slamming the door shut behind them. There was a low, moaning sound from the bed.

"Caramon!" Tas whispered. Hurriedly grabbing up the water pitcher, he dumped some water in the bowl and carried it over to the big warrior's bedside. "What did they do?" he asked softly, moistening the man's lips with water.

Caramon moaned again and shook his head weakly. Tas glanced quickly at the big man's body. There were no visible wounds, no blood, no swelling, no purple welts or whiplash marks. Yet he had been tortured, that much was obvious. The big man was in agony. His body was covered with sweat, his eyes had rolled back in his head. Every now and then, various muscles in his body twitched spasmodically and a groan of pain escaped his lips.

"Was . . . was it the rack?" Tas asked, gulping. "The wheel, maybe? Thumb-screws?" None of those left marks on the body, at least so he had heard.

Caramon mumbled a word.

"What?" Tas bent near him, bathing his face in water. "What did you say? Cali—cali—what? I didn't catch that." The kender's brow furrowed. "I never heard of a torture called calisomething," he muttered. "I wonder what it could be."

Caramon repeated it, moaning again.

"Cali . . . cali . . . calisthenics!" Tas said triumphantly. Then he dropped the water pitcher onto the floor. "Calisthenics? That's not torture!"

Caramon groaned again.

"That's exercises, you big baby!" Tas yelled. "Do you mean I've been waiting here, worried sick, imagining all sorts of horrible things, and you've been out doing exercises!"

Caramon had just strength enough to raise himself off the bed. Reaching out one big hand, he gripped Tas by the collar of his shirt and dragged him over to stare him in the eye.

"I was captured by goblins once," Caramon said in a hoarse whisper, "and they tied me to a tree and spent the night tormenting me. I was wounded by draconians in Xak Tsaroth. Baby dragons chewed on my leg in the dungeons of the Queen of Darkness. And, I swear to you, that I am in more pain now than I have ever been in my life! Leave me alone, and let me die in peace."

With another groan, Caramon's hand dropped weakly to his side. His eyes closed. Smothering a grin, Tas crept back to his bed.

"He thinks he's in pain now," the kender reflected, "wait until morning!"

Summer in Istar ended. Fall came, one of the most beautiful in anyone's memory. Caramon's training began, and the warrior did not die, though there were times when he thought death might be easier. Tas, too, was strongly tempted on more than one occasion to put the big, spoiled baby out of his misery. One of these time had been during the night, when Tas had been awakened by a heartbreaking sob.

"Caramon?" Tas said sleepily, sitting up in bed.

No answer, just another sob.

"What is it?" Tas asked, suddenly concerned. He got out of bed and trotted across the cold, stone floor. "Did you have a dream?"

He could see Caramon nod in the moonlight.

"Was it about Tika?" asked the tenderhearted kender, feeling tears come to his own eyes at the sight of the big man's grief. "No. Raistlin? No. Yourself? Are you afraid—"

"A muffin!" Caramon sobbed.

"What?" Tas asked blankly.

"A muffin!" Caramon blubbered. "Oh, Tas! I'm so hungry. And I had a dream about this muffin, like Tika used to bake, all covered with sticky honey and those little, crunchy nuts...."

Picking up a shoe, Tas threw it at him and went back to bed in disgust.

But by the end of the second month of rigorous training, Tas looked at Caramon, and the kender had to admit that this was just exactly what the big man had needed. The rolls of fat around the big man's waist were gone, the flabby thighs were once more hard and muscular, muscles rippled in his arms and across his chest and back. His eyes were bright and alert, the dull, vacant stare gone. The dwarf spirits had been sweated and soaked from his body, the red had gone from his nose, and the puffy look was gone from his face. His body was tanned a deep bronze from being out in the sun. The dwarf decreed that Caramon's brown hair be allowed to grow long, as this style was currently popular in Istar, and now it curled around his face and down his back.

He was a superbly skilled warrior now, too. Although Caramon had been well-trained before, it had been informal training, his weapons technique picked up mostly from his older half-sister, Kitiara. But Arack imported trainers from all over the world, and now Caramon was learning techniques from the best.

Not only this, but he was forced to hold his own in daily contests between the gladiators themselves. Once proud of his wrestling skill, Caramon had been deeply shamed to find himself flat on his back after only two rounds against the woman, Kiiri. The black man, Pheragas, sent Caramon's sword flying after one pass, then bashed him over the head with his own shield for good measure.

But Caramon was an apt, attentive pupil. His natural ability made him a quick study, and it wasn't long before Arack was watching in glee as the big man flipped Kiiri with ease, then coolly wrapped Pheragas up in his own net, pinning the black man to the arena floor with his own trident.

Caramon, himself, was happier than he had been in a long time. He still detested the iron collar, and rarely a day went by at first without his longing to break it and run. But, these feelings lessened as he became interested in his training. Caramon had always enjoyed military life. He liked having someone tell him what to do and when to do it. The only real problem he was having was with his acting abilities.

Always open and honest, even to a fault, the worst part of his training came when he had to pretend to be losing. He was supposed to cry out loudly in mock pain when Rolf stomped on his back. He had to learn how to collapse as though horribly wounded when the Barbarian lunged at him with the fake, collapsible swords.

"No! No! No! you big dummy!" Arack screamed over and over. Swearing at Caramon one day, the dwarf walked over and punched him hard, right in the face.

"Arrgh!" Caramon cried out in real pain, not daring to fight back with Raag watching in glee.

"There—" Arack said, standing back in triumph, his fists clenched, blood on the knuckles. "Remember that yell. The gulls'll love it."

But, in acting, Caramon appeared hopeless. Even when he did yell, it sounded "more like some wench getting her behind pinched than like anyone dying," Arack told Kiiri in disgust. And then, one day, the dwarf had an idea.

It came to him as he was watching the training sessions that afternoon. There happened to be a small audience at the time. Arack occasionally allowed certain members of the public in, having discovered that this was good for business. At this time, he was entertaining a nobleman, who had traveled here with his family from Solamnia. The nobleman had two very charming young daughters and, from the moment they entered the arena, they had never taken their eyes from Caramon.

"Why didn't we see him fight the other night?" one asked their father.

The nobleman looked inquiringly at the dwarf.

"He's new," Arack said gruffly. "He's still in training. He's just about ready, mind you. In fact, I was thinking of putting him in—when did you say you were coming back to the Games?"

"We weren't," the nobleman began, but his daughters both cried out in dismay. "Well," he amended, "perhaps—if we can get tickets."

The girls both clapped their hands, their eyes going back to Caramon, who was practicing his sword work with Pheragas. The young man's tanned body glistened with sweat, his hair clung in damp curls to his face, he moved with the grace of a well-trained athlete. Seeing the girls' admiring gaze, it suddenly occurred to the dwarf what a remarkably handsome young man Caramon was.

"He must win," said one of the girls, sighing. "I could not bear to see him lose!"

"He will win," said the other. "He was meant to win. He looks like a victor."

"Of course! That solves all my problems!" said the dwarf suddenly, causing the noblemen and his family to stare at him, puzzled. "The Victor! That's how I'll bill 'im. Never defeated! Doesn't know how to lose! Vowed to take his own life, he did, if anyone ever beat him!"

"Oh, no!" both girls cried in dismay. "Don't tell us that."

"It's true," the dwarf said solemnly, rubbing his hands.

"They'll come from miles around," he told Raag that night, "hoping to be there the night he loses. And, of course, he won't lose—not for a good, long while. Meanwhile, he'll be a heart-breaker. I can see that now. And I have just the costume..."

Tasslehoff, meanwhile, was finding his own life in the arena quite interesting. Although at first deeply wounded when told he couldn't be a gladiator (Tas had visions of himself as another Kronin Thistleknot—the hero of Kenderhome), Tas had moped around for a few days in boredom. This ended in his nearly getting killed by an enraged minotaur who discovered the kender happily going through his room.

The minotaurs were furious. Fighting at the arena for the love of the sport only, they considered themselves a superior race, living and eating apart from the others. Their quarters were sacrosanct and inviolate.

Dragging the kender before Arack, the minotaur demanded that he be allowed to slit him open and drink his blood. The dwarf might have agreed—not having overly much use for kenders himself—but Arack remembered the talk he'd had with Quarath shortly after he'd purchased these two slaves. For some reason, the highest church authority in the land was interested in seeing that nothing happened to these two. He had to refuse the minotaur's request, therefore, but mollified him by giving him a boar he could butcher in sport. Then, Arack took Tas aside, cuffed him across the face a few times, and finally gave him permission to leave the arena and explore the town if the kender promised to come back at night.

Tas, who had already been sneaking out of the arena anyway, was thrilled at this, and repaid the dwarf's kindness by bringing him back any little trinket he thought Arack might like. Appreciative of this attention, Arack only beat the kender with a stick when he caught Tas trying to sneak pastry to Caramon, instead of whipping him as he would have otherwise.

Thus, Tas came and went about Istar pretty much as he liked, learning quickly to dodge the town guards, who had a most unreasonable dislike for kender. And so it was that Tasslehoff was able to enter the Temple itself.

Amid his training and dieting and other problems, Caramon had never lost sight of his real goal. He had received a cold, terse message from Lady Crysania, so he knew she was all right. But that was all. Of Raistlin, there was no sign.

At first, Caramon despaired of finding his brother or Fistandantilus, since he was never allowed outside the arena. But he soon realized that Tas could go places and see things much easier than he could, even if he had been free. People had a tendency to treat kender the same way they treated children—as if they weren't there. And Tas was even more expert than most kender at melting into shadows and ducking behind curtains or sneaking quietly through halls.

Plus there was the advantage that the Temple itself was so vast and filled with so many people, coming and going at nearly all hours, that one kender was easily ignored or—at most—told irritably to get out of the way. This was made even easier by the fact that there were several kender slaves working in the kitchens and even a few kender clerics, who came and went freely.

Tas would have dearly loved to make friends of these and to ask questions about his homeland—particularly the kender clerics, since he'd never known these existed. But he didn't dare. Caramon had warned him about talking too much and, for once, Tas took this warning seriously. Finding it nerve-racking to be on constant guard against talking about dragons or the Cataclysm or something that would get everyone all upset, he decided it would be easier to avoid temptation altogether. So he contented himself with nosing around the Temple and gathering information.

"I've seen Crysania," he reported to Caramon one night after they'd returned from dinner and a game of arm wrestling with Pheragas. Tas lay down on the bed while Caramon practiced with a mace and chain in the center of the room, Arack wanting him skilled in weapons other than the sword. Seeing that Caramon still needed a lot of practice, Tas crept to the far end of the bed—well out of the way of some of the big man's wilder swings.

"How is she?" Caramon asked, glancing over at the kender with interest.

Tas shook his head. "I don't know. She *looks* all right, I guess. At least she doesn't look sick. But she doesn't look happy, either. Her face is pale and, when I tried to talk to her, she just ignored me. I don't think she recognized me."

Caramon frowned. "See if you can find out what the matter is," he said. "She was looking for Raistlin, too, remember. Maybe it has something to do with him."

"All right," the kender replied, then ducked as the mace whistled by his head. "Say, be careful! Move back a little." He felt his topknot anxiously to see if all his hair was still there.

"Speaking of Raistlin," Caramon said in a subdued voice. "I don't suppose you found out anything today either?"

Tas shook his head. "I've asked and asked. Fistandantilus has apprentices that come and go sometimes. But no one's seen anyone answering Raistlin's description. And, you know, people with golden skin and hourglass eyes do tend to stand out in a crowd. But"—the kender looked more cheerful—"I may find out something soon. Fistandantilus is back, I heard."

"He is?" Caramon stopped swinging the mace and turned to face Tas.

"Yes. I didn't see him, but some of the clerics were talking about it. I guess he reappeared last night, right in the Kingpriest's Hall of Audience. Just—poof! There he was. Quite dramatic."

"Yeah," Caramon grunted. Swinging the mace thoughtfully, he was quiet for so long that Tas yawned and started to drift off to sleep. Caramon's voice brought him back to consciousness with a start.

"Tas," Caramon said, "this is our chance."

"Our chance to what?" The kender yawned again.

"Our chance to murder Fistandantilus," the warrior said quietly.

Chapter 7

aramon's cold statement woke the kender up quickly.

"M-murder! I—uh—think you ought to think about this, Caramon," Tas stammered. "I mean, well, look at it this way. This Fistandantilus is a really, really *good,* I-I mean, *talented* magic-user. Better even than Raistlin and Par-Salian put together, if what they say is true. You just don't sneak up and murder a guy like that. Especially when you've never murdered anybody! Not that I'm saying we should practice, mind you, but—"

"He has to sleep, doesn't he?" Caramon asked.

"Well," Tas faltered, "I suppose so. Everybody has to sleep, I guess, even magic-users—"

"Magic-users most of all," Caramon interrupted coldly. "You remember how weak Raist'd be if he didn't sleep? And that holds true of all wizards, even the most powerful. That's one reason they lost the great battles—the Lost Battles. They had to rest. And quit talking about this 'we' stuff. *I'll* do it. You don't even have to come along. Just find out where his room is, what kind of defenses he has, and when he goes to bed. I'll take care of it from there."

"Caramon," Tas began hesitantly, "do you suppose it's right? I mean, I know that's why the mages sent you back here. At least I *think* that's why. It all got sort of muddled there at the end. And I know this Fistandantilus is supposed to be a really *evil* person and he wears the black robes and all that, but is it right to *murder* him? I mean, it seems to me that this just makes us as evil as he is, doesn't it?"

"I don't care," Caramon said without emotion, his eyes on the mace he was slowly swinging back and forth. "It's his life or Raistlin's, Tas. If I kill Fistandantilus now, back in this time, he won't be able to come forward and grab Raistlin. I could free Raistlin from that shattered body, Tas, and make him whole! Once I wrench this man's evil hold from him—then I know he'd be just like the old Raist. The little brother I loved." Caramon's voice grew wistful and his eyes moist. "He could come and live with us, Tas."

"What about Tika?" Tas asked hesitantly. "How's she going to feel about you murdering somebody?"

Caramon's brown eyes flashed in anger. "I told you before—don't talk about her, Tas!"

"But, Caramon—"

"I mean it, Tas!"

And this time the big man's voice held the tone that Tas knew meant he had gone too far. The kender sat hunched miserably in his bed. Looking over at him, Caramon sighed.

"Look, Tas," he said quietly, "I'll explain it once. I-I haven't been very good to Tika. She was right to throw me out, I see that now, though there was a time I thought I'd never forgive her." The big man was quiet a moment, sorting out his thoughts. Then, with another sigh, he continued. "I told her once that, as long as Raistlin lived, he'd come first in my thoughts. I warned her to find someone who could give her all his love. I thought at first *I* could, when Raistlin went off on his own. But"—he shook his head—"I dunno. It didn't work. Now, I've got to do this, don't you see? And I can't think about Tika! She-she only gets in the way. . . ."

"But Tika loves you so much!" was all Tas could say. And, of course, it was the wrong thing. Caramon scowled and began swinging the mace again.

"All right, Tas," he said, his voice so deep it might have come from beneath the kender's feet, "I guess this means good-bye. Ask the dwarf for a different room. I'm going to do this and, if anything goes wrong, I wouldn't want to get you into trouble—"

"Caramon, you know I didn't mean I wouldn't help," Tas mumbled. "You need me!"

"Yeah, I guess," Caramon muttered, flushing. Then, looking over at Tas, he smiled in apology. "I'm sorry. Just don't talk about Tika anymore, all right?"

"All right," Tas said unhappily. He smiled back at Caramon in return, watching as the big man put his weapons away and prepared for bed. But it was a sickly smile and, when Tas crawled into his own bed, he felt more depressed and unhappy than he had since Flint died.

"*He* wouldn't have approved, that's for sure," Tas said to himself, thinking of the gruff, old dwarf. "I can hear him now. 'Stupid, doorknob of a kender!' he'd say. 'Murdering wizards! Why don't you just save everyone trouble and do away with yourself!' And then there's Tanis," Tas thought, even more miserable. "I can just imagine what *he'd* say!" Rolling over, Tas pulled the blankets up around his chin. "I wish he was here! I wish *someone* was here to help us! Caramon's not thinking right, I know he isn't! But what can *I* do? I've got to help him. He's my friend. And he'd likely get into no end of trouble without me!"

The next day was Caramon's first day in the Games. Tas made his visit to the Temple in the early morning and was back in time to see Caramon's fight, which would take place that afternoon. Sitting on the bed, swinging his short legs back and forth, the kender made his report as Caramon paced the floor nervously, waiting for the dwarf and Pheragas to bring him his costume.

"You're right," Tas admitted reluctantly. "Fistandantilus needs lots of sleep, apparently. He goes to bed early every night and sleeps like the dead—I m-mean"—Tas stuttered—"sleeps soundly till morning."

Caramon looked at him grimly.

"Guards?"

"No," Tas said, shrugging. "He doesn't even lock his door. No one locks doors in the Temple. After all, it is a holy place, and I guess everyone either trusts everyone or they don't have anything to lock up. You know," the kender said on reflection, "I always detested door locks, but now I've decided that life without them would be really boring. I've been in a few rooms in the Temple"—Tas blissfully ignored Caramon's horrified glance—"and, believe me, it's not worth the bother. You'd think a magic-user would be different, but Fistandantilus doesn't keep any of his spell stuff there. I guess he just uses his room to spend the night when he's visiting the court. Besides," the kender pointed out with a sudden brilliant flash of logic, "he's the only evil person in the court, so he wouldn't need to protect himself from anyone other than himself!"

Caramon, who had quit listening long ago, muttered something and kept pacing. Tas frowned uncomfortably. It had suddenly occurred to him that he and Caramon now ranked right up there with evil magic-users. This helped him make up his mind.

"Look, I'm sorry, Caramon," Tas said, after a moment. "But I don't think I can help you, after all. Kender aren't very particular, sometimes, about their own things, or other people's for that matter, but I don't believe a kender ever in his life *murdered* anybody!" He sighed, then continued in a quivering voice. "And, I got to thinking about Flint and . . . and Sturm. You know Sturm wouldn't approve! He was so honorable. It just isn't right, Caramon! It makes us just as bad as Fistandantilus. Or maybe worse."

Caramon opened his mouth and was just about to reply when the door burst open and Arack marched in.

"How're we doing, big guy?" the dwarf said, leering up at Caramon. "Quite a change from when you first came here, ain't it?" He patted the big man's hard muscles admiringly, then—balling up his fist—suddenly slammed it into

Caramon's gut. "Hard as steel," he said, grinning and shaking his hand in pain.

Caramon glowered down at the dwarf in disgust, glanced at Tas, then sighed. "Where's my costume?" he grumbled. "It's nearly High Watch."

The dwarf held up a sack. "It's in here. Don't worry, it won't take you long to dress."

Grabbing the sack nervously, Caramon opened it. "Where's the rest of it?" he demanded of Pheragas, who had just entered the room.

"That's it!" Arack cackled. "I told you it wouldn't take long to dress!"

Caramon's face flushed a deep red. "I—I can't wear . . . just this. . . ." he stammered, shutting the sack hastily. "You said there'd be ladies. . . ."

"And they'll love every bronze inch!" Arack hooted. Then the laughter vanished from the dwarf's broken face, replaced by the dark and menacing scowl. "Put it on, you great oaf. What do you think they pay to see? A dancing school? No—they pay to see bodies covered in sweat and blood. The more body, the more sweat, the more blood— real blood—the better!"

"*Real* blood?" Caramon looked up, his brown eyes flaring. "What do you mean? I thought you said—"

"Bah! Get him ready, Pheragas. And while you're at it, explain the facts of life to the spoiled brat. Time to grow up, Caramon, my pretty poppet." With that and a grating laugh, the dwarf stalked out.

Pheragas stood aside to let the dwarf pass, then entered the small room. His face, usually jovial and cheerful, was a blank mask. There was no expression in his eyes, and he avoided looking directly at Caramon.

"What did he mean? Grow up?" Caramon asked. "Real blood?"

"Here," Pheragas said gruffly, ignoring the question. "I'll help with these buckles. It takes a bit of getting used to at first. They're strictly ornamental, made to break easily. The audience loves it if a piece comes loose or falls off."

He lifted an ornate shoulder guard from the bag and

began strapping it onto Caramon, working around behind him, keeping his eyes fixed on the buckles.

"This is made out of gold," Caramon said slowly.

Pheragas grunted.

"Butter would stop a knife sooner than this stuff," Caramon continued, feeling it. "And look at all these fancy dodads! A sword point'll catch and stick in any of 'em."

"Yeah." Pheragas laughed, but it was forced laughter. "As you can see, it's almost better to be naked than wear this stuff."

"I don't have much to worry about then," Caramon remarked grimly, pulling out the leather loincloth that was the only other object in the sack, besides an ornate helmet. The loincloth, too, was ornamented in gold and barely covered his private parts decently. When he and Pheragas had him dressed, even the kender blushed at the sight of Caramon from the rear.

Pheragas started to go, but Caramon stopped him, his hand on his arm. "You better tell me, my friend. That is, if you still are my friend."

Pheragas looked at Caramon intently, then shrugged. "I thought you'd have figured it out by now. We use edged weapons. Oh, the swords still collapse," he added, seeing Caramon's eyes narrow. "But, if you get hit, you bleed—for real. That's why we harped on your stabbing thrusts."

"You mean people really get hurt? I could hurt someone? Someone like Kiiri, or Rolf, or the Barbarian?" Caramon's voice raised in anger. "What else goes on! What else didn't you tell me—friend!"

Pheragas regarded Caramon coldly. "Where did you think I got these scars? Playing with my nanny? Look, someday you'll understand. There's not time to explain it now. Just trust us, Kiiri and I. Follow our lead. And—keep your eyes on the minotaurs. They fight for themselves, not for any masters or owners. They answer to no one. Oh, they agree to abide by the rules—they have to or the Kingpriest would ship them back to Mithas. But . . . well, they're favorites with the crowd. The people like to see them draw blood. And they can take as good as they give."

"Get out!" Caramon snarled.

Pheragas stood staring at him a moment, then he turned and started out the door. Once there, however, he stopped.

"Listen, friend," he said sternly, "these scars I get in the ring are badges of honor, every bit as good as some knight's spurs he wins in a contest! It's the only kind of honor we can salvage out of this tawdry show! The arena's got its own code, Caramon, and it doesn't have one damn thing to do with those knights and noblemen who sit out there and watch us slaves bleed for their own amusement. They talk of *their* honor. Well, we've got our own. It's what keeps us alive." He fell silent. It seemed he might say something more, but Caramon's gaze was on the floor, the big man stubbornly refusing to acknowledge his words or presence.

Finally, Pheragas said "You've got five minutes," and left, slamming the door behind him.

Tas longed to say something but, seeing Caramon's face, even the kender knew it was time to keep silent.

Go into a battle with bad blood, and it'll be spilled by nightfall. Caramon couldn't remember what gruff old commander had told him that, but he'd found it a good axiom. Your life often depended on the loyalty of those you fought with. It was a good idea to get any quarrels between you settled. He didn't like holding grudges either. It generally did nothing for him but upset his stomach.

It was an easy thing, therefore, to shake Pheragas's hand when the black man started to turn away from him prior to entering the arena and to make his apologies. Pheragas accepted these warmly, while Kiiri—who obviously had heard all about the episode from Pheragas—indicated her approval with a smile. She indicated her approval of Caramon's costume, too; looking at him with such open admiration in her flashing green eyes that Caramon flushed in embarrassment.

The three stood talking in the corridors that ran below the arena, waiting to make their entrance. With them were the other gladiators who would fight today, Rolf, the Barbarian, and the Red Minotaur. Above them, they could hear occasional roars from the crowd, but the sound was muffled.

Craning his neck, Caramon could see out the entryway door. He wished it was time to start. Rarely had he ever felt this nervous, more nervous than going into battle, he realized.

The others felt the tension, too. It was obvious in Kiiri's laughter that was too shrill and loud and the sweat that poured down Pheragas's face. But it was a good kind of tension, mingled with excitement. And, suddenly, Caramon realized he was looking forward to this.

"Arack's called our names," Kiiri said. She and Pheragas and Caramon walked forward—the dwarf having decided that since they worked well together they should fight as a team. (He also hoped that the two pros would cover up for any of Caramon's mistakes!)

The first thing Caramon noticed as he stepped out into the arena was the noise. It crashed over him in thunderous waves, one after another, coming seemingly from the sun-drenched sky above him. For a moment he felt lost in confusion. The by-now familiar arena—where he had worked and practiced so hard these last few months—was a strange place suddenly. His gaze went to the great circular rows of stands surrounding the arena, and he was overwhelmed at the sight of the thousands of people, all—it seemed—on their feet screaming and stomping and shouting.

The colors swam in his eyes—gaily fluttering banners that announced a Games Day, silk banners of all the noble families of Istar, and the more humble banners of those who sold everything from fruited ice to tarbean tea, depending on the season of the year. And it all seemed to be in motion, making him dizzy, and suddenly nauseous. Then he felt Kiiri's cool hand upon his arm. Turning, he saw her smile at him in reassurance. He saw the familiar arena behind her, he saw Pheragas and his other friends.

Feeling better, he quickly turned his attention back to the action. He had better keep his mind on business, he told himself sternly. If he missed a single rehearsed move, he would not only make himself look foolish, but he might accidentally hurt someone. He remembered how particular Kiiri had been that he timed his swordthrusts just right. Now, he thought grimly, he knew why.

Keeping his eyes on his partners and the arena, ignoring the noise and the crowd, he took his place, waiting to start. The arena looked different, somehow, and for a moment he couldn't figure it out. Then he realized that, just as they were in costume, the dwarf had decorated the arena, too. Here were the same old sawdust-covered platforms where he fought every day, but now they were tricked out with symbols representing the four corners of the world.

Around these four platforms, the hot coals blazed, the fire roared, the oil boiled and bubbled. Bridges of wood spanned the Death Pits as they were called, connecting the four platforms. These Pits had, at first, alarmed Caramon. But he had learned early in the game that they were for effect only. The audience loved it when a fighter was driven from the arena onto the bridges. They went wild when the Barbarian held Rolf by his heels over the boiling oil. Having seen it all in rehearsal, Caramon could laugh with Kiiri at the terrified expression on Rolf's face and the frantic efforts he made to save himself that resulted—as always—in the Barbarian being hit over the head by a blow from Rolf's powerful arms.

The sun reached its zenith and a flash of gold brought Caramon's eyes to the center of the arena. Here stood the Freedom Spire—a tall structure made of gold, so delicate and ornate that it seemed out of place in such crude surroundings. At the top hung a key—a key that would open a lock on any of the iron collars. Caramon had seen the spire often enough in practice, but he had never seen the key, which was kept locked in Arack's office. Just looking at it made the iron collar around his neck feel unusually heavy. His eyes filled with sudden tears. Freedom.... To wake in the morning and be able to walk out a door, to go anywhere in this wide world you wanted. It was such a simple thing. Now, how much he missed it!

Then he heard Arack call out his name, he saw him point at them. Gripping his weapon, Caramon turned to face Kiiri, the sight of the Golden Key still in his mind. At the end of the year, any slave who had done well in the Games could fight for the right to climb that spire and get the key. It was all fake, of course. Arack always selected those guaranteed to draw the biggest audiences. Caramon had never thought about it before—his only concern being his brother and Fistandantilus. But, now, he realized he had a new goal. With a wild yell, he raised his phony sword high in the air in salute.

Soon, Caramon began to relax and have fun. He found himself enjoying the roars and applause of the crowd. Caught up in their excitement, he discovered he was playing up to them—just as Kiiri had told him he would. The few wounds he'd received in the warm-up bouts were nothing, only scratches. He couldn't even feel the pain. He laughed at himself for his worry. Pheragas had been right not to mention such a silly thing. He was sorry he had made such a big deal of it.

"They like you," Kiiri said, grinning at him during one of their rest periods. Once again, her eyes swept admiringly over Caramon's muscular, practically nude body. "I don't blame them. I'm looking forward to our wrestling match."

Kiiri laughed at his blush, but Caramon saw in her eyes that she wasn't kidding and he was suddenly acutely aware of her femaleness—something that had never occurred to him in practice. Perhaps it was her own scanty costume, which seemed designed to reveal everything, yet hid all that was most desirable. Caramon's blood burned, both with passion and the pleasure he always found in battle. Confused memories of Tika came to his mind, and he looked away from Kiiri hurriedly, realizing he had been saying more with his own eyes than he intended.

This ploy was only partly successful, because he found himself staring into the stands—right into the eyes of many admiring and beautiful women, who were obviously trying to capture his attention.

"We're on again," Kiiri nudged him, and Caramon returned thankfully to the ring.

He grinned at the Barbarian as the tall man strode forward. This was their big number, and he and Caramon had practiced it many times. The Barbarian winked at Caramon as they faced each other, their faces twisted into looks of ferocious hatred. Growling and snarling like animals, both men crouched over, stalking each other around the ring a suitable amount of time to build up tension. Caramon caught himself about to grin and had to remind himself that he was supposed to look mean. He liked the Barbarian. A Plainsman, the man reminded him in many ways of Riverwind—tall, dark-haired, though not nearly as serious as the stern ranger.

The Barbarian was a slave as well, but the iron collar around his neck was old and scratched from countless battles. He would be one chosen to go after the golden key this year, that was certain.

Caramon thrust out with the collapsible sword. The Barbarian dodged with ease and, catching Caramon with his heel, neatly tripped him. Caramon went down with a roar. The audience groaned (the women sighed), but there were many cheers for the Barbarian, who was a favorite. The Barbarian lunged at the prone Caramon with a spear. The women screamed in terror. At the last moment, Caramon rolled to one side and, grabbing the Barbarian's foot, jerked him down to the sawdust platform.

Thunderous cheers. The two men grappled on the floor of the arena. Kiiri rushed out to aid her fallen comrade and the Barbarian fought them both off, to the crowd's delight. Then, Caramon, with a gallant gesture, ordered Kiiri back behind the line. It was obvious to the crowd that he would take care of this insolent opponent himself.

Kiiri patted Caramon on his rump (that wasn't in the script and nearly caused Caramon to forget his next move), then she ran off. The Barbarian lunged at Caramon, who pulled his collapsible dagger. This was the show-stopper—as they had planned. Ducking beneath the Barbarian's upraised arm with a skillful maneuver, Caramon thrust the dummy dagger right into the Barbarian's gut where a bladder of chicken blood was cleverly concealed beneath his feathered breastplate.

It worked! The chicken blood splashed out over Caramon, running down his hand and his arm. Caramon looked into the Barbarian's face, ready for another wink of triumph. . . .

Something was wrong.

The man's eyes had widened, as was in the script. But they had widened in true pain and in shock. He staggered forward—that was in the script, too—but not the gasp of agony.

As Caramon caught him, he realized in horror that the blood washing over his arm was warm!

Wrenching his dagger free, Caramon stared at it, even as he fought to hold onto the Barbarian, who was collapsing against him. The blade was real!

"Caramon . . ." The man choked. Blood spurted from his mouth.

The audience roared. They hadn't seen special effects like this in months!

"Barbarian! I didn't know!" Caramon cried, staring at dagger in horror. "I swear!"

And then Pheragas and Kiiri were by his side, helping to ease the dying Barbarian down onto the arena floor.

"Keep up the act!" Kiiri snapped harshly.

Caramon nearly struck her in his rage, but Pheragas caught his arm. "Your life, our lives depend on it!" the black man hissed. "*And* the life of your little friend!"

Caramon stared at them in confusion. What did they mean? What were they saying? He had just killed a man—a friend! Groaning, he jerked away from Pheragas and knelt beside the Barbarian. Dimly he could hear the crowd cheering, and he knew—somewhere inside of him—that they were eating this up. The Victor paying tribute to the "dead."

"Forgive me," he said to the Barbarian, who nodded.

"It's not your fault," the man whispered. "Don't blame yoursel—" His eyes fixed in his head, a bubble of blood burst on his lips.

"We've got to get him out of the arena," Pheragas whispered sharply to Caramon, "and make it look good. Like we rehearsed. Do you understand?"

Caramon nodded dully. *Your life . . . the life of your little friend.* I am a warrior. I've killed before. Death is nothing new. *The life of your little friend.* Obey orders. I'm used to that. Obey orders, then I'll figure out the answers. . . .

Repeating that over and over, Caramon was able to subdue the part of his mind that burned with rage and pain. Coolly and calmly, he helped Kiiri and Pheragas lift the Barbarian's "lifeless" corpse to its feet as they had done countless times in rehearsal. He even found the strength to turn and face the crowd and bow. Pheragas, with a skillful motion of his free arm, made it seem as if the "dead" Barbarian were bowing, too. The crowd loved it and cheered wildly. Then the three friends dragged the corpse off the stage, down into the dark aisles below.

Once there, Caramon helped them ease the Barbarian down onto the cold stone. For long moments, he stared at the corpse, dimly aware of the other gladiators, who had been waiting their turn to go up into the arena, looking at the lifeless body, then melting back into the shadows.

Slowly, Caramon stood up. Turning around, he grabbed hold of Pheragas and, with all his strength, hurled the black man up against the wall. Drawing the bloodstained dagger from his belt, Caramon held it up before Pheragas's eyes.

"It was an accident," Pheragas said through clenched teeth.

"Edged weapons!" Caramon cried, shoving Pheragas's head roughly into the stone wall. "Bleed a little! Now, you tell me! What in the name of the Abyss is going on!"

"It was an accident, oaf," came a sneering voice.

Caramon turned. The dwarf stood before him, his squat body a small, twisted shadow in the dark and dank corridor beneath the arena.

"And now I'll tell you about accidents," Arack said, his voice soft and malevolent. Behind him loomed the giant figure of Raag, his club in his huge hand. "Let Pheragas go. He and Kiiri have to get back to the arena and take their bows. You all were the winners today."

Caramon glanced at Pheragas for a moment, then dropped his hand. The dagger slipped from his nerveless fingers onto the floor, he slumped back against the wall. Kiiri regarded him in mute sympathy, laying her hand on his arm. Pheragas sighed, cast the smug dwarf a venomous glance, then both he and Kiiri left the corridor. They walked around the body of the Barbarian, which lay, untouched, on the stone.

"You told me no one got killed!" Caramon said in a voice choked with anger and pain.

The dwarf came over to stand in front of the big man. "It was an accident," Arack repeated. "Accidents happen around here. Particularly to people who aren't careful. They could happen to you, if you're not careful. Or to that little friend of yours. Now, the Barbarian, here, he wasn't careful. Or rather, his master wasn't careful."

Caramon raised his head, staring at the dwarf, his eyes wide with shock and horror.

"Ah, I see you finally got it figured out," Arack nodded.

"This man died because his owner crossed someone," Caramon said softly.

"Yeah." The dwarf grinned and tugged at his beard. "Civilized, ain't it? Not like the old days. And no one's the wiser. Except his master, of course. I saw his face this afternoon. He knew, as soon as you stuck the Barbarian. You might as well have thrust that dagger into him. He got the message all right."

"This was a warning?" Caramon asked in strangled tones.

The dwarf nodded again and shrugged.

"Who? Who was his owner?"

Arack hesitated, regarding Caramon quizzically, his broken face twisted into a leer. Caramon could almost see him calculating, figuring how much he could gain from telling, how much he might gain by keeping silent. Apparently, the money added up quickly in the "telling" column, because he didn't hesitate long. Motioning Caramon to lean down, he whispered a name in his ear.

Caramon looked puzzled.

"High cleric, a Revered Son of Paladine," the dwarf added. "Number two to the Kingpriest himself. But he's made a bad enemy, a bad enemy." Arack shook his head.

A burst of muffled cheering roared from above them. The dwarf glanced up, then back at Caramon. "You'll have to go up, take a bow. It's expected. You're a winner."

"What about him?" Caramon asked, his gaze going to the Barbarian. "He won't be going up. Won't they wonder?"

"Pulled muscle. Happens all the time. Can't make his final bow," the dwarf said casually. "We'll put the word out he retired, was given his freedom."

Given his freedom! Tears filled his eyes. He looked away, down the corridor. There was another cheer. He would have to go. *Your life. Our lives. The life of your little friend.*

"That's why," Caramon said thickly, "that's why you had me kill him! Because now you've got me! You know I won't talk—"

"I knew that anyway," Arack said, grinning wickedly. "Let's say having you kill him was just a little extra touch. The customers like that, shows I care. You see, it was *your* master who sent this warning! I thought he'd appreciate it, having his own slave carry it out. Course that puts you in a bit of danger. The Barbarian's death'll have to be avenged. But, it'll do wonders for business, once the rumor spreads."

"*My* master!" Caramon gasped. "But, you bought me! The school—"

"Ah, I acted as agent only." The dwarf cackled. "I thought maybe you didn't know!"

"But who is my—" And then Caramon knew the answer. He didn't even hear the words the dwarf said. He couldn't hear them over the sudden roaring sound that echoed in his brain. A blood-red tide surged over him, suffocating him. His lungs ached, his stomach heaved, and his legs gave way beneath him.

The next thing he knew, he was sitting in the corridor, the ogre holding his head down between his knees. The dizziness passed. Caramon gasped and lifted his head, shaking off the ogre's grasp.

"I'm all right," he said through bloodless lips.

Raag glanced at him, then up at the dwarf.

"We can't take him out there in this condition," Arack said, regarding Caramon with disgust. "Not looking like a fish gone belly up. Haul him to his room."

"No," said a small voice from the darkness. "I-I'll take care of him."

Tas crept out of the shadows, his face nearly as pale as Caramon's.

Arack hesitated, then snarled something and turned away. With a gesture to the ogre, he hurried off, clambering up the stairs to make the awards to the victors.

Tasslehoff knelt beside Caramon, his hand on the big man's arm. The kender's gaze went to the body that lay forgotten on the stone floor. Caramon's gaze followed. Seeing the pain and anguish in his eyes, Tas felt a lump come to his throat. He couldn't say a word, he could only pat Caramon's arm.

"How much did you hear?" Caramon asked thickly.

"Enough," Tas murmured. "Fistandantilus."

"He planned this all along," Caramon sighed and leaned his head back, wearily closing his eyes. "This is how he'll get rid of us. He won't even have to do it himself. Just let this . . . this cleric. . . ."

"Quarath."

"Yeah, he'll let this Quarath kill us." Caramon's fists clenched. "The wizard's hands will be clean! Raistlin will never suspect. And all the time, every fight from now on, I'll wonder. Is that dagger Kiiri holds real?" Opening his eyes, Caramon looked at the kender. "And you, Tas. You're in this, too. The dwarf said so. I can't leave, but you could! You've got to get out of here!"

"Where would I go?" Tas asked helplessly. "He'd find me, Caramon. He's the most powerful magic-user that ever lived. Even kender can't hide from people like him."

For a moment the two sat together in silence, the roar of the crowd echoing above them. Then Tas's eyes caught a gleam of metal across the corridor. Recognizing the object, he rose to his feet and crept over to retrieve it.

"I can get us inside the Temple," he said, taking a deep breath, trying to keep his voice steady. Picking up the bloodstained dagger, he brought it back and handed it to Caramon.

"I can get us in tonight."

Chapter 8

The silver moon, Solinari, flickered on the horizon. Rising up over the central tower of the Temple of the Kingpriest, the moon looked like a candle flame burning on a tall, fluted wick. Solinari was full and bright this night, so bright that the services of the light-walkers were not needed and the boys who earned their living lighting party-goers from one house to another with their quaint, silver lamps spent the night at home, cursing the bright moonlight that robbed them of their livelihood.

Solinari's twin, the blood-red Lunitari, had not risen, nor would it rise for several more hours, flooding the streets with its eerie purplish brilliance. As for the third moon, the black one, its dark roundness among the stars was noted by one man, who gazed at it briefly as he divested himself of his black robes, heavy with spell components, and put on the simpler, softer, black sleeping gown. Drawing the black hood up over his head to blot out Solinari's cold, piercing light, he lay down on his bed and drifted into the restful sleep so necessary to him and his Art.

At least that is what Caramon envisioned him doing as he and the kender walked the moonlit, crowded streets. The night was alive with fun. They passed group after group of merrymakers—parties of men laughing boisterously and discussing the games; parties of women, who clung together and shyly glanced at Caramon out of the corners of their eyes. Their filmy dresses floated around them in the soft breeze that was mild for late autumn. One such group recognized Caramon, and the big man almost ran, fearing they would call guards to take him back to the arena.

But Tas—wiser about the ways of the world—made him stay. The group was enchanted with him. They had seen him fight that afternoon and, already, he had won their hearts. They asked inane questions about the Games, then didn't listen to his answers—which was just as well. Caramon was so nervous, he made very little sense. Finally they went on their way, laughing and bidding him good fortune. Caramon glanced at the kender wonderingly at this, but Tas only shook his head.

"Why did you think I made you dress up?" he asked Caramon shortly.

Caramon had, in fact, been wondering about this very thing. Tas had insisted that he wear the golden, silken cape he wore in the ring, plus the helmet he had worn that afternoon. It didn't seem at all suitable for sneaking into Temples—Caramon had visions of crawling through sewers or climbing over rooftops. But when he balked, Tas's eyes had grown cold. Either Caramon did as he was told or he could forget it, he said sharply.

Caramon, sighing, dressed as ordered, putting the cape on over his regular loose shirt and leather breeches. He put the bloodstained dagger in his belt. Out of habit, he had started to clean it, then stopped. No, it would be more suitable this way.

It had been a simple matter for the kender to unlock their door after Raag locked them in that night, and the two had slipped through the sleeping section of the gladiators' quarters without incident; most of the fighters either being asleep or—in the case of the minotaurs—roaring drunk.

The two walked the streets openly, to Caramon's vast discomfort. But the kender seemed unperturbed. Unusually moody and silent, Tas continually ignored Caramon's repeated questions. They drew nearer and nearer the Temple. It loomed before them in all its pearl and silver radiance, and finally Caramon stopped.

"Wait a minute, Tas," he said softly, pulling the kender into a shadowy corner, "just how do you plan to get us in here?"

"Through the front doors," Tas answered quietly.

"The front doors?" Caramon repeated in blank astonishment. "Are you mad? The guards! They'll stop us—"

"It's a Temple, Caramon," Tas said with a sigh. "A Temple to the gods. Evil things just don't enter."

"Fistandantilus enters," Caramon said gruffly.

"But only because the Kingpriest allows it," Tas said, shrugging. "Otherwise, he *couldn't* get in here. The gods wouldn't permit it. At least that's what one of the clerics told me when I asked."

Caramon frowned. The dagger in his belt seemed heavy, the metal was hot against his skin. Just his imagination, he told himself. After all, he'd worn daggers before. Reaching beneath his cloak, he touched it reassuringly. Then, his lips pressed tightly together, he started walking toward the Temple. After a moment's hesitation, Tas caught up with him.

"Caramon," said the kender in a small voice, "I-I think I know what you were thinking. I've been thinking the same thing. What if the gods won't let *us* in?"

"We're out to destroy evil," Caramon said evenly, his hand on the dagger's hilt. "They'll help us, not hinder us. You'll see."

"But, Caramon—" Now it was Tas's turn to ask questions and Caramon's turn to grimly ignore him. Eventually, they reached the magnificent steps leading up to the Temple.

Caramon stopped, staring at the building. Seven towers rose to the heavens, as if praising the gods for their creation. But one spiraled above them all. Gleaming in Solinari's light, it seemed not to praise the gods but sought to rival them. The beauty of the Temple, its pearl and rose-colored marble gleaming softly in the moonlight, its still pools of water reflecting the stars, its vast gardens of lovely, fragrant flowers, its ornamentation of silver and of gold, all took Caramon's breath away, piercing his heart. He could not move but was held as though spellbound by the wonder.

And then, in the back of his mind, came a lurking feeling of horror. He had seen this before! Only he had seen it in a nightmare—the towers twisted and misshapen. . . . Confused, he closed his eyes. Where? How? Then, it came to him. The Temple at Neraka, where he'd been imprisoned! The Temple of the Queen of Darkness! It had been this very Temple, perverted by her evil, corrupted, turned to a thing of horror. Caramon trembled. Overwhelmed by this terrible memory, wondering at its portent, he thought for a moment of turning around and fleeing.

Then he felt Tas tug at his arm. "Keep moving!" the kender ordered. "You look suspicious!"

Caramon shook his head, clearing it of stupid memories that meant nothing, he told himself. The two approached the guards at the door.

"Tas!" Caramon said suddenly, gripping the kender by the shoulder so tightly he squeaked in pain. "Tas, this is a test! If the gods let us in, I'll know we're doing the right thing! We'll have their blessing!"

Tas paused. "Do you think so?" he asked hesitantly.

"Of course!" Caramon's eyes shone in Solinari's bright light. "You'll see. Come on." His confidence restored, the big man strode up the stairs. He was an imposing sight, the golden, silken cape fluttering about him, the golden helmet flashing in the moonlight. The guards stopped talking and turned to watch him. One nudged the other, saying something and making a swift, stabbing motion with his hand. The other guard grinned and shook his head, regarding Caramon with admiration.

Caramon knew immediately what the pantomime represented and he nearly stopped walking, feeling once again the warm blood splash over his hand and hearing the Barbarian's last, choked words. But he had come too far to quit now. And, perhaps this too was a sign, he told himself. The Barbarian's spirit, lingering near, anxious for its revenge.

Tas glanced up at him anxiously. "Better let me do the talking," the kender whispered.

Caramon nodded, swallowing nervously.

"Greetings, gladiator," called one of the guards. "You're new to the Games, are you not? I was telling my companion on watch, here, that he missed a pretty fight today. Not only that, but you won me six silver pieces, as well. What is it you are called?"

"He's the 'Victor,'" Tas said glibly. "And today was just the beginning. He's never been defeated in battle, and he never will be."

"And who are you, little cutpurse? His manager?"

This was met by roars of laughter from the other guard and nervous high-pitched laughter from Caramon. Then he glanced down at Tas and knew immediately they were in trouble. Tas's face was white. Cutpurse! The most dreadful insult, the worst thing in the world one could call a kender! Caramon's big hand clapped over Tas's mouth.

"Sure," said Caramon, keeping a firm grip on the wriggling kender, "and a good one, too."

"Well, keep an eye on him," the other guard added, laughing even harder. "We want to see you slit throats—not pockets!"

Tasslehoff's ears—the only part visible above Caramon's wide hand—flushed scarlet. Incoherent sounds came from behind Caramon's palm. "I-I think we better go on in," the big warrior stammered, wondering how long he could hold Tas. "We're late."

The guards winked at each other knowingly, one of them shook his head in envy. "I saw the women watching you today," he said, his gaze going to Caramon's broad shoulders. "I should have known you'd be invited here for—uh—dinner."

What were they talking about? Caramon's puzzled look caused the guards to break out in renewed laughter.

"Name of the gods!" One sputtered. "Look at him! He *is* new!"

"Go ahead," the other guard waved him on by. "Good appetite!"

More laughter. Flushing red, not knowing what to say and still trying to hold onto Tas, Caramon entered the Temple. But, as he walked, he heard crude jokes pass between the guards, giving him sudden clear insight into their meaning. Dragging the wriggling kender down a hallway, he darted around the first corner he came to. He hadn't the vaguest idea where he was.

Once the guards were out of sight and hearing, he let Tas go. The kender was pale, his eyes dilated.

"Why, those-those—I'll—They'll regret—"

"Tas!" Caramon shook him. "Stop it. Calm down. Remember why we're here!"

"Cutpurse! As if I were a common thief!" Tas was practically frothing at the mouth. "I—"

Caramon glowered at him, and the kender choked. Getting control of himself, he drew a deep breath and let it out again slowly. "I'm all right, now," he said sullenly. "I said I'm all right," he snapped as Caramon continued to regard him dubiously.

"Well, we got inside, though not quite the way I expected," Caramon muttered. "Did you hear what they were saying?"

"No, not after 'cu-cut' . . . after that word. You had part of your hand over my ears," Tas said accusingly.

"They . . . they sounded like . . . the ladies invited m-men here for-for . . . you know. . . ."

"Look, Caramon," Tas said, exasperated. "You got your sign. They let us in. They were probably just teasing you. You know how gullible you are. You'll believe anything! Tika's always saying so."

A memory of Tika came to Caramon's mind. He could hear her say those very words, laughing. It cut him like a knife. Glaring at Tas, he shoved the memory away immediately.

"Yeah," he said bitterly, flushing, "you're probably right. They're having their joke on me. And I fell for it, too! But"—he lifted his head and, for the first time, looked around at the splendor of the Temple. He began to realize where he was—this holy place, this palace of the gods. Once more he felt the reverence and awe he had experienced as he stood gazing at it, bathed in Solinari's radiant light—"you're right—the gods have given us our sign!"

There was a corridor in the Temple where few came and, of those that did, none went voluntarily. If forced to come here on some errand, they did their business quickly and left as swiftly as possible.

There was nothing wrong with the corridor itself. It was just as splendid as the other halls and corridors of the Temple. Beautiful tapestries done in muted colors graced its walls, soft carpets covered its marble floors, graceful statues filled its shadowy alcoves. Ornately carved wooden doors opened off of it, leading to rooms as pleasingly decorated as other rooms in the Temple. But the doors opened no longer. All were locked. All the rooms were empty—all except one.

That room was at the very far end of the corridor, which was dark and silent even in the daytime. It was as if the occupant of this one room cast a pall over the very floor he walked, the very air he breathed. Those who entered this corridor complained of feeling smothered. They gasped for breath like someone dying inside a burning house.

This room was the room of Fistandantilus. It had been his for years, since the Kingpriest came to power and drove the magic-users from their Tower in Palanthas—the Tower where Fistandantilus had reigned as Head of the Conclave.

What bargain had they struck—the leading powers of good and of evil in the world? What deal had been made that allowed the Dark One to live inside the most beautiful, most holy place on Krynn? None knew, many speculated. Most believed it was by the grace of the Kingpriest, a noble gesture to a defeated foe.

But even he—even the Kingpriest himself—did not walk this corridor. Here, at least, the great mage reigned in dark and terrifying supremacy.

At the far end of the corridor stood a tall window. Heavy plush curtains were drawn over it, blotting out the sunlight in the daytime, the moons' rays at night. Rarely did light penetrate the curtains' thick folds. But this night, perhaps because the servants had been driven by the Head of Household to clean and dust the corridor, the curtains were parted the slightest bit, letting Solinari's silver light shine into the bleak, empty corridor. The beams of the moon the dwarves call Night Candle pierced the darkness like a long, thin blade of glittering steel.

Or perhaps the thin, white finger of a corpse, Caramon thought, looking down that silent corridor. Stabbing through the glass, the finger of moonlight ran the length of the carpeted floor and, reaching the length of the hall, touched him where he stood at the end.

"That's his door," the kender said in such a soft whisper Caramon could barely hear him over the beating of his own heart. "On the left."

Caramon reached beneath his cloak once more, seeking the dagger's hilt, its reassuring presence. But the handle of the knife was cold. He shuddered as he touched it and quickly withdrew his hand.

It seemed a simple thing, to walk down this corridor. Yet he couldn't move. Perhaps it was the enormity of what he contemplated—to take a man's life, not in battle, but as he slept. To kill a man in his sleep—of all times, the time we are most defenseless, when we place ourselves in the hands of the gods. Was there a more heinous, cowardly crime?

The gods gave me a sign, Caramon reminded himself, and sternly he made himself remember the dying Barbarian. He made himself remember his brother's torment in the Tower. He remembered how powerful this evil mage was when awake. Caramon drew a deep breath and grasped the hilt of the dagger firmly. Holding it tightly, though he did not draw it from his belt, he began to walk down the still corridor, the moonlight seeming now to beckon him on.

He felt a presence behind him, so close that, when he stopped, Tas bumped into him.

"Stay here," Caramon ordered.

"No—" Tas began to protest, but Caramon hushed him.

"You've got to. Someone has to stand on watch at this end of the corridor. If anyone comes, make a noise or something."

"But—"

Caramon glared down at the kender. At the sight of the big man's grim expression and cold, emotionless glare, Tas gulped and nodded. "I-I'll just stand over there, in that shadow." He pointed and crept away.

Caramon waited until he was certain Tas wouldn't "accidentally" follow him. But the kender hunched miserably in the shadow of huge, potted tree that had died months ago. Caramon turned and continued on.

Standing next to the brittle skeleton whose dry leaves rustled when the kender moved, Tas watched Caramon walk down the hallway. He saw the big man reach the end, stretch out a hand, and wrap it around the door handle. He saw Caramon give it a gentle push. It yielded to his pressure and opened silently. Caramon disappeared inside the room.

Tasslehoff began to shake. A horrible, sick feeling spread from his stomach throughout his body, a whimper escaped his lips. Clasping his hand over his mouth so that he wouldn't yelp, the kender pressed himself up against the wall and thought about dying, alone, in the dark.

Caramon eased his big body around the door, opening it only a crack in case the hinges should squeak. But it was silent. Everything in the room was silent. No noise from anywhere in the Temple came into this chamber, as if all life itself had been swallowed by the choking darkness. Caramon felt his lungs burn, and he remembered vividly the time he had nearly drowned in the Blood Sea of Istar. Firmly, he resisted the urge to gasp for air.

He paused a moment in the doorway, trying to calm his racing heart, and looked around the room. Solinari's light streamed in through a gap in the heavy curtains that covered the window. A thin sliver of silver light slit the darkness, slicing through it in a narrow cut that led straight to the bed at the far end of the room.

The chamber was sparsely furnished. Caramon saw the shapeless bulk of a heavy black robe draped over a wooden chair. Soft leather boots stood next to it. No fire burned in the grate, the night was too warm. Gripping the hilt of the knife, Caramon drew it slowly and crossed the room, guided by the moon's silver light.

A sign from the gods, he thought, his pounding heartbeat nearly choking him. He felt fear, fear such as he had rarely experienced in his life—a raw, gut-wrenching, bowel-twisting fear that made his muscles jerk and dried his throat. Desperately, he forced himself to swallow so that he wouldn't cough and wake the sleeper.

I must do this quickly! he told himself, more than half afraid he might faint or be sick. He crossed the room, the soft carpet muffling his swift footsteps. Now he could see the bed and the figure asleep within it. He could see the figure clearly, the moonlight slicing a neat line across the floor, up the bedstead, over the coverlet, slanting upward to the head lying on the pillow, its hood pulled over the face to blot out the light.

"Thus the gods point my way," Caramon murmured, unaware that he was speaking. Creeping up to the side of the bed, he paused, the dagger in his hand, listening to the quiet breathing of his victim, trying to detect any change in the deep, even rhythm that would tell him he had been discovered.

In and out . . . in and out . . . the breathing was strong, deep, peaceful. The breathing of a healthy young man. Caramon shuddered, recalling how old this wizard was supposed to be, recalling the dark tales he had heard about how Fistandantilus renewed his youth. The man's breathing was steady, even. There was no break, no quickening. The moonlight poured in, cold, unwavering, a sign. . . .

Caramon raised the dagger. One thrust—swift and neat—deep in the chest and it would be over. Moving forward, Caramon hesitated. No, before he struck, he would look upon the face—the face of the man who had tortured his brother.

No! Fool! a voice screamed inside Caramon. Stab now, quickly! Caramon even lifted the knife again, but his hand shook. He *had* to see the face! Reaching out a trembling hand, he gently touched the black hood. The material was soft and yielding. He pushed it aside.

Solinari's silver moonlight touched Caramon's hand, then touched the face of the sleeping mage, bathing it in radiance. Caramon's hand stiffened, growing white and cold as that of a corpse as he stared down at the face on the pillow.

It was not the face of an ancient evil wizard, scarred with countless sins. It was not even the face of some tormented being whose life had been stolen from his body to keep the dying mage alive.

It was the face of a young magic-user, weary from long nights of study at his books, but now relaxed, finding welcome rest. It was the face of one whose tenacious endurance of constant pain was marked in the firm, unyielding lines about the mouth. It was a face as familiar to Caramon as his own, a face he had looked upon in sleep countless times, a face he had soothed with cooling water. . . .

The hand holding the dagger stabbed down, plunging the blade into the mattress. There was a wild, strangled shriek, and Caramon fell to his knees beside the bed, clutching at the coverlet with fingers curled in agony. His big body shook convulsively, wracked with shuddering sobs.

Raistlin opened his eyes and sat up, blinking in Solinari's bright light. He drew his hood over his eyes once more, then, sighing in irritation, reached out and carefully removed the dagger from his brother's nerveless grip.

Chapter 9

This was truly stupid, my brother," said Raistlin, turning the dagger over in his slender hands, studying it idly. "I find it hard to believe, even of you."

Kneeling on the floor by the bedside, Caramon looked up at his twin. His face was haggard, drawn and deathly pale. He opened his mouth.

"'I don't understand, Raist,'" Raistlin whined, mocking him.

Caramon clamped his lips shut, his face hardened into a dark, bitter mask. His eyes glanced at the dagger his brother still held. "Perhaps it would have been better if I hadn't drawn aside the hood," he muttered.

Raistlin smiled, though his brother did not see him.

"You had no choice," he replied. Then he sighed and shook his head. "My brother, did you honestly think to simply walk into my room and murder me as I slept? You know what a light sleeper I am, have always been."

"No, not you!" Caramon cried brokenly, lifting his gaze. "I thought—" He could not go on.

Raistlin stared at him, puzzled for a moment, then suddenly began to laugh. It was horrible laughter, ugly and taunting, and Tasslehoff—still standing at the end of the hall—clasped his hands over his ears at the sound, even as he began creeping down the corridor toward it to see what was going on.

"You were going to murder Fistandantilus!" Raistlin said, regarding his brother with amusement. He laughed again at the thought. "Dear brother," he said, "I had forgotten how entertaining you could be."

Caramon flushed, and rose unsteadily to his feet.

"I was going to do it . . . for you," he said. Walking over to the window, he pulled aside the curtain and stared moodily out into the courtyard of the Temple that shimmered with pearl and silver in Solinari's light.

"Of course you were," Raistlin snapped, a trace of the old bitterness creeping into his voice. "Why did you ever do anything, except for me?"

Speaking a sharp word of command, Raistlin caused a bright light to fill the room, gleaming from the Staff of Magius that leaned against the wall in a corner. The mage threw back the coverlet and rose from his bed. Walking over to the grate, he spoke another word and flames leaped up from the bare stone. Their orange light beat upon his pale, thin face and was reflected in the clear, brown eyes.

"Well, you are late, my brother," Raistlin continued, holding his hands out to warm them at the blaze, flexing and exercising his supple fingers. "Fistandantilus is dead. By my hands."

Caramon turned around sharply to stare at his brother, caught by the odd tone in Raistlin's voice. But his brother remained standing by the fire, staring into the flames.

"You thought to walk in and stab him as he slept," Raistlin murmured, a grim smile on his thin lips. "The greatest mage who ever lived—up until now."

Caramon saw his brother lean against the mantelpiece, as if suddenly weak.

"He was surprised to see me," said Raistlin softly. "And he mocked me, as he mocked me in the Tower. But he was afraid. I could see it in his eyes.

" 'So, little mage,' " Fistandantilus sneered, 'and how did you get here? Did the great Par-Salian send you?'

" 'I came on my own,' I told him. 'I am the Master of the Tower now.'

"He had not expected that. 'Impossible,' he said, laughing. '*I* am the one whose coming the prophecy foretold. *I* am master of past and present. When I am ready, I will return to my property.'

"But the fear grew in his eyes, even as he spoke, for he read my thoughts. 'Yes,' I answered his unspoken words, 'the prophecy did not work as you hoped. You intended to journey from the past to the present, using the lifeforce you wrenched from me to keep you alive. But you forgot, or perhaps you didn't care, that I could draw upon your *spiritual* force! You had to keep me alive in order to keep sucking out my living juices. And—to that end—you gave me the words and taught me to use the dragon orb. When I lay dying at Astinus's feet, you breathed air into this wretched body you had tortured. You brought me to the Dark Queen and beseeched her to give me the Key to unlock the mysteries of the ancient magic texts I could not read. And, when you were finally ready, you intended to enter the shattered husk of my body and claim it for your own.' "

Raistlin turned to face his brother, and Caramon stepped back a pace, frightened at the hatred and fury he saw burning within the eyes, brighter than the dancing flames of the fire.

"So he thought to keep me weak and frail. But I fought him! I fought him!" Raistlin repeated softly, intently, his gaze staring far away. "I used him! I used his spirit and I lived with the pain and I overcame it! '*You* are master of the past,' I told him, 'but you lack the strength to get into the present. *I* am master of the present, about to become master of the past!' "

Raistlin sighed, his hand dropped, the light flickered in his eyes and died, leaving them dark and haunted. "I killed him," he murmured, "but it was a bitter battle."

"You killed him? They-they said you came back to learn from him," Caramon stammered, confusion twisting his face.

"I did," Raistlin said softly. "Long months I spent with him, in another guise, revealing myself to him only when I was ready. This time, I sucked *him* dry!"

Caramon shook his head. "That's impossible. You didn't

leave until the same time we did, that night.... At least that's what the dark elf said—"

Raistlin shook his head irritably. "Time to you, my brother, is a journey from sunrise to sunset. Time to those of us who have mastered its secrets is a journey beyond suns. Seconds become years, hours—millennia. I have walked these halls as Fistandantilus for months now. These last few weeks I have traveled to all the Towers of High Sorcery—those still standing, that is—to study and to learn. I have been with Lorac, in the elven kingdom, and taught him to use the dragon orb—a deadly gift, for one as weak and vain as he. It will snare him, later on. I have spent long hours with Astinus in the Great Library. And, before that, I studied with the great Fistandantilus. Other places I have visited, seeing horrors and wonders beyond your imagining. But, to Dalamar, for example, I have been gone no more than a day and a night. As have you."

This was beyond Caramon. Desperately, he sought to grab at some fraction of reality.

"Then ... does this mean that you're ... all right, now? I mean, in the present? In our time?" He gestured. "Your skin isn't gold anymore, you've lost the hourglass eyes. You look ... like you did when you were young, and we rode to the Tower, seven years ago. Will you be like that when we go back?"

"No, my brother," Raistlin said, speaking with the patience one uses explaining things to a child. "Surely Par-Salian explained this? Well, perhaps not. Time is a river. I have not changed the course of its flow. I have simply climbed out and jumped in at a point farther upstream. It carries me along its course. I—"

Raistlin stopped suddenly, casting a sharp glance at the door. Then, with a swift motion of his hand, he caused the door to burst open and Tasslehoff Burrfoot tumbled inside, falling down face first.

"Oh, hullo," Tas said, cheerfully picking himself up off the floor. "I was just going to knock." Dusting himself off, he turned eagerly to Caramon. "*I have it figured out!* You see— it used to be Fistandantilus becoming Raistlin becoming Fistandantilus. Only now it's Fistandantilus becoming Raistlin becoming Fistandantilus, then becoming Raistlin again. See?"

No, Caramon did not. Tas turned around to the mage. "Isn't that right, Raist—"

The mage didn't answer. He was staring at Tasslehoff with such a queer, dangerous expression in his eyes that the kender glanced uneasily at Caramon and took a step or two nearer the warrior—just in case Caramon needed help, of course.

Suddenly Raistlin's hand made a swift, slight, summoning motion. Tasslehoff felt no sensation of movement, but there was a blurring in the room for half a heartbeat, and then he was being held by his collar within inches of Raistlin's thin face.

"Why did Par-Salian send *you*?" Raistlin asked in a soft voice that "shivered" the kender's skin, as Flint used to say.

"Well, he thought Caramon needed help, of course and—" Raistlin's grip tightened, his eyes narrowed. Tas faltered. "Uh, actually, I don't think he, uh, really intended to s-send me." Tas tried to twist his head around to look beseechingly at Caramon, but Raistlin's grip was strong and powerful, nearly choking the kender. "It-it was, more or less, an accident, I guess, at least as far as he was c-concerned. And I could t-talk better if you'd let me breathe . . . every once in awhile."

"Go on!" Raistlin ordered, shaking Tas slightly.

"Raist, stop—" Caramon began, taking a step toward him, his brow furrowed.

"Shut up!" Raistlin commanded furiously, never taking his burning eyes off the kender. "Continue."

"There-there was a ring someone had dropped . . . well, maybe not dropped—" Tas stammered, alarmed enough by the expression in Raistlin's eyes into telling the truth, or as near as was kenderly possible. "I-I guess I was sort of going into someone else's room, and it f-fell in-into my pouch, I suppose, because I don't know how it got there, but when th-the red-robed man sent Bupu home, I knew I was next. And I couldn't leave Caramon! So I-I said a prayer to F-Fizban—I mean Paladine—and I put the ring on and—poof!"—Tas held up his hands—"I was a mouse!"

The kender paused at this dramatic moment, hoping for an appropriately amazed response from his audience. But Raistlin's eyes only dilated with impatience and his hand twisted the kender's collar just a bit more, so Tas hurried on, finding it increasingly difficult to breathe.

"And so I was able to hide," he squeaked, not unlike the mouse he had been, "and sneaked into Par-Salian's labra-labora-lavaratory—and he was doing the most wonderful things and the rocks were singing and Crysania was lying there all pale and Caramon looked terrified and I *couldn't* let him go alone—so . . . so . . ." Tas shrugged and looked at Raistlin with disarming innocence, "here I am. . . ."

Raistlin continued clutching him for a moment, devouring him with his eyes, as if he would strip the skin from his bones and see inside his very soul. Then, apparently satisfied, the mage let the kender drop to the floor and turned back to stare into the fire, his thoughts abstracted.

"What does this mean?" he murmured. "A kender—by all the laws of magic forbidden! Does this mean the course of time *can* be altered? Is he telling the truth? Or is this how they plot to stop me?"

"What did you say?" Tas asked with interest, looking up from where he sat on the carpet, trying to catch his breath. "The course of time altered? By *me*? Do you mean that I could—"

Raistlin whirled, glaring at the kender so viciously that Tas shut his mouth and began edging his way back to where Caramon stood.

"I was sure surprised to find your brother. Weren't you?" Tas asked Caramon, ignoring the spasm of pain that crossed Caramon's face. "Raistlin was surprised to see me, too, wasn't he? That's odd, because I saw him in the slave market and I assumed he must have seen us—"

"Slave market!" Caramon said suddenly. Enough of this talk about rivers and time. This was something he could understand! "Raist—you said you've been here months! That means *you* are the one who made them think I attacked Crysania! You're the one who bought me! You're the one who sent me to the Games!"

Raistlin made an impatient gesture, irritated at having his thoughts interrupted.

But Caramon persisted. "Why!" he demanded angrily. "Why that place?"

"Oh, in the name of the gods, Caramon!" Raistlin turned around again, his eyes cold. "What possible use could you be to me in the condition you were in when you came here? I need a strong warrior where we're going next—not a fat drunk.'

"And . . . and you ordered the Barbarian's death?" Caramon asked, his eyes flashing. "You sent the warning to what's-his-name—Quarath?"

"Don't be a dolt, my brother," Raistlin said grimly. "What do I care for these petty court intrigues? Their little, mindless games? If I wanted to do away with an enemy, his life would be snuffed out in a matter of seconds. Quarath flatters himself to think I would take such an interest in him."

"But the dwarf said—"

"The dwarf hears only the sound of money being dropped into his palm. But, believe what you will," Raistlin shrugged.

"It matters little to me."

Caramon was silent long moments, pondering. Tas opened his mouth—there were at least a hundred questions he was dying to ask Raistlin—but Caramon glared at him and the kender closed it quickly. Caramon, slowly going over in his mind all that his brother had told him, suddenly raised his gaze.

"What do you mean—'where we go next'?"

"My counsel is mine to keep," Raistlin replied. "You will know when the time comes, so to speak. My work here progresses, but it is not quite finished. There is one other here besides you who must be beaten down and hammered into shape."

"Crysania," Caramon murmured. "This has something to do with challenging the-the Dark Queen, doesn't it? Like they said? You need a cleric—"

"I am very tired, my brother," Raistlin interrupted. At his gesture, the flames in the fireplace vanished. At a word, the light from the Staff winked out. Darkness, chill and bleak, descended on the three who stood there. Even Solinari's light was gone, the moon having sunk behind the buildings. Raistlin crossed the room, heading for his bed. His black robes rustled softly. "Leave me to my rest. You should not remain here long in any event. Undoubtedly, spies have reported your presence, and Quarath can be a deadly enemy. Try to avoid getting yourself killed. It would annoy me greatly to have to train another bodyguard. Farewell, my brother. Be ready. My summons will come soon. Remember the date."

Caramon opened his mouth, but he found himself talking to a door. He and Tas were standing outside in the now-dark corridor.

"That's really incredible!" the kender said, sighing in delight. "I didn't even feel myself moving, did you? One minute we were there, the next we're here. Just a wave of the hand. It must be wonderful being a mage," Tas said wistfully, staring at the closed door. "Zooming through time and space and closed doors."

"Come on," Caramon said abruptly, turning and stalking down the corridor.

"Say Caramon," Tas said softly, hurrying after him. "What did Raistlin mean—'remember the date'? Is it his Day of Life Gift coming up or something? Are you supposed to get him a present?"

"No," Caramon growled. "Don't be silly."

"I'm not being silly," Tas protested, offended. "After all, Yuletide is in a few weeks, and he's probably expecting a present for that. At least, I suppose they celebrate Yuletide back here in Istar the same as we celebrate it in our time. Do you think—"

Caramon came to a sudden halt.

"What is it?" Tas asked, alarmed at the horrified expression on the big man's face. Hurriedly, the kender glanced around, his hand closing over the hilt of a small knife he had tucked into his own belt. "What do you see? I don't—"

"The date!" Caramon cried. "The date, Tas! Yuletide! In Istar!" Whirling around, he grabbed the startled kender. "What year is it? What year?"

"Why . . ." Tas gulped, trying to think. "I believe, yes, someone told me it was—962."

Caramon groaned, his hands dropped Tas and clutched at his head.

'What *is* it?" Tas asked.

"Think, Tas, think!" Caramon muttered. Then, clutching at his head in misery, the big man stumbled blindly down the corridor in the darkness. "What do they want me to do? What *can* I do?"

Tas followed more slowly. "Let's see. This is Yuletide, year 962 I.A. Such a ridiculously high number. For some reason it sounds familiar. Yuletide, 962. . . . Oh, I remember!" he said triumphantly. "That was the last Yuletide right before . . . right before. . . ."

The thought took the kender's breath away.

"Right before the Cataclysm!" he whispered.

Chapter 10

enubis set down the quill pen and rubbed his eyes. He sat in the quiet of the copying room, his hand over his eyes, hoping that a brief moment of rest would help him. But it didn't. When he opened his eyes and grasped the quill pen to begin his work again, the words he was trying to translate still swam together in a meaningless jumble.

Sternly, he reprimanded himself and ordered himself to concentrate and—finally—the words began to make sense and sort themselves out. But it was difficult going. His head ached. It had ached, it seemed, for days now, with a dull, throbbing pain that was present even in his dreams.

"It's this strange weather," he told himself repeatedly. "Too hot for the beginning of Yule season."

It was too hot, strangely hot. And the air was thick with moisture, heavy and oppressive. The fresh breezes had seemingly been swallowed up by the heat. One hundred miles away at Kathay, so he had heard, the ocean lay flat and calm beneath the fiery sun, so calm that no ships could sail. They sat in the harbor, their captains cursing, their cargo rotting.

Mopping his forehead, Denubis tried to continue working diligently, translating the Disks of Mishakal into Solamnic. But his mind wandered. The words made him think of a tale he had heard some Solamnic knights discussing last night—a gruesome tale that Denubis kept trying to banish from his mind.

A knight named Soth had seduced a young elven cleric and then married her, bringing her home to his castle at Dargaard Keep as his bride. But this Soth had already been married, so the knights said, and there was more than one reason to believe that his first wife had met a most foul end.

The knights had sent a delegation to arrest Soth and hold him for trial, but Dargaard Keep, it was said, was now an armed fortress—Soth's own loyal knights defending their lord. What made it particularly haunting was that the elven woman the lord had deceived remained with him, steadfast in her love and loyalty to the man, even though his guilt had been proven.

Denubis shuddered and tried to banish the thought. There! He made an error. This was hopeless! He started to lay the quill down again, then heard the door to the copying room opening. Hastily, he lifted the quill pen and began to write rapidly.

"Denubis," said a soft, hesitant voice.

The cleric looked up. "Crysania, my dear," he said, with a smile.

"Am I disturbing your work? I can come back—"

"No, no," Denubis assured her. "I am glad to see you. Very glad." This was quite true. Crysania had a way of making him feel calm and tranquil. Even his headache seemed to lessen. Leaving his high-backed writing stool, he found a chair for her and one for himself, then sat down near her, wondering why she had come.

As if in answer, Crysania looked around the still, peaceful room and smiled. "I like it here," she said. "It's so quiet and, well, private." Her smile faded. "I sometimes get tired of . . . of so many people," she said, her gaze going to the door that led to the main part of the Temple.

"Yes, it is quiet," Denubis said. "Now, at any rate. It wasn't so, in past years. When I first came, it was filled with scribes, translating the words of the gods into languages so that everyone could read them. But the Kingpriest didn't think that was necessary and—one by one—they all left, finding more important things to do. Except me." He sighed. "I guess I'm too old," he added gently, apologetically. "I tried to think of something important to do, and I couldn't. So I stayed here. No one seemed to mind . . . very much."

He couldn't help frowning slightly, remembering those long talks with Revered Son, Quarath, prodding and poking at him to make something of himself. Eventually, the higher cleric gave up, telling Denubis he was hopeless. So Denubis had returned to his work, sitting day after day in peaceful solitude, translating the scrolls and the books and sending them off to Solamnia where they sat, unread, in some great library.

"But, enough about me," he added, seeing Crysania's wan face. "What is the matter, my dear? Are you not feeling well? Forgive me, but I couldn't help but notice, these past few weeks, how unhappy you've seemed."

Crysania stared down at her hands in silence, then glanced back up at the cleric. "Denubis," she began hesitantly, "do . . . do you think the church is . . . what it should be?"

That wasn't at all what he had expected. She had more the look of a young girl deceived by a lover. "Why, of course, my dear," Denubis said in some confusion.

"Really?" Lifting her gaze, she looked into his eyes with an intent stare that made Denubis pause. "You have been with the church for a long time, before the coming of the Kingpriest and Quar—his ministers. You talk about the old days. You have seen it change. Is it better?"

Denubis opened his mouth to say, certainly, yes, it was better. How could it be otherwise with such a good and holy man as the Kingpriest at its head? But Lady Crysania's gray eyes were staring straight into his soul, he realized suddenly, feeling their searching, seeking gaze bringing light to all the dark corners where he had been hiding things—he knew—for years. He was reminded, uncomfortably, of Fistandantilus.

"I—well—of course—it's just—" He was babbling and he knew it. Flushing, he fell silent. Crysania nodded gravely, as if she had expected the answer.

"No, it *is* better" he said firmly, not wanting to see her young faith bruised, as his had been. Taking her hand, he leaned forward. "I'm just a middle-aged old man, my dear. And middle-aged old men don't like change. That's all. To us, everything was better in the old days. Why"—he chuckled—"even the water tasted better, it seems. I'm not used to modern ways. It's hard for me to understand. The church is doing a world of good, my dear. It's bringing order to the land and structure to society—"

"Whether society wants it or not," Crysania muttered, but Denubis ignored her.

"It's eradicating evil," he continued, and suddenly the story of that knight—that Lord Soth—floated to the top of his mind, unbidden. He sank it hurriedly, but not before he had lost his place in his lecture. Lamely, he tried to pick it up again, but it was too late.

"Is it?" Lady Crysania was asking him. "Is it eradicating evil? Or are we like children, left alone in the house at night, who light candle after candle to keep away the darkness. We don't see that the darkness has a purpose—though we may not understand it—and so, in our terror, we end up burning down the house!"

Denubis blinked, not understanding this at all; but Crysania continued, growing more and more restless as she talked. It was obvious, Denubis realized uncomfortably, that she had kept this pent up inside her for weeks.

"We don't try to help those who have lost their way find it again! We turn our backs on them, calling them unworthy, or we get rid of them! Do you know"—she turned on Denubis— "that Quarath has proposed ridding the world of the ogre races?"

"But, my dear, ogres are, after all, a murderous, villainous lot—" Denubis ventured to protest feebly.

"Created by the gods, just as we were," Crysania said. "Do we have the right, in our imperfect understanding of the great scheme of things, to destroy anything the gods created?"

"Even spiders?" Denubis asked wistfully, without thinking. Seeing her irritated expression, he smiled. "Never mind. The ramblings of an old man."

"I came here, convinced that the church was everything good and true, and now I—I—" She put her head in her hands.

Denubis's heart ached nearly as much as his head. Reaching out a trembling hand, he gently stroked the smooth, blue-black hair, comforting her as he would have comforted the daughter he never had.

"Don't feel ashamed of your questioning, child," he said, trying to forget that he had been feeling ashamed of his. "Go, talk to the Kingpriest. He will answer your doubts. He has more wisdom than I."

Crysania looked up hopefully.

"Do you think—"

"Certainly," Denubis smiled. "See him tonight, my dear. He will be holding audience. Do not be afraid. Such questions do not anger him."

"Very well," Crysania said, her face filled with resolve. "You are right. It's been foolish of me to wrestle with this myself, without help. I'll ask the Kingpriest. Surely, he can make this darkness light."

Denubis smiled and rose to his feet as Crysania rose. Impulsively, she leaned over and kissed him gently on the cheek. "Thank you, my friend," she said softly. "I'll leave you to your work."

Watching her walk from the still, sunlit room, Denubis felt a sudden, inexplicable sorrow and, then, a very great fear. It was as if he stood in a place of bright light, watching her walk into a vast and terrible darkness. The light around him grew brighter and brighter, while the darkness around her grew more horrible, more dense.

Confused, Denubis put his hand to his eyes. The light was real! It was streaming into this room, bathing him in a radiance so brilliant and beautiful that he couldn't look upon it. The light pierced his brain, the pain in his head was excruciating. And still, he thought desperately, I must warn Crysania, I must stop her. . . .

The light engulfed him, filling his soul with its radiant brilliance. And then, suddenly, the bright light was gone. He was once more standing in the sunlit room. But he wasn't alone. Blinking, trying to accustom his eyes to the darkness, he looked around and saw an elf standing in the room with him, observing him coolly. The elf was elderly, balding, with a long, meticulously groomed, white beard. He was dressed in long, white robes, the medallion of Paladine hung about his neck. The expression on the elf's face was one of sadness, such sadness that Denubis was moved to tears, though he had no idea why.

"I'm sorry," Denubis said huskily. Putting his hand to his head, he suddenly realized it didn't hurt anymore. "I-I didn't see you come in. Can I help you? Are you looking for someone?"

"No, I have found the one I seek," the elf said calmly, but still with the same sad expression, "if you are Denubis."

"I am Denubis," the cleric replied, mystified. "But, forgive me, I can't place you—"

"My name is Loralon," said the elf.

Denubis gasped. The greatest of the elven clerics, Loralon had, years ago, fought Quarath's rise to power. But Quarath was too strong. Powerful forces backed him. Loralon's words of reconciliation and peace were not appreciated. In sorrow, the old cleric had returned to his people, to the wondrous land of Silvanesti that he loved, vowing never to look upon Istar again.

What was he doing here?

"Surely, you seek the Kingpriest," Denubis stammered, "I'll—"

"No, there is only one in this Temple I seek and that is you, Denubis," Loralon said. "Come, now. We have a long journey ahead of us."

"Journey!" Denubis repeated stupidly, wondering if he were going mad. "That's impossible. I've not left Istar since I came here, thirty years—"

"Come along, Denubis," said Loralon gently.

"Where? How? I don't understand—" Denubis cried. He saw Loralon standing in the center of the sunlit, peaceful room, watching him, still with that same expression of deep, unutterable sadness. Reaching up, Loralon touched the medallion he wore around his neck.

And then Denubis knew. Paladine gave his cleric insight. He saw the future. Blanching in horror, he shook his head.

"No," he whispered. "That is too dreadful."

"All is not decided. The scales of balance are tipping, but they have not yet been upset. This journey may be only temporary, or it may last for time beyond reckoning. Come, Denubis, you are needed here no longer."

The great elven cleric stretched out his hand. Denubis felt blessed with a sense of peace and understanding he had never before experienced, even in the presence of the Kingpriest. Bowing his head, he reached out and took Loralon's hand. But, as he did so, he could not help weeping. . . .

Crysania sat in a corner of the Kingpriest's sumptuous Hall of Audience, her hands folded calmly in her lap, her face pale but composed. Looking at her, no one would have guessed the turmoil in her soul. No one, perhaps, except one man, who had entered the room unnoticed by anyone and who now stood in a shadowy alcove, watching Crysania.

Sitting there, listening to the musical voice of the Kingpriest, hearing him discuss important matters of state with his ministers, hearing him go from politics to solving the great mysteries of the universe with other ministers, Crysania actually blushed to think she had even considered approaching him with her petty questions.

Words of Elistan's came to her mind. "Do not go to others for the answers. Look in your own heart, search your own faith. You will either find the answer or come to see that the answer is with the gods themselves, not with man."

And so Crysania sat, preoccupied with her thoughts, searching her heart. Unfortunately, the peace she sought eluded her. Perhaps there were no answers to her questions, she decided abruptly. Then she felt a hand on her arm. Starting, Crysania looked up.

"There *are* answers to your questions, Revered Daughter," said a voice that sent a thrill of shocked recognition through her nerves, "there are answers, but you refuse to listen to them."

She knew the voice, but—looking eagerly into the shadows of the hood, she could not recognize the face. She glanced at the hand on her shoulder, thinking she knew that hand. Black robes fell around it, and her heart lurched. But there were no silver runes upon the robes, such as *he* wore. Once more, she stared into the face. All she could see was the glitter of hidden eyes, pale skin.... Then the hand left her shoulder and, reaching up, turned back the front of the hood.

At first, Crysania felt bitter disappointment. The young man's eyes were not golden, not shaped like the hourglass that had become his symbol. The skin was not tinted gold, the face was not frail and sickly. This man's face was pale, as if from long hours of study, but it was healthy, even handsome, except for its look of perpetual, bitter cynicism. The eyes were brown, clear and cold as glass, reflecting back all they saw, revealing nothing within. The man's body was slender, but well-muscled. The black, unadorned robes he wore revealed the outline of strong shoulders, not the stooped and shattered frame of the mage. And then the man smiled, the thin lips parted slightly.

"It *is* you!" Crysania breathed, starting up from her chair.

The man placed his hand upon her shoulder again, exerting a gentle pressure that forced her back down. "Please, remain seated, Revered Daughter," he said. "I will join you. It is quiet here, and we can talk without interruption." Turning, he motioned with a graceful gesture and a chair that had been across the room suddenly stood next to him. Crysania gasped slightly and glanced around the room. But, if anyone else had noticed, they were all studiously intent upon ignoring the mage. Looking back, Crysania found Raistlin watching her in amusement, and she felt her skin grow warm.

"Raistlin," she said formally, to cover her confusion, "I am pleased to see you."

"And I am pleased to see you, Revered Daughter," he said in that mocking voice that grated on her nerves. "But my name is not Raistlin."

She stared at him, flushing even more now in her embarrassment. "Forgive me," she said, looking intently at his face, "but you reminded me strongly of someone I know— once knew."

"Perhaps this will clear up the mystery," he said softly. "My name, to those around here, is Fistandantilus."

Crysania shivered involuntarily, the lights in the room seemed to darken. "No," she said, shaking her head slowly, "that cannot be! You came back . . . to learn from him!"

"I came back to *become* him," Raistlin replied.

"But . . . I've heard stories. He's evil, foul—" She drew away from Raistlin, her gaze fixed on him in horror.

"The evil is no more," Raistlin replied. "He is dead."

"You?" The word was a whisper.

"He would have killed me, Crysania," Raistlin said simply, "as he has murdered countless others. It was my life or his."

"We have exchanged one evil for another," Crysania answered in a sad, hopeless voice. She turned away.

I am losing her! Raistlin realized instantly. Silently, he regarded her. She had shifted in her chair, turning her face from him. He could see her profile, cold and pure as Solinari's light. Coolly he studied her, much as he studied the small animals that came under his knife when he probed for the secrets of life itself. Just as he stripped away their skins to see the beating hearts beneath, so he mentally stripped away Crysania's outer defenses to see her soul.

She was listening to the beautiful voice of the Kingpriest, and on her face was a look of profound peace. But Raistlin remembered her face as he had seen it on entering. Long accustomed to observing others and reading the emotions they thought they hid, he had seen the slight line appear between her black eyebrows, he had seen her gray eyes grow dark and clouded.

She had kept her hands in her lap, but he had seen the fingers twist the cloth of her gown. He knew of her conversation with Denubis. He knew she doubted, that her faith was wavering, teetering on the edge of the precipice. It would take little to shove her over the edge. And, with a bit of patience on his part, she might even jump over of her own accord.

Raistlin remembered how she had flinched at his touch. Drawing near her, he reached out and took hold of her wrist. She started and almost immediately tried to break free of his hold. But his grip was firm. Crysania looked up into his eyes and could not move.

"Do you truly believe that of me?" Raistlin asked in the voice of one who has suffered long and then returned to find it was all for nothing. He saw his sorrow pierce her heart. She tried to speak, but Raistlin continued, twisting the knife in her soul.

"Fistandantilus planned to return to our time, destroy me, take my body, and pick up where the Queen of Darkness left off. He plotted to bring the evil dragons under his control. The Dragon Highlords, like my sister, Kitiara, would have flocked to his standard. The world would be plunged into war, once again," Raistlin paused. "That threat is now ended," he said softly.

His eyes held Crysania, just as his hand held her wrist. Looking in them, she saw herself reflected in their mirrorlike surface. And she saw herself, not as the pale, studious, severe cleric she had heard herself called more than once, but as someone beautiful and caring. This man had come to her in trust and she had let him down. The pain in his voice was unendurable, and Crysania tried once again to speak, but Raistlin continued, drawing her ever nearer.

"You know my ambitions," he said. "To you, I opened my heart. Is it my design to renew the war? Is it my desire to conquer the world? My sister, Kitiara, came to me to ask this very thing, to seek my help. I refused, and you, I fear, paid the consequences." Raistlin sighed and lowered his eyes. "I told her about you, Crysania, and of your goodness and your power. She was enraged and sent her death knight to destroy you, thinking to end your influence over me."

"Do I have influence over you then?" Crysania asked softly, no longer trying to break free of Raistlin's hold. Her voice trembled with joy. "Can I dare hope that you have seen the ways of the church and—"

"The ways of *this* church?" Raistlin asked, his voice once again bitter and mocking. Withdrawing his hand abruptly, he sat back in his chair, gathering his black robes about him and regarding Crysania with a sneering smile.

Embarrassment, anger, and guilt stained Crysania's cheeks a faint pink, her gray eyes darkened to deep blue. The color in her cheeks spread to her lips and suddenly she *was* beautiful, something Raistlin noticed without meaning to. The thought annoyed him beyond all bounds, threatening to disrupt his concentration. Irritably, he pushed it away.

"I know your doubts, Crysania," he continued abruptly. "I know what you have seen. You have found the church to be far more concerned with running the world than teaching the ways of the gods. You have seen its clerics double-dealing, dabbling in politics, spending money for show that might have fed the poor. You thought to vindicate the church, when you came back; to discover that others caused the gods in their righteous anger to hurl the fiery mountain down upon those who forsook them. You sought to blame . . . magic-users, perhaps."

Crysania's flush deepened, she could not look at him and turned her face away, but her pain and humiliation were obvious.

Raistlin continued mercilessly. "The time of the Cataclysm draws near. Already, the true clerics have left the land. . . . Yes, didn't you know? Your friend, Denubis, has gone. You, Crysania, are the only true cleric left in the land."

Crysania stared at Raistlin in shock. "That's . . . impossible," she whispered. Her eyes glanced around the room. And she could hear, for the first time, the conversations of those gathered in knots away from the Kingpriest. She heard talk of the Games, she heard arguments over the distribution of public funds, the routing of armies, the best means to bring a rebellious land under control—all in the name of the church.

And then, as if to drown out the other, harsh voices, the sweet, musical voice of the Kingpriest welled up in her soul, calming her troubled spirit. The Kingpriest was here, still. Turning from the darkness, she looked toward his light and felt her faith, once more strong and pure, rise up to defend her. Coolly, she looked back at Raistlin.

"There is still goodness in the world," she said sternly. Standing she started to leave. "As long as that holy man, who is surely blessed of the gods, rules, I cannot believe that the gods visited their wrath upon the church. Say, rather, it was on the world for ignoring the church," she continued, her voice low and passionate. Raistlin had risen as well and, watching her intently, moved nearer to her.

She did not seem to notice but kept on. "Or for ignoring the Kingpriest! He must foresee it! Perhaps even now he is trying to prevent it! Begging the gods to have mercy!"

"Look at this man," Raistlin whispered, " 'blessed' of the gods." Reaching out, the mage took hold of Crysania with his strong hands and forced her to face the Kingpriest. Overwhelmed with guilt for having doubted and angry with herself for having carelessly allowed Raistlin to see within her, Crysania angrily tried to free herself of his hold, but he gripped her firmly, his fingers burning into her skin.

"Look!" he repeated. Shaking her slightly, he made her raise her head to look directly into the light and glory that surrounded the Kingpriest.

Raistlin felt the body he held so near his own start to tremble, and he smiled in satisfaction. Moving his black-hooded head near hers, Raistlin whispered in her ear, his breath touching her cheek.

"What do you see, Revered Daughter?"

His only answer was a heartbroken moan.

Raistlin's smile deepened. "Tell me," he persisted.

"A man." Crysania faltered, her shocked gaze on the Kingpriest. "Only a human man. He looks weary and . . . and frightened. His skin sags, he hasn't slept for nights. Pale blue eyes dart here and there in fear—" Suddenly, she realized what she had been saying. Acutely aware of Raistlin's nearness, the warmth and the feel of the strong, muscled body beneath the soft, black robes, Crysania broke free of his grip.

"What spell is this you have cast over me?" she demanded angrily, turning to confront him.

"No spell, Revered Daughter," Raistlin said quietly. "I have broken the spell he weaves around himself in his fear. It is that fear which will prove his undoing and bring down destruction upon the world."

Crysania stared at Raistlin wildly. She wanted him to be lying, she willed him to be lying. But then she realized that, even if he was, it didn't matter. She could no longer lie to herself.

Confused, frightened, and bewildered, Crysania turned around and, half-blinded by her tears, ran out of the Hall of Audience.

Raistlin watched her go, feeling neither elation nor satisfaction at his victory. It was, after all, no more than he had expected. Sitting down again, near the fire, he selected an orange from a bowl of fruit sitting on a table and casually tore off its peel as he stared thoughtfully into the flames.

One other person in the room watched Crysania flee the audience chamber. He watched as Raistlin ate the orange, draining the fruit of its juice first, then devouring the pulp.

His face pale with anger vying with fear, Quarath left the Hall of Audience, returning to his own room, where he paced the floor until dawn.

Chapter II

It became known in later history as the Night of Doom, that night the true clerics left Krynn. Where they went and what their fate may have been, not even Astinus records. Some say they were seen during the bleak, bitter days of the War of the Lance, three hundred years later. There are many elves who will swear on all they hold dear that Loralon, greatest and most devout of the elven clerics, walked the tortured lands of Silvanesti, grieving at its downfall and blessing the efforts of those who gave of themselves to help in its rebuilding.

But, for most on Krynn, the passing of the true clerics went unnoticed. That night, however, proved to be a Night of Doom in many ways for others.

Crysania fled the Hall of Audience of the Kingpriest in confusion and fear. Her confusion was easily explained. She had seen that greatest of beings, the Kingpriest, the man that even clerics in her own day still revered, as a human afraid of his own shadow, a human who hid himself behind spells and who let others rule for him. All of the doubts and misgivings she had developed about the church and its purpose on Krynn returned.

As for what she feared, that she could not or would not define.

On first leaving the Hall, she stumbled along blindly without any clear idea of where she was going or what she was doing. Then she sought refuge in a corner, dried her tears, and pulled herself together. Ashamed of her momentary loss of control, she knew at once what she had to do.

She must find Denubis. She would prove Raistlin wrong.

Walking through the empty corridors lit by Solinari's waning light, Crysania went to Denubis's chamber. This tale of vanishing clerics could not be true. Crysania had, in fact, never believed in the old legends about the Night of Doom, considering them children's tales. Now, she still refused to believe it. Raistlin was . . . mistaken.

She hurried on without pause, familiar with the way. She had visited Denubis in his chambers several times to discuss theology or history, or to listen to his stories of his homeland. She knocked on the door.

There was no answer.

"He's asleep," Crysania said to herself, irritated at the sudden shiver that shook her body. "Of course, it's past Deep Watch. I'll return in the morning."

But she knocked again and even called out softly, "Denubis."

Still no answer.

"I'll come back. After all, it's only been a few hours since I saw him," she said to herself again, but she found her hand on the doorknob, gently turning it. "Denubis?" she whispered, her heart throbbing in her throat. The room was dark, it faced into an inner courtyard and so the window let in nothing of the moon's light. For a moment Crysania's will failed her. "This is ridiculous!" she reprimanded herself, already envisioning Denubis's embarrassment and her own if the man woke up to find her creeping into his bed chamber in the dead of night.

Firmly, Crysania threw open the door, letting the light from the torches in the corridor shine into the small room. It was just the way he had left it—neat, orderly . . . and empty.

Well, not quite empty. The man's books, his quill pens, even his clothes were still there, as if he had just stepped out for a few minutes, intending to return directly. But the spirit of the room was gone, leaving it cold and vacant as the still-made bed.

For a moment, the lights in the corridor blurred before Crysania's eyes. Her legs felt weak and she leaned against the door. Then, as before, she forced herself to be calm, to think rationally. Firmly, she shut the door and, even more firmly, made herself walk down the sleeping corridors toward her own room.

Very well, the Night of Doom had come. The true clerics were gone. It was nearly Yule. Thirteen days after Yule, the Cataclysm would strike. That thought brought her to a halt. Feeling weak and sick, she leaned against a window and stared unseeing into a garden bathed in white moonlight. So this was the end of her plans, her dreams, her goals. She would be forced to go back to her own time and report nothing but dismal failure.

The silver garden swam in her sight. She had found the church corrupt, the Kingpriest apparently at fault for the terrible destruction of the world. She had even failed in her original intent, to draw Raistlin from the folds of darkness. He would never listen to her. Right now, probably, he was laughing at her with that terrible, mocking laugh. . . .

"Revered Daughter?" came a voice.

Hastily wiping her eyes, Crysania turned. "Who is there?" she asked, trying to clear her throat. Blinking rapidly, she stared into the darkness, then caught her breath as a dark, robed figure emerged from the shadows. She could not speak, her voice failed.

"I was on my way to my chambers when I saw you standing here," said the voice, and it was not laughing or mocking. It was cool and tinged with cynicism, but there was a strange quality to it, a warmth, that made Crysania tremble.

"I hope you are not ill," Raistlin said, coming over to stand beside her. She could not see his face, hidden by the shadows of the dark hood. But she could see his eyes, glittering, clear and cold in the moonlight.

"No," Crysania murmured in confusion and turned her face away, devoutly hoping that all traces of tears were gone. But it did little good. Weariness, strain, and her own failings overwhelmed her. Though she sought desperately to control them, the tears came again, sliding down her cheeks.

"Go away, please," she said, squeezing her eyes shut, swallowing the tears like bitter medicine.

She felt warmth envelop her and the softness of velvet black robes brush against her bare arm. She smelled the sweet scent of spices and rose petals and a vaguely cloying scent of decay—bat's wings, perhaps, the skull of some animal—those mysterious things magicians used to cast their spells. And then she felt a hand touch her cheek, slender fingers, sensitive and strong and burning with that strange warmth.

Either the fingers brushed the tears away or they dried at their burning touch, Crysania wasn't certain. Then the fingers gently lifted her chin and turned her head away from the moonlight. Crysania couldn't breathe, her heartbeat stifled her. She kept her eyes closed, fearing what she might see. But she could feel Raistlin's slender body, hard beneath the soft robes, press against hers. She could feel that terrible warmth . . .

Crysania suddenly wanted his darkness to enfold her and hide her and comfort her. She wanted that warmth to burn away the cold inside of her. Eagerly, she raised her arms and reached out her hands . . . and he was gone. She could hear the rustle of his robes receding in the stillness of the corridor.

Startled, Crysania opened her eyes. Then, weeping once more, she pressed her cheek against the cold glass. But these were tears of joy.

"Paladine," she whispered, "thank you. My way is clear. I will not fail!"

A dark-robed figure stalked the Temple halls. Any who met it shrank away from it in terror, shrank from the anger that could be felt if not seen on the hooded face. Raistlin at last entered his own deserted corridor, hit the door to his room with a blast that nearly shattered it, and caused flames to leap up in the grate with nothing more than a glance. The fire roared up the chimney and Raistlin paced, hurling curses at himself until he was too tired to walk. Then he sank into a chair and stared at the fire with a feverish gaze.

"Fool!" he repeated. "I should have foreseen this!" His fist clenched. "I should have known. This body, for all its strength, has the great weakness common to mankind. No matter how intelligent, how disciplined the mind, how controlled the emotions, *that* waits in the shadows like a great beast, ready to leap out and take over." He snarled in rage and dug his nails into his palm until it bled. "I can still see her! I can see her ivory skin, her pale, soft lips. I can smell her hair and feel the curving softness of her body next to mine!"

"No!" This was fairly a shriek. "This must not, will not be allowed to happen! Or perhaps...." A thought. "What if I were to seduce her? Would that not put her even more in my power?" The thought was more than tempting, it brought such a rush of desire to the young man that his entire body shook.

But the cold and calculating, logical part of Raistlin's mind took over. "What do you know of lovemaking?" he asked himself with a sneer. "Of seduction? In this, you are a child, more stupid than your behemoth of a brother."

Memories of his youth came back to him in a flood. Frail and sickly, noted for his biting sarcasm and his sly ways, Raistlin had certainly never attracted the attention of women, not like his handsome brother. Absorbed, obsessed by his studies of magic, he had not felt the loss—much. Oh, once he had experimented. One of Caramon's girlfriends, bored by easy conquest, thought the big man's twin brother might prove more interesting. Goaded by his brother's gibes and those of his fellows, Raistlin had given way to her coarse overtures. It had been a disappointing experience for both of them. The girl returned gratefully to Caramon's arms. For Raistlin, it had simply proved what he had long suspected—that he found true ecstasy only in his magic.

But this body—younger, stronger, more like his brother's—ached with a passion he had never before experienced. Yet he could not give way to it. "I would end up destroying myself"— he saw with cold clarity—"and, far from furthering my objective, might well harm it. She is virgin, pure in mind and body. That purity is her strength. I need it tarnished, but I need it intact."

Having firmly resolved this and being long experienced in the practice of exerting strict mental control over his emotions, the young mage relaxed and sat back in his chair, letting weariness sweep over him. The fire died low, his eyes closed in the rest that would renew his flagging power.

But, before he drifted off to sleep, still sitting in the chair, he saw once more, with unwanted vividness, a single tear glistening in the moonlight.

The Night of Doom continued. An acolyte was awakened from a sound sleep and told to report to Quarath. He found the elven cleric sitting in his chambers.

"Did you send for me, my lord?" the acolyte asked, attempting to stifle a yawn. He looked sleepy and rumpled. Indeed, his outer robes had been put on backward in his haste to answer the summons that had come so late in the night.

"What is the meaning of this report?" Quarath demanded, tapping at a piece of paper on his desk.

The acolyte bent over to look, rubbing the sleep out of his eyes enough to make the writing coherent.

"Oh, that," he said after a moment. "Just what it says, my lord."

"That Fistandantilus was *not* responsible for the death of my slave? I find that very difficult to believe."

"Nonetheless, my lord, you may question the dwarf yourself. He confessed—after a great deal of monetary persuasion—that he had in reality been hired by the lord named there, who was apparently incensed at the church's takeover of his holdings on the outskirts of the city."

"I know what he's incensed about!" Quarath snapped. "And killing my slave would be just like Onygion—sneaky and underhanded. He doesn't dare face me directly."

Quarath sat, musing. "Then why did that big slave commit the deed?" he asked suddenly, giving the acolyte a shrewd glance.

"The dwarf stated that this was something arranged privately between himself and Fistandantilus. Apparently the first 'job' of this nature that came his way was to be given to the slave, Caramon."

"That wasn't in the report," Quarath said, eyeing the young man sternly.

"No," the acolyte admitted, flushing. "I-I really don't like putting anything about . . . the magic-user . . . down in writing. Anything like that, where he might read it—"

"No, I don't suppose I blame you," Quarath muttered. "Very well, you may go."

The acolyte nodded, bowed, and returned thankfully to his bed.

Quarath did not go to his bed for long hours, however, but sat in his study, going over and over the report. Then, he sighed. "I am becoming as bad as the Kingpriest, jumping at shadows that aren't there. If Fistandantilus wanted to do away with me, he could manage it within seconds. I should have realized—this is not his style." He rose to his feet, finally. "Still, he was with her tonight. I wonder what that means? Perhaps nothing. Perhaps the man is more human than I would have supposed. Certainly the body he has appeared in this time is better than those he usually dredges up."

The elf smiled grimly to himself as he straightened his desk and filed the report away carefully. "Yule is approaching. I will put this from my mind until the holiday season is past. After all, the time is fast coming when the Kingpriest will call upon the gods to eradicate evil from the face of Krynn. That will sweep this Fistandantilus and those who follow him back into the darkness which spawned them."

He yawned, then, and stretched. "But I'll take care of Lord Onygion first."

The Night of Doom was nearly ended. Morning lit the sky as Caramon lay in his cell, staring into the gray light. Tomorrow was another game, his first since the "accident."

Life had not been pleasant for the big warrior these last few days. Nothing had changed outwardly. The other gladiators were old campaigners, most of them, long accustomed to the ways of the Game.

"It is not a bad system," Pheragas said with a shrug when Caramon confronted him the day after his return from the Temple. "Certainly better than a thousand men killing each other on the fields of battle. Here, if one nobleman feels offended by another, their feud is handled secretly, in private, to the satisfaction of all."

"Except the innocent man who dies for a cause he doesn't care about or understand!" Caramon said angrily.

"Don't be such a baby!" Kiiri snorted, polishing one of her collapsible daggers. "By your own account, you did some mercenary work. Did you understand or care about the cause then? Didn't you fight and kill because you were being well paid? Would you have fought if you weren't? I don't see the difference."

"The difference is I had a choice!" Caramon responded, scowling. "And I knew the cause I fought for! I never would have fought for anyone I didn't believe was in the right! No matter how much money they paid me! My brother felt the same. He and I—" Caramon abruptly fell silent.

Kiiri looked at him strangely, then shook her head with a grin. "Besides," she added lightly, "it adds spice, an edge of real tension. You'll fight better from now on. You'll see."

Thinking of this conversation as he lay in the darkness, Caramon tried to reason it out in his slow, methodical fashion. Maybe Kiiri and Pheragas were correct, maybe he *was* being a baby, crying because the bright, glittering toy he had enjoyed playing with suddenly cut him. But—looking at it every way possible—he still couldn't believe it was right. A man deserved a choice, to choose his own way to live, his own way to die. No one else had the right to determine that for him.

And then, in the predawn, a crushing weight seemed to fall on Caramon. He sat up, leaning on one elbow, staring unseeing into the gray cell. If that was true, if every man deserved a choice, then what about his brother? Raistlin had made his choice—to walk the ways of night instead of day. Did Caramon have the right to drag his brother from those paths?

His mind went back to those days he had unwittingly recalled when talking to Kiiri and Pheragas—those days right before the Test, those days that had been the happiest in his life—the days of mercenary work with his brother.

The two fought well together, and they were always welcomed by nobles. Though warriors were common as leaves in the trees, magic-users who could and would join the fighting were another thing altogether. Though many nobles looked somewhat dubious when they saw Raistlin's frail and sickly appearance, they were soon impressed by his courage and his skill. The brothers were paid well and were soon much in demand.

But they always selected the cause they fought for with care.

"That was Raist's doing," Caramon whispered to himself wistfully. "I would have fought for anyone, the cause mattered little to me. But Raistlin insisted that the cause had to be a just one. We walked away from more than one job because he said it involved a strong man trying to grow stronger by devouring others...."

"But that's what Raistlin's doing!" Caramon said softly, staring up at the ceiling. "Or is it? That's what they *say he's* doing, those magic-users. But can I trust them? Par-Salian was the one who got him into this, he admitted that! Raistlin rid the world of this Fistandantilus creature. By all accounts, that's a good thing. And Raist told me he didn't have anything to do with the Barbarian's death. So he hasn't really done anything wrong. Maybe we've misjudged him.... Maybe we have *no right* to try to force him to change...."

Caramon sighed. "What should I do?" Closing his eyes in forlorn weariness, he fell asleep, and soon the smell of warm, freshly baked muffins filled his mind.

The sun lit the sky. The Night of Doom ended. Tasslehoff rose from his bed, eagerly greeted the new day, and decided that he—he personally—would stop the Cataclysm.

Chapter 12

"Alter time!" Tasslehoff said eagerly, slipping over the garden wall into the sacred Temple area and dropping down to land in the middle of a flower bed. Some clerics were walking in the garden, talking among themselves about the merriment of the forthcoming Yule season. Rather than interrupt their conversation, Tas did what he considered the polite thing and flattened himself down among the flowers until they left, although it meant getting his blue leggings dirty.

It was rather pleasant, lying among the red Yule roses, so called because they grew only during the Yule season. The weather was warm, too warm, most people said. Tas grinned. Trust humans. If the weather was cold, Yule-type weather, they'd complain about that, too. He thought the warmth was delightful. A trifle hard to breathe in the heavy air, perhaps, but—after all—you couldn't have everything.

Tas listened to the clerics with interest. The Yule parties must be splendid things, he thought, and briefly considered attending. The first one was tonight—Yule Welcoming. It would end early, since everyone wanted to get lots of sleep in preparation for the big Yule parties themselves, which would begin at dawn tomorrow and run for days—the last celebration before the harsh, dark winter set in.

"Perhaps I'll attend that party tomorrow," Tas thought. He had supposed that a Yule Welcoming party in the Temple would be solemn and grand and, therefore, dull and boring—at least from a kender viewpoint. But the way these clerics talked, it sounded quite lively.

Caramon was fighting tomorrow—the Games being one of the highlights of the Yule season. Tomorrow's fight determined which teams would have the right to face each other in the Final Bout—the last game of the year before winter forced the closing of the arena. The winners of this last game would win their freedom. Of course, it was already predetermined who would win tomorrow—Caramon's team. For some reason, this news had sent Caramon into a gloomy depression.

Tas shook his head. He never would understand that man, he decided. All this sulking about honor. After all, it was only a game. Anyway, it made things easy. It would be simple for Tas to sneak off and enjoy himself.

But then the kender sighed. No, he had serious business to attend to—stopping the Cataclysm was more important than a party, maybe even a couple of parties. He'd sacrifice his own amusement to this great cause.

Feeling very self-righteous and noble (and suddenly quite bored), the kender glared at the clerics irritably, wishing they'd hurry up. Finally, they strolled inside, leaving the garden empty. Heaving a sigh of relief, Tas picked himself up and brushed off the dirt. Plucking a Yule rose, he stuck it in his topknot for decoration in honor of the season, then slipped into the Temple.

It, too, was decorated for the Yule season, and the beauty and splendor took the kender's breath away. He stared around in delight, marveling at the thousands of Yule roses that had been raised in gardens all over Krynn and brought here to fill the Temple corridors with their sweet fragrance. Wreaths of everbloom added a spicy scent, sunlight glistened off its pointed, polished leaves twined with red velvet and swans' feathers. Baskets of rare and exotic fruits stood on nearly every table—gifts from all over Krynn to be enjoyed by everyone in the Temple. Plates of wonderful cakes and sweetmeats stood beside them. Thinking of Caramon, Tas stuffed his pouches full, happily picturing the big man's delight. He had never known Caramon to stay depressed in the face of a crystal sugared almond puff.

Tas roamed the halls, lost in happiness. He almost forgot why he had come and had to remind himself continually of his Important Mission. No one paid any attention to him. Everyone he passed was intent on the upcoming celebration or on the business of running the government or the church or both. Few even gave Tas a second glance. Occasionally, a guard stared sternly at him, but Tas just smiled cheerily, waved, and went on. It was an old kender proverb—*Don't change color to match the walls. Look like you belong and the walls will change color to match you.*

Finally, after many windings and turnings (and several stops to investigate interesting objects, some of which happened to fall into the kender's pouches), Tas found himself in the one corridor that was *not* decorated, that was *not* filled with merry people making gleeful party arrangements, that was *not* resounding with the sounds of choirs practicing their Yule hymns. In this corridor, the curtains were still drawn, denying the sun admittance. It was chill and dark and forbidding, more so than ever because of the contrast to the rest of the world.

Tas crept down the hall, not walking softly for any particular reason except that the corridor was so grimly silent and gloomy it seemed to expect everyone who entered to be the same and would be highly offended if he weren't. The last thing Tas wanted to do was offend a corridor, he told himself, so he walked quietly. The possibility that he might be able to sneak up on Raistlin without the mage knowing it and catch a glimpse of some wonderful magical experiment certainly never crossed the kender's mind.

Drawing near the door, he heard Raistlin speaking and, from the tone, it sounded like he had a visitor.

"Drat," was Tas's first thought. "Now I'll have to wait to talk to him until this person leaves. And I'm on an Important Mission, too. How inconsiderate. I wonder how long they're going to be."

Putting his ear to the keyhole—to see if he could figure out how much longer the person planned to stay—Tas was startled to hear a woman's voice answer the mage.

"That voice sounds familiar," said the kender to himself, pressing closer to listen. "Of course! Crysania! I wonder what she's doing here."

"You're right, Raistlin." Tas heard her say with a sigh, "this *is* much more restful than those garish corridors. When I first came here, I was frightened. You smile! But I was. I admit it. This corridor seemed so bleak and desolate and cold. But now the hallways of the Temple are filled with an oppressive, stifling warmth. Even the Yule decorations depress me. I see so much waste, money squandered that could be helping those in need."

She stopped speaking, and Tas heard a rustle. Since no one was talking, the kender quit listening and put his eyes to the keyhole. He could see inside the room quite clearly. The heavy curtains were drawn, but the chamber was lit with soft candlelight. Crysania sat in a chair, facing him. The rustling sound he heard was apparently her stirring in impatience or frustration. She rested her head on her hand, and the look on her face was one of confusion and perplexity.

But that was not what made the kender open his eyes wide. Crysania had changed! Gone were the plain, unadorned white robes, the severe hair style. She was dressed as the other female clerics in white robes, but these were decorated with fine embroidery. Her arms were bare, though a slender golden band adorned one, enhancing the pure whiteness of her skin. Her hair fell from a central part to sweep down around her shoulders with feathery softness. There was a flush of color in her cheeks, her eyes were warm and their gaze lingered on the black-robed figure that sat across from her, his back to Tas.

"Humpf," said the kender with interest. "Tika was right."

"I don't know why I come here," Tas heard Crysania say after a moment's pause.

I do, the kender thought gleefully, quickly moving his ear back to the keyhole so he could hear better.

Her voice continued. "I am filled with such hope when I come to visit you, but I always leave depressed and unhappy. I plan to show you the ways of righteousness and truth, to prove to you that only by following those ways can we hope to bring peace to our world. But you always turn my words upside down and inside out."

"Your questions are your own," Tas heard Raistlin say, and there was another rustling sound, as if the mage moved closer to the woman. "I simply open your heart so that you may hear them. Surely Elistan counsels against blind faith. . . ."

Tas heard a sarcastic note in the mage's voice, but apparently Crysania did not detect it, for she answered quickly and sincerely, "Of course. He encourages us to question and often tells us of Goldmoon's example—how her questioning led to the return of the true gods. But questions should lead one to better understanding, and your questions only make me confused and miserable!"

"How well I know that feeling." Raistlin murmured so softly that Tas almost didn't hear him. The kender heard Crysania move in her chair and risked a quick peep. The mage was near her, one hand resting on her arm. As he spoke those words, Crysania moved nearer him, impulsively placing her hand over his. When she spoke, there was such hope and love and joy in her voice that Tas felt warm all over.

"Do you mean that?" Crysania asked the mage. "Are my poor words touching some part of you? No, don't look away! I can see by your expression that you have thought of them and pondered them. We are so alike! I knew that the first time I met you. Ah, you smile again, mocking me. Go ahead. *I* know the truth. You told me the same thing, in the Tower. You said I was as ambitious as you were. I've thought about it, and you're right. Our ambitions take different forms, but perhaps they are not as dissimilar as I once believed. We both live lonely lives, dedicated to our studies. We open our hearts to no one, not even those who would be closest to us. You surround yourself with darkness, but, Raistlin, I have seen beyond that. The warmth, the light . . ."

Tas quickly put his eye back to the keyhole. He's going to kiss her! he thought, wildly excited. This is wonderful! Wait until I tell Caramon.

"Come on, fool!" he instructed Raistlin impatiently as the mage sat there, his hands on Crysania's arms. "How can he resist?" the kender muttered, looking at the woman's parted lips, her shining eyes.

Suddenly Raistlin let loose of Crysania and turned away from her, abruptly rising out of his chair. "You had better go," he said in a husky voice. Tas sighed and drew away from the door in disgust. Leaning against the wall, he shook his head.

There was the sound of coughing, deep and harsh, and Crysania's voice, gentle and filled with concern.

"It is nothing," Raistlin said as he opened the door. "I have felt unwell for several days. Can you not guess the reason?" he asked, pausing with the door half ajar. Tas pressed back against the wall so they wouldn't see him, not wanting to interrupt (or miss) anything. "Haven't you felt it?"

"I have felt something," Crysania murmured breathlessly. "What do you mean?"

"The anger of the gods," Raistlin answered, and it was obvious to Tas that this wasn't the answer Crysania had hoped for. She seemed to droop. Raistlin did not notice, but continued on. "Their fury beats upon me, as if the sun were drawing nearer and nearer to this wretched planet. Perhaps that is why you are feeling depressed and unhappy."

"Perhaps," murmured Crysania.

"Tomorrow is Yule," Raistlin continued softly. "Thirteen days after that, the Kingpriest will make his demand. Already, he and his ministers plan for it. The gods know. They have sent him a warning—the vanishing of the clerics. But he did not heed it. Every day, from Yule on, the warning signs will grow stronger, clearer. Have you ever read Astinus's *Chronicles of the Last Thirteen Days*? They are not pleasant reading, and they will be less pleasant to live through."

Crysania looked at him, her face brightening. "Come back with us before then," she said eagerly. "Par-Salian gave Caramon a magical device that will take us back to our own time. The kender told me—"

"What magical device?" Raistlin demanded suddenly, and the strange tone of his voice sent a thrill through the kender and startled Crysania. "What does it look like? How does it work?" His eyes burned feverishly.

"I-I don't know," Crysania faltered.

"Oh, I'll tell you," Tas offered, stepping out from against the wall. "Gee, I'm sorry. I didn't mean to scare you. It's just that I couldn't help overhearing. Merry Yule to you both, by the way," Tas extended his small hand, which no one took.

Both Raistlin and Crysania were staring at him with the same expressions worn on the faces of those who suddenly see a spider drop into their soup at dinner. Unabashed, Tas continued prattling cheerfully, putting his hand in his pocket. "What were we talking about? Oh, the magical device. Yes, well," Tas continued more hurriedly, seeing Raistlin's eyes narrow in an alarming fashion, "when it's unfolded, it's shaped like a . . . a sceptre and it has a . . . a ball at one end, all glittering with jewels. It's about this big." The kender spread his hands about an arm's length apart. "That's when it's stretched out. Then, Par-Salian did something to it and it—"

"Collapsed in upon itself," Raistlin finished, "until you could carry it in your pocket."

"Why, yes!" Tas said excitedly. "That's right! How did you know?"

"I am familiar with the object," Raistlin replied, and Tas noticed again a strange sound to the mage's voice, a quivering, a tenseness—fear? Or elation? The kender couldn't tell. Crysania noticed it, too.

"What is it?" she asked.

Raistlin didn't answer immediately, his face was suddenly a mask, unreadable, impassive, cold. "I hesitate to say," he told her. "I must study on this matter." Flicking a glance at the kender—"What is it you want? Or are you simply listening at keyholes!"

"Certainly not!" Tas said, insulted. "I came to talk to you, if you and Lady Crysania are finished, that is," he amended hastily, his glance going to Crysania.

She regarded him with quite an unfriendly expression, the kender thought, then turned away from him to Raistlin. "Will I see you tomorrow?" she asked.

"I think not," he said. "I will not, of course, be attending the Yule party."

"Oh, but I don't want to go either—" Crysania began.

"You will be expected," Raistlin said abruptly. "Besides, I have too long neglected my studies in the pleasure of your company."

"I see," Crysania said. Her own voice was cool and distant and, Tasslehoff could tell, hurt and disappointed.

"Farewell, gentlemen," she said after a moment, when it was apparent Raistlin wasn't going to add anything further. Bowing slightly, she turned and walked down the dark hall, her white robes seeming to take the light away as she left.

"I'll tell Caramon you send your regards," Tas called after her helpfully, but Crysania didn't turn around. The kender turned to Raistlin with a sigh. "I'm afraid Caramon didn't make much of an impression on her. But, then, he was all fuddled because of the dwarf spirits—"

Raistlin coughed. "Did you come here to discuss my brother?" he interrupted coldly, "because, if so, you can leave—"

"Oh, no!" Tas said hastily. Then he grinned up at the mage. "I came to stop the Cataclysm!"

For the first time in his life, the kender had the satisfaction of seeing his words absolutely stun Raistlin. It was not a satisfaction he enjoyed long, however. The mage's face went white and stiff, his mirrorlike eyes seemed to shatter, allowing Tas to see inside, into those dark, burning depths the mage kept hidden. Hands as strong as the claws of a predatory bird sank into the kender's shoulders, hurting him. Within seconds, Tas found himself thrown inside Raistlin's room. The door slammed shut with a shattering bang.

"What gave you this idea?" Raistlin demanded.

Tas shrank backward, startled, and glanced around the room uneasily, his kender instincts telling him he better look for someplace to hide.

"Uh—you d-did," Tas stammered. "Well, n-not exactly. But you said something about m-my coming back here and being able to alter time. And, I thought, st-stopping the Cataclysm would be a sort of good thing—"

"How did you plan to do it?" Raistlin asked, and his eyes burned with a hot fire that made Tas sweat just looking into it.

"Well, I planned to discuss it with you first, of course," the kender said, hoping Raistlin was still subject to flattery, "and then I thought—if you said it was all right—that I would just go and talk to the Kingpriest and tell him he was making a really big mistake—one of the All Time Big Mistakes, if you take my meaning. And, I'm sure, once I explained, that he'd listen—"

"I'm sure," Raistlin said, and his voice was cool and controlled. But Tas thought he detected, oddly, a note of vast relief. "So"—the mage turned away—"you intend to talk to the Kingpriest. And what if he refuses to listen? What then?"

Tas paused, his mouth open. "I guess I hadn't considered that," the kender said, after a moment. He sighed, then shrugged. "We'll go home."

"There's another way," Raistlin said softly, sitting down in his chair and regarding the kender with his mirrorlike eyes. "A sure way! A way you could stop the Cataclysm without fail."

"There is?" Tas said eagerly. "What?"

"The magical device," Raistlin answered, spreading his slender hands. "Its powers are great, far beyond what Par-Salian told that idiot brother of mine. Activate it on the Day of the Cataclysm, and its magic will destroy the fiery mountain high above the world, so that it harms no one."

"Really?" Tas gasped. "That's wonderful." Then he frowned. "But, how can I be sure. Suppose it doesn't work—"

"What have you got to lose?" Raistlin asked. "If, for some reason, it fails, and I truly doubt it." The mage smiled at the kender's naiveté. "It was, after all, created by the highest level magic-users—"

"Like dragon orbs?" Tas interrupted.

"Like dragon orbs," Raistlin snapped, irritated at the interruption. "But if it did fail, you could always use it to escape at the last moment."

"With Caramon and Crysania," Tas added.

Raistlin did not answer, but the kender didn't notice in his excitement. Then he thought of something.

"What if Caramon decides to leave before then?" he asked fearfully.

"He won't," Raistlin answered softly. "Trust me," he added, seeing Tas about to argue.

The kender pondered again, then sighed. "I just thought of something. I don't think Caramon will let me have the device.

DRAGONLANCE LEGENDS

Par-Salian told him to guard it with his life. He never lets it out of his sight and locks it up in a chest when he has to leave. And I'm sure he wouldn't believe me if I tried to explain why I wanted it."

"Don't tell him. The day of the Cataclysm is the day of the Final Bout," Raistlin said, shrugging. "If it is gone for a short time, he'll never miss it."

"But, that would be stealing!" Tas said, shocked.

Raistlin's lips twitched. "Let us say—borrowing," the mage amended soothingly. "It's for such a worthy cause! Caramon won't be angry. I know my brother. Think how proud he will be of you!"

"You're right," Tas said, his eyes shining. "I'd be a true hero, greater than Kronin Thistleknot himself! How do I find out how to work it?"

"I'll give you instructions," Raistlin said, rising. He began to cough again. "Come back . . . in three days' time. And now . . . I must rest."

"Sure," Tas said cheerfully, getting to his feet. "I hope you feel better." He started for the door. Once there, however, he hesitated. "Oh, say, I don't have a gift for you. I'm sorry—"

"You have given me a gift," Raistlin said, "a gift of inestimable value. Thank you."

"I have!" Tas said, astonished. "Oh, you must mean stopping the Cataclysm. Well, don't mention it. I—"

Tas suddenly found himself in the middle of the garden, staring at the rosebushes and an extremely surprised cleric who had seen the kender apparently materialize out of nowhere, right in the middle of the path.

"Great Reorx's beard! I wish I knew how to do that," Tasslehoff said wistfully.

Chapter 13

On Yule day came the first of what would be later known as the Thirteen Calamities, (note that Astinus records them in the *Chronicles* as the Thirteen Warnings).

The day dawned hot and breathless. It was the hottest Yule day anyone—even the elves—could remember. In the Temple, the Yule roses drooped and withered, the everbloom wreaths smelled as if they had been baked in an oven, the snow that cooled the wine in silver bowls melted so rapidly that the servants did nothing all day but run back and forth from the depths of the rock cellars to the party rooms, carrying buckets of slush.

Raistlin woke on that morning, in the dark hour before the dawn, so ill he could not rise from his bed. He lay naked, bathed in sweat, a prey to the fevered hallucinations that had caused him to rip off his robes and the bedcovers. The gods were indeed near, but it was the closeness of one god in particular—his goddess, the Queen of Darkness—that was affecting him. He could feel her anger, as he could sense the anger of all the gods at the Kingpriest's attempt to destroy the balance they sought to achieve in the world.

Thus he had dreamed of his Queen, but she had chosen not to appear to him in her anger as might have been expected. He had not dreamed of the terrible five-headed dragon, the Dragon of All Colors and of None that would try to enslave the world in the Wars of the Lance. He had not seen her as the Dark Warrior, leading her legions to death and destruction. No, she had appeared to him as the Dark Temptress, the most beautiful of all women, the most seductive, and thus she had spent the night with him, tantalizing him with the weakness, the glory of the flesh.

Closing his eyes, shivering in the room that was cool despite the heat outdoors, Raistlin pictured to himself once again the fragrant dark hair hanging over him; he felt her touch, her warmth. Reaching up his hands, letting himself sink beneath her spell, he had parted the tangled hair—and seen Crysania's face!

The dream ended, shattered as his mind took control once more. And now he lay awake, exultant in his victory, yet knowing the price it had cost. As if to remind him, a wrenching coughing fit seized him.

"I will not give in," he muttered when he could breathe. "You will not win me over so easily, my Queen," Staggering out of bed, so weak he had to pause more than once to rest, he put on the black robes and made his way to his desk. Cursing the pain in his chest, he opened an ancient text on magical paraphernalia and began his laborious search.

Crysania, too, had slept poorly. Like Raistlin, she felt the nearness of all the gods, but of her god—Paladine—most of all. She felt his anger, but it was tinged with a sorrow so deep and devastating that Crysania could not bear it. Overwhelmed with guilt, she turned away from that gentle face and began to run. She ran and ran, weeping, unable to see where she was going. She stumbled and was falling into nothingness, her soul torn with fear. Then strong arms caught her. She was enfolded in soft black robes, held near a muscular body. Slender fingers stroked her hair, soothing her. She looked into a face—

Bells. Bells broke the stillness. Startled, Crysania sat up in bed, looking around wildly. Then, remembering the face she had seen, remembering the warmth of his body and the comfort she had found there, she put her aching head in her hands and wept.

Tasslehoff, on waking, at first felt disappointment. Today was Yule, he remembered, and also the day Raistlin said Dire Things would begin to happen. Looking around in the gray light that filtered through their window, the only dire thing Tas saw was Caramon, down on the floor, huffing and puffing his way grimly through morning exercises.

Although Caramon's days were filled with weapons' practice, working out with his team members, developing new parts of their routine, the big man still fought a never-ending battle with his weight. He had been taken off his diet and allowed to eat the same food as the others. But the sharp-eyed dwarf soon noticed that Caramon was eating about five times more than anyone else!

Once, the big man had eaten for pleasure. Now, nervous and unhappy and obsessed by thoughts of his brother, Caramon sought consolation in food as another might seek consolation in drink. (Caramon had, in fact, tried that once, ordering Tas to sneak a bottle of dwarf spirits in to him. But, unused to the strong alcohol, it had made him violently sick—much to the kender's secret relief.)

Arack decreed, therefore, that Caramon could eat only if he performed a series of strenuous exercises each day. Caramon often wondered how the dwarf knew if he missed a day, since he did them early in the morning before anyone else was up. But Arack *did* know, somehow. The one morning Caramon had skipped the exercises, he had been denied access to the mess hall by a grinning, club-wielding Raag.

Growing bored with listening to Caramon grunt and groan and swear, Tas climbed up on a chair, peering out the window to see if there was anything dire happening outside. He felt cheered immediately.

"Caramon! Come look!" he called in excitement. "Have you ever seen a sky that peculiar shade before?"

"Ninety-nine, one hundred," puffed the big man. Then Tas heard a large "ooof." With a thud that shook the room,

Caramon flopped down on his now rock-hard belly to rest. Then the big man heaved himself up off the stone floor and came to look out the barred window, mopping the sweat from his body with a towel.

Casting a bored glance outside, expecting nothing but an ordinary sunrise, the big man blinked, then his eyes opened wide.

"No," he murmured, draping the towel around his neck and coming to stand behind Tas, "I never did. And I've seen some strange things in my time, too."

"Oh, Caramon!" Tas cried, "Raistlin was right. He said—"

"Raistlin!"

Tas gulped. He hadn't meant to bring that up.

"Where did you see Raistlin?" Caramon demanded, his voice deep and stern.

"In the Temple, of course," Tas answered as if it were the most common thing in the world. "Didn't I mention I went there yesterday?"

"Yes, but you—"

"Well, why else would I go except to see our friends?"

"You never—"

"I saw Lady Crysania and Raistlin. I'm sure I mentioned that. You never do listen to me, you know," Tas complained, wounded. "You sit there on that bed, every night, brooding and sulking and talking to yourself. 'Caramon,' I could say, 'the roof's caving in,' and you'd say, 'That's nice, Tas.' "

"Look, kender, I know that if I had heard you mention—"

"Lady Crysania, Raistlin, and I had a wonderful little chat," Tas hurried on, "all about Yule—by the way, Caramon, you should see how beautifully they've decorated the Temple! It's filled with roses and everbloom and, say, did I remember to give you that candy? Wait, it's right over there in my pouch. Just a minute"—the kender tried to jump off the chair but Caramon had him cornered—"well, I guess it can wait. Where was I? Oh, yes"—seeing Caramon scowl—"Raistlin and Lady Crysania and I were talking and, oh, Caramon! It's so exciting. Tika was right, she's in love with your brother."

Caramon blinked, having completely lost the thread of the

conversation, which Tas, being rather careless with his pronouns, didn't help.

"No, I don't mean Tika's in love with your brother," Tas amended, seeing Caramon's confusion. "I mean Lady Crysania's in love with your brother! It was great fun. I was sort of leaning against Raistlin's closed door, resting, waiting for them to finish their conversation, and I happened to glance in the keyhole and he almost kissed her, Caramon! Your brother! Can you imagine! But he didn't." The kender sighed. "He practically yelled at her to leave. She did, but she didn't want to, I could tell. She was all dressed up and looked really pretty."

Seeing Caramon's face darken and the preoccupied look steal over it, Tas began to breathe a bit easier. "We got to talking about the Cataclysm, and Raistlin mentioned how Dire Things would begin happening today—Yule—as the gods tried to warn the people to change."

"In love with him?" Caramon muttered. Frowning, he turned away, letting Tas slip off the chair.

"Right. Unmistakably," the kender said glibly, hurrying over to his pouch and digging through it until he came to the batch of sweetmeats he had brought back. They were half-melted, sticking together in a gooey mass, and they had also acquired an outer coating of various bits and pieces from the kender's pouch, but Tas was fairly certain Caramon would never notice. He was right. The big man accepted the treat and began to eat without even glancing at it.

"He needs a cleric, they said," Caramon mumbled, his mouth full. "Were they right, after all? Is he going to go through with it? Should I let him? Should I try to stop him? Do I have the right to stop him? If she chooses to go with him, isn't that her choice? Maybe that would be the best thing for him," Caramon said softly, licking his sticky fingers. "Maybe, if she loves him enough. . . ."

Tasslehoff sighed in relief and sank down on his bed to wait for the breakfast call. Caramon hadn't thought to ask the kender *why* he'd gone to see Raistlin in the first place. And Tas was certain now, that he'd never remember he hadn't. His secret was safe. . . .

The sky was clear that Yule day, so clear it seemed one could look up into the vast dome that covered the world and see realms beyond. But, though everyone glanced up, few cared to fix their gazes upon it long enough to see anything. For the sky was indeed "a peculiar shade," as Tas said—it was green.

A strange, noxious, ugly green that, combined with the stifling heat and the heavy, hard-to-breathe air, effectively sucked the joy and merriment out of Yule. Those forced to go outside to attend parties hurried through the sweltering streets, talking about the odd weather irritably, viewing it as a personal insult. But they spoke in hushed voices, each feeling a tiny sliver of fear prick their holiday spirit.

The party inside the Temple was somewhat more cheerful, being held in the Kingpriest's chambers that were shut away from the outside world. None could see the strange sky, and all those who came within the presence of the Kingpriest felt their irritation and fear melt away. Away from Raistlin, Crysania was once again under the Kingpriest's spell and sat near him a long time. She did not speak, she simply let his shining presence comfort her and banish the dark, nighttime thoughts. But she, too, had seen the green sky. Remembering Raistlin's words, she tried to recall what she had heard of the Thirteen Days.

But it was all children's tales that were muddled together with the dreams she had had last night. Surely, she thought, the Kingpriest will notice! He will heed the warnings.... She willed time to change or, if that were not possible, she willed the Kingpriest innocent. Sitting within his light, she banished from her mind the picture she had seen of the frightened mortal with his pale blue, darting eyes. She saw a strong man, denouncing the ministers who had deceived him, an innocent victim of their treachery....

The crowd at the arena that day was sparse, most not caring to sit out beneath the green sky, whose color deepened and darkened more and more fearfully as the day wore on.

The gladiators themselves were uneasy, nervous, and performed their acts half-heartedly. Those spectators who came were sullen, refusing to cheer, cat-calling and hurling gibes at even their favorites.

"Do you often have such skies?" Kiiri asked, glancing up with a shudder as she and Caramon and Pheragas stood in the corridors, awaiting their turn in the arena. "If so, I know why my people choose to live beneath the sea!"

"My father sailed the sea," growled Pheragas, "as did my grandfather before him, as did I, before I tried to knock some sense into the first mate's head with a belaying pin and got sent here for my pains. And I've never seen a sky this color. Or heard of one either. It bodes ill, I'll wager."

"No doubt," Caramon said uncomfortably. It had suddenly begun to sink into the big man that the Cataclysm was thirteen days away! Thirteen days . . . and these two friends, who had grown as dear to him as Sturm and Tanis, these two friends would perish! The rest of the inhabitants of Istar meant little to him. From what he had seen, they were a selfish lot, living mainly for pleasure and money (though he found he could not look upon the children without a pang of sorrow), but these two—He had to warn them, somehow. If they left the city, they might escape.

Lost in his thoughts, he had paid little attention to the fight in the arena. It was between the Red Minotaur, so called because the fur that covered his bestial face had a distinctly reddish-brown cast to it, and a young fighter—a new man, who had arrived only a few weeks before. Caramon had watched the young man's training with patronizing amusement.

But then he felt Pheragas, who was standing next to him, stiffen. Caramon's gaze went immediately to the ring. "What is it?"

"That trident," Pheragas said quietly, "have you ever seen one like it in the prop room?"

Caramon stared hard at the Red Minotaur's weapon, squinting against the harsh sun blazing in the green-glazed sky. Slowly, he shook his head, feeling anger stir inside of him. The young man was completely outclassed by the minotaur, who had fought in the arena for months and who, in fact, was rivaling Caramon's team for the championship. The only reason the young man had lasted as long as he had was the skilled showmanship of the minotaur, who blundered around in a pretended battle rage that actually won a few laughs from the audience.

"A real trident. Arack intends to blood the young man, no doubt," Caramon muttered. "Look there, I was right," pointing to three bleeding scratches that suddenly appeared on the young man's chest.

Pheragas said nothing, only flicked a glance at Kiiri, who shrugged.

"What is it?" Caramon shouted above the roar of the crowd. The Red Minotaur had just won by neatly tripping up his opponent and pinning him to the mat, thrusting the points of the trident down around his neck.

The young man staggered to his feet, feigning shame, anger, and humiliation as he had been taught. He even shook his fist at his victorious opponent before he stalked from the arena. But, instead of grinning as he passed Caramon and his team, enjoying a shared joke on the audience, the young man appeared strangely preoccupied and never looked at them. His face was pale, Caramon saw, and beads of sweat stood out on his forehead. His face twisted with pain, and he had his hand clasped over the bloody scratches.

"Lord Onygion's man," Pheragas said quietly, laying a hand on Caramon's arm. "Count yourself fortunate, my friend. You can quit worrying."

"What?" Caramon gaped at the two in confusion. Then he heard a shrill scream and a thud from within the underground tunnel. Whirling around, Caramon saw the young man fall into a writhing heap on the floor, clutching his chest and screaming in agony.

"No!" Kiiri commanded, holding onto Caramon. "Our turn next. Look, Red Minotaur comes off."

The minotaur sauntered past them, ignoring them as that race ignores all it considers beneath them. The Red Minotaur also walked past the dying young man without a glance. Arack came scurrying down the tunnel, Raag behind. With a gesture, the dwarf ordered the ogre to remove the now lifeless body.

Caramon hesitated, but Kiiri sank her nails into his arm, dragging him out into the hideous sunlight. "The score for the Barbarian is settled," she hissed out of the corner of her mouth. "Your master had nothing to do with it, apparently. It was Lord Onygion, and now he and Quarath are even."

The crowd began to cheer and the rest of Kiiri's words were lost. The spectators had begun to forget their oppression at the sight of their favorite trio. But Caramon didn't hear them. Raistlin had told him the truth! He hadn't had anything to do with the Barbarian's death. It had been coincidence, or perhaps the dwarf's perverted idea of a joke. Caramon felt a sensation of relief flow over him.

He could go home! At last he understood. Raistlin had tried to tell him. Their paths were different, but his brother had the right to walk his as he chose. Caramon was wrong, the magic-users were wrong, Lady Crysania was wrong. He would go home and explain. Raistlin wasn't harming anyone, he wasn't a threat. He simply wanted to pursue his studies in peace.

Walking out into the arena, Caramon waved back to the cheering crowd in elation.

The big man even enjoyed that day's fighting. The bout was rigged, of course, so that his team would win—setting up the final battle between them and the Red Minotaur on the day of the Cataclysm. But Caramon didn't need to worry about that. He would be long gone, back at home with Tika. He would warn his two friends first, of course, and urge them to leave this doomed city. Then he'd apologize to his brother, tell him he understood, take Lady Crysania and Tasslehoff back to their own time, and begin his life anew. He'd leave tomorrow, or perhaps the day after.

But it was at the moment when Caramon and his team were taking their bows after a well-acted battle that the cyclone struck the Temple of Istar.

The green sky had deepened to the color of dark and stagnant swamp water when the swirling clouds appeared, snaking down out of the vast emptiness to wrap their sinuous coils about one of the seven towers of the Temple and tear it from its foundations. Lifting it into the air, the cyclone broke the marble into fragments fine as hail and sent it rattling down upon the city in a stinging rain.

No one was hurt seriously, though many suffered small cuts from being struck by the sharp pieces of rock. The part of the Temple that was destroyed was used for study and for the work of the church. It had—fortunately—been empty during the holiday. But the inhabitants of the Temple and the city itself were thrown into a panic.

Fearing that cyclones might start descending everywhere, people fled the arena and clogged the streets in panicked efforts to reach their homes. Within the Temple, the Kingpriest's musical voice fell silent, his light wavered. After surveying the wreckage, he and his ministers—the Revered Sons and Daughters of Paladine—descended to an inner sanctuary to discuss the matter. Everyone else hurried about, trying to clean up, the wind having overturned furniture, knocked paintings off the walls, and sent clouds of dust drifting down over everything.

This is the beginning, Crysania thought fearfully, trying to force her numb hands to quit shaking as she picked up fragments of fine china from the dining hall. This is only the beginning . . .

And it will get worse.

Chapter 14

It is the forces of evil, working to defeat me," cried the Kingpriest, his musical voice sending a thrill of courage through the souls of those listening. "But I will not give in! Neither must you! We must be strong in the face of this threat. . . ."

"No," Crysania whispered to herself in despair. "No, you have it all wrong! You don't understand! How can you be so blind!"

She was sitting at Morning Prayers, twelve days after the First of the Thirteen Warnings had been given—but had not been heeded. Since then, reports had poured in from all parts of the continent, telling of other strange events—a new one each day.

"King Lorac reports that, in Silvanesti, the trees wept blood for an entire day," the Kingpriest recounted, his voice swelling with the awe and horror of the events he related. "The city of Palanthas is covered in a dense white fog so thick people wander around lost if they venture out into the streets.

"In Solamnia, no fires will burn. Their hearths lie cold and barren. The forges are shut down, the coals might as well be ice for all the warmth they give. Yet, on the plains of Abanasinia, the prairie grass has caught fire. The flames rage out of control, filling the skies with black smoke and driving the Plainsmen from their tribal lodges.

"Just this morning, the griffons carried word that the elven city of Qualinost is being invaded by the forest animals, suddenly turned strange and savage—"

Crysania could bear it no longer. Though the women glanced at her in shock as she stood up, she ignored their glowering looks and left the Services, fleeing into the corridors of the Temple.

A jagged flash of lightning blinded her, the vicious crack of thunder immediately following made her cover her face with her hands.

"This must cease or I will go mad!" she murmured brokenly, cowering in a corner.

For twelve days, ever since the cyclone, a thunderstorm raged over Istar, flooding the city with rain and hail. The flash of lightning and peals of thunder were almost continuous, shaking the Temple, destroying sleep, battering the mind. Tense, numb with fatigue and exhaustion and terror, Crysania sank down in a chair, her head in her hands.

A gentle touch on her arm made her start in alarm, jumping up. She faced a tall, handsome young man wrapped in a sopping wet cloak. She could see the outlines of strong, muscular shoulders.

"I'm sorry, Revered Daughter, I didn't mean to scare you," he said in a deep voice that was as vaguely familiar as his face.

"Caramon!" Crysania gasped in relief, clutching at him as something real and solid. There was another bright flash and explosion. Crysania squeezed her eyes shut, gritting her teeth, feeling even Caramon's strong, muscular body tense nervously. He held onto her, steadying her.

"I-I had to go to Morning Prayers," Crysania said when she could be heard. "It must be horrible out there. You're soaked to the skin!"

"I've tried for days to see you—" Caramon began.

"I-I know," Crysania faltered. "I'm sorry. It's just that I-I've been busy—"

"Lady Crysania," Caramon interrupted, trying to keep his voice steady. "We're not talking about an invitation to a Yule Party. Tomorrow this city will cease to exist! I—"

"Hush!" Crysania commanded. Nervously, she glanced about. "We cannot talk here!" A flash of lightning and a shattering crash made her cringe, but she regained control almost immediately. "Come with me."

Caramon hesitated then, frowning, followed her as she led the way through the Temple into one of several dark, inner rooms. Here, the lightning at least could not penetrate and the thunder was muffled. Shutting the door carefully, Crysania sat down in a chair and motioned Caramon to do the same.

Caramon stood a moment, then sat down, uncomfortable and on edge, acutely conscious of the circumstances of their last meeting when his drunkenness had nearly gotten them all killed. Crysania might have been thinking of this, too. She regarded him with eyes that were cold and gray as the dawn. Caramon flushed.

"I am glad to see your health has improved," Crysania said, trying to keep the severity out of her voice and failing entirely.

Caramon's flush grew deeper. He looked down at the floor.

"I'm sorry," Crysania said abruptly. "Please forgive me. I-I haven't slept for nights, ever since this started." She put a trembling hand to her forehead. "I can't think," she added hoarsely. "This incessant noise. . . ."

"I understand," Caramon said, glancing up at her. "And you have every right to despise me. I despise myself for what I was. But that really doesn't matter now. We've got to leave, Lady Crysania!"

"Yes, you're right" Crysania drew a deep breath. "We've got to get out of here. We have only hours left to escape. I am well aware of it, believe me." Sighing, she looked down at her hands. "I have failed," she said dully. "I kept hoping, up until this last moment, that somehow things might change. But the Kingpriest is blind! Blind!"

"That's not why you've been avoiding me though, is it?" Caramon asked, his voice expressionless. "Preventing me from leaving?"

Now it was Crysania who blushed. She looked down at her hands, twisting in her lap. "No," she said so softly Caramon barely heard. "No, I-I didn't want to leave without . . . without . . ."

"Raistlin," Caramon finished. "Lady Crysania, he has magic of his own. It brought him here in the first place. He has made his choice. I've come to realize that. We should leave—"

"Your brother has been terribly ill," Crysania said abruptly.

Caramon looked up quickly, his face drawn with concern.

"I have tried for days to see him, ever since Yule, but he refused admittance to all, even to me. And now, today, he has sent for me," Crysania continued, feeling her face burn under Caramon's penetrating gaze. "I am going to talk to him, to persuade him to come with us. If his health is impaired, he will not have the strength to use his magic."

"Yes," Caramon muttered, thinking about the difficulty involved in casting such a powerful, complex spell. It had taken Par-Salian days, and he was in good health. "What's wrong with Raist?" he asked suddenly.

"The nearness of the gods affects him," Crysania replied, "as it does others, though they refuse to admit it." Her voice died in sorrow, but she pressed her lips together tightly for a moment, then continued. "We must be prepared to move quickly, if he agrees to come with us—"

"If he doesn't?" Caramon interrupted.

Crysania blushed. "I think . . . he will," she said, overcome by confusion, her thoughts going back to the time in his chambers when he had been so near her, the look of longing and desire in his eyes, the admiration. "I've been . . . talking to him . . . about the wrongness of his ways. I've shown him how evil can never build or create, how it can only destroy and turn in upon itself. He has admitted the validity of my arguments and promised to think about them."

"And he loves you," Caramon said softly.

Crysania could not meet the man's gaze. She could not answer. Her heart beat so she could not, for a moment, hear above the pulsing of her blood. She could sense Caramon's dark eyes regarding her steadily as the thunder rumbled and shook the Temple around them. Crysania gripped her hands together to stop their trembling. Then she was aware of Caramon rising to his feet.

"My lady," he said in a hushed, solemn voice, "if you are right, if your goodness and your love can turn him from those dark paths that he walks and lead him—by his own choice—into the light, I would . . . I would—" Caramon choked and turned his head hurriedly.

Hearing so much love in the big man's voice and seeing the tears he tried to hide, Crysania was overcome with pain and remorse. She began to wonder if she had misjudged him. Standing up, she gently touched the man's huge arm, feeling its great muscles tense as Caramon fought to bring himself under control.

"Must you return? Can't you stay—"

"No." Caramon shook his head. "I've got to get Tas, and the device Par-Salian gave me. It's locked away. And then, I have friends. . . . I've been trying to convince them to leave the city. It may be too late, but I've got to make one more attempt—"

"Certainly," Crysania said. "I understand. Return as quickly as you can. Meet me . . . meet me in Raistlin's rooms."

"I will, my lady," he replied fervently. "And now I must go, before my friends leave for practice." Taking her hand in his, he clasped it firmly, then hurried away. Crysania watched him walk back out into the corridor, whose torchlights shone in the gloomy darkness. He moved swiftly and surely, not even flinching when he passed a window at the end of the corridor and was suddenly illuminated by a brilliant flash of lightning. It was hope that anchored his storm-tossed spirit, the same hope Crysania felt suddenly welling up inside her.

Caramon vanished into the darkness and Crysania, catching up her white robes in one hand, quickly turned and climbed the stairs to the part of the Temple that housed the black-robed mage.

Her good spirits and her hope failed slightly as she entered that corridor. Here the full fury of the storm seemed to rage unabated. Not even the heaviest curtains could keep out the blinding lightning, the thickest walls could not muffle the peals of thunder. Perhaps because of some ill-fitting window, even the wind itself seemed to have penetrated the Temple walls. Here no torches would burn, not that they were needed, so incessant was the lighting.

Crysania's black hair blew in her eyes, her robes fluttered around her. As she neared the mage's room at the end of the corridor, she could hear the rain beat against the glass. The air was cold and damp. Shivering, she hastened her steps and had raised her hand to knock upon the door when the corridor suddenly sizzled with a blue-white flash of lightning. The simultaneous explosion of thunder knocked Crysania against the door. It flew open, and she was in Raistlin's arms.

It was like her dream. Almost sobbing in her terror, she nestled close to the velvet softness of the black robes and warmed herself by the heat of his body. At first, that body next to hers was tense, then she felt it relax. His arms tightened around her almost convulsively, a hand reached up to stroke her hair, soothingly, comfortingly.

"There, there," he whispered as one might to a frightened child, "fear not the storm, Revered Daughter. Exult in it! Taste the power of the gods, Crysania! Thus do they frighten the foolish. They cannot harm us—not if you choose otherwise."

Gradually Crysania's sobs lessened. Raistlin's words were not the gentle murmurings of a mother. Their meaning struck home to her. She lifted her head, looking up at him.

"What do you mean?" she faltered, suddenly frightened. A crack had appeared in his mirrorlike eyes, permitting her to see the soul burning within.

Involuntarily, she started to push away from him, but he reached out and, smoothing the tangled black hair from her face with trembling hands, whispered, "Come with me, Crysania! Come with me to a time when you will be the only cleric in the world, to the time when we may enter the portal and challenge the gods, Crysania! Think of it! To rule, to show the world such power as this!"

Raistlin let go his grasp. Raising his arms, the black robes shimmering about him as the lightning flared and the thunder roared, he laughed. And then Crysania saw the feverish gleam in his eyes and the bright spots of color on his deathly pale cheeks. He was thin, far thinner than when she had seen him last.

"You're ill," she said, backing up, her hands behind her, reaching for the door. "I'll get help. . ."

"No!" Raistlin's shout was louder than the thunder. His eyes regained their mirrored surface, his face was cold and composed. Reaching out, he grasped her wrist with a painful grip and jerked her back into the room. The door slammed shut behind her. "I am ill," he said more quietly, "but there is no help, no cure for my malady but to escape this insanity. My plans are almost completed. Tomorrow, the day of the Cataclysm, the attention of the gods will be turned to the lesson they must inflict upon these poor wretches. The Dark Queen will not be able to stop me as I work my magic and carry myself forward to the one time in history when *she* is vulnerable to the power of a true cleric!"

"Let me go!" Crysania cried, pain and outrage submerging her fear. Angrily, she wrenched her arm free of his grasp. But she still remembered his embrace, the touch of his hands. . . . Hurt and ashamed, Crysania turned away. "You must work your evil without me," she said, her voice choked with her tears. "I will not go with you."

"Then you will die," Raistlin said grimly.

"Do you dare threaten me!" Crysania cried, whirling around to face him, shock and fury drying her eyes.

"Oh, not by my hand," Raistlin said with a strange smile. "You will die by the hands of those who sent you here."

Crysania blinked, stunned. Then she quickly regained her composure. "Another trick?" she asked coldly, backing away from him, the pain in her heart at his deception almost more than she could bear. She wanted only to leave before he saw how much he had been able to hurt her—

"No trick, Revered Daughter," Raistlin said simply. He gestured to a book with red binding that lay open upon his desk. "See for yourself. Long I studied—" He swept his hand about the rows and rows of books that lined the wall. Crysania gasped. These had not been here the last time. Looking at her, he nodded. "Yes, I brought them from far-off places. I traveled far in search of many of them. This one I finally found in the Tower of High Sorcery at Wayreth, as I suspected all along I might. Come, look at it."

"What is it?" Crysania stared at the volume as if it might have been a coiled, poisonous serpent.

"A book, nothing more." Raistlin smiled wearily. "I assure you it will not change into a dragon and carry you off at my command. I repeat—it is a book, an encyclopedia, if you will. A very ancient one, written during the Age of Dreams."

"Why do you want me to see this? What does it have to do with me?" Crysania asked suspiciously. But she had ceased edging her way toward the door. Raistlin's calm demeanor reassured her. She had even ceased to notice, for the moment, the lightning and cracking of the storm outside.

"It is an encyclopedia of magical devices produced during the Age of Dreams," Raistlin continued imperturbably, never taking his eyes from Crysania. seeming to draw her nearer with his gaze as he stood beside the desk. "Read—"

"I cannot read the language of magic," Crysania said, frowning, then her brow cleared. "Or are you going to 'translate' for me?" she inquired haughtily.

Raistlin's eyes flared in swift anger, but the anger was almost instantly replaced by a look of sadness and exhaustion that went straight to Crysania's heart. "It is not written in the language of magic," he said softly. "I would not have asked you here otherwise." Glancing down at the black robes he wore, he smiled the twisted, bitter smile. "Long ago, I willingly paid the penalty. I do not know why I should have hoped you would trust me."

Biting her lip, feeling deeply ashamed, though she had no idea why, Crysania crossed around to the other side of the desk. She stood there, hesitantly. Sitting down, Raistlin beckoned to her, and she took a step forward to stand beside the open book. The mage spoke a word of command, and the staff that leaned up against the wall near Crysania burst into a flood of yellow light, startling her nearly as much as the lightning.

"Read," Raistlin said, indicating the page.

Trying to compose herself, Crysania glanced down, scanning the page, though she had no idea what she sought. Then, her attention was captured. *Device of Time Journeying* read one of the entries and, beside it, was pictured a device similar to the one the kender had described.

"This is it?" she asked, looking up at Raistlin. "The device Par-Salian gave Caramon to get us back?"

The mage nodded, his eyes reflecting the yellow light of the staff.

"Read," he repeated softly.

Curious, Crysania scanned the text. There was little more than a paragraph, describing the device, the great mage—now long forgotten—who had designed and built it—the requirements for its use. Much of the description was beyond her understanding, dealing with things arcane. She grasped at bits and pieces—

... will carry the person already under a time spell forward or backward ... must be assembled correctly and the facets turned in the prescribed order. ... will transport one person only, the person to whom it is given at the time the spell is cast ... device's use is restricted to elves, humans, ogres ... no spell word required. ...

Crysania came to the end and glanced up at Raistlin uncertainly. He was watching her with a strange, expectant look. There was something there he was waiting for her to find. And, deep within, she felt a disquiet, a fear, a numbness, as if her heart understood the text more quickly than her brain.

"Again," Raistlin said.

Trying to concentrate, though she was now once more aware of the storm outside that seemed to be growing in intensity, Crysania looked back at the text.

And there it was. The words leaped out at her, reaching for her throat, choking her.

Transport one person only. ...

Transport one person only!

Crysania's legs gave way. Fortunately, Raistlin moved a chair behind her or she might have fallen to the floor.

For long moments she stared into the room. Though lit by lightning and the magical light of the staff, it had, for her, grown suddenly dark.

"Does he know?" she asked finally, through numb lips.

"Caramon?" Raistlin snorted. "Of course not. If they had told him, he would have broken his fool neck trying to get it to you and would beg you on his knees to use it and give him the privilege of dying in your stead. I can think of little else that would make him happier.

"No, Lady Crysania, he would have used it confidently, with you standing beside him as well as the kender, no doubt. And he would have been devastated when they explained to him why he returned alone. I wonder how Par-Salian would have managed that," Raistlin added with a grim smile. "Caramon is quite capable of tearing that Tower down around their ears. But that is neither here nor there."

His gaze caught hers, though she would have avoided it. He compelled her, by the force of his will, to look into his eyes. And, once again, she saw herself, but this time alone and terribly frightened.

"They sent you back here to die, Crysania," Raistlin said in a voice that was little more than a breath, yet it penetrated to Crysania's very core, echoing louder in her mind than the thunder. "This is the good you tell me about? Bah! They live in fear, as does the Kingpriest! They fear you as they fear me. The only path to good, Crysania, is my path! Help me defeat the evil. I need you...."

Crysania closed her eyes. She could see once again, vividly, Par-Salian's handwriting on the note she had found—*your life or your soul—gain one and you will lose the other! There are many ways back for you, one of which is through Caramon.* He had purposely misled her! What other way existed, besides Raistlin's? Is this what the mage meant? Who could answer her? Was there anyone, anyone in this bleak and desolate world she could trust?

Her muscles twitching, contracting, Crysania pushed herself up from her chair. She did not look at Raistlin, she stared ahead at nothing. "I must go . . ." she muttered brokenly, "I must think. . . ."

Raistlin did not try to stop her. He did not even stand. He spoke no word—until she reached the door.

"Tomorrow," he whispered. "Tomorrow. . . ."

CHAPTER 15

It took all of Caramon's strength, plus that of two of the Temple guards, to force the great doors of the Temple open and let him out into the storm. The wind hit him full force, driving the big man back against the stone wall and pinning him there for an instant, as if he were no bigger than Tas. Struggling, Caramon fought against it and finally won, the gale force relenting enough to allow him to continue down the stairs.

The fury of the storm was somewhat lessened as he walked among the tall buildings of the city, but it was still difficult going. Water ran a foot deep in some places, swirling about his legs, threatening more than once to sweep him off his feet. The lightning half-blinded him, the thunder was deafening.

Needless to say, he saw few other people. The inhabitants of Istar cowered indoors, alternately cursing or calling upon the gods. The occasional traveler he passed, driven out into the storm by who knows what desperate reason, clung to the sides of the buildings or stood huddled miserably in doorways.

But Caramon trudged on, anxious to get back to the arena. His heart was filled with hope, his spirits were high, despite the storm. Or perhaps because of the storm. Surely now Kiiri and Pheragas would listen to him instead of giving him strange, cold looks when he tried to persuade them to flee Istar.

"I can't tell you how I know, I just know!" he pleaded. "There's disaster coming, I can smell it!"

"And miss the final tournament?" Kiiri said coolly.

"They won't hold it in this weather!" Caramon waved his arms.

"No storm this fierce ever lasts long!" Pheragas said. "It will blow itself out, and we'll have a beautiful day. Besides"—his eyes narrowed—"what would you do without us in the arena?"

"Why, fight alone, if need be," Caramon said, somewhat flustered. He planned to be long gone by that time—he and Tas, Crysania and perhaps . . . perhaps. . . .

"If need be . . ." Kiiri had repeated in an odd, harsh tone, exchanging glances with Pheragas. "Thanks for thinking of us, friend," she said with a scathing glance at the iron collar Caramon wore, the collar that matched her own, "but no thanks. Our lives would be forfeit—runaway slaves! How long do you think we'd live out there?"

"It won't matter, not after . . . after . . ." Caramon sighed and shook his head miserably. What could he say? How could he make them understand? But they had not given him the chance. They walked off without another word, leaving him sitting alone in the mess hall.

But, surely, now they would listen! They would see that this was no ordinary storm. Would they have time to get away safely? Caramon frowned and wished, for the first time, he had paid more attention to books. He had no idea how wide an area the devastating effect of the fall of the fiery mountain encompassed. He shook his head. Maybe it was already too late.

Well, he had tried, he told himself, slogging along through the water. Wrenching his mind from the plight of his friends, he forced himself to think more cheerful thoughts. Soon he would be gone from this terrible place. Soon this would all seem like a bad dream.

He would be back home with Tika. Maybe with Raistlin! "I'll finish building the new house," he said, thinking regretfully of all the time he had wasted. A picture came into his mind. He could see himself, sitting by the fire in their new home, Tika's head resting in his lap. He'd tell her all about their adventures. Raistlin would sit with them, in the evenings; reading, studying, dressed in white robes. . . .

"Tika won't believe a word of this," Caramon said to himself. "But it won't matter. She'll have the man she fell in love with home again. And this time, he won't leave her, ever, for anything!" He sighed, feeling her crisp red curls wrap around his fingers, seeing them shine in the firelight.

These thoughts carried Caramon through the storm and to the arena. Pulling out the block in the wall that was used by all the gladiators on their nocturnal rambles. (Arack was aware of its existence but, by tacit arrangement, turned a blind eye to it as long as the privilege wasn't abused.) No one was in the arena, of course. Practice sessions had all been canceled. Everyone was huddled inside, cursing the foul weather and making bets on whether or not they would fight tomorrow.

Arack was in a mood nearly as foul as the elements, counting over and over the pieces of gold that would slip through his fingers if he had to cancel the Final Bout—the sporting event of the year in Istar. He tried to cheer himself up with the thought that *he* had promised him fine weather and *he*, if anyone, should know. Still, the dwarf stared gloomily outside.

From his vantage point, a window high above the grounds in the tower of the arena, he saw Caramon creep through the stone wall. "Raag!" He pointed. Looking down, Raag nodded in understanding and, grabbing the huge club, waited for the dwarf to put away his account books.

Caramon hurried to the cell he shared with the kender, eager to tell him about Crysania and Raistlin. But when he entered, the small room was empty.

"Tas?" he said, glancing around to make certain he hadn't overlooked him in the shadows. But a flash of lightning illuminated the room more brightly than daylight. There was no sign of the kender.

"Tas, come out! This is no time for games!" Caramon ordered sternly. Tasslehoff had nearly frightened him out of six years' growth one day by hiding under the bed, then leaping out when Caramon's back was turned. Lighting a torch, the big man got down, grumbling, on his hands and knees and flashed the light under the bed. No Tas.

"I hope the little fool didn't try to go out in this storm!" Caramon said to himself, his irritation changing to sudden concern. "He'd get blown back to Solace. Or maybe he's in the mess hall, waiting for me. Maybe he's with Kiiri and Pheragas. That's it! I'll just grab the device, then join him—"

Talking to himself, Caramon went over to the small, wooden chest where he kept his armor. Opening it, he took out the fancy, gold costume. Giving it a scornful glance, he tossed the pieces on the floor. "At least I won't have to wear that get-up again," he said thankfully. "Though"—he grinned somewhat shamefacedly—"it'd be fun to see Tika's reaction when I put that on! Wouldn't she laugh? But I'll bet she'd like it, just the same." Whistling cheerfully, Caramon quickly took everything out of the chest and, using the edge of one of the collapsible daggers, carefully prized up the false bottom he had built into it.

The whistle died on his lips.

The chest was empty.

Frantically, Caramon felt all over the inside of the chest, though it was quite obvious that a pendant as large as the magical device wouldn't have been likely to slip through a crack. His heart beating wildly with fear, Caramon scrambled to his feet and began to search the room, flashing the torchlight into every corner, peering once more under the beds. He even ripped up his straw mattress and was starting to work on Tas's when he suddenly noticed something.

Not only was the kender gone, but so were his pouches, all his beloved possessions. And so was his cloak.

And then Caramon knew. Tas had taken the device.

But why? . . . Caramon felt for a moment as if lightning had struck him, the sudden understanding sizzling his way from his brain to his body with a shock that paralyzed him.

Tas had seen Raistlin—he had told Caramon about that. But what had Tas been doing there? *Why* had he gone to see Raistlin? Caramon suddenly realized that the kender had skillfully steered the conversation away from that point.

Caramon groaned. The curious kender had, of course, questioned him about the device, but Tas had always seemed satisfied with Caramon's answers. Certainly, he had never bothered it. Caramon checked, occasionally, to make sure it was still there—one did that as a matter of habit when living with a kender. But, if Tas had been curious enough about it, he would have taken it to Raistlin. . . . He did that often in the old days, when he found something magical.

Or maybe Raistlin tricked Tas into bringing it to him! Once he had the device, Raistlin could force them to go with him. Had he been plotting this all along? Had he tricked Tas and deceived Crysania? Caramon's mind stumbled about his head in confusion. Or maybe—

"Tas!" Caramon cried, suddenly latching onto firm, positive action. "I have to find Tas! I have to stop him!"

Feverishly, the big man grabbed up his soaking wet cloak. He was barreling out the door when a huge dark shadow blocked his path.

"Out of my way, Raag," Caramon growled, completely forgetting, in his anxiety, where he was.

Raag reminded him instantly, his giant hand closing over Caramon's huge shoulder. "Where go, slave?"

Caramon tried to shake off the ogre's grip, but Raag's hand simply tightened its grip. There was a crunching sound, and Caramon gasped in pain.

"Don't hurt him, Raag," came a voice from somewhere around Caramon's kneecaps. "He's got to fight tomorrow. What's more, he's got to win!"

Raag pushed Caramon back into the cell with as little effort as a grown man playfully tosses a child. The big warrior stumbled backward, falling heavily on the stone floor.

"You sure are busy today," Arack said conversationally, entering the cell and plopping down on the bed.

Sitting up, Caramon rubbed his bruised shoulder. He cast a quick glance at Raag, who was still standing, blocking the door. Arack continued.

"You've already been out once in this foul weather, and now you're heading out again?" The dwarf shook his head. "No, no. I can't allow it. You might catch cold. . . ."

"Hey," Caramon said, grinning weakly and licking his dry lips. "I was just going to the mess hall to find Tas—" He cringed involuntarily as a bolt of lightning exploded outside. There was a cracking sound and a sudden odor of burning wood.

"Forget it. The kender left," Arack said, shrugging, "and it looked to me like he left for good—had his stuff all packed."

Caramon swallowed, clearing his throat. "Let me go find him then—" he began.

Arack's grin twisted suddenly into a vicious scowl. "I don't give a damn about the little bastard! I got my money's worth outta him, I figure, in what he stole for me already. But you—I've got quite an investment in you. Your little escape plan's failed, slave."

"Escape?" Caramon laughed hollowly. "I never—You don't understand—"

"So I don't understand?" Arack snarled. "I don't understand that you've been trying to get two of my best fighters to leave? Trying to ruin me, are you?" The dwarf's voice rose to a shrill shriek above the howl of the wind outside. "Who put you up to this?" Arack's expression became suddenly shrewd and cunning. "It wasn't your master, so don't lie. He's been to see me."

"Raist—er—Fist-Fistandantil—" Caramon stammered, his jaw dropping.

The dwarf smiled smugly. "Yeah. And Fistandantilus warned me you might try something like this. Said I should watch you carefully. He even suggested a fitting punishment for you. The final fight tomorrow will not be between your team and the minotaurs. It will be you against Kiiri and Pheragas and the Red Minotaur!" The dwarf leaned over, leering into Caramon's face. "And their weapons will be real!"

Caramon stared at Arack uncomprehendingly for a

moment. Then, "Why?" he murmured bleakly. "Why does he want to kill me?"

"Kill you?" The dwarf cackled. "He doesn't want to kill you! He thinks you'll win! 'It's a test,' he says to me, 'I don't want a slave who isn't the best! And this will prove it. Caramon showed me what he could do against the Barbarian. That was his first test. Let's make *this* test harder on him,' he says. Oh, he's a rare one, your master!"

The dwarf chuckled, slapping his knees at the thought, and even Raag gave a grunt that might have been indicative of amusement.

"I won't fight," Caramon said, his face hardening into firm, grim lines. "Kill me! I won't fight my friends. And they won't fight me!"

"He said you'd say that!" The dwarf roared. "Didn't he, Raag! The very words. By gar, he knows you! You'd think you two was kin! 'So,' he says to me, 'if he refuses to fight, and he will, I have no doubt, then you tell him that his friends will fight in his stead, only they will fight the Red Minotaur and it will be the minotaur who has the real weapons.' "

Caramon remembered vividly the young man writhing in agony on the stone floor as the poison from the minotaur's trident coursed through his body.

"As for your friends fighting you"—the dwarf sneered—"Fistandantilus took care of that, too. After what he told them, I think they're gonna be real eager to get in the arena!"

Caramon's head sank to his chest. He began to shake. His body convulsed with chills, his stomach wrenched. The enormity of his brother's evil overwhelmed him, his mind filled with darkness and despair.

Raistlin has deceived us all, deceived Crysania, Tas, me! It was Raistlin who made me kill the Barbarian. He lied to me! And he's lied to Crysania, too. He's no more capable of loving her than the dark moon is capable of lighting the night skies. He's using her! And Tas? Tas! Caramon closed his eyes. He remembered Raistlin's look when he discovered the kender, his words—"kender can alter time. . . . is this how they plan to stop me?" Tas was a danger to him, a threat! He had no doubt, now, where Tas had gone. . . .

The wind outside howled and shrieked, but not as loudly as the pain and anguish in Caramon's soul. Sick and nauseous, wracked by icy spasms of needle-sharp pain, the big warrior completely lost any comprehension of what was going on around him. He didn't see Arack's gesture, nor feel Raag's huge hands grab hold of him. He didn't even feel the bindings on his wrists....

It was only later, when the awful feelings of sickness and horror passed, that he woke to a realization of his surroundings. He was in tiny, windowless cell far underground, probably beneath the arena. Raag was fastening a chain to the iron collar around his neck and was bolting that chain to a ring in the stone wall. Then the ogre shoved him to the floor and checked the leather thongs that bound Caramon's wrists.

"Not too tight," Caramon heard the dwarf's voice warn, "he's got to fight tomorrow...."

There was a distant rumble of thunder, audible even this far beneath the ground. At the sound, Caramon looked up hopefully. *We can't fight in this weather*—

The dwarf grinned as he followed Raag out the wooden door. He started to slam it shut, then poked his head around the corner, his beard wagging in glee as he saw the look on Caramon's face.

"Oh, by the way. Fistandantilus says it's going to be a beautiful day tomorrow. A day that everyone on Krynn will long remember...."

The door slammed shut and locked.

Caramon sat alone in the dense, damp darkness. His mind was calm, the sickness and shock having wiped it clean as slate of any feeling, any emotion. He was alone. Even Tas was gone. There was no one he could turn to for advice, no one to make his decisions for him anymore. And then, he realized, he didn't need anyone. Not to make this decision.

Now he knew, now he understood. *This* is why the mages had sent him back. They knew the truth. They wanted him to learn it for himself. His twin was lost, never to be reclaimed.

Raistlin must die.

Chapter 16

No one slept in Istar that night.

The storm increased in fury until it seemed it must destroy everything in its path. The wind's keening was like the deadly wail of the banshee, piercing even the continuous crashing of the thunder. Splintered lightning danced among the streets, trees exploded at its fiery touch. Hail rattled and bounced among the streets, knocking bricks and stones from houses, shattering the thickest glass, allowing the wind and rain to rush into homes like savage conquerors. Flood waters roared through the streets, carrying away the market stalls, the slave pens, carts and carriages.

Yet, no one was hurt.

It was as if the gods, in this last hour, held their hands cupped protectively over the living; hoping, begging them to heed the warnings.

At dawn, the storm ceased. The world was suddenly filled with a profound silence. The gods waited, not even daring to breathe, lest they miss the one small cry that might yet save the world.

The sun rose in a pale blue, watery sky. No bird sang to welcome it, no leaves rustled in the morning breeze, for there was no morning breeze. The air was still and deathly calm. Smoke rose from the smoldering trees in straight lines to the heavens, the flood waters dwindled away rapidly as though whisked down a huge drain. The people crept outdoors, staring around in disbelief that there was not more damage and then, exhausted from sleepless nights preceding, went back to their beds.

But there was, after all, one person in Istar who slept peacefully through the night. The sudden silence, in fact, woke him up.

As Tasslehoff Burrfoot was fond of recounting—he had talked to spooks in Darken Wood, met several dragons (flown on two), come *very* near the accursed Shoikan Grove (how near improved with each telling), broke a dragon orb, and had been personally responsible for the defeat of the Queen of Darkness (with some help). A mere thunderstorm, even the likes of a thunderstorm such as this one, wasn't likely to frighten him, much less disturb his sleep.

It had been a simple matter to retrieve the magical device. Tas shook his head over Caramon's naive pride in the cleverness of his hiding place. Tas had refrained from telling the big man, but that false bottom could have been detected by any kender over the age of three.

Tas lifted the magical device out of the box eagerly, staring at it with wonder and delight. He had forgotten how charming and lovely it was, folded down into an oval pendant. It seemed impossible that his hands would transform it into a device that would perform such a miracle!

Hurriedly, Tas went over Raistlin's instructions in his mind. The mage had given them to him only a few days before and had made him memorize them—figuring that Tas would promptly lose written instructions, as Raistlin had told him caustically.

They were not difficult, and Tas had them in moments.

Thy time is thy own
Though across it you travel.
Its expanses you see
Whirling through forever,
Obstruct not its flow.
Grasp firmly the end and the beginning,
Turn them back upon themselves, and
All that is loose shall be secure.
Destiny be over your own head.

The device was so beautiful, Tas could have lingered, admiring it, for long moments. But he didn't have long moments, so he hastily thrust it into one of his pouches, grabbed his other pouches (just in case he found anything worth carrying along—or anything found him), put on his cloak and hurried out. On the way, he thought about his last conversation with the mage just a few days previous.

" 'Borrow' the object the night before," Raistlin had counseled him. "The storm will be frightening, and Caramon might take it into his head to leave. Besides, it will be easiest for you to slip into the room known as the Sacred Chamber of the Temple unnoticed while the storm rages. The storm will end in the morning, and then the Kingpriest and his ministers will begin the processional. They will be going to the Sacred Chamber, and it is there that the Kingpriest will make his demands of the gods.

"You must be in the chamber and you must activate the device at the very moment the Kingpriest ceases to speak—"

"How will it stop it?" Tas interrupted eagerly. "Will I see it shoot a ray of light up to heaven or something? Will it knock the Kingpriest flat?"

"No," Raistlin answered, coughing softly, "it will not—um— knock the Kingpriest flat. But you are right about the light."

"I am?" Tas's mouth gaped open. "I just guessed! That's fantastic! I must be getting good at this magic stuff."

"Yes," Raistlin replied dryly, "now, to continue before I was interrupted—"

"Sorry, it won't happen again," Tas apologized, then shut his mouth as Raistlin glared at him.

"You must sneak into the Sacred Chamber during the night. The area behind the altar is lined with curtains. Hide there and you will not be discovered."

"Then I'll stop the Cataclysm, go back to Caramon, and tell him all about it! I'll be a hero—" Tas stopped, a sudden thought crossing his mind. "But, how can I be a hero if I stop something that never started? I mean, how will they know I did anything if I didn't—"

"Oh, they'll know. . . ." said Raistlin softly.

"They will? But I still don't see—Oh, you're busy, I guess. I suppose I should go? All right. Say, well, you're leaving after this is all over," Tas said, being rather firmly propelled toward the door by Raistlin's hand on his shoulder. "Where are you going?"

"Where I choose," said Raistlin.

"Could I come with you?" Tas asked eagerly.

"No, you'll be needed back in your own time," Raistlin answered, staring at the kender very strangely—or so Tas thought at the time. "To look after Caramon. . . ."

"Yes, I guess you're right." The kender sighed. "He does take a lot of looking after." They reached the door. Tas regarded it for a moment, then looked up wistfully at Raistlin. "I don't suppose you could . . . sort of swoosh me somewhere, like you did the last time? It's great fun. . . ."

Checking a sigh, Raistlin obligingly "swooshed" the kender into a duck pond, to Tas's vast amusement. The kender couldn't recall, in fact, when Raistlin had been so nice to him.

It must be because of my ending the Cataclysm, Tas decided. He's probably really grateful, just doesn't know how to express it properly. Or maybe he's not allowed to be grateful since he's evil.

That was an interesting thought and one Tas considered as he waded out of the pond and went, dripping, back to the arena.

Tas recalled it again as he left the arena the night before the Cataclysm that wasn't going to happen, but his thoughts about Raistlin were rudely interrupted. He hadn't realized quite how bad the storm had grown and was somewhat amazed at the ferocity of the wind that literally picked him up and slammed him back against the stone wall of the arena when he first darted outside. After pausing a moment to recover his breath and check to see if anything was broken, the kender picked himself up and started off toward the Temple again, the magical device firmly in hand.

This time, he had presence of mind enough to hug the buildings, finding that the wind didn't buffet him so there. Walking through the storm proved to be rather an exhilarating experience, in fact. Once lightning struck a tree next to him, smashing it to smithereens. (He had often wondered, what exactly was a smithereen?) Another time he misjudged the depth of the water running in the street and found himself being washed down the block at a rapid rate. This was amusing and would have been even more fun if he had been able to breathe. Finally, the water dumped him rather abruptly in an alley, where he was able to get back onto his feet and continue his journey.

Tas was almost sorry to reach the Temple after so many adventures, but—reminding himself of his Important Mission—he crept through the garden and made his way inside. Once there, it was, as Raistlin had predicted, easy to lose himself in the confusion created by the storm. Clerics were running everywhere, trying to mop up water and broken glass from shattered windows, relighting blown out torches, comforting those who could no longer stand the strain.

He had no idea where the Sacred Chamber was, but there was nothing he enjoyed more than wandering around strange places. Two or three hours (and several bulging pouches later), he ran across a room that precisely matched Raistlin's description.

No torches lit the room; it was not being used at present, but flashes of lightning illuminated it brightly enough for the kender to see the altar and the curtains Raistlin had described. By this time, being rather fatigued, Tas was glad to rest. After investigating the room and finding it boringly empty, he made his way past the altar (empty as well) and ducked behind the curtains, rather hoping (even if he was tired) to find some kind of secret cave where the Kingpriest performed holy rites forbidden to the eyes of mortal men.

Looking around, he sighed. Nothing. Just a wall, covered by curtains. Sitting down behind the curtains, Tas spread out his cloak to dry, wrung the water out of his topknot, and—by the flashes of lightning coming through the stained glass windows—began to sort through the interesting objects that had made their way into his pouches.

After a while, his eyes grew too heavy to keep open and his yawns were beginning to hurt his jaws. Curling up on the floor, he drifted off to sleep, only mildly annoyed by the booming of the thunder. His last thought was to wonder if Caramon had missed him yet and, if so, was he very angry? . . .

The next thing Tas knew, it was quiet. Now, why that should have startled him out of perfectly sound sleep was at first a complete mystery. It was also somewhat of a mystery as to where he was, exactly, but then he remembered.

Oh, yes. He was in the Sacred Chamber of the Temple of the Kingpriest of Istar. Today was the day of the Cataclysm, or it would have been. Perhaps, more accurately, today wasn't the day of the Cataclysm. Or today *had been* the day of the Cataclysm. Finding this all very confusing—altering time was such a bother—Tas decided not to think about it and to try to figure out, instead, why it was so quiet.

Then, it occurred to him. The storm had stopped! Just like Raistlin said it would. Rising to his feet, he peeked out from between the curtains into the Sacred Chamber. Through the windows, he could see bright sunlight. Tas gulped in excitement.

He had no idea what time it was but, from the brilliance of the sunlight, it must be close to midmorning. The processional would start soon, he remembered, and would take a while to wind through the Temple. The Kingpriest had called upon the gods at High Watch, when the sun reached its zenith in the sky.

Sure enough, just as Tas was thinking about it, bells pealed out, right above him, it seemed, their clanging startling him more than the thunder. For a moment he wondered if he might be doomed to go through life hearing nothing but bonging sounds ring in his ears. Then the bells in the tower above stopped and, after a few moments more, so did the bells in his head. Heaving a sigh of relief, he peeked out between the curtains into the Chamber again and was just wondering if there was a chance someone might come back here to clean when he saw a shadowy figure slip into the room.

Tas drew back. Keeping the curtains open only a crack, he peered through with one eye. The figure's head was bowed, its steps were slow and uncertain. It paused a moment to lean against one of the stone benches that flanked the altar as if too tired to continue further, then it sank down to its knees. Though it was dressed in white robes like nearly everyone in the Temple, Tas thought this figure looked familiar, so, when he was fairly certain the figure's attention wasn't on him, he risked widening the opening.

"Crysania!" he said to himself with interest. "I wonder why she's here so early?" Then he was seized with a sudden overwhelming disappointment. Suppose she was here to stop the Cataclysm as well! "Drat! Raistlin said I could," Tas muttered.

Then, he realized she was talking—either to herself or praying—Tas wasn't sure which. Crowding as close to the curtain as he dared, he listened to her soft words.

"Paladine, greatest, wisest god of eternal goodness, hear my voice on this most tragic of days. I know I cannot stop what is to come. And, perhaps it is a sign of a lack of faith that I even question what you do. All I ask is this—help me to understand! If it is true that I must die, let me know why. Let me see that my death will serve some purpose. Show me that I have not failed in all I came back here to accomplish.

"Grant that I may stay here, unseen, and listen to what no mortal ever heard and lived to relate—the words of the Kingpriest. He is a good man, too good, perhaps." Crysania's head sank into her hands. "My faith hangs by a thread," she said so softly Tas could barely hear. "Show me some justification for this terrible act. If it is your capricious whim, I will die as I was intended to, perhaps, among those who long ago lost their faith in the true gods—"

"Say not that they lost their faith, Revered Daughter," came a voice from the air that so startled the kender he nearly fell through the curtains. "Say, rather, that their faith in the true gods was replaced by their faith in false ones—money, power, ambition. . . ."

Crysania raised her head with a gasp that Tas echoed, but it was the sight of her face, not the sight of a shimmering figure of white materializing beside her, that made the kender draw in his breath. Crysania had obviously not slept for nights, her eyes were dark and wide, sunken into her face. Her cheeks were hollow, her lips dry and cracked; She had not bothered to comb her hair—it fell down about her face like black cobwebs as she stared in fear and alarm at the strange, ghostly figure.

"Who-who are you?" she faltered.

"My name is Loralon. And I have come to take you away. You were not intended to die, Crysania. You are the last true cleric now on Krynn and you may join us, who left many days ago."

"Loralon, the great cleric of Silvanesti," Crysania murmured. For long moments, she looked at him, then, bowing her head, she turned away, her eyes looking toward the altar. "I cannot go," she said firmly, her hands clasped nervously before her as she knelt. "Not yet. I must hear the Kingpriest. I must understand. . . ."

"Don't you understand enough already?" Loralon asked sternly. "What have you felt in your soul this night?"

Crysania swallowed, then brushed back her hair with a trembling hand. "Awe, humility," she whispered. "Surely, all must feel that before the power of the gods. . . ."

"Nothing else?" Loralon pursued. "Envy, perhaps? A desire to emulate them? To exist on the same level?"

"No!" Crysania answered angrily, then flushed, averting her face.

"Come with me now, Crysania," Loralon persisted. "A true faith needs no demonstrations, no justification for believing what it knows in its heart to be right."

"The words my heart speaks echo hollow in my mind," Crysania returned. "They are no more than shadows. I must see the truth, shining in the clear light of day! No, I will not leave with you. I will stay and hear what he says! I will know if the gods are justified!"

Loralon regarded her with a look that was more pitying than angry. "You do not look into the light, you stand in front of it. The shadow you see cast before you is your own. The next time you will see clearly, Crysania, is when you are blinded by darkness . . . darkness unending. Farewell, Revered Daughter."

Tasslehoff blinked and looked around. The old elf was gone! Had he ever really been there? the kender wondered uneasily. But he must have, because Tas could still remember his words. He felt chilled and confused. What had he meant? It all sounded so strange. And what had Crysania meant—being sent here to die?

Then the kender cheered up. Neither of them knew that the Cataclysm wasn't going to happen. No wonder Crysania was feeling gloomy and out of sorts.

"She'll probably perk up quite a bit when she finds out that the world isn't going to be devastated after all," Tas said to himself.

And then the kender heard distant voices raised in song. The processional! It was beginning. Tas almost whooped in excitement. Fearing discovery, he quickly covered his mouth with his hands. Then he took a last, quick peek out at Crysania. She sat forlornly, cringing at the sound of the music. Distorted by distance, it was shrill, harsh, and unlovely. Her face was so ashen Tas was momentarily alarmed, but then he saw her lips press together firmly, her eyes darken. She stared, unseeing, at her folded hands.

"You'll feel better soon," Tas told her silently, then the kender ducked back behind the curtain to remove the wonderful magical device from his pouch. Sitting down, he held the device in his hands, and waited.

The processional lasted forever, at least as far as the kender was concerned. He yawned. Important Missions were certainly dull, he decided irritably, and hoped someone would appreciate what he'd gone through when it was all over. He would have dearly loved to tinker with the magical device, but Raistlin had impressed upon him that he was to *leave it alone* until the time came and then *follow the instructions to the letter*. So intent had been the look in Raistlin's eyes and so cold his voice that it had penetrated even the kender's careless attitude. Tas sat holding the magical object, almost afraid to move.

Then, just as he was beginning to give up in despair (and his left foot was slowing losing all sensation), he heard a burst of beautiful voices right outside the room! A brilliant light welled through the curtains. The kender fought his curiosity, but finally couldn't resist just one peep. He had, after all, never seen the Kingpriest. Telling himself that he needed to see what was going on, he peeked through the crack in the curtains again.

The light nearly blinded him.

"Great Reorx!" the kender muttered, covering his eyes with his hands. He recalled once looking up at the sun when a child, trying to figure out if it really *was* a giant gold coin and, if so, how he could get it out of the sky. He'd been forced to go to bed for three days with cold rags over his eyes.

"I wonder how he does that?" Tas asked, daring to peep through his fingers again. He stared into the heart of the light just as he had stared into the sun. And he saw the truth. The sun wasn't a golden coin. The Kingpriest was just a man.

The kender did not experience the terrible shock felt by Crysania when she saw through the illusion to the real man. Perhaps this was because Tas had no preconceived notions of what the Kingpriest *should* look like. Kender hold absolutely no one and nothing in awe (though Tas had to admit he felt a bit queer around the death knight, Lord Soth). He was, therefore, only mildly surprised to see that the most holy Kingpriest was simply a middle-aged human, balding, with pale blue eyes and the terrified look of a deer caught in a thicket. Tas was surprised—and disappointed.

"I've gone to all this trouble for nothing," the kender thought irritably. "There isn't going to be a Cataclysm. I don't think this man could make me angry enough to throw a pie at him, let alone a whole fiery mountain."

But Tas had nothing else to do (and he was really dying to work the magical device), so he decided to stick around and watch and listen. Something might happen after all. He tried to see Crysania, wondering how she felt about this, but the halo of light surrounding the Kingpriest was so bright he couldn't see anything else in the room.

The Kingpriest walked to the front of the altar, moving slowly, his eyes darting left and right. Tas wondered if the Kingpriest would see Crysania, but apparently he was blinded by his own light as well, for his eyes passed right over her. Arriving at the altar, he did not kneel to pray, as had Crysania. Tas thought he might have started to, but then the Kingpriest angrily shook his head and remained standing.

From his vantage point behind and slightly to the left of the altar, Tas had an excellent look at the man's face. Once again, the kender gripped the magical device in excitement. For, the look of sheer terror in the watery eyes had been hidden by a mask of arrogance.

"Paladine," the Kingpriest trumpeted, and Tas had the distinct impression that the man was conferring with some underling. "Paladine, you see the evil that surrounds me! You have been witness to the calamities that have been the scourge of Krynn these past days. You know that this evil is directed against me, personally, because I am the only one fighting it! Surely you must see now that this doctrine of balance will not work!"

The Kingpriest's voice lost the harsh blare, becoming soft as a flute. "I understand, of course. You had to practice this doctrine in the old days, when you were weak. But you have me now, your right arm, your true representative upon Krynn. With our combined might, I can sweep evil from this world! Destroy the ogre races! Bring the wayward humans into line! Find new homelands far away for the dwarves and kender and gnomes, those races not of your own creation—"

How insulting! Tas thought, incensed. I've half a mind to let them go ahead and drop a mountain on him!

"And I will rule in glory," the Kingpriest's voice rose to a crescendo, "creating an age to rival even the fabled Age of Dreams!" The Kingpriest spread his arms wide. "You gave this and more to Huma, Paladine, who was nothing but a renegade knight of low birth! I demand that you give me, too, the power to drive away the shadows of evil that darken this land!"

The Kingpriest fell silent, waiting, his arms upraised.

Tas held his breath, waiting, too, clutching the magical device in his hands.

And then, the kender felt it—the answer. A horror crept over him, a fear he'd never experienced before, not even in the presence of Lord Soth or the Shoikan Grove. Trembling, the kender sank to his knees and bowed his head, whimpering and shaking, pleading with some unseen force for mercy, for forgiveness. Beyond the curtain, he could hear his own incoherent mumblings echoed, and he knew Crysania was there and that she, too, felt the terrible hot anger that rolled over him like the thunder from the storm.

But the Kingpriest did not speak a word. He simply remained, staring up expectantly into the heavens he could not see through the vast walls and ceilings of his Temple . . . the heavens he could not see because of his own light.

Chapter 17

His mind firmly resolved upon a course of action, Caramon fell into an exhausted sleep and, for a few hours, was blessed with oblivion. He awakened with a start to find Raag bending over him, breaking his chains.

"What about these?" Caramon asked, raising his bound wrists.

Raag shook his head. Although Arack didn't really think even Caramon would be foolish enough to try and overpower the ogre unarmed, the dwarf had seen enough madness in the man's eyes last night not to risk taking chances.

Caramon sighed. He had, indeed, considered that possibility as he had considered many others last night, but had rejected it. The important thing was to stay alive—at least until he had made certain Raistlin was dead. After that, it didn't matter anymore. . . .

Poor Tika. . . . She would wait and wait, until one day she would wake and realize he was never coming home.

"Move!" Raag grunted.

Caramon moved, following the ogre up the damp and twisting stairs leading from the storage rooms beneath the arena. He shook his head, clearing it of thoughts of Tika. Those might weaken his resolve, and he could not afford that. Raistlin must die. It was as if the lightning last night had illuminated a part of Caramon's mind that had lain in darkness for years. At last he saw the true extent of his brother's ambition, his lust for power. At last Caramon quit making excuses for him. It galled him, but he had to admit that even that dark elf, Dalamar, knew Raistlin far better than he, his twin brother.

Love had blinded him, and it had, apparently, blinded Crysania, too. Caramon recalled a saying of Tanis's "I've never seen anything done out of love come to evil." Caramon snorted. Well, there was a first time for everything—that had been a favorite saying of old Flint's. A first time . . . and a last.

Just how he was going to kill his brother, Caramon didn't know. But he wasn't worried. There was a strange feeling of peace within him. He was thinking with a clarity and a logic that amazed him. He *knew* he could do it. Raistlin wouldn't be able to stop him either, not this time. The magic time travel spell would require the mage's complete concentration. The only thing that could possibly stop Caramon was death itself.

And therefore, Caramon said grimly to himself, I'll have to live.

He stood quietly without moving a muscle or speaking a word as Arack and Raag struggled to get him into his armor.

"I don't like it," the dwarf muttered more than once to the ogre as they dressed Caramon. The big man's calm, emotionless expression made the dwarf more uneasy than if he had been a raging bull. The only time Arack saw a flicker of life on Caramon's stoic face was when he buckled his shortsword onto his belt. Then the big man had glanced down at it, recognizing the useless prop for what it was. Arack saw him smile bitterly.

"Keep your eye on him," Arack instructed, and Raag nodded. "And keep him away from the others until he goes into the arena."

Raag nodded again, then led Caramon, hands bound, into the corridors beneath the arena where the others waited. Kiiri and Pheragas glanced over at Caramon as he entered. Kiiri's lip curled, and she turned coldly away. Caramon met Pheragas's gaze unflinchingly, his eyes neither begging nor pleading. This was not what Pheragas had expected, apparently. At first the black man seemed confused, then—after a few whispered words from Kiiri—he, too, turned away. But Caramon saw the man's shoulders slump and he saw him shake his head.

There was a roar from the crowd then, and Caramon shifted his gaze to what he could see of the stands. It was nearly midday, the Games started promptly at High Watch. The sun shone in the sky, the crowd—having had some sleep—was large and in a particularly good humor. There were some preliminary fights scheduled—to whet the crowd's appetite and to heighten the tension. But the true attraction was the Final Bout—the one that would determine the champion—the slave who wins either his freedom or—in the Red Minotaur's case—wealth enough to last him years.

Arack wisely kept up the pacing of the first few fights, making them light, even comic. He'd imported a few gully dwarves for the occasion. Giving them real weapons (which, of course, they had no idea how to use), he sent them into the arena. The audience howled its delight, laughing until many were in tears at the sight of the gully dwarves tripping over their own swords, viciously stabbing each other with the hilts of their daggers, or turning and running, shrieking, out of the arena. Of course, the audience didn't enjoy the event nearly as much as the gully dwarves themselves, who finally tossed aside all weapons and launched into a mud fight. They had to be forcibly removed from the ring.

The crowd applauded, but now many began to stomp their feet in good humored, if impatient, demand for the main attraction. Arack allowed this to go on for several moments, knowing—like the showman he was—that it merely heightened their excitement. He was right. Soon the stands were rocking as the crowd clapped and stomped and chanted.

And thus it was that no one in the crowd felt the first tremor.

Caramon felt it, and his stomach lurched as the ground shuddered beneath his feet. He was chilled with fear—not fear of dying, but fear that he might die without accomplishing his objective. Glancing up anxiously into the sky, he tried to recall every legend he had ever heard about the Cataclysm. It had struck near mid-afternoon, he thought he remembered. But there had been earthquakes, volcanic eruptions, dreadful natural disasters of all kinds throughout Krynn, even before the fiery mountain smashed the city of Istar so far beneath the ground that the seas rushed in to cover it.

Vividly, Caramon saw the wreckage of this doomed city as he had seen it after their ship had been sucked into the whirlpool of what was now known as the Blood Sea of Istar. The sea elves had rescued them then, but there would be no rescue for these people. Once more, he saw the twisted and shattered buildings. His soul recoiled in horror and he realized, with a start, that he had been keeping that terrible sight from his mind.

I never really believed it would happen, he realized, shivering with fear as the ground shivered in sympathy. *I have hours only, maybe not that long. I must get out of here! I must reach Raistlin!*

Then, he calmed down. Raistlin was expecting him. Raistlin needed him—or at least he needed a "trained fighter." Raistlin would ensure that he had plenty of time— time to win and get to him. Or time to lose and be replaced.

But it was with a feeling of vast relief that Caramon felt the tremor cease. Then he heard Arack's voice coming from the center of the arena, announcing the Final Bout.

"Once they fought as a team, ladies and gentlemen, and as all of you know, they were the best team we've seen here in long years. Many's the time you saw each one risk his or her life to save a teammate. They were like brothers"—Caramon flinched at this—"but now they're bitter enemies, ladies and gentlemen. For when it comes to freedom, to wealth, to winning this greatest of all the Games—love has to sit in the back row. They'll give their all, you may be sure of that, ladies and gentlemen. This is a fight to the death between Kiiri the Sirine, Pheragas of Ergoth, Caramon the Victor, and the Red Minotaur. They won't leave this arena unless it's feet first!"

The crowd cheered and roared. Even though they knew it was fake, they loved convincing themselves it wasn't. The roaring grew louder as the Red Minotaur entered, his bestial face disdainful as always. Kiiri and Pheragas glanced at him, then at the trident he held, then at each other. Kiiri's hand closed tightly around her dagger.

Caramon felt the ground shake again. Then Arack called his name. It was time for the Game to begin.

Tasslehoff felt the first tremors and for a moment thought it was just his imagination, a reaction to that terrible anger rolling around them. Then he saw the curtains swaying back and forth, and he realized that this was it. . . .

Activate the device! came a voice into Tasslehoff's brain. His hands trembling, looking down at the pendant, Tas repeated the instructions.

"*Thy time is thy own*, let's see, I turn the face toward me. There. *Though across it you travel*. I shift this plate from right to left. *Its expanses you see*—back plate drops to form two disks connected by rods . . . it works!" Highly excited, Tas continued. "*Whirling through forever*, twist top facing me counterclockwise from bottom. *Obstruct not its flow*. Make sure the pendant chain is clear. There, that's right. Now, *Grasp firmly the end and the beginning*. Hold the disks at both ends. *Turn them back upon themselves*, like so, and *All that is loose shall be secure*. The chain will wind itself into the body! Isn't this wonderful! It's doing it! Now, *Destiny be over your own head*. Hold it over my head and—Wait! Something's not right! I don't think this is supposed to be happening. . . ."

A tiny jeweled piece fell off the device, hitting Tas on the nose. Then another, and another, until the distraught kender was standing in a perfect rain of small, jeweled pieces.

"What?" Tas stared wildly at the device he held up over his head. Frantically he twisted the ends again. This time the rain of jeweled pieces became a positive downpour, clattering on the floor with bright, chime-like tones.

Tasslehoff wasn't sure, but he didn't think it was supposed to do this. Still, one never knew, especially about wizard's toys. He watched it, holding his breath, waiting for the light. . . .

The ground suddenly leaped beneath his feet, hurling him through the curtains and sending him sprawling on the floor at the feet of the Kingpriest. But the man never noticed the ashen-faced kender. The Kingpriest was staring about him in magnificent unconcern, watching with detached curiosity the curtains that rippled like waves, the tiny cracks that suddenly branched through the marble altar. Smiling to himself, as if assured that this was the acquiescence of the gods, the Kingpriest turned from the crumbling altar and made his way back down the central aisle, past the shuddering benches, and out into the main part of the Temple.

"No!" Tas moaned, rattling the device. At that moment, the tubes connecting either end of the sceptre separated in his hands. The chain slipped between his fingers. Slowly, trembling nearly as much as the floor on which he lay, Tasslehoff struggled to his feet. In his hand, he held the broken pieces of the magical device.

"What have I done?" Tas wailed. "I followed Raistlin's instructions, I'm sure I did! I—"

And suddenly the kender knew. Tears caused the glimmering, shattered pieces to blur in his gaze. "He was so nice to me," Tas murmured. "He made me repeat the instructions over and over—*to make certain you have them right*, he said." Tas squeezed shut his eyes, willing that when he opened them, this would all be a bad dream.

But when he did, it wasn't.

"I had them right. He *meant* for me to break it!" Tas whimpered, shivering. "Why? To strand us all back here? To leave us all to die? No! He wants Crysania, they said so, the mages in the Tower. That's it!" Tas whirled around. "Crysania!"

But the cleric neither heard nor saw him. Staring straight unhead, unmoved, even though the ground shook beneath her knees as she knelt, Crysania's gray eyes glowed with an eerie, inner light. Her hands, still folded as if in prayer, clenched each other so tightly that the fingers had turned purplish red, the knuckles white.

Her lips moved. Was she praying?

Scrambling back behind the curtains, Tas quickly picked up every tiny jeweled piece of the device, gathered up the chain that had nearly slipped down a crack in the floor, then stuck everything into one pouch, closing it securely. Giving the floor a final look, he crept out into the Sacred Chamber.

"Crysania," he whispered. He hated to disturb her prayers, but this was too urgent to give up.

"Crysania?" he said, coming over to stand in front of her, since it was obvious she wasn't even aware of his existence.

Watching her lips, he read their unspoken utterings.

"I know," she was saying, "I know his mistake! Perhaps for me, the gods will grant what they denied him!"

Drawing a deep breath, she lowered her head. "Paladine, thank you! Thank you!" Tas heard her intone fervently. Then, swiftly, she rose to her feet. Glancing around in some astonishment at the objects in the room that were moving in a deadly dance, her gaze flicked, unseeing, right over the kender.

"Crysania!" Tas babbled, this time clutching at her white robes. "Crysania, I broke it! Our only way back! I broke a dragon orb once. But that was on purpose! I never meant to break this. Poor Caramon! You've got to help me! Come with me, talk to Raistlin, make him fix it!"

The cleric stared down at Tasslehoff blankly, as if he were a stranger accosting her on the street. "Raistlin!" she murmured, gently but firmly detaching the kender's hands from her robes. "Of course! He tried to tell me, but I wouldn't listen. And now I know, now I know the truth!"

Thrusting Tas away from her, Crysania gathered up her flowing white robes, darted out from among the benches, and ran down the center aisle without a backward glance as the Temple shook on its very foundations.

It wasn't until Caramon started to mount the stairs leading out into the arena, that Raag finally removed the bindings from the gladiator's wrists. Flexing his fingers, grimacing, Caramon followed Kiiri and Pheragas and the Red Minotaur out into the center of the arena. The audience cheered. Caramon, taking his place between Kiiri and Pheragas, looked up at the sky nervously. It was past High Watch, the sun was beginning its slow descent.

Istar would never live to see the sunset.

Thinking of this, and thinking that he, too, would never again see the sun's red rays stream over a battlement, or melt into the sea, or light the tops of the vallenwoods, Caramon felt tears sting his eyes. He wept not so much for himself, but for those two who stood beside him, who must die this day, and for all those innocents who would perish without understanding why.

He wept, too, for the brother he had loved, but his tears for Raistlin were for someone who had died long ago.

"Kiiri, Pheragas," Caramon said in a low voice when the Minotaur strode forward to take his bow alone, "I don't know what the mage told you, but I never betrayed you."

Kiiri refused to even look at him. He saw her lip curl. Pheragas, glancing at him from the corner of his eye, saw the stain of tears upon Caramon's face and hesitated, frowning, before he, too, turned away.

"It doesn't matter, really," Caramon continued, "whether you believe me or not. You can kill each other for the key if you want, because I'm finding my freedom my own way."

Now Kiiri looked at him, her eyes wide in disbelief. The crowd was on its feet, yelling for the Minotaur, who was walking around the arena, waving his trident above his head.

"You're mad!" she whispered as loudly as she dared. Her gaze went meaningfully to Raag. As always, the ogre's huge, yellowish body blocked the only exit.

Caramon's gaze followed imperturbably, his face not changing expression.

"Our weapons are real, my friend," Pheragas said harshly. "Yours are not!"

Caramon nodded, but did not answer.

"Don't do this!" Kiiri edged closer. "We'll help you fake it in the arena today. I-I guess neither of us really believed the blackrobed one. You must admit, it seemed weird—you trying to get us to leave the city! We thought, like he said, that you wanted the prize all to yourself. Look, pretend you're injured real early. Get yourself carried off. We'll help you escape tonight—"

"There will be no tonight," Caramon said softly. "Not for me, not for any of us. I haven't got much time. I can't explain. All I ask is this—just don't try to stop me."

Pheragas took a breath, but the words died on his lips as another tremor, this one more severe, shook the ground.

Now, everyone noticed. The arena swayed on its stilts, the bridges over the Death Pits creaked, the floor rose and fell, nearly knocking the Red Minotaur to his feet. Kiiri grabbed hold of Caramon. Pheragas braced his legs like a sailor on board a heaving vessel. The crowd in the stands fell suddenly silent as their seats rocked beneath them. Hearing the cracking of the wood, some screamed. Several even rose to their feet. But the tremor stopped as quickly as it had begun.

Everything was quiet, too quiet. Caramon felt the hair rise on his neck and his skin prickle. No birds sang, not a dog barked. The crowd was silent, waiting in fear. *I have to get out of here!* Caramon resolved. His friends didn't matter anymore, nothing mattered. He had just one fixed objective—to stop Raistlin.

And he must act now, before the next shock hit and before people recovered from this one. Glancing quickly around, Caramon saw Raag standing beside the exit, the ogre's yellow, mottled face creased in puzzlement, his slow brain trying to figure out what was going on. Arack had appeared suddenly beside him, staring around, probably hoping he wouldn't be forced to refund his customers' money. Already the crowd was starting to settle down, though many glanced about uneasily.

Caramon drew a deep breath, then, gripping Kiiri in his arms, he heaved with all his strength, hurling the startled woman right into Pheragas, sending them both tumbling to the ground.

Seeing them fall, Caramon whirled around and propelled his massive body straight at the ogre, driving his shoulder into Raag's gut with all the strength his months of training had given him. It was a blow that would have killed a human, but it only knocked the wind out of the ogre. The force of Caramon's charge sent them both crashing backward into the wall.

Desperately, while Raag was gasping for breath, Caramon grappled for the ogre's stout club. But just as he yanked it out of Raag's grip, the ogre recovered. Howling in anger, Raag brought both massive hands up under Caramon's chin with a blow that sent the big warrior flying back into the arena.

Landing heavily, Caramon could see nothing for a moment except sky and arena whirling around and around him. Groggy from the blow his warrior's instincts took over. Catching a glimpse of movement to his left, Caramon rolled over just as the minotaur's trident came down where his sword arm had been. He could hear the minotaur snarling and growling in bestial fury.

Caramon struggled to regain his feet, shaking his head to clear it, but he knew he could never hope to avoid the minotaur's second strike. And then a black body was between him and the Red Minotaur. There was a flash of steel as Pheragas's sword blocked the trident blow that would have finished Caramon. Staggering, Caramon backed up to catch his breath and felt Kiiri's cool hands helping to support him.

"Are you all right?" she muttered.

"Weapon!" Caramon managed to gasp, his head still ringing from the ogre's blow.

"Take mine," Kiiri said, thrusting her shortsword into Caramon's hands. "Then rest a moment. I'll handle Raag."

The ogre, wild with rage and the excitement of battle, barreled toward them, his slavering jaws wide open.

"No! You need it—" Caramon began to protest, but Kiiri only grinned at him.

"Watch!" she said lightly, then spoke strange words that reminded Caramon vaguely of the language of magic. These, however, had a faint accent, almost elvish.

And, suddenly Kiiri was gone. In her place stood a gigantic she-bear. Caramon gasped, unable—for a moment—to comprehend what had happened. Then he remembered— Kiiri was a Sirine, gifted with the power to change her shape!

Rearing up on her hind legs, the she-bear towered over the huge ogre. Raag came to a halt, his eyes wide open in alarm at the sight. Kiiri roared in rage, her sharp teeth gleamed. The sunlight glinted off her claws as one of her giant paws lashed out and caught Raag across his mottled face.

The ogre howled in pain, streams of yellowish blood oozed from the claw marks, one eye disappeared in a mass of bleeding jelly. The bear leaped on the ogre. Watching in awe, Caramon could see nothing but yellow skin and blood and brown fur.

The crowd, too, although they had yelled in delight at the beginning, suddenly became aware that this fight wasn't faked. This was for real. People were going to die. There was a moment of shocked silence, then—here and there—someone cheered. Soon the applause and wild yells were deafening.

Caramon quickly forgot the people in the stands, however. He saw his chance. Only the dwarf stood blocking the exit now, and Arack's face, though twisted in anger, was twisted in fear as well. Caramon could easily get past him. . . .

At that moment, he heard a grunt of pleasure from the minotaur. Turning, Caramon saw Pheragas slump over in pain, catching the butt end of the trident in his solar plexus. The minotaur reversed the stroke, raising the weapon to kill, but Caramon yelled loudly, distracting the minotaur long enough to throw him off stride.

The Red Minotaur turned to face this new challenge, a grin on his red-furred face. Seeing Caramon armed only with a shortsword, the minotaur's grin broadened. Lunging at Caramon, the minotaur sought to end the fight quickly. But Caramon sidestepped deftly. Raising his foot, he kicked, shattering the minotaur's kneecap. It was a painful, crippling blow, and sent the minotaur stumbling to the ground.

Knowing his enemy was out for at least a few moments, Caramon ran over to Pheragas. The black man remained huddled over, grasping his stomach.

"C'mon," Caramon grunted, putting his arm around him. "I've seen you take a hit like that, get up, and eat a five-course meal. What's the matter?"

But there was no answer. Caramon felt the man's body shiver convulsively, and he saw that the shining black skin was wet with sweat. Then Caramon saw the three bleeding slashes the trident had cut in the man's arm. . . .

Pheragas looked up at his friend. Seeing Caramon's horrified gaze, he realized he understood. Shuddering in pain from the poison that was coursing through his veins, Pheragas sank to his knees. Caramon's big arms closed around him.

"Take . . . take my sword." Pheragas choked. "Quickly, fool!" Hearing from the sounds his enemy was making that the minotaur was back on his feet, Caramon hesitated only a second, then took the large sword from Pheragas's shaking hand.

Pheragas pitched over, writhing in pain.

Gripping the sword, tears blinding his eyes, Caramon rose and whirled, blocking the Red Minotaur's sudden thrust. Even though limping on one leg, the minotaur's strength was such that he easily compensated for the painful injury. Then, too, the minotaur knew that all it took was a scratch to kill his victim, and Caramon would have to come inside the trident's range to use his sword.

Slowly the two stalked each other, circling round and round. Caramon no longer heard the crowd that was stamping and whistling and cheering madly at the sight of real blood. He no longer thought of escape, he had no idea—even—where he was. His warrior's instincts had taken over. He knew one thing. He had to kill.

And so he waited. Minotaurs had one major fault, Pheragas taught him. Believing themselves to be superior to all other races, minotaurs generally underestimate an opponent. They make mistakes, if you wait them out. The Red Minotaur was no exception. The minotaur's thoughts became clear to Caramon—pain and anger, outrage at the insult, an eagerness to end the life of this dull-witted, puny human.

The two edged nearer and nearer the spot where Kiiri was still locked in a vicious battle with Raag, as Caramon could tell by the sounds of growling and shrieking from the ogre. Suddenly, apparently preoccupied with watching Kiiri, Caramon slipped in a pool of yellow, slimy blood. The Red Minotaur, howling in delight, lunged forward to impale the human's body on the trident.

But the slip had been feigned. Caramon's sword flashed in the sunlight. The minotaur, seeing he had been fooled, tried to recover from this forward lunge. But he had forgotten his crippled knee. It would not bear his weight, and the Red Minotaur fell to the arena floor, Caramon's sword cleaving cleanly through the bestial head.

Jerking his sword free, Caramon heard a horrible snarling behind him and turned just in time to see the great she-bear's jaws clamp over Raag's huge neck. With a shake of her head, Kiiri bit deeply into the jugular vein. The ogre's mouth opened wide in a scream none would ever hear.

Caramon started toward them when he caught sudden movement to his right. Quickly he turned, every sense alert as Arack hurtled past him, the dwarf's face an ugly mask of grief and fury. Caramon saw the dagger flash in the dwarf's hand and he hurled himself forward, but he was too late. He could not stop the blade that buried itself in the bear's chest. Instantly, the dwarf's hand was awash in red, warm blood. The great she-bear roared in pain and anger. One huge paw lashed out. Catching hold of the dwarf, with her last convulsive strength, Kiiri lifted Arack and threw him across the arena. The dwarf's body smashed against the Freedom Spire where hung the golden key, impaling it upon one of the countless ornate protrusions. The dwarf gave a fearsome shriek, then the entire pinnacle collapsed, crashing into the flame-filled pits below.

Kiiri fell, blood pouring from the gash in her breast. The crowd was going wild, screaming and yelling Caramon's name. The big man did not hear. Bending down, he took Kiiri in his arms. The magical spell she had woven unraveled. The bear was gone, and he held Kiiri close to his chest.

"You've won, Kiiri," Caramon whispered. "You're free."

Kiiri looked up at him and smiled. Then her eyes widened, the life left them. Their dying gaze remained fixed upon the sky, almost—it seemed to Caramon—expectantly, as if now she knew what was coming.

Gently laying her body down upon the blood-soaked arena floor, Caramon rose to his feet. He saw Pheragas's body frozen in its last, agonized throes. He saw Kiiri's sightless, staring eyes.

"You will answer for this, my brother," Caramon said softly.

There was a noise behind him, a murmuring like the angry roar of the sea before the storm. Grimly, Caramon gripped his sword and turned, preparing to face whatever new enemy awaited him. But there was no enemy, only the other gladiators. At the sight of Caramon's, tear-streaked and bloodstained face, one by one, they stood aside, making way for him to pass.

Looking at them, Caramon realized that—at last—*he* was free. Free to find his brother, free to put an end to this evil forever. He felt his soul soar, death held little meaning and no fear for him anymore. The smell of blood was in his nostrils, and he was filled with the sweet madness of battle.

Thirsting now with the desire for revenge, Caramon ran to the edge of the arena, preparing to descend the stairs that led down to the tunnels beneath it, when the first of the earthquakes shattered the doomed city of Istar.

Chapter 18

Crysania neither saw nor heard Tasslehoff. Her mind was blinded by a myriad colors that swirled within its depths, sparkling like splendid jewels, for suddenly she understood. *This* was why Paladine had brought her back here—not to redeem the memory of the Kingpriest—but to learn from his mistakes. And she knew, she knew in her soul, that she *had* learned. *She* could call upon the gods and they would answer—not with anger—but with power! The cold darkness within her broke open, and the freed creature sprang from its shell, bursting into the sunlight.

In a vision, she saw herself—one hand holding high the medallion of Paladine, its platinum flashing in the sun. With her other hand, she called forth legions of believers, and they swarmed around her with adoring, rapt expressions as she led them to lands of beauty beyond imagining.

She didn't have the Key yet to unlock the door, she knew. And it could not happen here, the wrath of the gods was too great for her to penetrate. But where to find the Key, where to find the door, even? The dancing colors made her dizzy, she could not see or think. And then she heard a voice, a small voice, and felt hands clutching at her robes. "Raistlin..." she heard the voice say, the rest of the words were lost. But suddenly her mind cleared. The colors vanished, as did the light, leaving her alone in the darkness that was calm and soothing to her soul.

"Raistlin," she murmured. "He tried to tell me...."

Still the hands clutched at her. Absently, she disengaged them and thrust them aside. Raistlin would take her to the Portal, he would help her find the Key. Evil turns in upon itself, Elistan said. So Raistlin would unwittingly help her. Crysania's soul sang in a joyous anthem to Paladine. *When I return in my glory, with goodness in my hand, when all the evil in the world is vanquished, then Raistlin himself will see my might, he will come to understand and believe.*

"Crysania!"

The ground shook beneath Crysania's feet, but she did not notice the tremor. She heard a voice call her name, a soft voice, broken by coughing.

"Crysania " It spoke again. "There is not much time. Hurry!"

Raistlin's voice! Looking around wildly, Crysania searched for him, but she saw no one. And then she realized, he was speaking to her mind, guiding her. "Raistlin," she murmured, "I hear you. I am coming"

Turning, she ran down the aisle and out into the Temple. The kender's cry behind her fell on deaf ears.

"Raistlin?" said Tas, puzzled, glancing around. Then he understood. Crysania was going to Raistlin! Somehow, magically, he was calling to her and she was going to find him! Tasslehoff dashed out into the corridor of the Temple after Crysania. Surely, she would make Raistlin fix the device....

Once in the corridor, Tas glanced up and down and spotted Crysania quickly. But his heart nearly jumped out on the floor—she was running so swiftly she had nearly reached the end of the hall.

Making certain the broken pieces of the magical device were secure in his pouch, Tas ran grimly after Crysania, keeping her fluttering white robes in his sight for as long as possible.

Unfortunately, that wasn't very long. She immediately vanished around a corner.

The kender ran as he had never run before, not even when the imagined terrors of Shoikan Grove had been chasing him. His topknot of hair streamed out behind him, his pouches bounced around wildly, spilling their contents, leaving behind a glittering trail of rings and bracelets and baubles.

Keeping a firm grip on the pouch with the magical device, Tas reached the end of the hall and skidded around it, slamming up against the opposite wall in his haste. Oh, no! His heart went from jumping around in his chest to land with a thud at his feet. He began to wish irritably that his heart would stay put. Its gyrations were making him nauseous.

The hall was filled with clerics, all dressed in white robes! How was he ever to spot Crysania? Then he saw her, about half-way down the hall, her black hair shining in the torchlight. He saw, too, that clerics swirled about in her wake, shouting or glowering after her as she ran by.

Tas leaped to the pursuit, hope rising again; Crysania had been necessarily slowed in her wild flight by the crowd of people in the Temple. The kender sped past them, ignoring cries of outrage, skipping out of the way of grasping hands.

"Crysania," he yelled desperately.

The crowd of clerics in the hall became thicker, everyone hurrying out to wonder about the strange tremblings of the ground, trying to guess what this portended.

Tas saw Crysania halt more than once, pushing her way through the crowd. She had just freed herself when Quarath came around the corner, calling for the Kingpriest. Not watching where she was going, Crysania ran right into him, and he caught hold of her.

"Stop! My dear," Quarath cried, shaking her, thinking her hysterical. "Calm yourself!"

"Let me go!" Crysania struggled in his grasp.

"She's gone mad with terror! Help me hold her!" Quarath called to several other clerics standing nearby.

It suddenly occurred to Tas that Crysania *did* look mad. He could see her face as he drew near her, now. Her black hair was a tangled mass, her eyes were deep, deep gray, the color of the storm clouds, and her face was flushed with exertion. She seemed to hear nothing, no voices penetrated her consciousness, except, perhaps, one.

Other clerics caught hold of her at Quarath's command. Screaming incoherently, Crysania fought them, too. Desperation gave her strength, she came close to escaping more than once. Her white robes tore in their hands as they tried to hold her, Tas thought he saw blood on more than one cleric's face.

Running up, he was just about to leap on the back of the nearest cleric and bop him over the head when he was blinded by a brilliant light that brought everyone—even Crysania—to a halt.

No one moved. All Tas could hear for a moment were Crysania's gasps for breath and the heavy breathing of those who had tried to stop her. Then a voice spoke.

"The gods come," said the musical voice from out of the center of the light, "at my command—"

The ground beneath Tasslehoff's feet leaped high in the air, tossing the kender up like a feather. It sank rapidly as Tas was going up, then flew up to meet him as he was coming down. The kender slammed into the floor, the impact knocking the breath from his small body.

The air exploded with dust and glass and splinters, screams and shrieks and crashes. Tas could do nothing except fight to try to breathe. Lying on the marble floor as it jumped and rocked and shook beneath him, he watched in amazement as columns cracked and crumbled, walls split, pillars fell, and people died.

The Temple of Istar was collapsing.

Crawling forward on his hands and knees, Tas tried desperately to keep Crysania in sight. She seemed oblivious to what was happening around her. Those who had been holding her let go in their terror, and Crysania, still hearing only Raistlin's voice, started on her way again. Tas yelled, Quarath was lunging at her, but, even as the cleric hurtled toward her, a huge marble column next to her toppled and fell.

Tas caught his breath. He couldn't see a thing for an instant then the marble dust settled. Quarath was nothing but a bloody mass on the floor. Crysania, apparently unhurt, stood staring dazedly down at the elf, whose blood had spattered all over her white robes.

"Crysania!" Tasslehoff shouted hoarsely. But she didn't notice him. Turning away, she stumbled through the wreckage, unseeing, hearing nothing but the voice that called to her more urgently now than ever.

Staggering to his feet, his body bruised and aching, Tas ran after her. Nearing the end of the hall, he saw Crysania make a turn to her right and go down a flight of stairs. Before he followed her, Tas risked a quick look behind him, drawn by a terrible curiosity.

The brilliant light still filled the corridor, illuminating the bodies of the dead and dying. Cracks gaped in the Temple walls, the ceiling sagged, dust choked the air. And within that light, Tas could still hear the voice, only now its lovely music had faded. It sounded harsh, shrill, and off-key.

"The gods come...."

Outside the great arena, running through Istar, Caramon fought his way through death-choked streets. Much like Crysania's, his mind, too, heard Raistlin's voice. But it was not calling to him. No, Caramon heard it as he had heard it in their mother's womb, he heard the voice of his twin, the voice of the blood they shared.

And so Caramon paid no heed to the screams of the dying, or the pleas for help from those trapped beneath the wreckage. He paid no heed to what was happening around him. Buildings tumbled down practically on top of him, stones plummeted into the streets, narrowly missing him. His arms and upper body were soon bleeding from small, jagged cuts. His legs were gashed in a hundred places.

But he did not stop. He did not even feel the pain. Climbing over debris, lifting giant beams of wood and hurling them out of his way, Caramon slowly made his way through the dying streets of Istar to the Temple that gleamed in the sun before him. In his hand, he carried a bloodstained sword.

Tasslehoff followed Crysania down, down, down into the very bowels of the ground—or so it seemed to the kender. He hadn't even known such places in the Temple existed, and he wondered how he had come to miss all these hidden staircases in his many ramblings. He wondered, too, how Crysania came to know of their existence. She passed through secret doors that were not visible even to Tas's kender eyes.

The earthquake ended, the Temple shook a moment longer in horrified memory, then shivered and was still once more. Outside was death and chaos, but inside all was still and silent. It seemed to Tas as if everything in the world was holding its breath, waiting. . . .

Down here—wherever *here* was—Tas saw little damage, perhaps because it was so far beneath the ground. Dust clouded the air, making it hard to breathe or see and occasionally a crack appeared in a wall, or a torch fell to the floor. But most of the torches were still in their sconces on the wall, still burning, casting an eerie glow in the drifting dust.

Crysania never paused or hesitated, but pressed on rapidly, though Tas soon lost all sense of direction or of where he was. He had managed to keep up with her fairly easily, but he was growing more and more tired and hoped that they would get to wherever they were going soon. His ribs hurt dreadfully. Each breath he drew burned like fire, and his legs felt like they must belong to a thick-legged, ironshod dwarf.

He followed Crysania down another flight of marble stairs, forcing his aching muscles to keep moving. Once at the bottom, Tas looked up wearily and his heart rose for a change. They were in a dark, narrow hallway that ended, thankfully, in a wall, not another staircase!

Here, a single torch burned in a sconce above a darkened doorway.

With a glad cry, Crysania hurried through the doorway, vanishing into the darkness beyond.

"Of course!" Tas realized thankfully. "Raistlin's laboratory! It must be down here."

Hurrying forward, he was very near the door when a great, dark shape bore down on him from him behind, tripping him. Tas tumbled to the floor, the pain in his ribs making him catch his breath.

Looking up, fighting the pain, the kender saw the flash of golden armor and the torchlight glisten upon the blade of a sword. He recognized the man's bronze, muscular body, but the man's face—the face that should have been so familiar—was the face of someone Tas had never seen before.

"Caramon?" he whispered as the man surged past him. But Caramon neither saw him nor heard him. Frantically, Tas tried to stand up.

Then the aftershock hit and the ground rocked out from beneath Tas's feet. Lurching back against a wall, he heard a cracking sound above him and saw the ceiling start to give way.

"Caramon!" he cried, but his voice was lost in the sound of wood tumbling down on top of him, knocking him in the head. Tas struggled to stay conscious, despite the pain. But his brain, as if stubbornly refusing to have anything more to do with this mess, snuffed out the lights. Tas sank into darkness.

Chapter 19

Hearing in her mind Raistlin's calm voice drawing her past death and destruction, Crysania ran without hesitation into the room that lay far below the Temple. But, on entering, her eager steps faltered. Hesitantly, she glanced around, her pulse beating achingly in her throat.

She had been blind to the horrors of the stricken Temple. Even now, she glanced at the blood on her dress and could not remember how it got there. But here, in this room, things stood out with vivid clarity, though the laboratory was lit only by light streaming from a crystal atop a magical staff. Staring around, overawed by a sense of evil, she could not make herself walk beyond the door.

Suddenly, she heard a sound and felt a touch on her arm. Whirling in alarm, she saw dark, living, shapeless creatures, trapped and held in cages. Smelling her warm blood, they stirred in the staff's light, and it was the touch of one of their grasping hands she had felt. Shuddering, Crysania backed out of their way and bumped into something solid.

It was an open casket containing the body of what might have once been a young man. But the skin was stretched like parchment across his bones, his mouth was open in a ghastly, silent scream. The ground lurched beneath her feet, and the body in the casket bounced up wildly, staring at her from empty eye sockets.

Crysania gasped, no sound came from her throat, her body was chilled by cold sweat. Clutching her head in shaking hands, she squeezed her eyes shut to blot out the horrible sight. The world started to slip away, then she heard a soft voice.

"Come, my dear," said the voice that had been in her mind. "Come. You are safe with me, now. The creatures of Fistandantilus's evil cannot harm you while I am here."

Crysania felt life return to her body. Raistlin's voice brought comfort. The sickness passed, the ground quit shaking, the dust settled. The world lapsed into deathly silence.

Thankfully, Crysania opened her eyes. She saw Raistlin standing some distance from her, watching her from the shadows of his hooded head, his eyes glittering in the light of his staff. But, even as Crysania looked at him, she caught a glimpse of the writhing, caged shapes. Shuddering, she kept her gaze on Raistlin's pale face.

"Fistandantilus?" she asked through dry lips. "He built this?"

"Yes, this laboratory is his," Raistlin replied coolly. "It is one he created years and years ago. Unbeknownst to any of the clerics, he used his great magic to burrow beneath the Temple like a worm, eating away solid rock, forming it into stairs and secret doors, casting his spells upon them so that few knew of their existence."

Crysania saw a thin-lipped sardonic smile cross Raistlin's face as he turned to the light.

"He showed it to few, over the years. Only a handful of apprentices were ever allowed to share the secret," Raistlin shrugged. "And none of these lived to tell about it." His voice softened. "But then Fistandantilus made a mistake. He showed it to one young apprentice. A frail, brilliant, sharp-tongued young man, who observed and memorized every turn and twist of the hidden corridors, who studied every word of every spell that revealed secret doorways, reciting them over and over, committing them to memory, before he slept, night after night. And thus, we stand here, you and I, safe—for the moment—from the anger of the gods."

Making a motion with his hand, he gestured for Crysania to come to the back part of the room where he stood at a large, ornately carved, wooden desk. On it rested a silver-bound spellbook he had been reading. A circle of silver powder was spread around the desk. "That's right. Keep your eyes on me. The darkness is not so terrifying then, is it?"

Crysania could not answer. She realized that, once again, she had allowed him, in her weakness, to read more in her eyes than she had intended him to see. Flushing, she looked quickly away.

"I-I was only startled, that's all," she said. But she could not repress a shudder as she glanced back at the casket. "What is—or was—that?" she whispered in horror.

"One of the Fistandantilus's apprentices, no doubt," Raistlin answered. "The mage sucked the life force from him to extend his own life. It was something he did . . . frequently."

Raistlin coughed, his eyes grew shadowed and dark with some terrible memory, and Crysania saw a spasm of fear and pain pass over his usually impassive face. But before she could ask more, there was the sound of a crash in the doorway. The black-robed mage quickly regained his composure. He looked up, his gaze going past Crysania.

"Ah, enter, my brother. I was just thinking of the Test, which naturally brought you to mind."

Caramon! Faint with relief, Crysania turned to welcome the big man with his solid, reassuring presence, his jovial, good-natured face. But her words of greeting died on her lips, swallowed up by the darkness that only seemed to grow deeper with the warrior's arrival.

"Speaking of tests, I am pleased you survived yours, brother," Raistlin said, his sardonic smile returned. "This lady"—he glanced at Crysania—"will have need of a bodyguard where we go. I can't tell you how much it means to me to have someone along I know and trust."

Crysania shrank from the terrible sarcasm, and she saw Caramon flinch as though Raistlin's words had been tiny, poisoned barbs, shooting in his flesh. The mage seemed neither to notice nor care, however. He was reading his spellbook, murmuring soft words and tracing symbols in the air with his delicate hands.

"Yes, I survived your test," Caramon said quietly. Entering the room, he came into the light of the staff. Crysania caught her breath in fear.

"Raistlin!" she cried, backing away from Caramon as the big man came slowly forward, the bloody sword in his hand. "Raistlin, look!" Crysania said, stumbling into the desk near where the mage was standing, unknowingly stepping into the circle of silver powder. Grains of it clung to the bottom of her robe, shimmering in the staff's light.

Irritated at the interruption, the mage glanced up.

"I survived your test," Caramon repeated, "as you survived the Test in the Tower. There, they shattered your body. Here, you shattered my heart. In its place is nothing now, just a cold emptiness as black as your robes. And, like this swordblade, it is stained with blood. A poor wretch of a minotaur died upon this blade. A friend gave his life for me, another died in my arms. You've sent the kender to *his* death, haven't you? And how many more have died to further your evil designs?" Caramon's voice dropped to a lethal whisper. "This ends it, my brother. No more will die because of you. Except one—myself. It's fitting, isn't it, Raist? We came into this world together; together, we'll leave it."

He took another step forward. Raistlin seemed about to speak, but Caramon interrupted.

"You cannot use your magic to stop me, not this time. I know about this spell you plan to cast. I know it will take all of your power, all of your concentration. If you use even the smallest bit of magic against me, you will not have the strength to leave this place, and my end will be accomplished all the same. If you do not die at my hands, you will die at the hands of the gods."

Raistlin gazed at his brother without comment, then, shrugging, he turned back to read in his book. It was only when Caramon took one more step forward, and Raistlin heard the man's golden armor clank, that the mage sighed in exasperation and glanced up at his twin. His eyes, glittering from the depths of his hood, seemed the only points of light in the room.

"You are wrong, my brother," Raistlin said softly. "There is one other who will die." His mirrorlike gaze went to Crysania, who stood alone, her white robes shimmering in the darkness, between the two brothers.

Caramon's eyes were soft with pity as he, too, looked at Crysania, but the resolution on his face did not waver. "The gods will take her to them," he said gently. "She is a true cleric. None of the true clerics died in the Cataclysm. That is why Par-Salian sent her back." Holding out his hand, he pointed. "Look, there stands one, waiting."

Crysania had no need to turn and look, she felt Loralon's presence.

"Go to him, Revered Daughter," Caramon told her. "Your place is in the light, not here in the darkness."

Raistlin said nothing, he made no motion of any kind, just stood quietly at the desk, his slender hand resting upon the spellbook.

Crysania did not move. Caramon's words beat in her mind like the wings of the evil creatures who fluttered about the Tower of High Sorcery. She heard the words, yet they held no meaning for her. All she could see was herself, holding the shining light in her hand, leading the people. The Key . . . the Portal. . . . She saw Raistlin holding the Key in his hand, she saw him beckoning to her. Once more, she felt the touch of Raistlin's lips, burning, upon her forehead.

A light flickered and died. Loralon was gone.

"I cannot," Crysania tried to say, but no voice came. None was needed. Caramon understood. He hesitated, looking at her for one, long moment, then he sighed.

"So be it," Caramon said coolly, as he, too, advanced into the silver circle. "Another death will not matter much to either of us now, will it, my brother?"

Crysania stared, fascinated, at the bloodstained sword shining in the staff's light. Vividly, she pictured it piercing her body and, looking up into Caramon's eyes, she saw that he pictured the same thing, and that even this would not deter him. She was nothing to him, not even a living, breathing human. She was merely an obstacle in his path, keeping him from his true objective—his brother.

What terrible hatred, Crysania thought, and then, looking deep into the eyes that were so near her own now, she had a sudden flash of insight—what terrible love!

Caramon lunged at her with an outstretched hand, thinking to catch her and hurl her aside. Acting out of panic, Crysania dodged his grasp, stumbling back up against Raistlin, who made no move to touch her. Caramon's hand gripped nothing but a sleeve of her robe, ripping and tearing it. In a fury, he cast the white cloth to the ground, and now Crysania knew she must die. Still, she kept her body between him and his brother.

Caramon's sword flashed.

In desperation, Crysania clutched the medallion of Paladine she wore around her throat.

"Halt!" She cried the word of command even as she shut her eyes in fear. Her body cringed, waiting for the terrible pain as the steel tore through her flesh. Then, she heard a moan and the clatter of a sword falling to the stone. Relief surged through her body, making her weak and faint. Sobbing, she felt herself falling.

But slender hands caught and held her; thin, muscular arms gathered her near, a soft voice spoke her name in triumph. She was enveloped in warm blackness, drowning in warm blackness, sinking down and down. And in her ear, she heard whispered the words of the strange language of magic.

Like spiders or caressing hands, the words crawled over her body. The chanting of the words grew louder and louder, Raistlin's voice stronger and stronger. Silver light flared, then vanished. The grip of Raistlin's arms around Crysania tightened in ecstasy, and she was spinning around and around, caught up in that ecstasy, whirling away with him into the blackness.

She put her arms about him and laid her head on his chest and let herself sink into the darkness. As she fell, the words of magic mingled with the singing of her blood and the singing of the stones in the Temple. . . .

And through it all, one discordant note—a harsh, heart-broken moan.

Tasslehoff Burrfoot heard the stones singing, and he smiled dreamily. He was a mouse, he remembered, scampering forward through the silver powder while the stones sang. . . .

Tas woke up suddenly. He was lying on a cold stone floor, covered with dust and debris. The ground beneath him was beginning to shiver and shake once more. Tas knew, from the strange and unfamiliar feeling of fear building up inside of him that this time the gods meant business. This time, the earthquake would not end.

"Crysania! Caramon!" Tas shouted, but he heard only the echo of his shrill voice come back, bouncing hollowly off the shivering walls.

Staggering to his feet, ignoring the pain in his head, Tas saw that the torch still shone above that darkened room Crysania had entered, that part of the building seemingly the only part untouched by the convulsive heaving of the ground. *Magic*, Tas thought vaguely, making his way inside and recognizing wizardly things. He looked for signs of life, but all he saw were the horrible caged creatures, hurling themselves upon their cell doors, knowing the end of their tortured existence was near, yet unwilling to give up life, no matter how painful.

Tas stared around wildly. Where had everyone gone? "Caramon?" he said in a small voice. But there was no answer, only a distant rumbling as the shaking of the ground grew worse and worse. Then, in the dim light of the torch outside, Tas caught a glimpse of metal shining on the floor near a desk. Staggering across the floor, Tas managed to reach it.

His hand closed about the golden hilt of a gladiator's sword. Leaning back against the desk for support, he stared at the silver blade, stained black with blood. Then he lifted something else that had been lying on the floor beneath the sword—a remnant of white cloth. He saw golden embroidery portraying the symbol of Paladine shine dully in the torchlight. There was a circle of powder on the floor, powder that once might have been silver but was now burned black.

"They've gone," Tas said softly to the caged, gibbering creatures. "They've gone. . . . I'm all alone."

A sudden heaving of the ground sent the kender to the floor on his hands and knees. There was a snapping and rending sound, so loud it nearly deafened him, causing Tas to raise his head. As he stared up at the ceiling in awe, it split wide open. The rock cracked. The foundation of the Temple parted.

And then the Temple itself shattered. The walls flew asunder. The marble separated. Floor after floor burst open, like the petals of a rose spreading in the morning's light, a rose that would die by nightfall. The kender's gaze followed the dreadful progress until, finally, he saw the very tower of the Temple itself split wide, falling to the ground with a crash that was more devastating than the earthquake.

Unable to move, protected by the powerful dark spells cast by an evil mage long dead, Tas stood in the laboratory of Fistandantilus, looking up into the heavens.

And he saw the sky begin to rain fire.

The War of Souls ends now.

The New York Times best-seller from DRAGONLANCE® world co-creators

Margaret Weis & Tracy Hickman

available for the first time in paperback!

The stirring conclusion to the epic trilogy

DRAGONS OF A VANISHED MOON
The War of Souls, Volume III

A small band of heroes, led by an incorrigible kender, prepares to battle an army of the dead led by a seemingly invincible female warrior. A dragon overlord provides a glimmer of hope to those who fight the darkness, but true victory —or utter defeat—lies in the secret of time's riddles.

DRAGONLANCE and its logo are trademarks of Wizards of the Coast, Inc.,
in the U.S.A. and other countries.
©2003 Wizards.

The Minotaur Wars

From *New York Times* best-selling author Richard A. Knaak comes a powerful new chapter in the DRAGONLANCE® saga.

The continent of Ansalon, reeling from the destruction of the War of Souls, slowly crawls from beneath the rubble to rebuild – but the fires of war, once stirred, are difficult to quench. Another war comes to Ansalon, one that will change the balance of power throughout Krynn.

NIGHT OF BLOOD
Volume I

Change comes violently to the land of the minotaurs. Usurpers overthrow the emperor, murder all rivals, and dishonor minotaur tradition. The new emperor's wife presides over a cult of the dead, while the new government makes a secret pact with a deadly enemy. But betrayal is never easy, and rebellion lurks in the shadows.

The Minotaur Wars have begun.

DRAGONLANCE and its logo are trademarks of Wizards of the Coast, Inc., in the U.S.A. and other countries.
©2003 Wizards.

Collections of the best of the DRAGONLANCE® saga

From *New York Times* best-selling authors Margaret Weis & Tracy Hickman.

THE ANNOTATED LEGENDS

A striking new three-in-one hardcover collection that complements *The Annotated Chronicles*. Includes *Time of the Twins*, *War of the Twins*, and *Test of the Twins*.

For the first time, DRAGONLANCE saga co-creators Weis & Hickman share their insights, inspirations, and memories of the writing of this epic trilogy. Follow their thoughts as they craft a story of ambition, pride, and sacrifice, told through the annals of time and beyond the edge of the world.

THE WAR OF SOULS Boxed Set

Copies of the *New York Times* best-selling War of Souls trilogy paperbacks in a beautiful slipcover case. Includes *Dragons of a Fallen Sun*, *Dragons of a Lost Star*, and *Dragons of a Vanished Moon*.

The gods have abandoned Krynn. An army of the dead marches under the leadership of a strange and mystical warrior. A kender holds the key to the vanishing of time. Through it all, an epic struggle for the past and future unfolds.

DRAGONLANCE and its logo are trademarks of Wizards of the Coast, Inc., in the U.S.A. and other countries.
©2003 Wizards.

Before the War of the Lance, there were other adventures.

Check out these new editions of the popular Preludes series!

DARKNESS & LIGHT
Sturm Brightblade and Kitiara are on their way to Solamnia when they run into a band of gnomes in jeopardy.

KENDERMORE
Tasslehoff Burrfoot is arrested for violating the kender laws of prearranged marriage – but his bride pulls a disappearing act of her own.

BROTHERS MAJERE
Desperate for money, Raistlin and Caramon Majere agree to take on a job in the backwater village of Mereklar, but they soon discover they may be in over their heads.

RIVERWIND THE PLAINSMAN
A barbarian princess and her beloved walked into the Inn of the Last Home, and thus began the DRAGONLANCE® Saga. This is the adventure that led to that fateful moment.

FLINT THE KING
Flint Fireforge's comfortable life turns to chaos when he travels to his ancestral home.

TANIS: THE SHADOW YEARS
When an old dwarf offers Tanis Halfelven the chance to find his father, he embarks on an adventure that will change him forever.

DRAGONLANCE and its logo are trademarks of Wizards of the Coast, Inc., in the U.S.A. and other countries.
©2003 Wizards.

Strife throughout the land of Krynn

CITY OF THE LOST
The Linsha Trilogy, Volume One
Mary H. Herbert

After the near-disaster chronicled in *The Clandestine Circle*, the Knights of Solamnia send Linsha Majere to an outpost in the backend of nowhere. But trouble seems to run in her family, and Linsha soon finds herself involved in a war between two dragon overlords, the Knights of Solamnia, the Legion of Steel, and invaders from across the sea.

DARK THANE
The Age of Mortals
Jeff Crook

Beneath Thorbardin, a spellbinding fanatic preaches revolution, turning the hearts of those who are caught up in the cause. The ancient dwarven nation is bloodily divided, and the true leadership banished.

DRAGONLANCE and its logo are trademarks of Wizards of the Coast, Inc., in the U.S.A. and other countries.
©2003 Wizards.